CHAPTER 1

PROVIDENCE, RHODE ISLAND, OCTOBER, 1788

FILTHY RICH EDMAN ROCHE accosted me on the street. "Bouncin' Bet," he rumbled, baring clean but feral-looking fangs, "tonight you're bouncin' wit' me." He clamped a meaty hand around my arm. If I didn't know him, the fear of death would've gripped me. I never met him proper, but his swarthy swagger and tailor-cut clothes made up for his brass.

All I wanted was a meal. "It'll cost you a steak dinner and a bottle of Malmsey Madeira," I cooed. Oh, how my mouth watered for a steak. My empty tum rumbled.

His crawling fingers sent shivers up my arm, yet he aroused my primitive urges.

He pulled me over the muddy cobblestones to a spit-shined carriage.

I slid inside the coach and sank into the plush seat cushion. Stroking the red velvet sides and top, I marveled, *blimey, if his rooms are half as posh...*

As the coach rolled along, an easy chat cooled our ardor. To my delight, he told me he saw *Who's the Dupe?* by Hannah Cowley, on a New York stage.

"I love reading *The Scottish Village,*" I gushed about one of Hannah's poems.

The carriage slowed to a halt at his three-story mansion, a symbol of wealth and luxury. No knee-tremblers for me tonight.

He led me through a marble foyer into his parlor. I ogled the velvet draperies, the artwork in fancy gold frames.

As I gawked, he answered my wordless question: "My late wife did the décor here. She perished of fever three years ago. Or was it four?" He gave a dismissive wave.

"Oh ... I'm sorry," I mumbled.

"I'm not." He plucked my fingers between his, as in a minuet, and sat me next to him on a plush settee. "The strumpet, she gave me a dose ..." He paused and placed his thumb under my chin to shut my gaping gob. "No worries. I got cured."

I heaved a relieved sigh. Rich, handsome, cultured ... and pox-free.

He lit a cheroot. I inhaled the sweet smoky fragrance. "Now, business before pleasure." He slid a hand into his trouser pocket, pulled out a fistful of bank notes, and tossed them on the table. "It's more than your usual take, but I'm taking more than usual." The leer returned with a cock of his brow.

Bloomin' blazes, money too! *This'll pay a week's rent, with some left over for flub dubs.* I wiped my sweaty fingers on my gown, leaving streaks. "And you'll have it, sir."

"Ed to you, Bets," he rumbled as we leaned toward each other, our arms entwined in a crushing embrace.

I shucked off my clothes and stripped him bare. We mated on the sofa, lusting, moaning, sweating. I earned it, all right. I

MRS. AARON BURR

I'M ELIZA TO YOU

THE SASSY LADIES SERIES
BOOK TWO

DIANA RUBINO

To Eliza Jumel Burr, a truly sassy lady; I'm so glad I was able to make you laugh when I visited your mansion.

PART I
BETSY BOWEN

could get used to this ... and the money. As I caught my breath, hunger gnawed at me.

He poured me a glass of dark liquid. That Malmsey Madeira I'd requested?

I sipped. Warm sweetness coated my tongue. After I swallowed my head reeled. "Thish ish heady shtuff," I slurred, the glass now a blur. My thirst demanding I quaff more, I drained it down my parched throat. Dizzy and delirious, I dropped the glass and fell into a dead stupor.

I woke alone on the settee, my skirt covering my lower half. I struggled to sit up but gasped in horror at my wrist handcuffed to a chain.

I tugged at it with all my strength, but it bound me tight. It clanked, mocking me, shackling me to the settee leg. I yelled, screamed, begged for help. But the echo of my pleas faded into the expanse.

I squared my shoulders. *I'll break free – somehow*. Meanwhile, I clasped my hands and passed endless hours in prayer.

As I dozed, weak with hunger, the front door opened and shut. My tongue curled, ready to give him a lashing he'd never heard from his dead cheating wife. He glided in and half-leered, half-sneered as I narrowed my eyes into slits of rage.

"What's the bloody idea?" I shook my shackled fist. The chain rattled. "Bondage was not part of the deal. I demand you release me."

"Or what?" His eyes smoldered with lust. As he lunged forward in an attempt to grope me, I clenched a fist, socked his jaw, and slammed my knee into his groin.

He doubled over. "You'll pay for that," he rasped and lumbered out, leaving me chained up and imprisoned. My stomach growled as I lay lightheaded and famishing.

In the dead of night, he slunk back in, did something disgusting to me, and unlocked the chain. He drug me down a hallway, shoved me down a staircase into a root cellar, and shackled me to a wall. He plunked a chamber pot in the corner.

I lost track of time. Days slid into nights. When he felt like it, he tossedme a stale hunk of bread with a tin cup of putrid water. Too weak to yell, scream, or pound on the walls, I curled up on the thin pile of straw and prayed. After what seemed an eternity, someone answered my prayers in the most unlikely way.

The next time he entered, I bolted for the chamber pot and knelt, as if retching into it.

"You sick?" He approached me.

In one swift move, I grasped the pot and slammed it against his head. He crumpled to the floor. I bashed his face to a bloody pulp with that pot until his dead eyes stared up at me.

As his blood soaked the straw, I rummaged through his pockets, begging, *please, the – key, please* …

No key. In my rage, I kicked him with the bit of strength I had left.

Legs buckling under me, I stumbled from my prison until the chain strained taut.

A square of daylight shone through a small window. I yelled for help through a scratchy throat. No help came. I groped in the near-darkness back to Edman Roche's corpse and the only other object in sight, the chamber pot. I hurled it at the window. The glass shattered, but the pot clanged to the floor. Straining against the chain, I screamed at the top of my lungs and rattled the clanking chain. Outside sounds floated in – the crunch of wheels on gravel, a horse's neigh – but no one heard my desperate cries.

I staggered back to the body, dragging the chain on the dirt floor. I yanked the boots off his feet, grunting in my struggle. I faced the broken window and hurled one boot at the gaping hole. It missed.

I flung the other boot, but in my weakened state, it landed way short of its mark.

Shattered with despair, I crawled back to the straw and clawed through it for something to eat – a bug, rotted fruit – anything.

My fingers grasped a hard object. I pulled it out – leg irons. I shuddered. He'd shackled another victim down here. But this instrument of torture could be my saving grace.

I tottered back to the window. The sun sank as a steady rain pounded the ground. I prayed. At dusk, footsteps slogged down the street. *Here goes my last chance.* I hurled the leg irons through the gaping hole.

It struck the passerby outside. "Hey!" he yelled.

"Help me!" I stomped on the dirt floor and rattled the chain.

A man peered in, startled at the sight of me. "Hold tight, lass."

The front door crashed open. Footsteps pounded above my head. "I'm down here, down here!" Two figures clattered down the steps.

"What happened?" A man in shipyard worker's clothes approached me.

I pointed to Roche's body. "He kidnapped me, starved me, raped me, tried to murder me ..." I gulped as my voice faltered.

The other man knelt to get a closer look. "Roche, you piece of filth." He turned to me. "You'd have been the fourth woman this year."

"He ... killed before?" I rasped, my mouth too dry to speak.

"Aye, but he bribed his way out of prison. Not anymore." He kicked Roche's bloody head. "Take that, ya scum." He gave me an earnest look. "He strangled my sister. A prostitute, but she didn't deserve that. I'm gonna chop his body in pieces and feed it to my pigs. He ain't nothin' but pig slop anyways."

The other man smashed the chain apart with a hammer. I pulled free and collapsed into their arms.

"Thank you, thank you ..." I gasped. "You saved me."

They helped me up the stairs to light and sweet freedom. But first things first. I ransacked the pantry.

As I stuffed my belly with bread, raw carrots, turnips, and onions like a starving animal, voices floated down the hall. I took a few cautious steps to see a horrific sight: two constables handcuffing my rescuers.

"You're under arrest for the murder of Edman Roche," one of the constables barked. Cuffs clinked.

"No!" I burst into the hall, waving my arms. "No, they saved me! They're innocent!"

Four pairs of eyes froze on me. The other constable looked down at me with a sneer of disgust. "A filthy streetwalker? Lay off the booze, you tawdry whore."

They pushed me away and herded my saviors out the door.

"You'll go free, I swear, as God is my witness!" I wailed as the constables loaded their captives, alive and dead, into a cart and rumbled away.

I stood on the pavement, shivering. I needed my shawl but couldn't bear to re-enter that house of horror. I took a deep breath. The odor of horse dung smelled like sweet roses after that suffocating dungeon.

I read in the *Providence Gazette* that Judge David Howell was to preside over their trials. I begged an audience with him.

"Your honor, I killed Edman Roche in self-defense. Go to the house, look at the place, he chained me up, look at the prison in the cellar he kept me in." I gulped air. "He raped me, starved me, beat me ..."

He listened, rapt, his eyes fixed on me in morbid fascination. I went on, "He killed before. When I got the chance, I smashed his head with a chamber pot ..." I paused for breath.

8

"Those kind men rescued me. Please let them go. They saved my life, they didn't take his!"

He stood and gestured at a bench. "Wait there."

When the judge went to that house of horror and beheld my cellar prison, flinched at the chain that bound me, retched at the vermin-infested bed of straw, and smelled the filth, he believed me.

He released the innocent men awaiting the trial that would've resulted in their hanging.

I promised to reward my rescuers someday, and kept my promise. Now I'm stinking rich, and after I bought them each a house, I bought Roche's mansion and knocked it down to build the Providence Home for Orphans.

New York was the only place I wanted to go then, and for one reason: to meet my father, George Washington.

I ached to look up into his blue eyes and hear him say, "I love you, Betsy." So I paid three of my last five shillings to a ship captain in Providence Harbor and sailed up the coast to New York. Papa and I live four blocks apart. But those blocks may as well be oceans.

I planned to seek a private audience with him – but will he deny he ever knew Mamma and throw me out? How will he feel looking at his own image, the same sturdy build, red hair, and blue eyes? Most of all, I want to ask, *Papa, why did you leave us?*

CHAPTER 2

EVERYONE, including George Washington himself, believed he was childless. But one cold evening, Mamma knelt beside my bed, tucked my threadbare blanket around me, and told me a story.

"One sultry night in Providence, General Washington came to the home of Mr. Hopkins, a Rhode Island delegate. I heard he was dining there and snuck in. I gathered my courage and strode up to him. Not knowing me from any other neighbor lady, for I dressed in a borrowed silk gown, he asked me to dance. We drank wine and laughed and drank more wine..." Mamma's eyes brightened in the fire-glow. "He later took me to his bed, and I gave myself to him." She focused on my eyes. "General Washington and I created you that night, Betsy."

I stared at her, struck dumb.

"I wrote to him so many times," she went on, "telling him of his beautiful new daughter. He never answered." Her voice cracked as her shoulders slumped. "But I don't believe he ever got my letters. Someone, likely Lady Washington, read them and burnt them. If he'd read one of them, he'd have sent for us."

I nodded, believing that with all my heart.

"Being so poor, we couldn't travel to Mount Vernon. So I gave up. I'm sure he's long forgotten the evening that meant so much to me." Her eyes left mine and gazed into the night.

"So my Papa isn't a sailor who drowned in Newport. He's the most famous man in our country." I shook my head in wonder. "My name is Betsy Washington." I glowed with pride —at first. But as I digested her story, how he left us and ignored her letters, that pride vanished. The weight of disappointment sat on my chest. My body ached, as if he'd knocked me down, kicked me, and walked away. I wept from a hollow space deep in my gut. As a child, I hadn't the judgment to handle or define the emotions assaulting me.

I escaped from my bed, flung the blanket off, and crouched on the front step, hugging my knees. Mamma's story tore me asunder. Why did Papa leave his only little girl to beg on the streets and shiver on a bed of straw with gnawing hunger?

Growing into a young lady, I learned to manage those emotions that sucker-punched me as a child. As a woman, I understood why he couldn't take us with him. But no matter what he did to us, I still needed my Papa.

NEW YORK CITY, THURSDAY, APRIL 30, 1789

"*About 2 o'clock P.M. General Washington, the illustrious President of the United States, arrived in this city. He approached in a barge which was built here for his use. On his passing the Battery, a federal salute was fired, which was followed by an instantaneous display of colors from all the shipping in the harbour. On his landing the federal salute was repeated and all the bells in the city rang peals of joy upon the glad occasion.*" — U.S. District Court Clerk Henry Sewall

. . .

On this inaugural morn, me and my best friend Sukie Shippen stood in front of Federal Hall. She insisted on getting here at daybreak for the best view.

"C'mon, he should be here by now." As my heart leapt in eagerness to see Papa, the plangent bells of Saint Paul's chimed the noon hour. But I would've stood in the street until I dropped. My stomach growled as I twisted the folds of my skirt.

Breathing in stale sweat and the rank odor of horse manure, I surveyed the pressing crowd. Rich and poor, young and old, black and white, Sukie and me, all Americans under one flag: dandies fitted up in the red and blue of patriots; ladies draped in silk finery; threadbare shirts and ripped breeches hanging from laborers' gaunt forms. The excited buzz swarmed like flies.

I bumped up against a pretty girl about my age, light-skinned with dark hair coiled atop her head—a mulatto, I reckoned. She fanned her face with her cotton cap. "Oops, 'xcuse me." I sidestepped, giving her what room I could. "It's one blended mass of humanity, ain't it?"

"Yeah." She flashed a smile as her golden brown eyes met mine. "I wouldn'a missed it for the world, not that I had a choice. They brang us all here."

"Who brang you?" I admired her dainty flowered frock, newer and cleaner than mine—pressed, too. *What bigwig takes care of her?* I wondered with a twinge of envy.

"The Washingtons," she answered both my questions.

"Oh." My heart plummeted. My face dropped, but I forced a smile.

"I am Lady Washington's house servant." Raising her chin, she looked mighty pleased to boast that title.

"Well, how d'you do? I'm Betsy, this here's Sukie." I

gestured at Sukie, busy chatting up a dandy.

"I am Ona Judge." She glanced over her shoulder. "Oh, well, they musta got a better spot. I gotta go find 'em; we're s'posed to stick together. Nice to meet you, Betsy."

"Yeah, you too..." She vanished into the crowd. Lady Washington sure relaxed her rules, letting servants scatter about on their own. But I full well knew what "servant" meant for real. The girl was a slave, and barring some miracle, always would be. Yet I envied her just the same—she knew my father, likely since birth. A string of vexing questions bombarded me: *Are they fond of each other? Does he treat her like the daughter he doesn't know he has? Do they banter and laugh together?* I shoved those questions aside and assured myself: *it don't matter how he feels about a slave girl. I'll meet him someday and call him Papa.*

Sukie returned to my side as I scanned the crowd some more. My breath halted as a flash of dark eyes caught the sunlight like jewels. "Who is he?" I gaped, wide-eyed, as those piercing eyes met mine. He smiled, leaving me weak in the knees.

Sukie poked me out of my trance and pointed yonder. "Bets, look! There he is! There's your Papa!"

Cheers and applause burst out. Four bobtailed grays pulled a shiny coach emblazoned with a coat of arms. Footmen fitted in scarlet and white livery walked alongside. Goosebumps prickled my arms. Bursting with excitement, I whistled through my teeth and clapped until my hands throbbed.

The coach door opened. Papa ducked out and unfolded his long body, his hair cloud-white. Gold buttons studded his tobacco brown jacket. Silk stockings and velvet breeches molded to his strong legs. A gleaming sword hung at his hip. For an instant, his blue eyes met mine. In my shabby attire, I cringed. He bowed to his senators, walked past the soldiers, and vanished inside Federal Hall. The stream of gents followed. The doors slammed, shutting me out. They shut everybody out, but it hurt me more.

My broken heart sent a sob to my throat. The emptiness of abandonment crushed me as on that day Mamma recalled how he left her.

Sukie frowned at me. "What's wrong, Bets? Why you cryin'?"

"Nothing, I'm... I'm goin' light in the head." She didn't understand what I felt as that door slammed in my face. Sukie still had both her parents.

"We'll eat soon." She glanced down the street. "When this is over, we'll go to the tavern. Just be patient for once."

Papa stepped onto the second-story balcony and stood between two columns.

Men followed and surrounded him. Cheers rang in my ears, but I just stood and stared. He approached the iron rail and placed his hand over his heart. A fierce jealousy shot through me. *He belongs to me!*

A man—one of our judges?—holding a huge book on a crimson cushion stood before Papa and looked up at him.

Papa flattened his right palm on it, raised his left hand, and repeated the presidential oath after the judge. Our first president then bent forward, kissed the Bible, and pled, "So help me God," his voice cracking in the fervent prayer.

Three cheers of 'hip, hip, hooray!' and clapping exploded around me. The great man – my Papa – turned to the mob and spoke his first words as our president: "God bless you and God bless the United States of America." He bowed. A surge of pride swelled my heart. The judge proclaimed, "It is done! Long live President George Washington!"

When a soldier hoisted our flag over Federal Hall, hot tears spilled down my cheeks. A thirteen-gun salute boomed. "Oh,

Sukie, how I wish Papa knew who I was." My voice shook with emotion.

"He will, Bets, you'll get to meet him. And soon if I know you."

I smiled with trembling lips. A cannon boomed. Church bells chimed.

Papa, the *president*, turned and re-entered the building. The other men, now his humble servants, followed on his heels.

The mob headed in all directions. Following Sukie, I scanned the mass of departing bodies. Again, those lustrous eyes I saw before... they sparkled like jewels. His bottle-green coat, brocaded waistcoat, and breeches fit him as if painted on with expert strokes. Black riding boots clung to his calves. His raw sensuality sent shivers down my body. I tried to wrench my gaze away but couldn't. My breath caught. He approached us, pinning me with those eyes.

I pinched Sukie's arm. "Sukie, do you know who he is?" slid out the side of my mouth, my lips barely moving.

"Who?" She looked around.

"Himmmm!" I jerked my head in his direction. "I can't bloody well point. Coming toward us." My mouth dried to dust. Trembles raced across my skin.

She gave a casual nod. "Of course, I know him. He's practically my stepbrother." She waved, and he waved back. My muscles froze. "Come on..." She dragged me towards him. Laugh lines creased at the corners of his eyes, adding to his charm. He had to be at least thirty-five, even older than I thought before. He grasped my cold hand with warm, tapering fingers. I melted when he touched me.

Our eyes stayed locked. Oh, his dark, piercing eyes...

"Betsy Bowen," Sukie's voice reached my ears, as if from far away. "Meet Aaron Burr."

He's Aaron Burr? I heard his name in the taverns and saw it in the papers, but our paths never crossed.

He flipped off his tricorn hat. A wavy mane of chestnut hair, shining and unpowdered, crowned his head. "Miss Bowen, I regret I've never had the pleasure of making your acquaintance." His voice swirled around me like an orchestra – the voice of a practiced orator, but tinged with playfulness.

"M-me, too." These would be the last words I'd ever speak to him unless I showed some sangfroid. I cleared my throat and raised my chin. "Do not nurture regrets, Mr. Burr. Let us look forward from this moment on." It came out too slinky. I drew on the English grammar lessons I'd got from my step-pa.

"Susannah, Miss Bowen, I must return to work, but I hope to enjoy your company in due course." He nodded.

"I'll call on you by week's end, Aaron." Sukie waved. "My love to all your ladies, dear brother."

She tugged me in the other direction, but tearing my gaze from him burned like pulling a scab off a wound.

"I need a drink – now!" Gasping in thirst and the after-effects of that intense encounter, I stumbled towards the John Street Tavern.

Women weren't allowed in taverns unescorted except in the parlor or the snug in back, but the proprietress, Mrs. Fortune, knew me.

Ale-swilling, reveling citizens packed the smoky tavern. Coughing, eyes stinging, I nudged my way through unwashed bodies. At the bar, I plunked down the coins I'd saved for supper.

A flustered Mrs. Fortune, gray strands falling from her cap, poured our Madeira – President Washington's favorite was also mine. Papa and I had something in common besides red hair and blood.

I gulped the syrupy liquid. Not an empty seat in sight, Sukie and I edged over to the wall near the outdoor privy.

I leaned against a wooden beam. "Now will you tell me why you never introduced me to your..." I harrumphed, "...step-brother?"

She laughed. "Mr. Burr Senior passed away when Aaron was an infant, and Mrs. Burr passed two years later, from a smallpox inoculation. When their grandmother journeyed to them to care for them, she died of dysentery." Sukie sipped her wine. "So Aaron and his sister Sally lived with my Uncle William. We grew up as brother and sister." She took a breath to speak but shut her lips.

"And?" Closer than sisters since Mamma's death in February, Sukie and I shared everything. Almost. My cheeks heated with private, sensuous thoughts.

"He was my affianced..." She took a breath.

I held mine.

"... but only briefly," she continued. "My parents arranged it. But he could not interest me in that way, nor could I him. He went on to wed Theodosia."

"What a powerful name," I said. "Means 'God's gift'. Where's she from?" I drained the last drops of wine onto my tongue.

"When they met, she dwelt in New Jersey." Sukie tossed a glance around. "Her husband was a Red Coat officer. When she became widowed, Aaron proposed. She's ten years older than him with five young 'uns. Together they have a lovely daughter, also named Theodosia, who will be four in June. He also has a year-old baby daughter, Louisa, by their servant, Mary Emmons, a woman from India." She went on, "He adopted a son, Aaron Columbus Burr. A lad of four. And two girls, Frances, going on three, I believe, and Elizabeth. He acknowledges them and supports them – and their mothers."

"But why ain't I ever seen him around?" I shook my head, stumped. Why had Sukie never sought him out to introduce us?

"He doesn't socialize all that much," Sukie said. "The odd levee or soirée, but work comes first." She turned and coughed as I waved away cheroot smoke.

She added, "Aaron is also a member of the New York State Assembly. Governor Clinton just appointed him New York's Attorney General." She gave me a smug, pride-filled smile.

I couldn't quit shaking my head in wonder. "And why didn't I ever lay eyes on him?"

"That is all you'll ever lay on him," she warned. Oh, how she knew me. "Dash any designs in that devilish head of yours."

"I couldn't have sparked interest in him – not the way I look now anyways." Peering down, I cringed at my homespun skirt, my thin shawl, my scruffy shoes – and with my hair pulled under a mob cap, I looked the fishwife. "But is he a rogue like the rest of 'em?" I wondered out loud, hardly expecting Sukie to know.

"He's a favorite among the ladies. They pet and caress him when he's among them, and titter about him when he isn't. But a rogue?" She shook her head. "No, he's unlike the rest of 'em."

"That's a relief." I allowed myself a dreamy smile. But I burned with curiosity about him. I planned to learn more – after my evening performance at the John Street Theater.

My acquaintances – James Reynolds and his cousin Sim, the upstart lawyers and Congressmen – were bound to know Mr. Burr. And tonight, they'd all flock to Little's Porter House on

Pine Street, the place to debate and brawl. I planned to steer the topic towards New York's next Attorney General.

By seven that evening, every tavern blazed in the growing dusk. Sukie and I plodded through the tangle of stuck coaches, neighing horses, and chattering folk. Bodies still jammed Hanover Square as we passed Federal Hall.

As we turned onto Wall Street, a chorus of church bells gonged seven times. In their dying echo, guns boomed. We stared with wonder at the skyrockets and crackers fired into the night. What a shattering climax to an unforgettable day.

CHAPTER 3

The John Street Theater: my escape from cold, hunger, and bug-ridden hovels.

As a tyke in Providence, I snuggled in my step-pa Jon Clarke's lap, and he spun tales of kings and queens. "Performers act out stories on a stage before hundreds of spectators. It's called a play," Jon told me. "In a place called a theater."

"Can we see a play in a theater, pretty please?" I begged Jon.

"We have no theaters in Providence. The good folk consider theater immoral," he replied to my pout.

"Then I shall find one someplace that ain't so moral." I clapped my little hands.

"But you must buy tickets, and they are very dear," Jon said, "at least ten shillings apiece. We're too poor to ever attend."

"I won't always be poor!" I yelled out. I began saying that again and again, I'd be running a shirt over a washboard and close my eyes, smelling the wax candles and the stage's polished boards beneath me ... or I'd be chewing my dinner of hard bread and cheese, shut my eyes and sit on a throne, a crown atop my head ... these dreams got me through another day of drudgery.

Trudging to work, my feet covered in mud, I thought, *so what if actresses are equal to whores?* Compared to the slums, hunger, and filth I suffered on the streets, theater life was fit for a queen!

Jon taught me to read by age four. Hungry for books, I sold my cloak and shivered through winter, patched my threadbare blouses, and ate bird seed. I bought Sterne, Voltaire, Fielding, and plays by Aphra Benn.

When I debarked the boat in New York Harbor, I stopped at a vendor. With only enough money to rent a room, but not for any of his fruit, I asked, "Where is John Street?" Ignoring my hunger, I scampered over cobblestones to the theater, my head pounding. Catching my breath, I stood before the structure's warped clapboards. I pressed my hand over my pounding heart. *Someday I'll stride in there and step onto that stage, a queen.*

Next morn, I donned the only presentable raiment I owned: a worn but clean green skirt with a matching bodice. I headed down the Broad Way, past the fashionable clothes and hat shops, ignored the costermongers and fishmongers hawking succulent fare. Tummy growling, I approached the John Street Theater, pushed open the creaky door, and stepped into the lobby. A man walked past me.

"Can you please show me to the manager?" I asked him.

"And you are?" He eyed me up and down as a fishwife dissects a pork shank. So I did the same.

"I ..." I cleared my throat. "I am Betsy Bowen of Providence." I made my voice singsong-like. "If you'll escort me to the manager, I'll be much obliged."

He smiled, showing a row of straight teeth. Not one missing. Must be false. "I'm happy to escort and oblige you, Miss Bowen."

He led me to a door and down a flight of narrow stairs. The air smelled musty. I itched to peek in at the stage and sweep my eyes over the seats and balcony, but there was plenty of time for that.

I followed him through a maze of crates and painted scenery – red houses, green trees, a full moon against a blue backdrop of a sky. He led me into a small office with a desk covered in papers, bank notes, and coin.

He sat behind the desk. The worn leather chair groaned on its springs. "Sit, Miss Bowen." He gestured to the settee across from him.

"Sir, is it proper for you to sit at the manager's desk – with all this ..." I waved my hand at the loot. "He'll think we're pilfering."

"Not to worry, Miss Bowen." He flashed that straight-toothed grin again. "For I am he. William Dunlap at your service."

I fell back against the lumpy seat and hid a giggle of relief. "Bloomin' blazes, Mr. Dunlap, why didn't you tell me? I made a right prat out of myself!"

"Because I found you utterly charming and frankly, I enjoyed leading you on." He sat up and leaned forward, propping his elbows on the piles of notes. "Now what can I do for you?"

He was handsome in a rugged, workman sort of way. Wavy gray-streaked hair framed his ruddy cheeks. Thick brows arched over his eyes. But that smile snagged me. And it wasn't a leer, which I fended off all the time.

"Mr. Dunlap ..." I matched his smile with one of my own. He wasn't the only one who took care of what teeth he had. "I am newly here from Providence." I leaned forward to give him a gander of my décolletage, "But I don't know a soul here who can help me. Except you now, kind sir."

"Have you ever acted on the stage, Miss Bowen?" His eyes slid to my breasts and back up to my eyes. Oh, yeah, I caught his fancy, all right.

"Not yet, sir. I prayed to meet someone in the theater who will give me my first chance." I hiked my skirt up to reveal an ankle, glad I'd scrubbed my worn shoes.

"I tend to discourage pretty young ladies from acting, Miss Bowen. It's a hard life." He ran a finger around the inside of his collar.

"My life is harder than you can imagine, sir. To me, acting is living in a fairy tale. I'd be superb at it. Not to boast." I held up a hand. "I mean, becoming someone else on stage I can escape my real life."

He screwed up his eyes. "How hard is your life that you're so desperate to escape it?"

I looked down at the sawdust-covered floor. "Nothing I want to talk about. I need to put it behind me. And ..." My body hunched forward, tense with hope, "...I know you can help me."

"How could I resist?" Another smile nearly lit up the room.

"I can well handle the scorn from folk who find it immoral," I assured him with a steady tone.

He glanced up and tapped his lips with a finger. "I see nothing immoral about the theater. Much drama is immoral, but it can teach morality by showing the consequences of good and evil acts."

"Such as Shakespeare did," I added. "On stage, I trust his

sentiments reach those who never read books." I omitted that I'd never seen a play—Shakespeare or otherwise.

You've read a book, missy? his wide eyes asked. But he said, "Precisely why I'm here managing this theater and writing plays."

"You write plays, sir?" Now my eyes and mouth gaped.

"Please – call me Will. I'm no sir." He raised his head and thrust out his chest. "I've written several. My latest, *The Father of an Only – Child*, is enjoying a long run. I don't intend to close it until summer. I pack the house every evening." Pride gleamed in his eyes.

"And are you the father of the 'only child' in question, Will?" I couldn't get sassy yet but wanted to show my interest. So I studied him. How much older than me was he? Curiosity stirred in me.

"No, but will be soon. My wife is expecting our first. I am the only child in question. Long story." He stopped there.

I kept it going. "Ah ...another father story. I have a few of my own." I sighed as the image flashed through my mind ... Papa turning his back and walking into Federal Hall, the door slamming behind him.

"I would greatly enjoy sitting down with you at the Tea Garden and discussing the fine arts, Miss Bowen. Perhaps there's a part for you in my next play, *Love in New York* – if you have a knack for comedy." He curled his smile into a wry grin.

"I see comedy in life every day. And trust me, Will ... it ain't easy, with my life." The steady bang of a hammer – a stagehand building a scene? – further prickled my blood for theater life.

"Then perhaps we can enter into an arrangement, sooner than later." His voice softened to a quiet rumble.

I bit back a laugh. This was easier than I thought. Of course, he was married. Married men cut right to the chase. They hadn't the time to waste.

"May I invite you to the parlor of my boarding house this evening?" I batted my lashes.

"Yes, tonight after the theater closes. But you must be my guest at tonight's performance." His voice lowered, his tone intense. "I believe a lady with such an interest in theater will find *The Father of an Only Child* very entertaining – and hardly immoral."

"There's enough immorality in real life. We don't need it in our theater," I told him what he already knew.

He stood, skirted the desk, and clasped my fingertips. I shivered with excitement. I knew we'd share our passion for the theater and each other. As mischief lightened my heart, I coaxed, "Do I pick up my ticket at the box office, Mr. Dunlap – Will?" I lifted one brow.

"Oh ..." He cleared his throat, a gleam in his eye. "Right you are. And will you have an escort?"

"I certainly shall." I nodded. "You."

He tripped backward, bumping into his desk. "That can be arranged."

Yea, he's married, all right.

He cupped my elbow and led me up the stairs, through the lobby, and into daylight. As I shielded my eyes from the glare, he took my hand again and kissed it this time. What punctilio! In polite circles, a kiss on the hand was an invitation to go way further and could destroy a lady's reputation – but I was no lady – yet.

I skipped down the street. When had my heart swelled with this much joy? But my hollow tum rumbled. With the few coppers I had left over after paying rent, I went to the bakery. The baker, rolling pin in hand, raised his arm, about to clobber an urchin.

"Go on, scram, ya thief!" He shook the rolling pin as the ragamuffin skittered down the street.

I turned and ran after the waif, catching him by his grimy collar. He twisted around and made to kick me, but my skirt swished as his bare foot skimmed it.

"Hey, kiddo, I ain't gonna hurt you."

He quit scrambling and looked up at me with sad blue eyes. When I saw that delicate face, I gasped. "Great God above, you're a girl!" I knelt and brushed loose strands of hair from her eyes. "Why are you dressed like a boy?"

"Cause that's all I have is boys' pants and shirts. Me sister and me, we're desperate hungry, and she's with child," she wailed.

Watching her teary eyes and quivering lip, I looked into a reflection of myself from not long ago. I dug out my coppers. "Here, lass, take these and buy yourself and sis some eats."

Her eyes bugged out at the coppers I dropped in her palm. "Lord bless ye, miss."

"I understand, lassie. I been chased outta stores for copping vittles myself when times were hard. I'd tell you not to steal, but hunger makes folk do things they oughtn't. Now scurry along." I patted her head.

Her grimy fingers closed around the coins, and she scampered away. Now ... whether to eat now and beg my breakfast in the morning or t'other way round?

Someday I'll be rich and give away a lot more. I ignored my starvation as I headed down the street.

CHAPTER 4

On inaugural evening, the theater stayed half empty. William and I hunched over his desk and counted the receipts, him smiling and whistling the entire time. My mouth watered for Little's Porter House oysters. I also craved some lively debate about our country's brilliant future with other like-minded patriots.

Most of all, I wanted to learn about Aaron Burr.

When we got to the Porter House, William held the door for me and warned, "I shan't stay long, Betsy. I can walk you home, or we'll borrow a hackney."

"Splendid by me, Will." I knew he wanted to get home to his wife.

Entering the low-ceilinged room, I squinted and brushed away clouds of cheroot smoke. Folks sat at tables and stood at the bar, chatting, eating, and swilling ale. Bright fires danced in the hearths. I inhaled the aroma of roasting meats.

Across the room, I spotted James Reynolds, his cousin Simeon, Fisher Ames, and Gertrude Meredith, the niece of Gouverneur Morris, one of our founding fathers. They all sat at a table with a few empty chairs. "Yoo-hoo!" I called out and waved.

James stood and waved us over. "Betsy, Will, come join us," he called in his thick Scottish lilt.

James, ever the gentleman, held out my chair. Fisher had just been elected to Congress. He shared my ideas of a strong central government. But I liked to play devil's advocate with him and fire him up.

I hiked my skirt up and sat, crossing my legs under the table, where the gents couldn't ogle my knees. "How's the missus, Jim?"

"Grand. She's practicing her fiddle. How went the theater this evening? Not much of a crowd, I peg." He took a swig from his tankard.

"Barely a sprinkling," William grumbled as James signaled the barmaid. "I should've closed in honor of President Washington."

"That was some mob at the inauguration." The vision of Aaron Burr's eyes flashed before me. I shivered with a surge of excitement. I clasped my hands to stop them trembling.

The noise around us loudened as more men stomped in, some escorting ladies, banging the door shut behind them.

A barmaid set a glass of wine before me.

Though my tongue tingled with the desire to talk about Mr. Burr, I held it in. I curled my hands around my glass.

Our new president became tonight's topic as a platter of steaming oysters and lampreys arrived. My mouth watered at the warm aroma. James grabbed one, so I followed, trying not to stuff it in my hungry face. But, aah, that first bite! I sucked it into my mouth and breathed in the succulent scent.

"Now that he's president, he'll be judged by every news-paper and politician and citizen down to the beggars on the streets." James held his empty tankard up to the barmaid as she scurried by. "It comes with the territory. And the best thing about not having a King George the First here is that if he doesn't serve us right, we can kick his arse out!" James guffawed as the barmaid stopped and refilled his glass, suds spilling over the rim.

Fisher shifted in his creaky chair. "William, can you show the president your support by sending him and Lady Washington free tickets? Or does he find theater lewd, too?" He snickered.

"No, not at all." A droll smile curled William's lips as he parted them to sip more ale. "I daresay there's not much he finds immoral. When Lady Washington keeps the home fires burning at Mount Vernon, he finds a way to keep his own fires burning."

The others listened wide-eyed, then pretended they didn't hear it. Gertrude and I shared a furtive glance and a smile.

"Now that he's our president, we should forbear spreading rumors," ventured Gertrude. She dabbed at her lips with a napkin.

"They ain't rumors, lass," William shot back, tossing his head.

And didn't I know the truth of that. The man was my Papa. I longed to blurt it all out, but couldn't let my precious secret out before its time.

As I chewed my lamprey, I realized I'd forgotten to ask Sukie whether Aaron Burr was a Federalist. I'd pay no mind if he was. We didn't need to talk politics. A hot thrill went through me as I thought about what we *could* do.

James looked over towards the entrance and rolled his eyes. "Ah, shite. That ponce Hambone and his gladiators just pranced in."

I turned to see Alexander Hamilton with some men who towered over him. I hadn't realized he was so elfin.

"Don't invite him over," Fisher scowled. "I'm in no mood for effete snobbery."

"Ye got no fear o'that, Fish," James assured him with a nod. I knew James didn't like Hamilton and his monarchist leanings. I wasn't sure if I liked him or not. I never met him. But I'd shut my gob until after I saw how Mr. Treasury Secretary handled the nation's money. And mine.

"That's Mac with him," Gertrude said, as Senator William Maclay parted company with Hamilton and loped over to our table, leaning on his walking stick. Maclay placed a meaty hand on Sim's shoulder.

"Evening, ladies and gentlemen." He raised his stick in greeting as James stood and offered him the chair next to him. "I trust you're reveling in our new administration." Built sturdy as a fort, he battled rheumatiz or gout. Both he and the chair groaned when he sat.

We ganged up on Maclay, all wanting to know what happened inside the Hall after the balcony doors shut in our faces. "Did you speak to the president? What did you talk about? Does he ever smile? Does he really have wooden teeth?" We hammered him with the questions of the curious.

Maclay leaned forward. "The president looks far different up close. And his teeth are human – he buys them from his slaves. But they're ill-fitting and do pain him quite a bit."

"Will you be painting another portrait of the president, Will?" Sim asked my escort.

"Another portrait?" Fisher's eyes bugged out at William. "You painted the president?"

Oh, here we go. I needed another drink to sit through this. Much as I admired William's endless artistic talents, he needed no goading to brag about his painting General and Mrs. Washington at age 17.

"Ah, yes, at Princeton, the winter of eighty-three. Besides a crayon sketch, I painted a full-length oil portrait of the general. I took it to England to study under Ben West." He shook his head. "Alas, it's still there. I hope to fetch it back. Would be a fitting tribute to him in the theater lobby."

William leaned over to me. "Do these folk know that you're the progeny of our revered president?"

Heat rushed to my face and dried my mouth. "No, and they won't know till I'm ready!" I whispered out the side of my mouth, spreading it into a smile when James held up his glass.

"To George Washington. The king is dead, long live the president."

Maclay lifted his glass. "A cobweb pair of breeches, a porcupine saddle, and a hard-trotting horse to all the enemies of freedom."

As we toasted our future, some men across the room burst into song.

Sung to the tune of God Save the King, which everyone knew, more joined in. "God save the thirteen states! Long rule the United States! God save our states!

Make us victorious, happy and glorious, no tyrants over us, God save our states!"

It seemed Hamilton led the singing, raising his glass as his cronies clapped. Another song followed, sung to Rule Britannia's tune.

Then to my utter astonishment, William stood and belted out a song that brought me to tears. The entire room rose to its feet and joined in.

"Great Washington the hero's come, each heart exulting hears the sound,

Thousands to their deliverer throng, and shout him welcome around.

Now in full chorus join the song, and shout out loud, great Washington!"

We sang it thrice, and by then, all knew the words. It ended in a burst of applause, a rollicking roar and a *huzzah!* for our new president.

"Your breeches and your very balls be blessed, Will!" Mac clinked his glass to ours.

I wept with pride for my country, my president—and my papa.

The meal devoured, William asked around the table, "Will one of you gents make sure Betsy has a safe escort home?"

Maclay volunteered. "We live the bray of an ass apart. I can see the lady home. Miss Bowen…" He held the door for me. I bristled with excitement. Now I would find out everything Sukie wouldn't tell me about Aaron Burr.

As I stepped outside and stumbled over a hog trotting by, Maclay said, "I saw you in *Love in New York* and your performance was superb. Comedy suits you."

My cheeks heated. Much as I reveled in flattery, I never got used to it. "Thank you, Senator. A statesman must act at times – or should I say perform. Must he not?" I pulled my shawl closer around my shoulders as a breeze chilled me.

"I concede some are actors," Maclay said, "in it for the fame and glory."

How to steer the conversation to Mr. Burr while making it seem his idea? Aha! Get him crabbing about his pet peeve – the city of New York itself. We livened our step past a pile of horse dung. "I enjoy New York. It's much more civilized than Providence. Fashionable. And sophisticated." I counted on my fingers. "And theatre ain't immoral here. New England Puritans need to learn to have fun – it's why their population is in decline."

My underlying meaning would've scandalized other gents, but I knew how far I could push old Mac.

"Miss Bowen!" he boomed, feigning shock, pressing his

hand to his chest in a theatrical gesture. "Wherever did you learn such boldness?"

"Dunno." I shrugged. "I never learned it, simply inherited it from my Mamma. Or my Papa," I added without thinking. "It runs in my blood. What about the city do you mislike?"

He looked up and shook his head. "I was never in so inhospitable a place. I visited the new president at his house on Cherry Street yestermorn and the streets are ripped up a great part of the way."

"The streets are worse in Providence," I offered.

"And this city plainly stinks," he went on. "I simply feel a stranger here." We skirted a water pump.

"You will grow used to it as I have. But you're right, sir, it does reek."

"They'll move the capital somewhere cleaner," he commented.

Now to steer the conversation to Mr. Burr. "Perhaps our new government will make cleaning up our streets a priority. After all, injuries lead to lawsuits. Speaking of lawyers – do you know who the governor appointed as the new Attorney General?" I tapped the side of my head and snapped my fingers. "Oh, what is his name? I had it on the tip of my tongue not long ago."

Ahh, to have *anything* of Mr. Burr's on the tip of my tongue!

"Aaron Burr," he replied, and I held in my sigh at the sound of his name. "It'll snow in hell before the president honors him with a cabinet post."

"Huh? Why?" I nearly halted.

"Because during the war, Burr joined the expedition to Canada. He became aide-de-camp to General Montgomery. Benedict Arnold launched his attack and was shocked that Monty had left most of his men behind in Montreal. He arrived at Quebec with only half that of the British."

I let out a long whistle. "Why did Monty have such a small force?"

"Illness, short-term enlistments, long supply line, and short-ages. The men attacked amidst an ice storm." Maclay stepped around another hog rooting in a smelly trash heap and went on, "The story goes that Captain Burr arrived with Monty, and as the men charged through the barricades, Burr turned to see his commander face down in the snow, dying from a cannon shot to the head. He then unsheathed his sword and shouted, 'Follow me to the citadel!' "The panicked troops fled." Maclay gave a flourish with his cane. "And Burr got promoted to major."

I awaited a tale of gore and blood.

"Burr refused to leave Monty's body behind. It was a brave task, for Monty was over fifty pounds heavier than Burr, but he managed to carry and drag the remains back to the American camp."

"A war hero," I said over a sigh. "So why doesn't Gen— President Washington like him?"

"They never got along. I heard that General Washington gave him a few good chewings-out. It remains to be seen. He has a brilliant political mind. If he plays the game right he'll rise in political ranks."

I couldn't let him see me float in reverie. I had to keep the conversation grounded. "Ah, yes. I recently learned my dear friend Susannah Shippen—Sukie—is well acquainted with him."

"Shippen? Any relation to Margaret Shippen who married Benedict Arnold?"

"They're cousins." But I didn't want to discuss Sukie or Benedict Arnold.

"I don't know Burr well, but I've made his acquaintance around town," he went on, to my delight. "He's the antithesis of

Hamilton, who's a pompous derrière, pardon my French. Strange because they do socialize. Burr is much more personable, down to earth. From pure stock but doesn't flaunt it."

I was about to open my mouth to ask another barrage of questions when he cut in with, "Why the sudden interest in Burr?"

"Sudden? Oh ..." With Mr. Burr's striking figure in my mind's eye, I slammed into a hitching post. "Owww!" Stars flashed before my eyes. Rubbing my arm, I went on, "I met him today. Sukie introduced us. He seemed – charming. Cordial. Approachable." I shut up there.

"Far too old for you, young lady," his stern tone warned.

"I am hardly young, Senator," I shot back.

"I strongly advise you to stay away from Burr, Hamilton, and their ilk," he warned. "Especially Hamilton. He'll use you. And that is no gossip."

"I've no interest in Hamilton," I declared.

"Good. Because you will be merely a notch on his bedpost. And he's a deadbeat." Maclay scowled. "Never leaves the serving wenches a gratuity. More often than not shows up with no money, expecting others to pay—as if swilling ale in his company is a privilege."

"A wise choice then for Treasury Secretary. I do not want my nation's money in the hands of a spendthrift and squandered on frippery."

"We can only hope for the best," he said as we reached my boarding house.

I dug into my pocket for my key, and we bade each other good evening.

I entered and locked up. A flickering oil lamp on the hall table cast a glow on an envelope. The fancy lettering drew me to it, "Betsy" in spidery, slanted penmanship.

Which suitor could it be from? I tore it open. My eyes

scanned an invitation to dinner at the Queen's Head, one of New York City's fanciest eating places ... Mozart's opera *The Marriage of Figaro* ... a carriage ride ... on Monday evening next. The only night the theater was shut. He must've known I was in the cast. My breath caught in my throat.

It was signed with bold confidence: A.B.

CHAPTER 5

"You are my destiny, Aaron Burr," I vowed.

Trembling, I set my eyes on the top line of the invite and savored every word, hearing his voice in my mind. As my fingertips grazed the "A.B.," I imagined touching his face. Hugging the note to my breast, I vowed to cherish it forever. To hold a part of him so close – a thrill warmed me to my toes. But only four days to prepare? I didn't dare wear my shabby raiment. What could I do, with a few coppers to my name? *Oh, please, Will, grant me another loan.* I cringed at the humiliation of asking him for more money.

Folding the note, I climbed the steps and entered my room under the eaves. I forced open the window and stuck my head out. "Aaron Burr wants to be seen in public with me!" I sang out into the night. It proved I was respectable enough for his company, making me feel worthwhile. I wanted to sing it from the rooftops, to the tune of the *Figaro* overture.

A breeze carried the sea's briny smell. I gazed at the crescent moon. The stars spattered like jewels. "Thank you so very much," I proclaimed to the heavens. "I've waited so long for this blessing!" I turned and flung myself onto my creaky bed, laughing with delight.

I clutched the note all night. As sunlight streamed through the shutters, I leapt from the bed and splashed yesterday's water on my face from the washbowl. I would bathe properly later.

I hoped Sukie was up and about. The note tucked into my bodice, I rushed to her house on Water Street, tripping over uneven cobbles. I crashed into a trudging milkman bellowing, "Milk, ho," tin pails swinging from a wooden yoke balanced on his shoulders.

The vendors shouting, "Clams! Hot corn! Fresh eggs by the dozen!" should've made my belly growl, but didn't.

I banged the brass knocker against her door. "Sukie! Sukie, open up! Be home, please!"

An aproned maid opened the door. I dashed past her, calling up the stairs, "Sukie! Get down here, make haste!"

"She ain't here, Miss Bowen, she gone out."

I spun around. "Oh, damn!" I never swore in front of servants or gentlemen, but I couldn't think straight. "Sorry 'bout that, thanks, I'll see myself out."

The maid vanished down the corridor. I snuck up the stairs, tiptoed into Sukie's bedroom, and crept to her wardrobe. I chose one of her hooped dresses with a drawn-in waist in a gay pattern of pink roses. I grabbed a matching bonnet with streaming ribbons. Footwear of every hue covered her closet floor. I plucked up a pair of pink quilted slippers, and on my way out, swiped a jar of face powder from her dressing table. Someday I'd have my own modiste, booter, and hairdresser.

"Forgive me, Sukie, I'll pay you back and then some," I vowed as I slid her property into her travel satchel and stole back downstairs, leaning over the banister to make sure the coast was clear. Bacon sizzled, its delicious aroma wafting down the hall. My mouth watered as I licked my dry lips.

When would I eat today? I'd spent last week's pay on that street urchin, a cake of French soap, and a new novel, *The Power of Sympathy*, with Sukie's breathless warning, "It exposes the fatal consequences of seduction!" The few coppers I had wouldn't buy me breakfast. Hence I hid the satchel under the stairs and strolled into the kitchen. I helped myself to a rasher of bacon and quaffed ale from a pitcher. I saw myself out, clutching Sukie's satchel.

Now I had the proper raiment to be seen with Mr. Burr, but needed something much more important. I'd inherited nerves of steel from my papa, but now I needed nerves of rock.

I headed for William's boarding house. I needed some fast lessons. His place was not as shabby as mine, being decades newer. He rented here to write his scripts without his wife and mother-in-law nosing about – "bedlam," he griped. The cackling and nagging drove him here most nights. I went to his door in the rear and knocked.

"C'min!"

I entered, skipped up to him at his desk, perched myself on his knee, and knocked over his old inkpot, but caught it.

"Hell's tooth, Betsy, watch it. Ink is dear, and I don't care to be seen around town with blue legs!"

I placed the inkpot back on the desk. "Take heed, Will, I received an invitation from the most brilliant handsome man in these thirteen states, if you count Rhode Island."

"I don't recall sending you an invitation." He gave me a saucy smile.

I gave his cheek a playful swat in return. "I wasn't going to blabber but you'd find out anyways, when me and him attend the opera and dinner at the Queen's Head. I want to be honest with you, as you are with me. I want—"

"Then quit waffling and tell me who he is, for the love of Saint Genesius!"

I pranced across the room and sprawled on his bed. "He is the suave and polished next Attorney General of New York, Aaron Burr, Esquire. And he wants to escort me to dinner and *The Marriage of Figaro*."

"*The* Aaron Burr?" He struggled to keep his eyes from popping. "Asked you to *Marriage of Figaro*? What for? To hold his opera glasses atop his nose?"

"You vex me not a whit, Will." I gave him an airy wave. "I am on my climb up, and Attorney General Burr squiring me boosts me a thousand rungs."

"But why did he ask you?" Will egged on. "Did Biddy Cummings raise her rates?"

"If she did, then you can't afford her no more!" I shot back, and he nodded as if to say, "Can't top that one."

"Then what's on your mind, Betsy?" He cocked a brow. "You should be soaking in a tin tub if you're seeing him tonight."

"I ain't seeing him tonight. I have a performance. Sides, I need to prepare. And not just with a bath. I need your help, Will. I *got* him interested in me, so how do I *keep* him interested?" My heart raced.

He rattled his head as if shaking off fleas and shot me a questioning glare. "You need *me*..." He jabbed a thumb at his chest, "...to tell *you* how to interest him? Ye gods, Betsy, must I join you over there and work your limbs like a puppeteer?"

"I don't mean that way. I mean up heeere." I tapped the side of my head. "I want this to mean something. My entire future is at stake."

"What future?" He splayed his fingers. "He's married."

"What's that worth to someone like him? He ain't so attached that he's above asking me for an evening out." I smoothed my skirts and straightened my back.

He shrugged. "Perhaps his missus don't like Mozart."

"Somethin' told me from the moment mine and Attorney General Burr's eyes met across the mobbed street, not just our bodies but our souls connected. Both our fates put us there at that time and place, and I can't disobey fate. I need your help. Please." I clasped my hands and met his gaze with pleading eyes. Bells jangled outside. They matched my jangling nerves.

"Ah, no, don't go all John Donne on me again. If you want to talk metaphysical, go see your occult friend, what's his name, the Frenchie crêpe suzette—"

"Etteilla," I nudged his memory. "The pseudonym of Jean Alliette."

"Yeah, him."

"He's back in France." I wiggled my fingers as if in farewell. "But I do need the earthly help only you can give me, Will."

"Very well." He slid his quill behind his ear. "You may have two free tickets. On your night off."

My cocksure smile told him: *two tickets ain't gonna make this custard.* "I need more'n that. I need a crash course. In literature. In music. In the fine art of dining when everybody has two forks, these things that'll show that I'm a lady – but not of the evening," I added, drawing imaginary circles on his quilt.

He rose from his squeaky chair and sat beside me. He warned, "Betsy, he can easily find out who you are, if he hasn't already. He knows you didn't attend King's College."

"I don't have to. I'm a quick study. So, when can we get started?" I squirmed. "We'll begin with Mozart since that's where we're supposed to be going. I need to get cultured – and proper – and I have four blasted days to do it!" I raised my arms in entreaty.

"Where to begin?" He made a theatrical show of despair, holding his head in his hands.

I jabbed him in the arm. "First things first. Procure a *Figaro* libretto in English and I'll study it till I can sing it backwards. Then we'll work on making me Mr. Burr's intellectual equal. That should be the easy part." I gave him a smile and a wink.

"All joshing aside, I believe in you, Betsy." He clasped my hand between his ink-stained fingers. I clasped back. "You're capable of surpassing him intellectually. Then what?"

"Then nothing because I'll never let him know," I answered with a resolute nod.

William sat me down at his kitchen table and gave me a *Marriage of Figaro* lesson over tea and plum cakes. Then he made a list of words I use, and the "real" words they should be.

"'Ain't' is not a word." He checked off each one from his list. "Don't ever swear. Do not drop your g's – or, worse, your h's. Makes you sound like a bloody Cockney. And never say 'bloody'."

He coached me on the authors someone like Mr. Burr would read. Most matched mine – Sterne, Voltaire, Shakespeare – "...and it is well known that he believes women should have all the advantages of men. He's giving his daughter a classical education."

"A man after my own heart!" I gave that heart of mine a theatrical clutch. "Oh, I am growing to love Mr. Burr more each minute." I took rapid breaths to calm myself. "If he starts talking women's equality, I won't have no trouble keepin' up."

"Won't have *any* trouble! Stop using double negatives. And stop droppin'—er,

dropping your g's."

I swallowed another mouthful of tea. "Oh, would I love to see him in action – in the courtroom, that is."

"On his courtroom performances I once heard an admirer comment, 'honey drips off his tongue.' Perhaps he should be an actor." William grabbed another cake.

Is true love in my future? I slapped the side of my head for even thinking that – so soon.

On Monday, I bathed twice and decided not to tell Sukie about my upcoming rendezvous. I knew she'd balk at his seeking out my company. As would everyone else, simply because he was Aaron Burr.

All dressed, perfumed, and ready for him, I waited – and waited. I stood at the window, my breath steaming up the glass, neck craned, heart thump-thumping against my blouse. I paced, looked in the mirror, paced again, unable to sit.

The clock struck seven, then half past. I pulled the curtain aside again and stared out the window, went to the porch and peered down the street. Alas, no sign of a shiny carriage with matched grays or whatever a man of his status owned. I went back in and counted the ticking minutes in time with the clock. As hoofbeats clopped on the cobbles outside, my heart did a somersault. "Here he is."

I threw the door open. But a man in a shabby jacket slid off an old gray horse. No shiny carriage, no carriage at all, not even a wagon.

"Miss Bowen?"

I nodded, too crushed to utter a yes.

He gave me a note, touched the brim of his hat, and left. I ripped into it. My gaze slid to the bottom – A. B. I read the few lines again and again. "I regret I cannot keep our appointment tonight." No word as to whether he'd call on me at some future date. My body numbed with disbelief. Had Sukie told him about my sordid past? What did it matter? "He's not coming." My shoulders fell.

As I dragged my feet down the hall, loneliness wrapped me in its bleak shroud. I fled the house. Wandering the streets, I vowed out loud: "I'll find out what detained him. I have my ways."

I picked up two tickets at the box office and sealed them in a sheet of William's fancy stationery. I addressed the packet, "Mr. A. Burr, Esq., Nassau Street," not knowing the number, but the post would know where to deliver it. He was the only Mr. A. Burr, Esq. on Nassau Street – and as far as I cared, in the world.

All through my performance the following evening, I peered out into the packed house to spot him in the audience. *He'll come backstage and thank me for the tickets*, I assured myself over and over. At closing time, William tallied the receipts, the stagehands swept up. But no sign of my guest.

As I sat at my vanity table pinning up my hair, a stagehand delivered a folded note. I recognized the elegant script on the outside. My heart leapt and I ripped it open. Just as I feared, more regrets. I read it thrice, my eyes lingering on his words. This time he had a reason. He needed to meet with some of his staff.

Believable enough. This one I didn't hug to my breast or inhale. But I didn't throw it out either.

Next morn I went to the stationer's with the money I saved for shoes. Whatever it cost, I would purchase a quire of the thickest, creamiest stationery. I asked the clerk behind the counter, "Can you print my name on top in that posh script you do for rich swells?" I spilt my coin-filled purse onto his counter. "Betsy – *Miss* Betsy Bowen is my name. Oh, and add the middle initial, P." I had no middle name, but Phebe was Mamma's name.

On my new posh stationery I penned a letter. *Dear Mr. Burr, I respectfully request an audience next evening at eight.* But I reckoned he'd asked around town and decided to have nothing to do with me. At mine and William's favorite tea house, Tyler's Washington Garden on Spring Street, Mr. Tyler rented me the upstairs room. I added a few embellishments to the letter, "I regret missing Mozart's opera and hope you did not cancel because of an unfortunate occurrence." Which I spelled right, having copied the words from a Fielding novel. I posted it to Aaron Burr, Esquire on Nassau Street.

I planned to convince him that my past had no bearing on my present. How many chances would I give him? Until he said yes. I refused to give up.

After a quiet supper with William, I told him my bold plan. "Mr. Burr backed out last time. So this time, I'm making sure we meet in a private room, not an opera house. Armed with my new knowledge of his pet subjects." I tossed my head. "I'm rather chuffed that I took matters into my own hands."

He wagged his finger at me. "Ah, but Betsy, inviting him to rendezvous alone in a room with no escorts? That's untoward. Don't forget, he's not a young'un like you."

"I see nothing untoward about it. It's a public house. I ain't inviting him to my boudoir." I stared him down, my heart racing at the thought of meeting Aaron on a level playing ground, but also because William tried to throw a wrench into it. "Don't toss salt into my coffee, Will."

Standing, I smoothed my new evergreen skirt. "You didn't even notice my skirt. I bought it because it matches the jacket Aaron wore the first time I saw him." I twirled around for him.

He nodded his approval. "I'm not salting your coffee. But you can be... uh, forward at times and don't want this to backfire on you, alone in a rented room with the object of your ardor."

"You needn't worry. I'll mind my p's and q's. And whatever else needs minding."

After telling him *he* needn't worry.

CHAPTER 6

"He was catnip to women."
— Historian Ray Swick, on Aaron Burr

THE EVENING of my private assignation with Aaron, I shook all over. I wiggled back into Sukie's raiment, my fingers catching in the bonnet strings. I applied the rouge too streakily and did it over. Too poor to hire a carriage, I walked the few blocks to the Washington Garden. Mr. Tyler greeted me with a glass of Madeira. I nearly spilled it down Sukie's satin bodice with my trembling hand.

Clutching my skirts in my other fist, I climbed the stairs to the tomb-quiet room. Tables and chairs were placed far apart enough for privacy. This being a private room for rental by the hour, the décor was more posh than the tavern downstairs. Blue velvet drapes hung from the windows, a glowing six-candle silver candelabra centered on each sill. The aroma of beeswax floated up from the floorboards, scrubbed clean of spittle and spat-out tobacco globs. The corners were swept free of cobwebs.

I waited next to a window, trying to occupy my mind with my Mary Wollstonecraft book, glancing out, quaffing wine. At the first of nine chimes in the clock belowstairs, a carriage rolled up to the door. Not a big fancy conveyance boasting emblems or gilded wheels, no matched grays, none of that phony flash some senators got carted around in. The door opened and in the shadows of the night, I knew his form – lean and lithe. My breath caught. My heart leapt. I sneaked my reflection in a table knife. His footsteps grew louder. I looked up and there he stood. He swept off his hat. His jacket and breeches matched his eyes and hair. A gold brocade waistcoat peeked out from the open jacket, matching his gold shoe buckles.

"Miss Bowen." He gave me a bow low enough to look gentlemanly, not bootlicky. I stared in wonder. What a dashing figure.

"Mr. Burr, I am pleased to see you again – after the other evening." We approached each other. I held back so as not to appear hasty, and we met under a blazing chandelier. "What detained you, if I may ask?" Ah, I couldn't wait to hear this!

"Miss Bowen – Betsy – may we sit?" His voice poured over me like nectar. "And it is Aaron to you."

"Of course—Aaron." My voice cracked. I cleared my throat and grabbed the glass, but the blasted thing was long empty.

We sat on the settee, knees nearly touching. "I shall get to the point without ado," he said.

A lawyer without ado? I couldn't help but smile.

"I found out something about you that I regret wouldn't go over well if we're to associate. Of course, I give you the chance to confirm or refute its veracity."

Now I had to call on my acting skills. I swallowed my fear of what was coming next. Something about my background? I'd bet my petticoat on it. "Of course. Tell me what it is then." I delivered my line in a voice that better not crack again. I raised my chin and drew my shoulders back.

He inhaled. "I heard you are President Washington's daughter."

Oh, no, not that. I recoiled as if he'd struck the bloomin' wind outta me. My chest tightened and my fists clenched. All thoughts of my sordid past vanished. No, I wasn't ready to talk about Papa with him. I feared spilling too much of myself too soon. Besides, I couldn't think of Papa without unresolved feelings welling up. "Uh ... well, I ... who told you?" I used the grand master of stalling, answering questions with questions.

He shook his head, flecks of gold glittering in his eyes, reflected in the candles' glow. "It matters not who told me."

"Then tell me why it's a problem." I was no lawyer, but as the one on the stand, I had a right to ask a question in my own defense.

"Because I haven't declared myself to be staunchly either Federalist or not. Our president does not quite favor me ..." He hesitated and took a breath, raising his hands. "To be blunt, he can't stand me. If he hears I'm associating with his daughter, he'll ruin my political career so that I cannot run for village idiot."

My whirring mind raced ahead – did he equally dislike Papa? How could we ever get along? Any man despising Papa despises me, knowing I adore him so.

You're racing too far ahead, Bets, I told myself. *Cease the what-ifs.*

I brought my acting talents to the forefront. "Is that all?" I forced a steady tone. "I'll tell you the truth. The president – my father – doesn't know I exist."

His gaze intensified, and he sat forward. "I'm sorry, I didn't mean to—"

"When the time is proper, I intend to let him know who I

am. I desperately want him to accept me. If you cannot associate with me because of that, then good evening, sir." I forced myself to my feet and stepped around him. But I couldn't stop myself from turning to look back at him. Here the acting ended and my heart came to the fore.

He pulled me back down, and I burst with happiness. My eyes found his and locked. I couldn't stop staring. "Tell me why he doesn't know you exist. Tell me the story. Then I have a few of my own. I know how it is to be orphaned, with both parents dead by age two. I never knew my father, either. I know who he was but have no memory of him. Please understand, Betsy ..." his voice softened, "...I know our president better than most, and now that we call him the father of our country – I meant no disrespect, to you or him."

I began, "My mother told me about an ... the only encounter she had with Pa—with then-General Washington, in Providence, where we come from. I was born nine months later. Her revelation shocked me." The memory brought back that stunned stare as I did now. "I'll never feel complete till he acknowledges me as his daughter." I paused and took a deep breath. "There, I said it. I wasn't ready to share this, and hope you won't think less of me for telling you."

"Why would I think less of you for wanting to bond with your own father?" He raised one brow over a quizzical eye.

I had a ready answer for that. "I feared you might find my claim false. I mean, what girl wouldn't want George Washington to be her father?" I caught my hands fluttering and clasped them. "But I assure you, I sit here before you as his daughter." Pride steadied my voice.

"I don't doubt you, Betsy. Did you ever try to verify his whereabouts that year?" He inched towards me. I didn't move.

"No, but Mamma never lied to me," I stated.

"What year was this?" he asked.

"Seventy-four." Which I knew gave away my age, but I couldn't lie if he was going to 'verify' this for me.

He nodded. Candlelight glinted in his hair. "That was the year he was elected to the first Continental Congress in Philadelphia."

"He wasn't there the whole year. If my Mamma says he was in Providence, then he was there," I declared. "He was in Providence after that, too – and I met him. But that's a memory too painful to think about."

His eyes widened. "I don't want to dredge up painful memories, but ... when was this?"

"Not long after Mamma told me he was my father, he and his officers were invited to the mansions of the rich." Head down, I peered at him. "Anyways, for a week, General – my father – attended balls, torch-light parades, parties, dinners – every evening a celebration. My father took refuge in the Ballou house, home of my Aunt Freelove. Aunt Free presented me to him, and I'll never forget his face when he looked at me."

I shut my eyes, his image in vivid color as if he stood before me now. "He stood so tall, he had to kneel on one knee. He looked into my eyes as if he knew me, but didn't know from where. I can't remember what he said, but he took my small hand in his big one and clasped it." I clasped my own hands. "I curtsied, and he bowed to me. Then some lady swept him away, and there was dancing – lots of dancing." I opened my eyes to Aaron, waiting for me to go on.

"I twirled about the ballroom with all the grown-ups till Aunt Free dragged me outside, exhausted. I remember one last thing – looking back to see him. But he wasn't there." Aaron blurred before my teary eyes. "It felt as if he left me again. Then those same feelings flooded back on inauguration day. When he turned and went inside Federal Hall, I stood there, that abandoned little girl." My voice quivered as I wiped away unwelcome tears.

"I'm sorry, I wasn't aware ..." His voice soothed me. He gestured, palms up, shaking his head.

I took a fortifying breath. "I intend to prove it." Tears gone, I spoke with the resolve that settled in my breast long ago. "Someone must know he was in Providence then. I haven't yet found anyone who can tell me. Perhaps someday he will. I plan to call on him when he's not so busy."

"If it means that much to you," he said. "Being his daughter is indeed a privilege. But you're still you, no matter who your parents were. Who is your mother?"

"It ain't—is not Lady Washington," I stated in haste. "My Mamma's name was Phebe. She didn't know where she was born. Tall and slim, as I am – and my father. She lived a hard-scrabble life. Her mother left her to be sold at pauper auction when she was five years old."

I looked straight into his eyes, though it would've been easier to look at the floor. "I'm not sure you know this, being from well-bred stock, but unlike slaves, paupers were sold to the lowest, not the highest, bidder. She met a sailor named John Bowen and moved to Providence. In circumstances with my brother, she changed her name to Bowen – even though Bowen left her to fend for herself and my brother when he was born. With no means of support from Bowen, she was forced into prostitution."

I paused, waiting for his reaction. With none forthcoming, I went on, "Providence is Puritanical and righteous. If you're a vagrant or a public charge, unless a resident posted bond, they could run you out of town. They warned her out, and she found shelter in a brothel, the first of many, where me and my sister – my sister Polly and I were born. The whores were good to us."

I stopped and took a deep breath. "The soldiers and sailors made us their pets. I learned to get things from men by being nice to them. The whores earned a lot of French money that year. When they left, two years later, Providence hated its prostitutes enough to throw them all out.

"Mamma found work in another brothel, but us girls were put in the workhouse. We were the only ones not blind, limbless, maimed, old or too wretched to be sold at pauper auction. But where else could we go?" I shrugged. "I spent my time picking oakum, pulling old ropes apart for ship's caulking. It was a horrible place."

I shivered as it rushed back to haunt me. "Those too lazy to work were gagged, forced to wear a wooden yoke around their necks, thrown in the dungeon on bread and water – like what I read about Newgate Prison." A long-forgotten emotion surged – helplessness.

"Then what?" he asked quickly, as a lawyer would.

"Mamma came back. Henry Bowen, the Town Sergeant, took charge of her worldly goods. Mamma seemed to like men named Bowen. We got shunted in and out of the workhouse, but Mr. Bowen got us tutored in reading. Mamma's so-called husband, John Bowen, the sailor, died and got buried in a pauper's grave. My father's... er, General Washington's dispatch rider, Reuben Ballou, paid Mamma's bond. He and his wife Freelove saved us from the streets. She became my Aunt Free, who I love to this day."

"Then what happened?" he urged me on.

"Mamma had another baby, Lavinia. The Ballous raised her. Then I was bound to Colonel Sam Adams. I learned a lot from his wife in the womanly arts. When Mistress Adams died, I could not live as the Colonel's concubine, so I made a living how I could."

"How did you?" He continued his line of questioning.

"How I could," I repeated, more deliberate. How could he not know what that meant? "Mamma married Jon Clark from Boston. He was a war veteran and left a wife and six young 'uns for Mamma. He was most times unemployed, but a smart man – I mean book smart. But being a vagrant at heart, the law warned he and Mamma out. They went from jail to jail, but they left me and Polly behind. They lived in a cave for a spell. Next I heard they were both dead. Murdered, perhaps."

Long-buried grief made me sob. "I came here on a packet and I joined the theater because my step-pa, Jon, taught me about it. There's no theater in Providence. They're still Puritans in New England."

"An amazing story, Betsy," he admitted, eyes downcast. "I admire your courage." Now he looked right at me.

"Thank you." I fluttered my lashes. "There's more to admire about me." This drew a grin from him. "I intend to use the resources God gave me to better my standing. Not that there's anything wrong with being poor." I held my head higher.

"I have no disdain for the poor," he assured me. "On the contrary, they deserve every bit of help the fortunate can give them. That is true democracy, and as an American, I feel it's my duty. I place my money where my mouth is in the form of *pro bono* work." His voice stayed calm and even, not in the least bragging, which he had every right to do.

"Why, that's right noble of you, Attorney Burr. I'll need legal advice down the line, but I plan to be a woman of enough means that you need not work *pro bono* for me."

"How do you plan to improve your lot, if you don't mind my asking?" He sat back and crossed one leg over the other.

"By buying property and renting it out. When they build more estates north of here, in Haarlem, for instance, mine will be one of them. The surface of this city has barely been scratched. I mean that in the true sense. You will see in coming years when the wilderness is cleared away and built upon. And populated." I held up one finger. "With dwellings." Then two fingers. "And businesses."

His eyes bored into me as if he tried to reach into my soul and pluck out some of this foresight for himself. "I confess I hadn't thought that far ahead, Betsy. My predictions and hopes lie in other fields, and I don't mean fields to develop buildings on. I've been concentrating on our political future."

"Are you part of it?" I leaned forward, eyes wide, the thumping of my heart visible through my blouse. My curiosity gnawed like hunger, and I knew hunger. "Where do you fit into our nation's future?" I added silently: *And mine?*

"I'm not one to sit on the sidelines and watch history pass me by. Now, more than ever, when our nation is in her infancy. Much the same as watching my daughter grow, from birth to the budding lady she is now." Pride brightened those dark eyes. "I hope when our nation is her age, it will also be on its way to great achievements."

"You plan to run for public office? Other than Attorney General?"

He blinked for the first time since he got here. "Eventually," was all he said. Then he drew his gaze away and glanced at the wall clock. "A glass of Madeira would do me a world of good right now. What about you? A refill?"

"Please." But I noticed the clock's spindly arms marking our last fifteen minutes to have the room. Panic swept through me. Where to go then?

"Excuse me for a moment." He stood, smoothed his breeches, and headed down the stairs.

CHAPTER 7

I NEEDED A PRIVY. Badly. Holding up Sukie's skirt, I tore down the back stairs and out to the privy in the yard. Never before had a man's presence jolted my nerves to the point of my needing to void my bladder like a plow horse. I envied Sukie, her wardrobe, and her knowing Aaron Burr as a brother all her life.

As I smoothed the skirt over my thighs and headed back up the stairs, I knew Aaron and I fit together. No better word for it. We fit.

I settled on the settee, the skirt spread about me, ankles crossed. He returned with two glasses of what I hoped was Madeira, but anything would do. I sipped. Ah, yes. It warmed me like a hug.

Eager to continue our exchange, I sat forward, almost spilling out of Sukie's bodice. Now I was glad I'd chosen it, despite the low décolletage, but his eyes hadn't strayed downwards yet. No, he was interested in what lay between my ears. "I have a confession to make now," I said. "Sukie never told me she knew you. Not till we stood in the crowd at Federal Hall."

"Why would she tell you?" came his casual reply as my practiced eye slid down his physique. I could size up a man between heartbeats.

"We've become close as sisters since Mamma's death," I told him. "My real sister Polly is so different from me, but me and—Sukie and I are a lot alike. Yet I know hardly anything about her childhood."

"Perhaps she stayed coy on the subject for a reason." His eyes twinkled as the ghost of a grin hovered upon his lips. "She didn't want us to meet any sooner than this."

"She didn't want us to meet at all," I replied bluntly. "Neither did anyone else I know, all males, I daresay. Except William Dunlap, that is. The theater manager."

"Ah, yes, Dunlap." He nodded as if he knew him. "I appreciate your candor."

Any man who could say that without his eyes sliding up my front, I had to respect.

"Very upfront, Aaron. What about you? Do you intend to make the game of politics your career? Or is law truth enough for you?" I started my own line of questioning.

His lips curved into an inviting smile. "Yes, the law is enough for me for now. But I do intend to grow with the country. One step at a time, though. The president hates political parties, but I daresay, as he decided he didn't want to be a king, Congress will overrule any of his wishes they don't like. And he's no politician. But they are."

"I like politicians," I admitted. "They're always up for a good row. They're actors, as I am." I found that easy to smile about. "Remember that, and your debates with them will never come to physical blows." My muscles relaxed as I eased up. Although his presence disarmed me, he had the knack of putting me at ease.

"Ah, but some do take themselves and each other too seriously." He took a mouthful of wine. "I've seen my share of brawls, and I don't mean in taprooms. And look at some of the things they write about each other in the papers." He shook his head, disapproval narrowing his eyes. "Petty, derogatory drivel. Far beneath their dignity."

"Those are the ones who don't have any dignity. We know so much better, don't we?" I gave him a knowing smile and something I didn't dare think I'd give him this evening – a wink. I knew we approached a comfortable place.

"I never goad anyone deliberately," he said. "I stay out of the ruckus. But if I do intend a career in the political arena, I'm not naïve enough to think I can always avoid it. I'll be running into opponents and will make enemies. Such as acting – you can't please all the critics."

I smiled at that. "I'm glad you understand how politics mimic the theater. Not to brag, but I never had a bad review." I beamed. "I give it my all. I become the person I'm portraying. It comes from a lifetime of pretending I was someone else."

"Do you believe the theater is your lifetime calling?" He sipped his wine.

I shook my head. "It will cease to be fun someday, or when I'm too old to get any roles. I plan to marry a worthy man and help build his fortune. Not live off him, mind you. Make my own fortune. But help each other."

"And do you have the lucky gent in mind?" He worded the question as any lawyer would. Yet he kept his tone casual.

"No, no one in mind – yet." My gaze strayed, and I noticed a spittoon in the corner. I traced circles on the velvet armrest with my finger. "I never met anyone I wanted to marry."

"I am married," he stated, his tone flat.

I answered too fast, "I know." I asked the obvious: "So what are you doing here?"

He skipped one beat and gave me a broad smile. "I'm

married, not dead." But without skipping another beat, his eyes drifted downwards, lingered, then captured mine once again. His timing was flawless. Courtroom tactics, I knew. I wondered when we'd fall into each other's arms. "And if I may be so bold as to say, if our president isn't your father, he ought to be."

In one private conversation, we'd made the connection of a lifetime. Never before had I needed to share every facet of my being with someone. Only Sukie and William had come close. But Aaron reached in and grasped my soul. Now I wished he'd take my body, too.

"I need to wait for the proper time," I went on. "I wanted my father to come back to me from the moment Mamma told me. It wasn't that long ago, but far before anyone dreamt he'd be president."

"How do you plan to convince him?" he asked.

"We share so many of the same traits. If that isn't enough, I can remind him he was in Providence in seventy-four. I can observe his reaction. I'm very good at reading a person. It came from my theater experience. It's all in the way the eyes blink, the brow lifts, the lips and hands tremble, and the tightening of the muscles."

I acted out those gestures. "I can't rightly explain it. It's an art." My hands got to fluttering again, but I didn't clench them this time. "The way a soothsayer can contact spirits. A third eye, if you will. Then it's up to him, how he reacts to my telling him."

"Betsy..." He paused. "I daresay you're not the first to do this. I was an aide-de-camp of his during the war, and though he was always discreet, he was away from Lady Washington for long stretches – and no one was fool enough to believe he cantered off into the night to play bid whist with General Gage. Some evenings he vanished into the darkness and did not return till morn. We all did. But when he rode off into the moonlit night, we took notice."

Afraid to ask, I plowed on, "He has other children?" I held my breath. *Please* say *no!*

"No one knows for sure."

I released a relieved sigh.

"If he does," Aaron continued, "he's never said a word. It depends. If a woman presents him with a child who's his spitting image, I suppose he'd be hard-pressed to turn his back."

"I wouldn't say we're the spittin' image. But we both have the same red hair, and Mamma didn't." In one sweeping gesture, I pulled the bonnet off. My hair tumbled past my shoulders. "And the same strong features." I turned my profile to him and raised my chin. "And the same take-charge determination. Deep down I know. I can neither explain nor prove it. But till the day I face him and tell him who I am, please keep all this to yourself. Now that you know – you know my bloodline, or what I'm praying is my bloodline. Whoever told you betrayed me."

"No one betrayed you, Betsy." He took my hand. I cringed, knowing how cold and clammy it was. But his heat seeped into me. "I'll tell you who it was if you must know."

"Never mind. I'm not dumb enough to believe I can tell someone something like that and expect them to keep their gob shut. There's no such thing as a secret, and three can't keep a secret unless two are dead." I tightened my fingers around his. "Someday it will no longer be a private matter. But till then, I'm simple Betsy Bowen."

"You're hardly simple." While his hand enveloped mine, I tingled. I thirsted for his lips upon mine, but waiting was delicious. Oh, was he worth the wait.

"I mean as in 'not renowned'. Yet. I have every faith you

will succeed in whatever endeavor you pursue, Betsy." His voice caressed me like a velvet glove.

"As will you. Then may we attend that opera?" I hoped I didn't sound too eager.

"I'll be happy to escort you." He released my hand. "Just tell me one thing."

"What?" I hoped for an intensely intimate question, to bring us even closer.

He glanced over at my book on the windowsill. "Why are you reading Miss Wollstonecraft?"

I hoped my eyes didn't show my disappointment. Discussing books was challenging and gave me a chance to show off, but I hoped we'd exhausted intellectual subjects for now. "I share a lot of her ideas and aspire to be like her – in some ways. She provokes deep discussion and outright outrage. Why?"

"She happens to be my favorite author." He finished his wine and placed the glass on the table.

"William was right!" I broke into a grin, biting my lip to suppress it. "The insults I've seen printed about her: 'a hyena in petticoats', 'a man-hater,' and those are the ones I can repeat. Why do you admire her?" Oh, God help me, I was falling in love with Aaron Burr by the minute!

"Because I believe women should have equal treatment and that they have souls," he said. "Call me a renegade, but that's what I believe. I have encountered intelligent, well-read, and well-spoken women, such as yourself. I'm bringing my daughter up that way. At seven, she's a scholar."

"I heard that from Sukie." I went over and fetched the book, sat back down, and ran my thumb over the pages. Knowing we'd struck a common chord thrilled me. "I'll never be a scholar, but I have logical reasons why I feel that way about things. Knowing we both admire Miss Wollstonecraft – that will make things much easier between us, Aaron." I inched closer. He didn't move. "We share beliefs few men share with women. A man whose thinking so matches mine – that man owns my heart."

Intensity gleamed in his eyes, but he still didn't make a move.

Mr. Tyler popped his head over the railing. "Miss Bowen, we need the room now. I'm sorry."

"Of course." Oh, why hadn't I rented the room for an hour? I knew the time would fly.

"We'd best depart, then." Aaron got to his feet and helped me to mine. This time his eye roved, but fast. "The opera it is, then, the next evening you're free."

"That would be Monday next." Crikey, a few days away. Now my mind whirred. How to get another dress? Shoes? A hat? Gloves? Would Sukie oblige me again, knowing the reason? If she refused me, who—er, whom could I borrow from?

"I can call for you at half past seven, if you'll let me." He led me to the stairs.

"Of course. But before we take this..." I scrambled for words I never needed before, "...take another step, what of your wife?" I didn't want to ask, but had to know, curious how he'd answer.

"She's at home. She has a chronic illness. And she understands I require companionship she cannot provide." His voice lowered.

Ah, had he rehearsed this line, or was it tried and true?

Something told me it was God's honest truth. As I stood, I nearly fell, dizzy from hunger, the wine, and the bedazzlement of him.

He clutched my elbows in his powerful grip. "Are you all right?"

I raised my head. Our lips nearly touched. I pushed myself away, or I'd have lunged into his arms. Oh, and he smelled so good! Pine and leather and... if moonlight had a fragrance, it would be him.

He walked me to his coach. The coachman opened the door as I lifted Sukie's skirts and slid inside. It smelled of that same leather, the seat plush and cushiony. He slid in beside me, but not close enough for our thighs to touch.

At my boarding house door, the carriage slowed to a halt. He helped me out and clasped my hand. "Betsy, please accept my sincere apology for being so unjust to you about your connection to President Washington. The evening we were to attend the opera, I was summoned by the governor, which is why I sent my regrets. I hope you understand, your being the president's daughter would be a big problem for me if he found out about us."

Us? I shivered with delight. "Let us cross that bridge when we get to it. I may not get to see him as long as he's president, but once he's out of office, it shouldn't be a problem for you. Should it?" I lifted my left brow and tilted my chin.

He shook his head, his eyes fixed on mine. "You're right, I'll be well on my way by then. He won't be interested in me once he quits politics and is back on his plantation. But that's far into the future. Let us enjoy the now, and next time we meet, I care to explore more of your mind."

"It is yours for the exploring." I didn't mean to sound whispery, it just came out that way.

Until we meet again, then, Betsy." His voice fondled me.

I opened the door and watched him turn on a heel and stride back to his carriage. I'd be up all night, I knew it.

CHAPTER 8

I LAY WIDE AWAKE, my mind whirring and my heart pounding. With Aaron as my future, I sloughed off my past. I unloaded those bitter memories.

When streaks of dawn peeked through the slatted shutters, I leapt out of bed, bursting with energy. I danced around my small room, giddy as a child with her first dolly.

But Aaron was hardly my first dolly. He was my first love.

I headed to William's dwelling, knowing he had rolls and coffee ready. More than breaking my fast, I wanted to know if he had blabbed to Aaron. But if he had, I owed him a show of gratitude.

"Betsy!" He greeted me, steaming cup in hand. "Care to partake of some soda bread and Wensleydale cheese?"

"Sounds like a deadly combination. Isn't one Irish and one British?" I seated myself at his messy writing table, eyeing the pile of unpaid bills. "Someday I'll help you pay those. Will, I've shared parts of my past with you that I've never told another person, so before we break bread, I need to ask: did you tell Aaron about my being the president's daughter?"

His downcast look told me he was the guilty party before he opened his mouth.

"I'm not angry," I assured him. "I'm simply curious. There has to be a reason you told him."

"He is Aaron to you now?" was all he could say.

"So you did tell him. Well, I wound up telling him everything. Then a painful weight lifted from my shoulders. Now we're on more intimate terms. So I must thank you. But just tell me why. I'm dying to know. What was in it for you?" I placed fists on hips, waiting.

He sputtered, "Wha-wha—nothing! Betsy, I'm so sorry, you know I would never say anything – on purpose. But it happened so fast the words tumbled out of my mouth before I heard them."

"What happened so fast?" For a second I thought Aaron, with his lawyerly skill, tricked it out of him. The coffee burnt a hole in my tum. I set the cup down, curling all ten icy fingers around it.

"One of Burr's clerks came to the theater, inquiring about your background – where you were from, who your family was. I told him, pardon my Anglo Saxon, 'None of your effing business,' but I was livid." His face reddened. "He threatened to close the house down. I blurted out, 'Who do you think you're sparring with? Her father is President Washington. Get away with your strong-arm tactics.' Only after it was out of my mouth did I realize I'd revealed it, but my blood was already boiling. Seems the aide went back to Burr and told him, 'Don't touch Betsy Bowen with a barge pole or President Washington will destroy you!' It's the only reason I can see why Burr sent his regrets that evening." His voice calmed and his words slowed. "I'm ever so sorry, Betsy. Please forgive me."

I leaned back in the squeaky chair and nearly fell backward. I righted myself, a grin spreading across my lips. "Oh,

Will, I know you'd never betray me on purpose. I reckoned it to be some mistake or blunder or bribe—"

His jaw fell.

"I don't mean a bribe, but ... there's nothing to forgive." I waved my hand. "You're too honest for your own good. You'll never make a politician. Stay in the arts."

"I intend to." He plopped into his chair, massaging his eyes with thumb and forefinger. "Ugh. I could've kicked myself in the arse."

"Relax, Will. You haven't a malicious bone in that wiry body of yours. You're too soft," I granted him sincere praise.

"Thanks – I think." He lowered his head, his eyes round like a wounded hound dog's.

"Soft-hearted, that is." I stood, walked over, and kissed him. "So he knows I am President Washington's daughter. I would've told him anyways. I just wasn't ready to bare my soul at the first meeting. But I'm glad I did. After a few minutes as we chit-chatted, I felt I'd known him all my life. I told him everything. I can't explain it, we have a ... a bond."

"He's a New York City lawyer, not a backwoodsman, Betsy. Your fears were unfounded," he assured me.

"This meeting meant the world to me. It's because he's who he is I didn't want to tell him my history. I've been rejected by too many men. I couldn't bear to let it happen again. Especially with the man I'm convinced is my future."

I lowered myself onto his lap and wound my arm around his shoulders. "Me and Aaron – I mean *Aaron and I* – got to talking, and after he'd told me he knew who my father is, it became so easy to talk."

I sighed. "When he told me he was orphaned and lived with Sukie's family, I realized life had thrust us into the same story, but we took different paths – him to college and the military, me to here and the theater. We faced our fates head-on. We're cut from the same cloth."

"I don't know which of you will get to the top first, but you will get there, I know it." He added in a softer tone, "With or without the help of him – or any man."

I rested my hands in my lap. "Oh, I didn't ask for any help. Stone the crows, we've just only met. But I see him going great places – the Senate, the governorship, even the presidency."

"All this from one meeting?" He raised his brows. "Perhaps you did pick up some skills from that crystal-ball-gazing French friend of yours."

"No ..." I trailed off. "Something he conveys. Energy. No, confidence. No ... there ain't even a word for it in English."

He pulled me closer to him. "Ah, now this is where Voltaire's Greek word fits perfectly: *charisma*. The word you use when someone's quality is so ethereal, every other word fails. And guess what? You have it, too." He kissed the tip of my nose. "Which is why you and Burr are kindred souls. It's a rare gift you both possess."

"Why, thank you." My heart burst with joy.

"And did future Governor-Senator-President Burr charm the petticoats off you with said charisma?" He faltered, as if not wanting to know the answer.

"No. The gloves, but not the petticoats. That won't happen any time soon." I smoothed down my skirt. "I am taking my time with him."

"You have time with him?"

"He wants to see me again. And again." I gave a firm nod.

"Meaning what? You intend to be the next Mrs. Burr? What about the present one?" he quizzed.

"His wife is ill. He told me, in his eloquent fashion, that her illness – oh, I forgot his phrasing, but he made it clear what her illness implied. Must I spell it out for you?"

"And you believe that?" he asked, as if I shouldn't.

"Of course. Sukie even mentioned something about it. But I'm privileged just to be his companion for now. For later – I will steer this ship on the right course."

"I know you will. You're your father's daughter. And now that Burr knows that, he'll tread carefully. And so you don't lack fitting raiment in his company ..." William opened his billfold and handed me ten dollars, "... go buy some fancy gewgaws."

After thanking him, I dashed to the second-hand store. I bought a plum taffeta dress with a blue bodice and a brocade hoopskirt. I pulled it on and let the frock slide over it, spun around until I went dizzy. Head high, I sauntered through the store with all the assurance of the magnate I'd someday be. I stopped to preen in the full-length looking glass. I tried on shoes until I found my first ever that truly fit. The cream satin mules would make me a smidge taller than Aaron, but that bothered me none. With the remaining two dollars of William's ten, I bought kid gloves and a ribboned lace cap.

When Aaron's carriage halted at the curb next Monday evening, I stood at the threshold, sweat trickling down my back.

He got out, and the sight of him turned me into trembling jelly.

"Betsy, a pleasure to see you again." He grasped my hand. I made sure to wipe it first. But sweat drenched me all over.

"As it is to see you ... uh, likewise." I tripped over my tongue. We laughed, easing the tension, but it hardly eased my fumbling. Would I ever calm down in his presence?

His coach was different than before. A rental? No one save the president owned two coaches. Roomier and with velvet seats, it didn't jostle as much over the cobbles. I glanced out the window at the familiar shop fronts, closed for the night. "A nice half-moon tonight," I commented.

He turned to look at me. "I'd like to see you under it when it's full."

At that suggestion, I sweated more. *Could I wait until it's full?*

Seated in the Queen's Head with a sip of Madeira in me, I took a deep breath. Whew, what a relief. I didn't tremble or sweat as before. My heart ticked, rather than slammed.

Calm enough, I went all serious. "One of my favorite subjects, besides theater and books and history, is the state of our new nation. Please tell me of your leanings." I clasped my hands on the table. My elbows crept up, but I pushed them down, remembering my table manners.

"I approved the Constitution's ratification. But in general, I have more anti-Federalist leanings, which is why our president doesn't favor me. I've not committed myself either way, so he knows not what camp I'm in. Till then, he cannot trust me, I'm sorry to say." He lowered his eyes and took a sip of wine.

"Why do you favor the anti-Federalist side?" I already knew it would be easy to keep this topic going.

"I'm a local politician with local concerns for people outside the privileged families." He twirled his glass. "I oppose the moneyed group that led the New York Federalists. As I told you before, I often work *pro bono*. Hence, I'm neither Federalist nor anti-Federalist in the national view." The sparkle in his eyes told me he enjoyed women with opinions. "What about you?"

I cleared my throat, ready to impress him. "Well, having

read the Constitution in the *Gazette*, I reckon it makes sense, so I lean more towards the Federalists – but not completely. Some of those items make more sense than others. I disagree with Hamilton's monarchist leanings, but Jefferson is too provincial. I fear they're all self-serving in the end."

"Most of them, sadly." He nodded and we got to chatting about Mozart and another chap named Bach who was as prolific at making music as at making babies.

We dined on broiled sturgeon with carrots, parsnips, and delicate boiled potatoes, and for afters, a creamy frothy drink called syllabub which I'd never delighted in before. The opera was like a fairy tale; I enjoyed it so much more having read it first.

The evening flew by. When it seemed ten minutes had passed, he bade me *au revoir* at my door. And *"au revoir"* is what he said. He held my hand and kissed it. I went weak. I pressed my fists to my sides, longing to throw my arms around his neck and ravish him.

Oh, how he left me wanting more. As my hand grasped his, my fingers lingered. I memorized all his dark beauty and forced myself to let go. I breached protocol, but I'd always treasure those seconds.

"Au revoir," I whispered, as my voice had left me. Dizzy and sighing, I backed into the hall, tripping and catching myself over a warped floorboard. I turned and floated upstairs. Did I sleep that night? Not a wink. He filled my thoughts every minute.

As morning dawned, a sharp rap on my door jarred me.

"Betsy, open up, it's Sukie. I need to see you."

I slid from bed, splashed water on my face, and rinsed my

mouth out. I unlatched the door and headed back to finish my toilette.

Sukie swept in, morning air swirling around her. "Betsy, do you plan to make this a regular ... occurrence?"

I glanced at her over my shoulder. "I should hope so. I never leave the house without washing up and donning decent raiment."

"You know what I mean." She removed her gloves one finger at a time, something I never did. Mine, the few times I had gloves, came off inside out, pulled from the bottoms. "Your liaison with Aaron."

"Ah, going all French on me, are you, Sukie? I ain't— haven't done nothing— anything with him that needs French. Hence no *liaison*, only visits. All in English. Except the opera. That was in German."

Her mouth tightened, in what I called her lemon lips. "I cannot lend you any more clothes if you wear them to entertain Aaron."

I combed my hair and pinned it up. "Crikey, I need a hair-cut. Heed me, Sukie. He told me in his eloquent way that his wife is ill and what that implies, but he didn't lay a finger on me. We clasped hands is all. All is upfront and with the utmost decorum."

"Hmph." She flicked her gloves through the air.

I twirled my hair around the brush. "I know our destinies are meant to be entwined. I've dreamt of someone like him all my life. And, as will be to your delight, we've no definite plans to see each other again. You can keep your frocks clean and tidy. I spent next week's pay on a new skirt and shoes and gloves. And rouge."

She sat on my bed, pushing aside the rumpled covers. "I'm sorry, take what you want from my wardrobe, it's only ... well, I feel ... protective of Aaron, as a little brother, even though he's four years older. He always seemed..." She waved her hands around, "...fragile. He was a sickly child. I love you both and don't want either of you to get hurt."

"Sukie, I hardly plan to spit him out onto a bone pile. This may sound dotty coming from me, but what I feel for him is ..." I swallowed. "Precious. I savor it, cherish it. I've never felt that way, ever, and I'd be daft to risk losing it. I've found a treasure." I clutched my comb between my clasped hands.

She gave me a heartfelt smile. "Oh, Betsy, I never thought I'd hear you say words so pretty that weren't from a written script. But be careful. Yes, Theo is ill and truth be told, she will not regain her health, and I hope you're not thinking ... uh ..." She stammered.

"I know what you're trying to spit out." A rush of shame crushed me. "I'm not thinking I'll replace her. What a morbid thought."

I flitted across the room. "Look what I bought." I modeled my new attire.

She gasped. "Betsy, that dress, that bodice – they were mine! I donated them on Tuesday. I would have given them to you. Oh, you could have saved all that money."

I leaned against the wall, shaking my head. Why was my life one dose of irony after another?

CHAPTER 9

NEWS CAME the next day that made my heart leap for joy. After William announced that *As You Like It* would end its run in ten days, we'd begin rehearsals for the raucous comedy *School for Scandal*. I would be the leading lady, Lady Sneerwell, a character I adored and despised at the same time.

"Will, why only ten days of rehearsal?" We strolled to the City Coffee House for a late tipple.

"Because of your sire—President George Washington, my dear Lady Sneerwell. He finally responded to my invitation and commanded a performance of *School for Scandal*. We shall perform before him and his entourage in our presidential box on opening night."

Ecstatic, I clutched his arm. A brisk breeze revived me. "My father is attending on opening night? Presidential box? What on earth is that?"

"I am widening the box at stage left to accommodate our president, Lady Washington, and ten distinguished guests. You shall meet him in a private audience after the show. He may even accept my invitation to dine with us afterward."

A rush of emotion brought tears to my eyes. "This is the best gift anyone has ever given me."

He cast me a sly look. "Just know your lines. Then I'll give you the second-best gift you'll ever get."

I hoped May 11 would be an evening I'd never forget—I'd come face to face with Papa, talk of our blood ties, and share the name Washington forevermore.

As the curtain rose, I became Lady Sneerwell, hot and dripping with sweat in my outrageous costume, and entered that absurd world of scandal-mongering. I never stopped glancing at that presidential box. I could only make out a meadow of bewigged and powdered heads, but a niggling hunch told me he was there.

After the show, I entered the dressing room I shared with three other female players. "Ladies," I addressed, each of them in various stages of *déshabillé*, "I need the room for a private audience—the most important of my life."

They didn't question me, thank heaven. They dressed and graciously vanished.

Heart pounding, palms sweating, I sat and watched the clock. The pendulum swung back and forth until I went cross-eyed watching it.

By eleven, my heart sank. *He's not coming.* He hated the play! He hated my performance! He'd never want to meet me now, an actress in a bawdy farce! Before the next minute passed, I broke into sobs. "No, not again," I cried, that abandoned little girl once more. I couldn't bear another rebuff. I vowed never to attempt another audience with him. Rejection stung as hard tonight as all those years ago.

I dragged myself out and ran smack into Governor Clinton

in the corridor. He pulled away with a glowing smile. "Miss Bowen, you were hilarious. I nearly laughed my teeth out."

"Why, thank you, sir." I looked over his shoulder, dreading, but hoping for Papa to come striding towards me. I blurted, "And what of the president? Did he enjoy the play as well?" I held my breath and braced myself against the wall for his answer.

"We thought the Regulars were invading again, the way he fled that theater. I can't tell you what or who called him out so suddenly." He shook his head and clucked. "We'll need to wait till morning to find that out."

"Oh, dear," I sighed, struggling to keep more tears back, but they stung my eyes and soaked my lashes. My stomach in knots, I clutched my middle. "You must excuse me, Governor. I'm not feeling very fit."

"Of course. Good evening to you."

I ran to William's office. "Papa fled the theater before the applause ended, Will. He didn't come backstage. He hates me."

He looked up from counting receipts. "Oh, no, love, he doesn't. Perhaps he had an emergency Cabinet meeting." He came around the desk, and I dropped into his outstretched arms. "We'll fetch a drink. Take your mind off it."

"I shall never seek him again." A breeze chilled me as we walked to Little's Tavern. I clutched my cloak tighter around my shoulders. "The wound from my father's rejection will fester as long as I live."

"You say that now, but you'll change your mind. I know you. You don't give up easily." He gave me an encouraging nod.

We entered the tavern, and I scanned the room for familiar faces. James and Sim sat with a few fellows, and over in the corner, Senator Maclay dug into a plate of something messy. He beckoned us over. I needed his praise but could not talk about my shattering let-down. I'd come here for distraction, not pity.

"Betsy, William, sit, sit, have some bangers and pickles." Maclay spoke and chewed. "Betsy, you were sensational. I haven't laughed so much since *The Magic Flute* when Papageno's feathers set on fire."

I forced a smile. "I don't feel like laughing now. Thank you anyway, Senator. You enjoyed the play?" I sat in the nearest chair.

"Indeed, I think it an indecent representation before ladies of character and virtue. I thought the players acted well, especially you, my dear lady." He nodded my way.

"God's foot, old bean!" William pounded the table with his fist. "Did you like it or not?"

"No—but I laughed till my buttons popped." Maclay turned to face me. "And how went your meeting with the president, my lady? Was that not a magnificent bouquet he presented you?"

I sat up. "What... what bouquet? Governor Clinton told me the president fled the theater as if engulfed in flames."

"You silly bird, he fled the box to buy you a bouquet off a flower girl. I saw him in the lobby. He said he went backstage to present it to you, but you'd already left. The posies must still be there, unless he brought them home to the missus."

"I... I'd already left, I was upset he'd gone..." My heart hollow, I muttered, "My one and only chance ruined."

"It wasn't your only chance," Maclay assured me with a warm pat on the hand. "You'll meet him again. I'll see if I can arrange it."

I shook my head. "No, it wasn't meant to be. It's greatly kind of you, Senator, but it's not meant to be."

"Don't give up, lass. You must make things happen, not surrender to fate. You will meet him someday. Even if it's not till you're Mrs. Aaron Burr, he will meet you."

Stunned by those words, I went dizzy. I cleared my throat, relieved to change the subject. "You believe I'll be Mrs. Burr someday?"

William watched this exchange with an amused curl to his lips.

"It's a hunch," Maclay said. "And my hunch got me elected to the Senate. But don't take my word for it. Rely on fate."

"He is married, you know. Please make no mistake. I have no immediate designs on him or becoming his missus." I hadn't thought that far ahead, even in my wildest fantasies.

"Yes, and his wife is gravely ill. A pity." He drained his stein, bade us good evening, and hobbled out on his cane. My heart went out to the poor woman I'd never met.

"He's right about not surrendering to fate," William said. "You have to steer your ship."

My ship foundered the next evening. The biggest part of my life ended. I rapped thrice, then twice on the theater door. This code told the scene-shifters or stagehands inside that it was cast or crew. When the door opened, I gaped. William opened it himself. Shoulders slumped, eyes downcast, he stepped back to let me in. No greeting, not a word.

I stepped into darkness. Goosebumps ridged my arms. I clutched his hand. "Will, what is it?"

"I wish I could've got word to you sooner, love." He rubbed his eyes. "Speculators bought the lot we stand on and plan to demolish the building."

I gasped, stumbling back into the door. "What happens now?" I searched his eyes.

He shrugged. "Some cultured swell will build a new theater. Someday."

I held him close and forced out, "We will survive."

"I know you will. But me..." He shook his head. "I haven't a groat. I live out of the receipt box."

He had more than me—I had no receipt box. Once again, my only source of income would be my wits and wares. Feminine wares, that is. I'd need to return to the streets until I could find a decent occupation.

"Betsy, you won't take up your former, uh... profession, will you?"

Did he read my mind? I sighed. "I hope not."

We pulled apart and looked into each other's eyes.

"Promise me. You can be a laundress, a chambermaid, anything but *that*." His eyes begged me.

"I have at least a day to think about it. I'm three meals from starvation. Do you need money?" I offered. "I can spare a coin or two."

"No, love, that's mighty generous of you, but keep your money. I'll survive. I may go back to painting or..." His shoulders slumped. "Oh, God's truth, I just don't know."

I couldn't bear to go inside, to see that quaint old house for the last time, so I promised him, "I'll visit soon, when I find another situation, and do please send me a note when you do. I'll have the landlady forward my post. I fear I won't be living there after next week's rent is due."

"You will write?" His eyes begged once more.

"Of course. Let us not tarry here and make it harder on us." I forced myself to turn and walk away. It pained me like a stab wound. But I knew I'd see William again soon.

I strode down the Broad Way towards Little's Tavern and

entered through the forbidden front, head high, daring anyone to confront me. Scanning the room, I saw the usual faces. James Reynolds and a nondescript chap sat at a table for two.

They stood, and James brought a chair over. He introduced his mate as Oliver Wolcott. We exchanged polite nods and Oliver asked, "Would you care for a glass of anything?"

"Yes!" I licked my dry lips. "A glass of anything...but make it strong."

Oliver ordered me a glass of strong ale.

"What is it, Betsy?" James asked. "Ain't you in the show tonight?"

"There ain't gonna be no more shows. The house is being demolished. Who knows when another will be built?" I twisted my fingers around each other.

They looked at me with pity, a blessing at that moment.

"Jimmy, I'll be blunt." I shifted in my chair and sat straight up. "I need work. Can you afford a housemaid?"

He shook his head. "Nay, lass, not right now. My fortunes hit bottom. We kin barely afford a meal this sennight."

Oliver offered, "I'm no better off, but I can ask around. What do you do?"

Oh, I could've laughed at that, if the moment weren't so somber. The barmaid set my ale down. I took a long pull. "Well, I, uh... I can polish and wax and launder and perform most domestic duties."

James gave me a raised brow. I stared him down. "*Most* domestic duties," I repeated.

"Wait, I know someone." James's eyes lit up. "Sally Marshall. On Barclay Street, next door to the grog shop. Go to her."

"What does she need in the way of services?" I asked.

Oliver excused himself, whether on purpose I knew not,

but I later reckoned so, when James told me Sally Marshall ran a 'house of debauchery'.

"But," he hastened to add, "of the highest class. Senators and swells. It's no bawdyhouse. It stands in the Holy Ground."

"What Holy Ground? Does the church own it?" I asked, joking.

To my surprise, he nodded. "Aye. The Episcopal church owns the land—two blocks along Church, Vesey, and Barclay Streets—the highest-priced bordellos run along those streets."

"How do you know?" I prodded. Could James be acquainted with anything *but* a bawdyhouse?

"I bin there now and again. In my salad days." He smirked.

I had to laugh this time. "I didn't know salad days ended at thirty."

"What I mean is—in my richer days." He smoothed his hair back. "Tell her I sent you. She hires by recommendation. In my day, I was not only her best recommender, but one of her best customers. My word carries its weight in gold."

That convinced me. I finished the drink, thanked him, and headed for Mrs. Marshall's non-bawdyhouse. Perhaps a generous senator would engage my services or—oh, God forbid if our next Attorney General stopped by for a bit of fun. I needed to make it clear to Marshall that I was off limits to Mr. Burr. But I doubted he ever paid for female company.

CHAPTER 10

ON THE WALK to Mrs. Marshall's not-a-bawdy-house, I asked myself some hard questions: *Do you want to do this, Betsy? Return to the world's oldest profession? Is not mucking out stalls more respectable?*

Yes, but it's a heap dirtier! And no one ever thanked me after mucking out a stall. Nor did I relish toiling over a wash tub or sidestepping advances from a liquorish lord of the manor.

I escaped Providence to break with my past. But my past was the streets – poverty, starvation, turning tricks for a meal at a time. Now, I headed to the 'Holy Ground' – where swells sought classy entertainment. I needn't stoop to trawling the streets of Lispenard Meadows on the north edge of town, the infamous area crawling with street harlots since the war. *Only until a new theater is built,* I convinced myself.

I turned the corner of Barclay Street and spotted Mrs. Marshall's fine residence as James had described, a white-washed townhouse wedged between the grog shop and tobacconist. Convenient spot for the customers fore and aft: a grog afore, a seegar after. I wondered if she'd located her establishment in that tactical place by design. If so, I applauded her shrewdness and liked her already.

The woman – girl, rather – who swung the door open looked younger than me by a few trips around the block. She sized me up, head to toes, and met my eyes with a toothbrushed smile.

I had to get the important bit out first. "Mr. James Reynolds sent me. I am Miss Betsy Bowen."

"I've heard your name." Before I could ask her if she ever attended the theater, she beat me to it. "Aha! You're *that* Betsy Bowen! Pray what happened, love? The theater burn down?"

"Worse. It is being demolished. Land speculators." Over her gasp, I explained, "We're hoping some smart investor with vision and love for the arts will build a new one. No telling when that'll be, though." My professional bearing broke down as tears filled my eyes. But I wept not for me. I ached for William and the anguish in his eyes when we said goodbye.

"Oh, I'm so sorry, Miss Bowen ... come in, do come in." She waved her hand in a 'come-along' gesture.

I inhaled lemon polish and beeswax. The floor gleamed under lighted sconces. James was spot on – this was no bawdy house.

I followed her into a sitting room that struck me as quite posh. Mirrored walls gave the illusion of vast expanse. They reflected the glow of candles in holders, on the flowery papered walls, and in a chandelier aglitter with sparkling crystals. High-backed settees upholstered in red and gold brocade faced each other. A table held a chessboard with pieces modeled after Red Coats and Patriots. A harpsichord stood against the wall.

"Sally Marshall." She held out her hand.

I grasped it, using my acting skills to conceal my astonishment. I clamped my lips, itching to ask, even more than I wanted to ask for employment. *Crikey, lass, how did you attain all this so young?*

But I needn't ask. She explained straightaway, "I was left a sizable inheritance from my uncle who raised me. With the advice of some knowledgeable ladies here in town, I set up shop. My house is known as the Second Senate Chamber," her voice lilted here, "where the gentlemen all 'retire', if you know my meaning, for the evening after a long day's toil." She winked, leaving a speck of black against her pale cheek.

My gaze adhered to the coating on her long lashes. Horrors, they looked like a pair of crawly centipedes. I'd read in an ancient Egypt book that ladies painted their lashes with kohl, crocodile dung, and honey. I reckoned it was the devil's agony washing that concoction off. I never wore the muck, even though actresses slathered on the spider-lash potions. And now, I learned, so did high-class madams.

"I shan't be coy, Mrs. Marshall. I am impressed, as you can see. I'm all agog." And gawk I did, as my eyes landed on each posh appointment: the velvet draperies, the marble mantel, the glittering chandelier... "I admire any woman who succeeds in business, especially of the compassionate type, relieving men of their pressures, as it were."

"Thank you, Miss Bowen. It's actually *Miss* Marshall, but call me Sally." She offered a welcoming grin. "And yes, I do pride myself on my, uh ... compassion. Not to brag, but I do *pro bono* work here, too, mostly for the lawyers, who offer legal advice when the need arises. When my needs arise, they help me. When their needs arise, I help them."

"That's called *quid pro quo* in lawyer-speak, ain't it, Sally?" We shared a laugh. "And I'm Betsy to you."

"Have you any experience in this field, Betsy?"

Oh, if she only knew the half of it! "I grew up on the streets of Providence." I reckoned that said it all. "Because of the ... er, experience I gained there, I feel more than adequate for your establishment." My voice rose a notch. "I feel almost proud to tell you, I can find my way around a man blindfolded – and I daresay, I have."

"When can you start?" She glanced at her mantel clock and looked back at me, as if hoping I could start before the next chime.

With no other plans – or hopes – I answered, "I'm at your service as we speak." From that moment, I needn't fear sleeping in the park. She showed me upstairs to a boudoir decorated with matching frilly pink curtains and bed coverings and – Jeminy! – a four-poster bed! Even Sukie didn't have one of those. Its pink canopy also matched. What else matched around here? Would she give me pink petticoats?

"The ladies and I split fifty-fifty. You get room and board, and you supply your own sheaths. We entertain by appointment only. No one off the street." She brought me down to the kitchen where a servant girl stood at a flour-sprinkled table rolling dough, and offered me bread and cheese with ale. I stuffed my hollow tum as we chatted about the theater, books – she also admired Miss Wollstonecraft – and our future goals.

"I intend to be a wealthy businesswoman someday, too, Sally, but not to worry – I won't set up in competition." I wiped crumbs from my mouth. "I want to begin by renting houses. Then buy land to build on and lease out to businesses. They're more reliable as renters than private citizens."

She studied me with that cock-browed 'show me' look I'd seen on numerous faces, especially men, when I shared my lofty ambitions. Without a discouraging word, she asked me how I planned on getting my hands on that much dough, since I hardly looked able to lease a cemetery plot.

"I'm counting on Mr. Hamilton's bank to pay a generous rate of interest on shares. I'll start slow, and as you must know,

Sally, interest begets interest that begets more interest. That's called compounding. I'm well acquainted with senators, congressmen, and a few upstart lawyers who are even more well acquainted with Mr. Hamilton. I'm also good friends with Gouverneur Morris's niece, Gertrude Meredith. We talk about these things all the time in the taverns and coffee houses."

Listening intently, she poured herself some tea and sat back down, eyes agog, gesturing with her hands for more of what I'd learned. "You know senators and congressmen? Who? Do tell!"

"Senator Maclay and I have a grand rapport, but he's too much of a rummy cove to partake of your ... *our* services. There's also Fisher Ames, Fred Muhlenberg – a few others." I didn't dare mention Aaron. Not yet.

"Have you met William North?" she asked.

I quit chewing and almost blurted, *That pompous ass?* "Uh ... yes, briefly." I could not refuse him if Sally sent him to me. It wasn't worth losing the job over puffed-up Billy North.

"If the Weeks brothers request you, you'll conclude many an evening with a bulging purse. They're especially generous. And I don't only mean with their money." Her saucy smile said it all, lashes aflutter.

"Weeks..." I tapped my chin with my forefinger. "I know that name ... aren't they builders?"

"They're builders, all right. Ezra is the most prominent builder in town. His younger brother Levi is his carpenter. They built City Hall and many a grand establishment in these parts. I could never afford their rates. But I'm glad they can afford mine." Her lips curved.

"Oh, of course, City Hall." I nodded, picturing the graceful building. "Right out of the French Renaissance. They're regulars here?"

"Tried and true. Ezra is married, but Levi is quite the

ladies' man. Confirmed bachelor. Insists he'll never let a lass snag him." She chuckled. "That's what they all say."

"Then send them to me if their needs so arise ... but one at a time, if you please. I know they work side by side, but they don't ..." I gestured, "... play side by side, do they? I've never been one for a ménage."

She shook her head. "Never requested it. But you'd be surprised who does. And not just with two women either."

I waved a dismissive hand. "I don't wanna know." We shared a chuckle.

We parted company for the time being, with a promise to meet up next morning. She bade me good evening with a parting wink. "Blindfolds, huh? I'll be sure to purchase a bolt of satin." She chuckled as she shut her door.

I skipped back to my old quarters, so happy I'd found employment that I vowed to buy James Reynolds a steak with all the trimmings for leading me to Sally's genteel brothel. It being the poshest place I'd ever worked at, I needed new raiment. Now employed in a field that demanded the highest quality, from the petticoats on out, I planned to establish credit at elite Broad Way shops.

I had a few shillings, which I brought to John Turner on William Street, one of the city's best-known tailors and dressmakers. Knowing Sukie purchased there and sang his praises, I sauntered in next morning wearing my best skirt and bodice. I ordered two new dresses, using what money I had as a deposit. At the till with my purchases, I made sure to mention, "I'm one of Miss Marshall's ladies." The dressmaker struggled to hide a smirk.

I next visited the milliner, not that I wore a hat in the boudoir, but I still strove to look fashionable.

"What's new in headwear?" I asked the young girl at the counter, wearing a grass green bonnet three times the size of her head.

"This is the calash hat, milady." She turned her head to and fro. "Or if you prefer something more modest, in appearance and in price, we have some lovely butterfly caps with lace ... but we can add pearls if you care to be extravagant."

"Modesty's not my strong point." I smiled and pointed to a straw hat decorated with bows and ribbons. "This says who I am."

She took it off the form and approached me. About to set it on my head, she nearly dropped it at my feet. "Why, you're ... Miss Bowen! I've seen all your plays!"

"Why, thank you, dear. But you won't see me on the boards any time soon. They're knocking down the theater. Bloomin' shame." Again I fought back tears, unable to forget the look in William's eyes.

"Oh, no." She bowed her head, her hat shading her face in shadow. "What will you do?"

Trying to keep a straight face, I said, "Oh, I won't go begging." I needn't give her the sordid details. "In fact, I'll be doing more hat shopping along the way, to complete some new ensembles. Speaking of completing ensembles, do you know a good jeweler in the area?"

"Why, yes, any jeweler in Maiden Lane, the center of the jewelry district. I enjoy strolling past the stores, hoping someday a beau will buy me a trinket there ..." She trailed off, her eyes taking on a dreamy look.

"Well, I'm sure you'll catch a suitor before long. You're too pretty to go unnoticed." I positioned the hat atop my head and preened in the mirror.

"Thank you, Miss Bowen. Coming from a beauty like you that's mighty kind."

I swept my new purchase off and admired it. "It's Betsy to you. How much for the *chapeau*?"

"Three dollars, Betsy. And I'm Gulielma Sands. But my friends call me Elma. My cousin Catharine owns this shop."

I handed her the money and perched the hat on my head. "Well, Elma, when I browse those jeweler shops, I won't be a bit surprised to see you there soon – with an ardent beau."

She beamed as if I'd just predicted her fortune with a crystal ball.

At another store, I purchased three pairs of gloves and another pair of shoes, all on credit.

This was the way Mr. Hamilton planned to run the country's finances – on credit. Jefferson and his ilk hated it, but they were farmers – what did they know about high finance? Heck, I knew more about handling money than those macaronis did.

The following evening, Sally sent me my first assignment – none other than the aforementioned Billy North.

I awaited him in the parlor, skimming *The Taming of the Shrew*, reciting Kate's part out loud. When he arrived, I itched to see his haughty face at the sight of me.

"Betsy! What are you doing here?" His eyes bugged out so far I thought they'd bounce on the floor. A crimson flush crawled up his cheeks.

"As you can see, I'm not beating rugs or scrubbing floors, Billy. What do you think I'm doing here? I'm here to do what ladies do here – take your money. Unless, of course, you want Miss Marshall to bring someone else—"

"No!" His refusal nearly knocked me over. "To engage the desirable Betsy Bowen for an evening will be a bigger victory than the Battle of Monmouth. May I escort you to your boudoir, my lady?"

He enticed me in the same sort of way as horseradish – pungent and overpowering – yet I never refused it. He was at least Aaron's age and retained that same spark of youth, though lines of maturity etched his face with character. But unlike Aaron, he was a self-important braggart. The times I endured his company at Sukie's house, I heard all about his and Benedict Arnold's doomed expedition to Canada ... his part in the Battle of Monmouth ... the surrender of Cornwallis which he witnessed ...

I didn't need another re-enactment. Egad, I heard it so many times, I could tell it better than he.

I got it – and him – off within the next five minutes. I almost felt sorry for him, for he'd hardly gotten his money's worth, it was over so fast.

"Give me a few more minutes, I'll be raring like a stallion at the gate," he panted as he rolled off me and slapped my bottom.

"Uh-uh, business is business." I sliced the air with my hand. "Another romp will cost you another three dollars."

"What?" He huffed. "But you know me already!"

"Then make it six."

"Blast it." He pulled his breeches back up.

"You have an hour." I glanced at the wall clock.

"And how do we pass the remainder of the hour? Play bid whist?" He sneered.

"You're the paying customer, Billy."

"As long as I'm paying." He dragged his fingers over my curves. "I'm sure you're obliged to tell me the truth when I ask. What were you doing with Colonel Burr at the opera?"

I stayed in *déshabillé* to further frustrate him. I propped myself up on my elbow. "I was watching the opera. What do you think I was doing?"

"I considered greeting the both of you, but wasn't sure he wanted to be greeted."

"Oh, because I'm a courtesan?" I sharpened my tone. "Well, I wasn't then. He'll find out soon enough. I'm ashamed to tell him. But what's worse is that he'll hear it from some gossipmonger. And I'll tell you the truth, as I'll tell whoever asks – I am a companion. His wife is an invalid, as you might know."

"His companion?" He snickered. "A delicate way to put it. Meaning he gets it for free."

"Not yet." I shot him a saucy smile.

"Are you serious, Bet? I thought you were pulling my leg. You and ... Colonel Burr ... companions? Squiring you around town sits well with Mrs. Burr? And with him?"

"Obviously." My lips spread into a dreamy smile. "We enjoy each other's company. And he doesn't gloat about his military exploits. I heard, but not from him, that he carried Monty's corpse through the snow. Colonel Aaron doesn't brag. Or gloat. He is the salt of the earth."

"Hmmph." Green envy seeped from his pores.

CHAPTER 11

I GREETED MY NEXT CUSTOMER, the prominent builder Ezra Weeks. "When Sally told me you were her newest, er ... lady, I couldn't resist, Miss Bowen." Ezra opened the bottle of Madeira he brought and poured us each a glass.

"Likewise, I cannot resist a gent who provides his own libation. And since we're hardly in polite circles, let's dispense with formality. I'm Betsy." His wavy hair and sleek physique stirred me. "I'm ready when you are."

Ezra became my regular, shunning the others. "You're my favorite now," he lavished praise while twirling my hair around his fingers. He liked to linger afterward and chat. "I enjoy your mind even more than your ..." He cleared his throat, "... services. And I do want to see you become successful. From what you've told me so far, you've got your entire strategy mapped out. And that's more than ninety-nine percent of entrepreneurs do. So many of them go bust. No business plan."

I covered my *décolletage* with my bodice, finding it awkward talking business in *déshabillé*. "Perhaps we can join in some venture in the future, when I'm solvent enough," I proposed, never one to let an opportunity slip by, even if it was years into the future.

"Oh, we'll see more of each other, Betsy, all over town." His nod and wink assured me he had no intention of letting me slip by either.

I already had four new hats...far too many for one head, but ladies wore hats, the bigger the better. And I needed to convince myself I was a lady. So, with Ezra Weeks's fee burning a hole in my purse, I strolled into the milliner's. Sweet Elma's eyes lit up when she saw me.

"Betsy! What timing. We just received a shipment from London. This is to swoon for." She placed a wide-brimmed burgundy *chapeau* in my hands. Tiny red roses encircled it.

"Oh, it's darling. What else came in?"

As she bustled around to show me their latest headwear, I noticed a blue and white cameo brooch fastened to her blouse. "Why, that's lovely. I knew it wouldn't be long before a suitor gifted you a fitting token."

She tittered, blushed, and fluttered her hands, stroking the brooch like a beloved pet. "Ah, yes, and I have you to thank for giving me the confidence to return his ardor. I was way too shy before, but he's a new boarder where I'm living with my cousins. So it's ... rather convenient." She pursed her pretty lips.

"Well, you're positively glowing. Ah, young love ..." I thought of Aaron and my pulse surged. "I'm in love, too. Isn't it grand?"

We clasped hands and at that moment I knew I'd made a friend for life. I bought three more hats that day, wishing I had multiple heads to perch them on!

Breathing in the night air, pungent with another full day's odors, I trudged to the tavern, too spent to walk at my usual brisk pace, but alert and wound up enough to know I was nowhere ready for sleep. I needed some continuing male companionship of the nonromantic sort, and this was the place for it.

Since I was still a lady, I entered the snug. I passed right through to the tap room, for I desired not the company of other ladies. I wanted to listen to some lively debate about our new nation, which politicians were corrupt, and when our backs would break under the burden of taxation.

"Evening, gents. I trust you haven't drunk the place dry yet." Senator Mac popped up, more sprightly than usual, and pulled out a free chair from the table he and James Reynolds shared.

"Nay, Fish ain't here tonight. Or we'd be knocking back the dregs," James answered as he stood to greet me.

"Where is everybody?" I glanced at the tall clock in the corner. 'Twas barely past nine.

"They're not as efficient as we, so they must return to their labors while we can enjoy our leisure," Mac offered, but I didn't believe it. I had a feeling Fish, a staunch Federalist, and his cronies were letting their political views compromise their camaraderie with these gents, as the nation grew and factions became more solid and opposed. Soon the taverns would be divided down the middle as was the senate chamber, so I'd read in the papers.

"How goes it, Senator Mac?" I asked as James ordered me a Madeira when a plate of steaming oysters arrived. "It is naught like hearing the news of our great government from the horse's mouth—oops"—I covered my mouth, "I didn't mean that literally. I meant the lion's mouth."

"'Tis an honor to be compared to a horse's mouth," he replied, picking up a shell and poising it at his lips. "Better than half those burks I'm thrown together with every day, more aptly described as horses' arses. Most of all that puffed-up superficial mimic Schuyler. A poor imitation of his son-in-law Sandy Hamilton."

"And speaking of Sandy, here comes the skite now." Mac nodded towards the door, where Hamilton and a few well-tailored-looking gents stepped in and helped themselves to the table nearest the window. Hamilton glanced our way and for an instant our eyes met. I saw the trace of a smile play upon his lips before he turned his attention back to his cronies. But for that split second we connected, a heart-stopping jolt hit me. Not of sexual desire, but something even more basic than that. A need, on both our parts, to share something. But I knew not what.

Neither James nor Mac acknowledged their arrival. Hamilton and his men seemed just as happy to ignore them, too. "We need someone to speak furr us, not the monarchists and the aristocrats, and tis what I stood furr when I ran furr the Continental Congress," James said.

"I'm sorry you lost that seat, Jimmy. You'd have brought a splash of color to that otherwise drab, gray day of a group." As a failed candidate, James was branded a loser in elevated Hamilton circles.

"Gray is the word. Like petticoats that've been washed too many times."

"The sooner Schuyler is out, the better," Mac said around a mouthful of oyster. "Just last week, the appropriation bill was taken up. And Schuyler brought forward an account of eight thousand dollars expended in repairing and furnishing the house in which the president lives. This was a great surprise to me, although a vote had originated in the House for furnishing the president's mansion. Yet I considered that allowance for all this had been made in the president's salary."

But why shouldn't my father live in a repaired and furnished house? "We have to show the Brits how far we've come in securing our freedom from their bonds," I argued. "We cannot have our commander living in a hovel, can we?"

"Should he require repairs and furnishings and gewgaws he can bloody well pay for it himself," Mac tossed off as he plucked the last oyster from the platter.

I could see that Mac and I would have our differences, now that my father, the president, was running things. I liked Mac as a person and didn't want to let a difference of opinion ruin our friendly rapport, but now I was doubly glad he wasn't representing me—unless I moved to Pennsylvania. And if 'twas all right with him for my president to have gewgaws at taxpayer expense, I'd love him even more.

"Come now, Senator Mac," I derided him, but in a light tone, "were you president, you'd want to live in high style."

"Not too high so I can only see above my subjects'—er, citizens' heads. I'd have an open house, so they could come right in and do their bidding, rather than these levees that some liken to holding court in the great hall of Windsor Castle. Nothing is regarded or valued at such meetings," he snapped, "But the qualifications that flow from the tailor, barber, or dancing master. Levees may be useful in old countries where men of great fortune are collected, as it may keep the idle from being much worse employed. But here I think they are hurtful."

"Just because you ain't been invited to one," James retorted as Mac snapped his fingers and signaled for another round.

"I certainly have, I just haven't had time to attend. I have work to do."

I lowered my head as a heavy sadness came over me. I longed for that great man to take me in his arms and accept me as his child. I cared not what the rest of the nation called him, how outrageous the title. All I wanted was to call him was Papa.

One late night, after Ezra Weeks buttoned his breeches and bade me good evening with a polite kiss to my hand, I wanted to share my newfound accomplishments with Aaron. I sharpened my quill and placed a sheet of creamy paper on Sally's desk. "*I now have some money. I am almost ready to invest.*" I then couldn't help showing off. "*I read* Candide *and am eager to discuss it ... I've been following Congress and envision many hostile factions forming_ ... I dined on roast duck for the first time ...*"

But I did not write about my occupation. No, I'd tell him in person. I dreaded it, but I had to.

A week went by, then two.

I penned another chatty letter about books and plays, my enjoyment of a Haydn concert where James Reynolds's wife played the violin, and how much I misliked Hamilton's policies.

Then, with boldness that came with my growing pile of stash, I strode up to Nassau Street.

Aaron's office was on the ground floor of a brick townhouse with a scrubbed porch, the tidiest on the block. Pansies bloomed in the flower boxes. Whitewashed picket fences separated it from the neighbors. The leafy trees brought dappled sunlight to the bow windows, hung with curtains I assumed were velvet.

He was not in, so I left a note with a clerk. "Make sure Attorney Burr gets this." My instructions accompanied two shillings, the first time I'd ever been able to afford a gratuity. As he bowed and held the door open and called me "ma'am", I sensed Mamma's presence at my shoulder. As her spirit engulfed me with love and support, I heard her voice in my mind: "You are doing the right thing, my girl."

I fetched more coin and passed it out to every street urchin I passed. Then I went into the snug at Fraunces and treated myself to shepherd's pie. I'd never eaten meat until arriving in New York. In Providence we scraped by on gruel, a crust of stale bread, or perhaps a chunk of moldy cheese the grocer had tossed out. My step-pa couldn't afford meat – except the occasional chicken, and when he made pigeon stew, I stayed hungry. The thought of eating a bird after seeing it shite on the ledge didn't whet my appetite.

But now I could afford meat. And could no longer button my skirts.

I did not curb my appetite. I simply purchased larger skirts. Bugger whoever didn't like it. I now had curves where I'd never had them before. Men began asking for "that voluptuous red-haired one."

I'd been called a lot of things, but never voluptuous. I looked it up and grinned wider than my hips.

Next morn, Sally surprised me with a knock at my door. "This letter just arrived. How was last evening?"

I rubbed my eyes. "I bade farewell to Ezra Weeks at midnight and sat reading till my eyes shut. A book I've been wanting to read for ages and couldn't put down. Richardson's *Pamela*. You'd like Pamela. She's a lass of high merit, but dim-witted at the same time." I grinned.

"Sounds like many women I know. A novel or biography?" she asked.

"A novel. I reckon some woman wrote it for him." I scowled.

"Well, this is for you, doll. I can get some eggs cooked for you after you've tidied yourself up," Sally offered.

I tossed the letter onto the bed unread, likely an invite to a soirée from one of my gents. I went about my morning toilette, not giving it another thought, until I went to make up the bed. I yawned as I decided to open it.

My eyes flew over the familiar script and landed on the signature. A gasp broke my yawn.

"Oh, Aaron, of course I'll join you in a late supper tomorrow evening," I accepted out loud, pressing the letter to my heart. Then dread wrapped its tentacles around me: I now had to tell him where I worked.

If I wanted his advice on how to invest this stash I'd earned, I had to tell him how I earned it. All day long, as I went about my business, I prepared myself for his expected reply – and the dreaded *adieu*.

Aaron's coach rolled to a halt at the curb. I gathered my taffeta skirt and descended Sally's porch steps.

He alighted from the carriage and stood before me. Our eyes met. My knees wobbled. I fumbled for something to grab onto and stumbled into his arms. Was that Sally tittering through the window?

Aaron steadied me on my feet. "Betsy, are you sporting new shoes? Heavens, wear some that you've already broken in." He escorted me to the coach.

I hardly wanted to admit my shoes hadn't made me lose my footing. It was the sight of him. But I opted for the more believable, "I got so engrossed in the last installment of *The Federalist*, I skipped the midday meal."

He helped me in as the coachman held the door. "I haven't

yet read that one. You must enlighten me. Is that how you pass the time since the theater closed? I wish I could spend my time as you do."

Ah, sweet irony. *No, dear Aaron, you wouldn't want to spend your time as I do*, I silently corrected him.

"I do try to make the best of my time." Words jumbled in my head and tied my tongue in knots.

Dreading yet prepared to accept this as our last encounter, I told myself *it doesn't matter when the subject comes up. He's too gallant to walk out on me in the middle of a meal and stick me with the bill.*

As we rolled down the bumpy street under a lit streetlight, a glowing aura framed his head and shoulders.

"How goes your new occupation?" I steered the conversation away from me for the time being. "I haven't read much in the papers about you."

"Keeps me occupied, all right." As we passed the street-lamp, darkness engulfed us. "Along with watching my cronies running our nation. It's kindling my political ambitions. I'm ready to jump into the fray, yet I don't feel the nation is quite ready for me."

Oh, we need you, I wanted to gush.

The carriage halted at The Queen's Head and the coachman handed me down. Only the second or third ride of my life, I felt I was living in the fanciful stories I read about, my prince at my side. Something about alighting from a shiny carriage seemed unreal. Oh, if only the folks back in Providence could see me now – dripping in new raiment, Sally's borrowed emerald earbobs glistening, and the Attorney General of New York escorting me.

Over a lavish meal of venison and partridge with artichokes and string beans drizzled with butter, our banter stayed light. "I'm engrossed in a novel, *The Coquette*, based on a true story about Eliza Whitman, who died last year and is reported to be a relative of yours," I said.

"Whitman? I have no relations with that name." He shook his head. "How are we supposed to be related?"

"Someone in her family intermarried with Jonathan Edwards's family. He's your grandfather, is he not?"

"Yes, my mother's father." His eyes searched back and forth as he thought. "But I never knew of an Eliza Whitman."

"I'll lend you the book," I offered, my tone eager. "She's involved with two men, has a secret affair with a married man, births a stillborn babe in a roadside tavern and then dies. But it speaks to readers. The underlying message is that women are constrained. Eliza went against conformity, sinned, and paid the ultimate price – death."

"Why is she a coquette?" He sprinkled salt on his venison.

"Because she's independent and a flirter, and looked down upon." I cut some of my beans in half. "She wanted more than what is available to women. We now have freedom from the Mother Country, but not from society, if we want to be moral and respected." Leaning forward, I awaited his response to all that.

"I can see why you identify with Eliza." He slid some venison onto his fork.

Had he read my mind? "I didn't say that."

"You didn't need to. But I would like to read it. Not because she might be related to me. A girl's education should fit her for any position, any sphere, and be equal to any circumstances. That is how I'm raising my daughter. You did see yourself in this heroine, did you not?"

He nailed me to the floor that time. I grinned. "In almost every way. Down to our shared name. But if you find your family connection, I'd like to hear about it."

"I don't doubt a family connection." He sipped some wine. "We're apparently of the same mind."

I admitted, "This is no false flattery, but I've never met any man who regarded women as much more than ornaments. You see, I've never been treated kindly by men. Except my step-pa. He gave me books and taught me sums and – and he listened to what I had to say. He never told me to shut up or my mind was inferior." My words rushed as I relived those days. "But all the others in my Providence milieu, if it can be called that, regarded me as a piece of trash."

"Men of that ilk, I have no respect for." He emptied our second bottle of Madeira into my glass. "And what has occupied your leisure time since the theater closed, Betsy? Besides quenching your well of curiosity?"

CHAPTER 12

Now THAT's a sudden change of subject! I raised the glass to my lips. *Oh, why didn't I rehearse this?* "I cannot conceal this, Aaron," I spoke from my heart. "Are you at all familiar with the house where you called for me?"

"No, I've never been there." He sipped his wine. "It does appear to be a decent dwelling."

"Yes, it is decent." I fiddled with my table napkin. "But it is no boarding house. Needing to find work or starve when the theater closed, I went there. Miss Sally Marshall owns it. I work for her. I needn't explain more, need I? I don't want to deceive you. Now, if you wish to never associate with me again, I understand." I could no longer look him in the eye.

"Why would I do that?" His voice soothed me—for two seconds.

"I ... uh ..." My poise flew out the window.

"I've heard of Miss Marshall and know what sort of house she runs. A man would have to inhabit another planet not to know. I would never end my association with you because you're employed there. That wasn't even what I asked you. I asked how you spent your *leisure* time." He smiled.

Burning with mortification, I gulped. "Oh, sorry, I didn't ... did you ..." My voice croaked, weak and brittle. "I just wanted to make sure you knew, and that I wasn't hiding it from you. But right now ..." I dropped the coquetry as native Providence overtook me, "...I feel like a nincompoop."

He waved his hand. "Don't. Your ego is bruised. Don't pay it any mind."

"Ego?" I asked. "I didn't know I had one."

"Everyone has. Some are bigger than others. It's not a part of anatomy. From the Latin, it means self-importance. Don Juan said 'self-importance is man's greatest enemy. It requires that one spend most of one's life offended by something or someone.' I remember that every time I try a case or want to enter politics. Men's greatest enemies are their egos – and trust me, that's one area where size does matter." His grin melted me.

I nodded, wishing he'd fill my wine glass a third time. "You don't ... you won't ... it matters not that I'm employed at Sally's? I don't intend to stay there. If you need to know what made me seek her out, I can tell you."

"I'm sure you have your reasons. They're none of my business. Betsy, you're you, no matter where you work. I'd never look down on you. I'm no saint myself. Yes, I have an ego I often put into its place. You'll see as we get to know each other better."

I reeled with relief. "I need to tell you what made me seek out Miss Marshall. One thing and one thing only – and that was *my* ego. I couldn't bear to beg or toil as a washerwoman or maid. I need a profession as close to the theater as I'm capable of because it makes me feel wanted. And keeps me in shelter and nourishment and growing capital. But if you think that's a show of my ego, Aaron, believe me when I say this, and I will never lie to you, my good man – you ain't seen nothin' yet." I winked.

He winked back.

I almost swooned.

All the way back to Sally's, I fretted. Invite him inside and sound forward? Don't invite him in and risk sounding dismissive? Would he take an invite as an invitation to my bedroom? I so wanted to extend this evening, exchange more ideas about politicians, critique more books ... revel in his company.

The coach pulled up to Sally's door. "Would you join me – *in the parlor* ..." I stressed those words, "...for some wine and chat and meet Miss Marshall?" I blurted in one breath.

"I've an early morn and need to do some work, but another evening, I will be glad to join you – *in the parlor*. I'd like to make Miss Marshall's acquaintance as well."

I sighed with a mixture of relief and disappointment. He walked me to the door and bade me good evening. Oh, I longed to ravish him! I gazed out the window until his carriage vanished from sight.

Climbing the stairs, unpinning my hair, and scratching my itchy scalp, I admitted out loud, "Of course I'm falling in love with him." Thank fortune he hadn't shunned me when I bared the truth. I stepped lighter, as if a boulder had rolled off my back. But I needed to keep reverie to a minimum. My customers deserved better than my fantasizing they were Aaron.

Next morn I purchased a dainty sandalwood fan, my very first. Embracing my extravagant mood, I purchased a blue bonnet for Sukie from Elma Sands. I banged on Sukie's door, bursting to share my joy of last evening. A servant led me into the sitting room where Sukie sat concentrating on needlepoint.

"Be with you in a moment, let me complete these stitches." Her hands worked with nimble dexterity, her eyes fixed on her work.

"Take your time. I don't care to be disturbed when I'm working, either."

I browsed her flub-dubs – wooden figurines of Indians, oil portraits of Sukie and her family, and a silver bowl. I picked it up to peek at the engraving. My eyes popped. Paul Revere!

"Finished," came her voice from across the room. "Sorry, I had to complete that row, or it would look like I stopped and started again. Care for tea?"

"Surely. And whatever you have to eat. I'm famishing." I rubbed my empty tum. "I've been too excited to eat till now." I bustled over to sit beside her and spread my new taffeta skirt about me. I handed her my gift, wrapped in pink tissue paper that cost me an extra shilling.

"Too excited to eat? You?" She tore the paper and looked up. "Ah, that means you went out with Aaron again?" Her voice wavered in doubt with a hint of warning.

"Yes, and he is the one true gentleman I've ever met. Aside from my father, of course. Oh, if only one day, me, Aaron, and him – I mean he, Aaron and I – can sit and enjoy one another's company ..." I sighed as my fancy carried me away.

"You never know, Betsy. That very well may happen some-day. But all the world is not a stage. You can write the script, but other players write their own, too – and not always do they coincide."

"I know, but I'm his only daughter. You can't say it ain't ..." I quickly corrected myself, "...isn't possible."

She slid the bonnet on and popped up to admire herself in the mirror above the mantel. "Thank you so much, that was so thoughtful of you."

I smiled at her delight. "It's to thank you for letting me pilfer your raiment. I'm wearing all new frocks and shoes and blouses and petticoats." I pulled up my skirt to show her. "Now that I'm... I can afford it."

"Do you really earn so much more than in the theater?" She sat beside me, wide-eyed.

"I will return to the theater when a new one is built, but it'll be a hardship sinking back to near-poverty. I've stashed funds I didn't plan to earn for another ten years. I have a head start on my business ventures." Another of my wishful sighs escaped my lips. "Oh, but I do enjoy the money. I'm torn, Sukie. Ever feel torn between two things? As if they pull you apart?"

Her eyes wandered, and she shook her head. "Cannot say I have. Perhaps if you invest in a new theater, you can reap the profits."

"No. There's no profit in theater. Entertaining is a labor of love. I need a business venture I can profit from, so I can support a theater, or an opera company or some such."

"You need not decide right away." She ran the bonnet's silk ribbons through her fingers.

"I'm afeard the longer I'm away in Sally's employ, the farther the theater will stray from my heart. But I cannot remain in a brothel. I've been lucky so far, but—" I stopped short, not wanting it to come out that way.

"But what?" She fixed her eyes on me. "You mean if Aaron finds out?"

"He already did."

She screwed up her face as if she'd stepped in chicken leavings. "Oh, dear. Who told him?"

"Me, thank heaven." I grinned.

Her jaw dropped. "Why, you live bravely."

"What was I to do?" My arms rose and fell against my sides. "Have some mealymouth like Billy North tell him? I had to come clean and tell him the truth."

She gave me the same approving nod as if I'd wiped my feet before coming in. "I know Aaron to be prim at times. But he has an understanding heart. And he so loves women." She gazed past me in a dreamy way but focused back on me. "I mean that in a good way – I mean, he holds women in high regard."

"Yes, thank the good God above." I clasped my hands and glanced heavenward.

"You could have talked it over with me first," she chided.

"I didn't want to bother you, Sukie. I've been reading and writing and – oh, I can tell you. But don't repeat this. I've taken some of my extra income and hired a tutor, Mr. O'Shammusy. We study sums and geography and history. Another reason I feel torn about leaving Sally's and giving up the income. Do you know that Shakespeare may not have written all those beautiful works?"

She shook her head. "He's an impostor?"

"It's likely. Experts ponder how someone with so little schooling could write about monarchs and rich folk stuff. Think about it."

"I will. Later. I'm ever so proud of you, Betsy. And I understand your dilemma. Me, I'd rather be a poor actress. Your ambitions greatly surpass mine. Because you're you, I know you'll earn enough to succeed in business. Then you can buy your heart anything it wants." She folded the bonnet and wrapped it back in its tissue paper.

I clasped my hands with joy. "Aaron is understanding and nonjudgmental, and I truly admire that about him. James Reynolds steered me to Sally's. Billy North showed up there – thrice already. With his big gob, he all but published it in the *Gazette*." I stopped to take a breath. "If I want Aaron in my life, the way I want him in my life, I cannot be a lady of the evening."

"Then you must decide." Her servant brought the teapot and accessories on a silver tray. The aroma of fresh mint floated from the steaming cups. "But I warned you before, as long as Theodosia lives, he is not interested beyond companionship."

I sensed something lurking between those lines. Had his wife's health worsened? A cloud of sorrow hung over me. "Do you mean something by 'as long as Theodosia lives'?"

Her cup trembled in her hand and she placed it down. "I spoke to Aaron the evening before last, and he tells me her health is 'wavering and precarious'. Two physicians saw to her and concur that she's..." She paused and I didn't push. I knew what she was trying to say.

An overpowering wave of guilt nearly drowned me.

"What's wrong, Betsy?" She grasped my hand. "You look as if you grieve. You never met her, did you?"

"No." I lowered my head. "I know she's a devoted wife and mother. But I hope Aaron will turn to me when he does need me – when she turns for the worse."

"She's a brave woman, braver than I'll ever be." Her voice softened.

"Oh, how I wish I could be there for him." But how presumptuous. "No..." I corrected myself, "I need to step back and stop letting my fantasies take flight."

What I later heard in the coffee house struck me blind and dumb.

Sukie and I went for a midday meal, and as we took our

seats at the last empty table, I overheard two gents next to us, the tables barely inches apart. "His health seems to be declining," said the one closer to me, covering his eyes as if to hide tears. His table mate agreed, lips in a tight grimace. "Our great and good man is unwell this spring. His heavy cold and slow fever has developed into pneumonia. He caught it from James Madison."

Who could they be talking about? It had to be somebody important. Sukie had heard, too. She looked at me, screwing up her eyes in puzzlement. I glanced over and saw the man next to me was George Clymer, one of our Congressmen. I knew him by sight, never spoke to him, but I simply had to know.

"Pardon me, Congressman." I leaned towards him. "But who is so ill, sir?"

"President Washington."

CHAPTER 13

I FELT as if he'd punched me in the gut.

"B-but the president's still attending office, is he not? I read the papers and know he caught a cold, but sat for a portrait by Edward Savage. How sick can he be?" I asked desperately.

"No, my lady," Clymer's voice quivered. "He's confined to bed. Madison told us the president suffers from labored breathing, sharp pains in his side, harsh coughing, and his spittle's got blood. Last time I saw him, his eyes were rheumy. They didn't put it in the papers, 'cause the press doesn't know, but Dr. Rush told us he fears the president is dying."

Numb with shock, my only instinct was the desperate need to go see him. *No, Papa cannot die!* I gave Sukie a desperate look. She grabbed my hand. "He'll be all right, he's been sick before," she assured me.

The barmaid stopped by, hovering over us. "'Scuse me." I fled and burst through the door, gulping air.

Sukie followed and held me as I crumbled. "He'll pull through, I know it. He's a strong man."

"I pray you're right." Struck with grief, for I feared the

worst, I went back and wrote him a letter. *"My fervent prayers are with you for a full recovery..."* I wrote, but of course, I couldn't tell him who I was. I brought the letter to his house, slid it through the mail slot, and stood back to gaze at the upper windows. Whichever room he was in, I knew not, but I stood there and begged God to spare him. The front door opened, and my heart jumped. Three men came out carrying black bags. I recognized Doctors Rush and McKnight, having seen them around town.

Forgetting manners and decorum, I grabbed Rush's arm as he strode by. "Doctor, how is the president?"

"His fever dropped," he replied with characteristic detachment.

But that wasn't enough for me. "Will he recover?" I wouldn't let go of his arm.

"We expect so." He gently shook me off, and I stood rooted to the ground. I sobbed in anguish and relief, yet the fear of losing Papa still haunted me. As servants began spreading straw on the street to muffle the noises, I departed.

Shaken, I couldn't work that night. I stayed in my room and devoured the evening papers. They printed not a word about Papa. I resented that they kept this from his public. Congress could be so sly and devious.

Next morning, I stood across the street from Papa's house and prayed, hoping my closeness would strengthen my imploring. Of course, I'd never be invited in.

I didn't hear from Aaron. As I serviced my gents, I shut my eyes and thought of him, despite my earlier promise. After each gent departed, I rinsed off, dressed, and added to my growing ledger. Now it was time to bank some.

I did not feel comfortable arranging a private audience with Secretary Hamilton to give me financial advice. That was not his line of work. My tavern gents could hardly qualify as businessmen – and Senator Mac was so tight his arse squeaked. He'd strongly advise me to keep my stash under the mattress, as I'm sure he did. Ezra Weeks plowed all his profits back into his growing enterprise.

James Reynolds lost every fortune he'd ever made on one scheme after another: his latest, a looking glass he claimed magnified a louse to twelve feet, put him back in the poorhouse.

I tried to steady my hand as I wrote Aaron once again. My quire of paper grew thin as I ripped up one draft after another.

"*I request the honor of your advice on my fiscal matters,*" I wrote as if I had a treasure chest, when for real, it was less than fifty dollars under a mattress.

Sally started making offers on row houses in Philadelphia to open a gentleman's brothel there. The lady sure was savvy. There never seemed to be enough brothels ...it gave me ideas. Collecting rents was profitable, but a brothel's rapid turnaround generated better cash flow.

Something to think about ...not that I'd open one across the street and compete.

Perhaps open one across the river in New Jersey ...

Just a thought.

I read that Papa had recovered. "The President of the United States has been exceedingly indisposed for several days past," announced the *New York Journal*, "but we are rejoiced at the authentic information of his being much relieved last evening."

Thank you, God! Each day the press, so silent on his brush with death, reported another item to assure his citizens – and his frantic daughter – that he was on the mend. They quoted Lady Washington: 'He seems less concerned as to the event than perhaps any other person in ye United States. Happily, he is now perfectly recovered.'

Next day, Philip Schuyler said: 'The President is again on his legs.'

Jefferson reported he was 'well enough to resume business.'

My prayers were answered! I felt alive again.

Almost.

I did my chores and readied for the evening, but every time I thought of Aaron, my heart lurched. His reply came on Saturday, of all days. *"I shall send my carriage for you at seven this evening."* Very short notice. And the busiest night at the house. But I told Sally the truth. "I'll make it up to you, I promise."

The truth always worked with me, all my life. I never told a lie. Perhaps I inherited that from Papa.

I bathed and brushed my locks until they tumbled like a sun-soaked waterfall. But I pinned it all up and used Sally's tongs to curl a few tendrils around my face. When his carriage rolled up to the door not a minute after seven, Sally squirted me with *Jacinthe Fleurs* perfume. I hoped the heady aroma wouldn't knock him out.

I wasn't sure if his Nassau Street townhouse was only his office, or if he resided upstairs. I found out when we arrived there.

He opened the door, took my hand, and led me down a beeswax-scented hallway to his office. The first thing I noticed atop his desk was a wooden box painted to look like a book, brimming over with money – piles of banknotes and stacks of coins.

"Anyone in need can come into my office and help themselves," he explained as if reading my mind. "I thought I'd let you know, since you didn't ask. But everyone who walks through this door does ask: 'Colonel Burr, why do you keep a box of money on your desk?' Sometimes I say it's to light my seegars." He chuckled. "And let us hope Hamilton's policies won't make money so worthless, that's all it'll be good for."

I couldn't stop staring – not at him this time, but at that box of money. What a heart of gold! "I just didn't reckon ... believe it was any of my business."

"But you did wonder." He slid his jacket off.

"Of course." We shared a smile as I sat at one end of his settee. He sat across from me but not close enough. "I've never known anyone with a big enough heart to keep a box of money on his desk."

His eyes darted side to side. "I do what I can."

"And that is what I want to do, when I have enough. Help those who really need it. One reason – I mean the reason I'm here right now – to ask you to help me make sound decisions. If you don't mind. I don't know anyone else I can trust, or who knows about investing. Not that I have much to invest—" I needed to hush up and let him get a word in.

He folded his hands and leaned back. "To start with, shares in the Bank of the United States are a safe investment. You can lend money privately at a higher rate of interest, but that is risky. How far ahead are you thinking?"

"Oh, ten years, till I have enough to buy real estate," I answered.

"My word, that will be the nineteenth century." He crossed one leg over the other and grabbed his ankle. His black leather boots sported a sheen I could see myself in.

"The nineteenth century will come and go with us or without us," I spoke the obvious. "And when it does, I want to know where I'm going."

He nodded, glints of gold shining in his eyes. "I'm beginning to think in four-year increments. Election years."

"Are you serious about running for office?" I knew he was born to hold high office and be part of our history, but voicing that would sound too fawning.

"Yes, but I need to be much better known and liked first." He drew a deep breath. "Considering who's out there, that's not easy."

"Our country needs you," slipped out of my mouth before I could shut it. So I qualified, "I mean, you are not of those other politicians' ilk. You work for the people, not rule from a lofty perch for self-glorification."

"You have that kind of faith in me already?" His tone teased.

"I feel I've known you since the day I was born," came out breathier than I wanted.

"And how well do you think you know me, Betsy?" His voice stayed light and inquisitive.

Before I could answer, he leaned forward and twirled one of my tendrils around his finger. Our lips within kissing range, our eyes locked. My heart pounded, and my breath came fast.

I said, "I know you're charming, brilliant, and compassionate. I know if I touch you, I'll never let go." I did not want to say that. Someone else said it for me. That alter-ego I read about. *She* wanted Aaron even more than I did! I tried to calm myself by leaning back, but he placed a finger under my chin, raising my lips to his, and drew me even closer.

I slanted my lips until they brushed his. My fingertips stroked his cheek. His mouth met mine in a sweet but intense kiss. Oh, I wanted this since the first time I drank in those fiery eyes and that lean body.

From that moment on, I knew we could only move forward. I touched his hair. It was surprisingly soft. My fingers didn't stop there; they ran down his neck as my thumb toyed with his earlobe. In one concerted move, his arms encircled me, and our lips played upon each other. Again, riotous pangs visited me.

I agonized over whether to nudge him away or let him continue. His hand played through my hair, working it free. He brushed it back, bringing me to dizzying heights with those long fingers. His breathing in my ear made heat sear through me. "I want you, Betsy."

I leaned back, which meant yes. In a frenzy of pent-up desire, we unbuttoned blouses, shirts, breeches, petticoats, and under-petticoats. His nimble hands set me aflame. Oh, he fulfilled me...

Only later did I realize we hadn't used a sheath. That would have been a mite more useful than a box of money.

We lay in each other's arms, neither wanting to let go.

"Why did we wait so long?" His voice washed over me like cool rain on a hot day.

"Long?" I planted kisses on his neck. "When else could it have been?"

"The minute I saw you, I wanted to ravish you. But that was neither the time nor the place," he answered.

"Outside Federal Hall? I think not." We laughed as I tried to catch my breath. My head spun. I'd never felt this shattered afterward. Now I knew what the French meant by *la petite mort*. Had I died a little death and was slowly coming back?

With the fire reduced to glowing embers, we swept our clothing off the floor and somehow got it back on. He invited me for a meal, but I needed drink. He gave me some wine, and I gulped it too fast.

When he stood to summon the carriage, I stopped him. "No, let's walk. I need air." Truth was, I didn't want the evening to end so soon.

So, he walked me. At the door, we kissed, but not hungrily, as we were both sated. He struggled to keep his eyes open. My nurturing instincts surged.

"My dear, I don't want you to walk back. Stay here ..." I offered, but it sounded preposterous. Of course, he declined.

I don't remember how we ended the evening. I don't even remember stumbling up the stairs, but I do remember waking up fully dressed.

Not a moment went by when I didn't think of him – or dream of him.

Three weeks went by, then a month. I stayed busy. Working. Reading. Saving money. Keeping up with developments around our city and our nation. One blustery day, a newspaper item made my heart leap with much-needed joy. A builder was erecting a theater designed by French architect Marc Brunel, on Park Row, across from the City Coffee House. I rushed over and, right as rain, workers hammered away at framing.

From there, I ran straight to William Dunlap's boarding house and rapped on the door. He opened it, and his eyes lit up.

We embraced. "Oh, Will, how good to feel you in my arms. I missed you."

He hustled me in and poured me a glass of ale. I fought the urge to stare at the tattered shirt or the ripped knee of his breeches.

"When will the new theater open?" rushed out of my mouth. "I passed by to see—"

"They plan to open the doors in January!" he gushed. "How did you know it would be called the New Theater?"

"I didn't. Is it the New Theater?"

He nodded. "They always call something new –the new this or the new that –till a real name emerges. I was about to sit down and write you and the other players. I've already secured the position as manager, and once again we're in business. A few kind souls offered me credit to run notices and print flyers."

"What will the play be?" Too excited to drink the ale, I left it untouched.

"As *Cato* is so popular, I expect receipts will come pouring in. You will join us, Betsy? Of course, you'll play Marcia." His encouraging tone dared me to resist.

"Of course, I will! I love *Cato*!" I clapped. "Do you know that famous quotations from the war came from *Cato*? Patrick Henry's 'Give me liberty or give me death' and Nathan Hale's 'I regret that I have but one life to lose for my country' are direct quotes from the play."

"Ah, yes, quotes plucked easily as chicken feathers. Good to know that plagiarism is alive and well in our government." He smirked.

"Oh, how long I've waited to return to the make-believe world I love, to shut out the ugliness of reality and act a part, always knowing the ending." My heart danced a jig to an imaginary hornpipe.

But that night as I pored over my ledger, now with a bank account earning interest, I knew this would end. No more weekly deposits, no more new frocks and shoes and hats and gloves, no more steak and malmsey, a delay to reaching my goal and my dreams. At least I had a week to think about it.

But on the day before opening night at the New Theater, someone else made up my mind for me.

I needed no magic or crystal ball. I knew from the first episode of morning sickness, then counting two months from my last flux – I was going to be a mother.

CHAPTER 14

I SCRAMBLED to the chamber pot, hung onto the edges, and retched. I staggered back to bed and fell in. As I lay there weak and dizzy, my mind raced weeks ahead, months ahead – what would I name him? Aaron Burr the Third? George Washington Bowen Burr? And if 'he' was a girl? Name her after Mamma? Phebe Bowen Burr? Or after me? Little Betsy Bowen Burr?

After dozing on and off, hunger pangs sat me up. Then I had a terrible recollection – I didn't use a sheath the last time I was with Billy North.

The only other time, in the heat of unplanned and impulsive passion, was with Aaron.

I prayed that night. "That was the first time I ever *made love* with a man. Please, God, let the father be Aaron." Oh, how badly I wanted my baby to be his! I hoped I'd sealed my child's fate during that night of passion, and Aaron's seed had given it life.

I struggled to my feet, cradling the life inside me, with an all-consuming vigilance I'd never felt before. "We will be fine, little one. You will never beg for food or sleep on the ground in an alley. And you will be respected. Safe from scandal and cruelty." That meant one thing. I needed to leave New York City and return to Providence.

I tidied myself and went downstairs to seek out Sally. As I stepped into the kitchen, the smell of sizzling bacon made bile rise to my throat. I turned and fled to the outdoor privy but collapsed with dry heaves. I sat, head between knees, to calm my roiling stomach. I shuffled back in and managed to choke down a crust of bread but couldn't swallow the bitter coffee and spat it out.

Sally wasn't about, so I went to Sukie. I dragged myself to her house, handkerchief pressed to my nose to quell the sickening odors of rotting animal carcasses and raw sewage.

I dreaded leaving the city I called home. I'd settled so well here, made friends, and cherished my blossoming union with Aaron. All this had to end – at least until my baby was born. But would I dare return? This hit me like a sack of bricks. *No, Betsy, you're thinking way too far ahead.*

A buxom servant admitted me, holding a whisk broom. Lightheaded, I sat on the bottom step in Sukie's hallway, head between knees again. I greeted the whisper of satin slippers scurrying down the steps. Sukie helped me to my feet, but I hung onto the banister as a wave of dizziness dazed me.

"What is wrong? You look positively cadaverous. Sit down in here." She draped my arm around her shoulders and led me to her parlor. "Do you want tea, some—"

"God, no," I groaned as I slid onto her settee. "Not a thing. Sukie, I'm with child."

The color drained from her face. "By God, when? How?"

"*When* could have been one of two occasions. *How*, I'm sure you know. I feel strangely alone, yet not alone. I'm carrying another life here." I placed my hands upon my belly. "I'm going back to Providence. I can't stay here."

"Oh, Betsy." She leaned forward and gave me a hug, careful not to crush me. "Are you sure? I've had times where I thought I was ..." She spread her hands and shrugged.

"My flux is nearly two months late, and I can't keep any food down." A wave of sickness hit me when I mentioned food. "I feel it, in my gut, I mean, I know it. And twice I did not protect myself."

"Do you know who the father is?" she asked.

"Not for certain. But ..." My lips clamped. I couldn't tell her it might be Aaron. Not yet. "I didn't want to leave town and not tell you. You've done so much for me." Tears stung my eyes at the finality of this goodbye. "And it was all going so well, all to plan, and then some."

"You can return when the baby's older and say you adopted. Who has to know? It's no one's business anyway."

"Oh, I will return. My future, my life is here. But it kills me to leave." Sudden weakness drained me. "I'll miss you, Gertrude and the chaps, the theater, the taverns – and Aaron."

She grasped my chin in a firm grip. "Betsy, look at me. May he be your baby's father?"

I had to tell her. I'd never lied in my life, and would not start with my dearest friend. "Sukie ..." I clasped her hand. "When I said I didn't protect myself, what I meant was ..." I choked on my words. "When Aaron and I made love, we ... he did not wear a sheath, nor did I ask him to. We fell into each other's arms and surrendered to our passion and ... yes, it can be his. I don't hold him responsible. But he will find out, as everyone will. I refuse to hide. So I'm a disgraced, fallen woman." I hung my head. "It will be his decision – or anyone else's –whether to shun me."

She looked more despondent than I felt. I knew why. Because she wanted a baby of her own and hadn't been blessed with one. I wished I could ease her shock. "No, Aaron won't shun you. But I say wait till the baby is born, and see who it resembles. If the child is the spitting image of Aaron, tell him. He will do the honorable thing and give the child his name. He gave all his other children his name."

"Even if the babe is his," my voice limped, "I won't tell him. He doesn't need the extra burden." It broke my heart to say this. I longed for that moment of pride, to tell him we were parents together ...

"Oh, he loves children, Betsy. He treats Theodosia's brood as his own. I'm just telling you, be sure. Because he's not sure, without a doubt, the others are his. He's just honorable to a fault."

A rush of respect for him filled me. And saddened me even more. "No, if this babe is his, I can't tell him. He doesn't need another bastard."

"You needn't leave right away, you know." She rang her servant bell. "You won't be quickening for a while yet."

"I need a head start. And a place to live and – to be honest, I don't know if I can work another night. I was so ill this morning, I thought I'd died." My mouth soured at the memory. "How can I perform on stage or in real life feeling this way?"

Her mouth turned down, and she slunk back, shoulders slumped. I knew she wanted to provide an instant solution. But there was none.

A servant came in, and Sukie asked for a pot of tea.

"I appreciate your willingness to help, Sukie. If I could take you to Providence with me, I would. I'll tell Aaron in a few years, when it no longer matters."

"That means you intend to stay in touch with him?" Her voice sharpened.

"Of course. There is a future for us," I gave a determined nod. "My name will live on in history beside his."

"Did your French spiritual friend tell you that?" She gave

me a dubious grin, unbeliever that she was. Well-grounded Sukie did not attend church either.

"No." I gave an emphatic shake of my head. "I don't need him to tell me, I know. Aaron is my destiny."

A vivid image flashed before me: a church with soaring arches, colored bands of sunlight streaming through stained glass windows, the sweet scent of incense. I walk towards the altar on the arm of my father, about to give me away to my groom...

I blinked and returned to reality. I'd never seen myself as a bride before. Where did that image come from?

A sob escaped the back of my throat as I realized I'd never share this precious moment with Papa. He'd never give me away, and saddest of all, I couldn't share the joy of his first grandchild.

Sukie leaned forward and placed a hand on my arm. "Worry not. It will all work out. Take one step at a time."

I forced the painful thoughts away. "I might never share special times with my father."

"You still plan an audience with him, do you not?"

I nodded. "Of course, when the time is right. But I cannot count on his accepting me, at least publicly. It will have to be our secret. He cannot keep his public image and let it be known that he has an illegitimate daughter. I so want him in my life, but it may never be."

"If it's meant to be, it will happen. Don't dwell on that now." She leaned over and hugged me. "Concentrate on the new life inside you. All will fall into place. I know you, Betsy. You're at the helm of your fate, not the other way around. I will be extremely proud of you, not that I am not already. Just don't forget those you leave behind."

"I cannot leave anyone behind. They are all a part of who I am." I looked down at my midriff. When would I feel that quickening, that first kick, the first sign of life within? "Including my baby's father. And grandfather."

"Sure you do not want to stay for tea?" She glanced at the doorway to the kitchen. "It should be steeped shortly."

"No, I can't stomach anything right now." We embraced and said farewell over tear-soaked hankies.

"Please stay in touch." Sukie dabbed at her eyes. "I know he'll ask about you."

My heart broke ... I was about to leave one life and start another. Bittersweet it was, but more bitter than sweet.

Sally's house was empty when I returned. I trudged up the stairs to my room, opened one of Aaron's letters, and breathed it in.

"Aaron, I miss you so much," I whispered into the words he'd written, brimming with his essence. "Oh, to be the next Mrs. Burr," I said out loud for the first time.

Like a hovering ghost, guilt haunted me. I could be the next Mrs. Burr only if the first one died. Perhaps she would enjoy a full recovery and divorce him. Now, that lessened my guilt!

Elation overtook my sadness as when sunbeams break through the dark cover of a storm. I had two things to look forward to – giving life to my baby and the hope of becoming the next Mrs. Burr.

Leaving New York City, only temporarily, didn't seem so wrenching now.

Before my joy faded, I wrote Aaron the honest truth, that I needed to go back home for a family matter. I promised to write on a regular basis and wished he'd do the same. I made the promise I planned to keep – that I would return and we'd pick up exactly where we left off. I wrapped it with a copy of the new Almanack by Benjamin Banneker, a freed slave, now a brilliant astronomer. I'd devoured each page and wanted him to have it. I signed it with the bold sentiment, *"Love from ..."* about to write *Betsy*, I dipped the quill and boldly wrote what I hoped would seal our future: *"your Betsy."* That was even closer to the truth. My baby's father had to be Aaron! Fate couldn't be so cruel to give this child Billy North for a father.

CHAPTER 15

*"She was a loose woman, but likely looking, I guess. I used to
see her laughing with the girls as she walked down Cheap-
side. That was the great promenade for ladies of her sort –
painted women."*
   – An old Providence mariner on Betsy Bowen

PROVIDENCE, Rhode Island, back to whence I came, and still a
painted woman – painted and pregnant.

As the swaying boat approached the pier, I grasped the
wooden rail. My gaze wandered past the shoreline to the ware-
houses, taverns, and shabby dwellings that trapped me since
birth. Rancid odors of fish, waste, and sewage assaulted me. As
the boat bumped the dock, I staggered and clutched my middle.

"Here we are, little one," I whispered. "Our birthplace.
Time to start your new life."

On the narrow streets and at the noisy market, I retraced
childhood journeys. Pigs and chickens squealed at my feet.
Vendors shouted, "Fresh chickens, fresh cod, fresh trotters!"
Carts and carriages rumbled around me. It wasn't as refined,

cultured, or developed as New York, but it didn't try to be. No one thought to put the nation's capital here. Theaters were still banned. More vagrants and beggars wandered the hilly lanes than on New York streets.

But a sense of belonging comforted me. New York was my future, but I came from these streets. Here I took my first breath, toiled, begged, starved – and killed.

I knew the layout of the town as if etched in my mind. With nowhere to go, I wandered. I turned familiar corners, peered in shop windows, and held my breath against the rotting innards piled on trash heaps.

I headed to the place of my fondest memory, the home of Reuben and Freelove Ballou. I escaped my guardians Sam and Lydia Allen after Lydia, plagued by one of her fits, beat me with a broom. I scrambled out to find Massachusetts, where my mother and Jon had fled, but Freelove took me in.

Now, as I walked, I remembered …

A tyke of seven, I'd gone in the only direction I knew, towards the docks. A soothing comfort enveloped me as I caught sight of the Muddy Dock Tavern, where Mamma brought me to sleep upstairs when she got busy downstairs. Where to go? On Charles Street, I passed a stately brick house.

Exhausted and ravenous, I longed to live in a palace like that. A portly woman hanging petticoats on a line spotted me. As I turned to scamper away, she grabbed a lock of hair that had escaped my cap.

"Where you be going, little girl?" She peered down at me with a stern eye.

"To Massachusetts." I prepared to bolt.

"You walking there?" She clapped her hands on my shoulders.

I nodded.

"You'll starve first. Come in and I'll feed you before you drop right here." She took my hand and led me to her big house.

Wide-eyed, I gaped at the posh surroundings through seven-year-old eyes that had seen only squalor. The furniture gleamed in the airy parlor. The wide clean-swept floorboards told me she was far from poor.

As I devoured johnnycake and gulped strong tea, she asked my name.

"Betsy Bowen."

She studied my face. "I'd wager your Mamma is Phebe Bowen."

"Aye, do you know her?" I perked up.

"Very well." She nodded. "I know Phebe Bowen quite well indeed. I know all her stories."

"How do you know her?" My spirits soared. I jumped up and down on my toes. She'd tell me how to get to Mamma!

"I know her because I helped her birth you. Right here in this house."

"I was born here?" At that moment, I knew I'd stay. I snuggled into the soft armchair. I truly belonged.

"Up those steps, in the first room." She waved toward the stairs. "I also helped birth your half-sister Lavinia. She's taking her lessons at present. You'll meet her at supper."

"A half-sister?" I gushed. "I have a real family right here? And I can stay for supper?"

With tears in her eyes, she nodded. "Yes, child. As long as you wish. You are home."

Searching her face over the rim of my teacup, I noticed she and Mamma shared distinct features – hooded eyelids, high cheekbones, pointed chin. The same chestnut blonde hair peeked out from her lacy cap.

She didn't come out and say it, but even at that young age, I had the strongest hunch she and Mamma were kin.

"Are you my auntie?" I held my breath, awaiting her answer.

"Till you find your Mamma, you can call me Aunt Free," came her answer.

So began my stay. Aunt Free wasn't a mere midwife – she ran a brothel, lower in social order than Sally's but higher than a bawdy house for sailors.

When she took me in, her name was Freelove Whipple. But on Christmas Eve, she brought home a strapping dark-haired giant she presented as Reuben Ballou, a widower. His wife, Chloe, had died in Cumberland. Freelove and Reuben married in the parlor a month later and let me and Lavinia be flower girls.

It was in her ballroom where I met Papa for the first time. Now I knew it was under this very roof he and Mamma created me.

Aunt Free always knew. That's why she called me Miss Washington.

Now, carrying a child of my own, I approached the Ballou house, where I'd spent my happiest childhood years. Sweet nostalgia tugged at my heart. I quickened my step, climbed the same porch Papa climbed, and banged the knocker on the door, plopping down my duffel bag. "Aunt Free! Open up, it's me, Betsy!"

The door opened, and there she stood, mouth agape. "Miss Washington! You've come home!"

At the sound of "home," I fell into her strong arms. She squeezed me. "Don't hug too tight, Aunt Free – I'm in circumstances. Another Washington is on the way."

"Oh, my child." She held me at arm's length and looked me up and down, her gaze landing at my middle. "How many is this for you?"

"My first, of course. Why do you think I'm here? I had to leave New York. I couldn't very well stay there."

"Well, home you are. Come in, child, come in." The rooms looked smaller. I helped myself to that same chair and plopped before the hearth, though no fire burned on this hot day. Just like the morning she took me in at age seven, she gave me cakes and tea. I jabbered about New York until my voice cracked.

"And who is your baby's father?" She put aside her knitting and sat across from me.

I told her what I longed for in my heart. "Aaron Burr."

"Who?"

I blinked in surprise, then realized she wouldn't know. "He's New York's Attorney General. Dashing and brilliant. We read the same books and we relish each other's company and he is the man I love and ..." I finally caught my breath, "...he'll be president someday."

"And you will be right at his side when he does." She nodded, wiping her mouth.

"Oh, well, much as I want to..." I didn't want to tell her Aaron was married, and about my gamut of emotions from guilt to acceptance to hoping they'd divorce – it was all too much. I just needed a place to lay my head. "I cannot rush ahead. I need to settle here for now, and someone to assist me in the birth. You will help me, won't you?"

"Of course, Miss Washington." She gave me a gap-toothed grin. "Anything for you. But now that our president is about to be a grandpapa, Reuben and I must invite him back."

That hit me like a sack of feed. "No! I'm not ready. Wait till the baby is born. Then I'll have a better chance of him accepting me and..." The words caught in my throat, "...loving me and his grandchild."

"Uh-uh." She shook her head. "Waiting never solved anything. He needs to know. And the sooner the better." She got up and went to her writing desk, plucked up a quill, and slid it behind her ear.

I could never stop Aunt Free from doing anything. She'd held me down for baths and force-fed me parsnips when I craved sweets. Could I stop her from writing to Papa? Never.

"Aunt Free, let me write the letter. I'm ready to contact him myself." I waved the newspaper through the air to dry, wanting to cherish it as my most prized keepsake.

"Not a good idea, Betsy." She shuffled around the table and leaned against her sideboard, folding her arms across her ample chest. "Too abrupt. He would doubt it's genuine. But from Reuben and me, he already knows who we are. Then when he does arrive, we shall present you to him—just as when you were a child—and this time we will make sure he knows who you are. Hence it is your good fortune you haven't yet called on him in New York. Perhaps that's why fate brought you back here for a meeting that bears fruit."

That made sense to me. If Aunt Free hadn't voiced her reason, I'd have dashed to the desk, scrawled out a letter, and run to the post. But I knew this would work out, and he would come here.

She worked magic – and I mean real magic. She used the 16th-century book *Natural Magick* by John Porta. It was all in Italian, but somehow she translated the whole book and followed the – what she called 'recipes' but to me, they were spells – to the letter. People paid Aunt Free in currency or vegetables or even hogs for her spells on unfaithful husbands and wives – chanting in Latin over a bowl of henbane seeds steeped in juice of sage with a handful of St. John's Wort in each palm, surrounded by candles. I shuddered and hid beneath my covers when she told me yet another 'recipe' of toadstool spores, mandrake, and foxglove had worked. How could I stop her from writing to the president about his daughter and grandchild?

So she sat and wrote to Papa.

Worry not, Betsy, I assured myself. *He won't receive the letter for months, and even then, will he even read it? It's best to knock at his door in New York.* I stopped talking to myself when I remembered who was in charge: Aunt Free – and I'd seen her magic in action. If anyone could sway a president's belief, she could.

"At least let me see it when you're finished," I called out. "He resides at Number Three Cherry Street, New York City."

Aunt Free's husband, Reuben, came home. He looked at me, scratching his head as if he knew me from somewhere.

"Hello, Reuben. I'm Betsy Bowen – Miss Washington." I stood to greet him.

He opened his arms and clasped them around me. "Ah, little Betsy, come home to the roost. What brings you back?"

I told him. He drew back. His eyes landed on my middle, and I knew this would happen a lot. "You sure? You're thin as a coat of varnish."

"I'm sure."

He didn't ask who the father was, nor did he mention Mamma. He let his wife do all the talking, wheeling and dealing. A major during the war, he was General Washington's dispatch rider, and posted bond for Mamma when she was run out of town. I remembered he hated Tories: "I done shot a Red Coat, dug a grave and planted the varmint under that tree out back," he'd boasted, giving me the willies.

I didn't hate Tories or Red Coats, but held a grudging respect for Reuben, despite my horror at what he'd done. I never ventured anywhere near that tree, knowing a Red Coat lay buried there.

"You'll stay with us?" He opened his mahogany cabinet and took out a bottle.

"For the time being." Elation lightened my tone.

"You shouldn't have this." He popped the cork. "I'll fetch a glass of milk."

"I don't want any more milk, I want some of that – I'll wager it's Madeira." It was his favorite, too. I remembered as a child climbing to the attic to fetch bottles for him. He taught me Madeira's aroma and taste improved with heat.

I wanted to tell Reuben about Papa, about his inauguration, and about Aunt Free writing him, but Reuben never discussed the war or the other soldiers. He was wounded in the Battle of Rhode Island and limped. So I respected his wishes and never spoke of it.

But I let him bring me a glass of warmed milk.

His servants brought up a bed and a stand from the cellar and put it in a room on the second floor, overlooking that tree. I pulled the curtains shut and waved away billowing dust, shuddering at the thought of that shallow grave.

I snuggled into bed, safe and cozy in my childhood home.

I longed to feel Aaron's arms around me, to hear him promise, "We'll be a family." But I slapped the side of my head. *Stop it, Betsy, stop this wistful wishing!* These thoughts were as fanciful as the plays I acted in.

I needed to make a living, to continue saving for my – our future, our success. I needed to earn my keep. I didn't mean only sweeping and dusting—I had to go back to earning my living as I always had. Aunt Free's was the best place in Providence for that.

Hence I returned to the business I was best at – for now.

No one famous came to Providence as a matter of course—only on official visits. They passed through on their way to the major cities, Baltimore, Philadelphia, New York. Thusly, I had no fear of having to entertain the likes of Tom Jefferson or Jemmy Madison. Just randy gents out for a romp came here.

"You needn't do this," Aunt Free repeated as I entered the parlor in my finest satin skirt and cotton blouse. "You can earn your keep other ways."

"Providence is too provincial to have theater, and I care not to ruin my knees and knuckles scrubbing and scouring, Aunt Free. I care not to earn my keep any other way at present." I grasped her hand. "I've made grand plans for the future. I will show our nation what the president's only daughter is capable of. And they needn't know how I got there. So let me do what I must."

Her smile brought back memories – Aunt Free throwing her false teeth into the fire because they were ill-fitting, swearing never to wear anything false again. "I cannot stop you from following your plans, Betsy. Just as you cannot stop me from writing to your father. Two headstrong women we are." She swiped a tin of snuff from her desktop and held it out to me. I shook my head in polite refusal. She flipped it open, took a pinch and gave a good snort. "It being Saturday evening, we'll have our fill of gents. I'll make sure you entertain only the ablest and most charming."

"It would help if they do not know me from before." I'd been popular with the sailors *and* the natives.

She tilted her head and pursed her lips. "Then you'd best try another town, lass. They all know Bouncin' Bet here."

I tittered, but the memory didn't amuse me. Bouncin' Bet was the moniker sailors slapped on me in my early days. Bouncin' Bet I became once again.

Next morning before breaking my fast, I sat down at Aunt Free's desk and with her borrowed paper, ink, and quill, wrote to Sukie. "*I miss New York so, but I returned to my happiest childhood home with a woman I believe is kinfolk. I needn't worry about meals nor shelter nor a midwife to birth my baby—what will happen beyond that point, I know not.*" I couldn't help but ask after Aaron. Realizing this was too forward, only having been gone a few days, I tried to cross that part out but ended up ruining the entire page, so I began again. But once again I couldn't help myself. My sweaty hand smudged the ink as I told Sukie to give him my regards. "*Please keep my secret for the time being,*" I repeated. Writing about him made my hand tremble so the lettering looked as shaky as I felt.

The days grew hotter and I grew larger. Aunt Free let me spend lazy days lounging on the porch chaise. In the evenings I read out loud to her other ladies and servants on the porch, all in wide-eyed fascination. I took them to the worlds of kings, queens, palaces, and castles—the worlds of my fantasies.

Some evenings, Aunt Free worked her magic for lost souls or those bent on revenge. When not busy plying my trade, I sat in on these sessions, rapt. She read from the medieval Italian book and had me fetch her tools of the trade – candles, a sieve, linseed, ivy berries, dried chamomile flowers, sundry other herbs, flowers, and potions she stored in the root cellar.

I took the hocus-pocus with a pinch of salt, but seeing the results almost made me a believer.

One night, I couldn't help but ask her to do a spell for me.

"Who will I marry, Aunt Free? The soothsayer Jean Alliette told me I'd marry for love, but can you tell me more?"

"I ain't no fortune-teller, my child, but I can send my life force out into the ether to attract that right man to you."

My heart leapt. Of course, I hungered for that right man to be Aaron. "Let's do it this evening!"

"Why so intent on knowing who you'll marry? I thought you wanted to storm the world yourself."

"I intend to, but I want to find true love. I believe I've found it, but—my being here, and—" I glanced down at my now-bulging middle, "—I'd hardly expected to ever leave New York. I was just wondering if—" My hands fluttered and I stumbled over my words, which I never did, especially with Aunt Free. But every time I thought of telling Aaron he had another child, I needed to know the next step, so desperate, it hurt.

"Go fetch a crow's egg from out back and the juice of the crow's foot plant, and I will mix them with honey and say the chant." She fetched some spoons.

"Mix them with honey and then what?"

She arched a brow at me. "That is the part most women shy away from, but I know you will not. You must anoint your—" She waved in the general direction of my nether region, "honey pot with them."

"What?" I shuddered. "Isn't there a less messy one?"

"Perhaps, but this has been known to work."

"On who?" I smirked. "Grizzly bears?"

She grasped my hands and shut her eyes. "My child, I've never felt what I'm feeling now, but a vibrating sensation nearly felled me. I'm as if lit afire. Look at my hands." She let go and I watched her hands quiver. I grasped them again to steady them, but that strange charge she described ran through me. "What is that, Aunt Free?"

"The life force, my child. It lives all around us. We bring it to ourselves, either good or bad, with our thoughts. Right now, this is all good. Positive. Something good will happen to you. I don't just feel it, I know it. Oh, you will marry a prominent man. A love match, and it will change your life. Your names will survive in history together."

"What's his name? What is it?" I squeezed her hands so tight, my knuckles turned white.

"I know not. You'll have to find out. But believe me, my child, once your name becomes linked with his, it will live on without his. And will never be forgotten."

Oh, please, I begged that invisible vortex surrounding us. *Let me be the next Mrs. Burr!*

CHAPTER 16

AUGUST ROLLED in on a thunderstorm that brought torrential rains. Flashes of blue-white lit the night sky. Aunt Free fetched the soggy newspaper and spread it on the table. "Look at this, Betsy!" She summoned me into the dining room as I broke eggs for a meringue pie. "President Washington is coming!"

"When? Where?" Wiping my hands on my apron, I squeezed my bulk through the door frame. "Here to the house? He answered your letter?" My voice screeched.

"No, alas, he never answered it. It says here he's visiting Providence to celebrate our ratification of the Federal Constitution." She read, "Our governor will welcome them at Newport, the 17th. That's ..." She counted on her fingers. "Only a fortnight away. If Reuben and I send an invitation, he may receive it in time and can dine here, as when you first met him. Wouldn't that be grand?" She pumped her fists.

That news nearly knocked me over. "Grand." I hung onto the door frame for support. My mind whirred in a thousand frantic directions. Reunite with Papa – right here in this room exactly as we met years ago. What a beautiful way to cherish a memory, and introduce myself as his daughter. I waddled over to the table and snatched up the droopy paper.

"It says here: '...in the past, he declined to visit Rhode Island, considering it foreign territory. He will lodge at the Golden Ball Inn on Benefit Street.'"

Oh, to have him walk through Aunt Free's front door and up to me – a dream come true! I ran through the dialogue like a rehearsed script again and again. I knew every word.

"Hear that, little one?" I placed my hand over my middle. "You're going to meet Grandpapa!"

Aunt Free and Reuben wrote a gracious letter, inviting Papa and his party to a dinner dance. They reminded him of his last visit with General Rochambeau, that visit when he met me – but they wisely left that out.

On the morning of the dinner dance, I heard Aunt Free scream. Believing she'd fallen or had an attack of some sort, I clattered down the stairs. Her trembling hand held a letter embossed with a gold seal.

"What is it?" It couldn't be from Aaron, still on my mind day and night.

"Wonderful, magical news!" She held it out to me. I scanned each line, rushing to the bottom. My eyes stuck to the signature splayed across the page in a confident hand, a decorative loop crossing the 't'.

"He signed it himself! He's coming, he's truly coming here. I'm going to meet Papa! Thank you, God, thank you!" I'd never burst with such gratitude before. Even the life inside me was a different kind of miracle, something I created. But the love for my father bordered on reverence.

The letter fluttered to the floor as Aunt Free and I

embraced and danced a little jig, President Washington's grandbaby floating between us.

"Yes, you are, right here in this room. That is why this town is called Providence—*divine* providence for you."

On the most important day of my life, we all bustled to scrub floors, polish silver, and set the table. Cooks got to work broiling and roasting beef and mutton, and more broiling and basting after Aunt Free hand-picked the fattest ducks, geese, and other fowls from the market. I hoped our guests wouldn't object to Reuben's non-*de rigueur* custom of doing his own carving at the table.

He ordered ten bottles of Madeira, ten more of claret, port, and Champagne, and a hogshead of ale.

"A hogshead!" Aunt Free quit her sweeping and held the broom like a rifle. "You think these men are lushes, Mr. Reuben? They'll roll outta here in hearses after swilling that much!"

"I'd rather too much than suffer the embarrassment of coming up short," came his terse answer, but we both knew he'd be the sole imbiber long after our presidential party departed.

The final touch was the musicians – a string quartet of students with hopes of joining major orchestras.

Reuben suggested they play some patriotic songs. They knew a few and began rehearsing *Washington's March at the Battle of Trenton*, and *Norah, Dear Norah* from an English opera *The Poor Soldier*, Papa's favorite. If only I could sing. But it was a man's part, sung by Pat, the poor soldier himself.

We expected the coach of state to arrive at seven that evening, so I began preparing at noon. I took a long bath, washed my hair, and brushed it until it shone. Lavinia curled it with tongs, piled it on my head with dangling tendrils, and topped it off with a rosette-adorned crown of gauze.

At seven chimes, I could no longer stand the wait. My bones rattling, I stepped onto the porch and peered up and down the street. Only a squeaky cart rumbled by, carrying burlap sacks. At five minutes past seven, I feared they wouldn't arrive. A sip of Madeira went down nice and smooth.

"Betsy! They're here!" Aunt Free's voice boomed down the hallway. I took a ragged breath. Hanging onto the wall for support, I stood back as Aunt Free and Reuben filled the open doorway.

I recognized Governor Clinton and the russet-headed Jefferson. Two other men entered. The ladies fussed about them, taking their hats. Then Papa entered, majestic as any king, towering above them, his white hair gathered back in a queue. His sky blue jacket displayed gleaming buttons. Matching breeches were tucked into dark brown boots. He bowed and returned to his imposing height. I couldn't move. Aunt Free clutched my elbow and brought me to him. My knees wobbled.

"Mr. President, this is my dear charge, Miss Betsy Bowen. You met when she was much younger, in this very room."

"Pleased to see you again, Miss Bowen."

"Thank you, sir." How badly I wanted to say "Papa." His hand took mine and swallowed it. *Do I tell him now?* I glanced at Aunt Free.

I blurted out my well-rehearsed lines: "Mr. President, sir, I ... I need to tell you something. I've been—"

A jab to my ribs knocked the breath out of me. Aunt Free glared daggers. "Not now!" her stern expression told me.

Not missing a beat, I went on, "I've been your most loyal citizen and proud to be American to the bottom of my heart."

As he smiled, I caught a glimpse of his teeth, reported to be made of everything from whale bone to polished oak to elephant ivory. But those of us who read the *New York Gazette* knew they came from slaves and animal corpses. They fit him well enough.

After that, Jefferson seemed like a footman. But I stayed polite and cordial.

At eight o'clock, one of Aunt Free's servants rang the dinner bell and seated us. Reuben sat at one end of the table, Papa at the other.

I sat mid-table at a safe distance from my sire, between Jefferson – we exchanged small talk about operas, for we had nothing else in common – and Mr. Foster, of Rhode Island's legislative branch.

The dinner began with French onion soup and lamb stew, peas, carrots, boiled cod, and roast pork arranged around a centerpiece of hothouse orchids and gladiolas on ice. At the end of the first course, the servers placed the 'remove' dishes at each end of the table – dishes of the duck, goose, and fowl Reuben carved right there. And my contribution – the oysters I'd bought at market. I'd struck a hard bargain, paying half the fishmonger's asking price. The 'remove' dishes filled the time it took to bring in the second course: smoked salmon, sweet potatoes, and cauliflower, with a peacock pie and 'gumballs' – a sweet confection with aniseed and caraway seeds. I craved the 'cheese wigs' – bread buns coated with cheese sauce so they resembled a wig on a stand.

For me, the highlight was dessert – apple tansey, gingerbread, and a variety of teas and coffee.

Our guests raved over the oysters. "I hand-picked each one," I boasted, but bucked my urge to gloat over the bargain I wrangled for them.

Dinner finished, the men retreated to the vestibule to smoke seegars – I noticed Papa did not smoke but enjoyed his

Madeira – and we ladies prattled with the musicians. Then the dancing began – first the customary minuet, which I danced with Jefferson. I couldn't tear my eyes from the sight of Papa dancing with Aunt Free. With his height, dignity, and courtliness, he made a striking figure gliding across the floor. I glowed with pride. *That is my Papa!* I wanted to proclaim. When the dance ended, Governor Clinton and Mr. Smith rushed out of the ballroom, clutching their middles.

At the sound of the next piece, a formal gavotte, Mr. Foster asked for my hand. Before the gavotte ended, one of Reuben's merchants dashed out as the others had. Only one thing was out there – the privy.

Then Mr. Gilman ran out the door, and I heard him retch. *Uh-oh. Something is amiss.*

A buzz began to circulate as the music played on. I took Reuben aside. "Several of the men went ill. Was something undercooked?" I scanned the room and noticed Mr. Smith returned, his face a sickly green.

Reuben glanced around, wringing his hands. "Do you feel ill?"

"No. Do you?" I asked.

He shook his head as Aunt Free approached and whispered, "Mr. Gilman is resting in an upstairs bedroom."

I stood in a daze. By God, the bloomin' oysters! Two storekeepers fell ill earlier, after eating the blasted bivalves, so went the gossip. And here stood I, guilty as sin, having fed them to my guests!

The quartet struck up a rollicking Virginia Reel in homage to Papa. He stood across from me and held out his hand. "Miss Bowen, care to dance with your president?"

"Of course, sir." Using my acting skill to keep my dignity, I ached to hug him and cry, *Papa, please take me home with you, I love you so!*

It passed in a blur. I managed to dance the right steps and not tread on his toes. Then I took the breath I'd waited so long to take and began to speak the words embedded in my memory: "Mr. President, sir, I need to tell you something I've been waiting many years to tell you."

"And what may that be?"

Music swirled around us. Our feet moved in tandem. "Mr. President, I am not a Bowen. I understand you may not believe this at first. But I am—"

He broke away from me as if I'd bitten him. He turned and doubled over. "Pardon, I must excuse myself—" He vanished, leaving me stunned.

"Dear God, the president is ill!" No one heard me above the music. Frantic, I found Aunt Free and pulled her aside. "Now the president is ill! He ran out! Go see if he's all right!"

"I ain't following him to the privy, you silly pillock," she shot back, "but I'll take care of it." She vanished out the same door the others had fled.

Jefferson sat on the settee in the corner, that same green tinge to his face.

God above, the entire evening ruined because of bad oysters! There I was, about to tell the president he was dancing with his one and only daughter, who now carried his first and only grandbaby, and some lousy bleedin' oysters had to get between us!

The quartet quit playing, and only a few guests lingered. Reuben gathered the group around him and gave a heartfelt apology. They all took it in good humor, since they weren't the ones crouching in the privy.

I stood at the window as they filed out. Reuben assisted Papa, recovered enough to walk to his carriage. I heard him mumble, "I'll spend the rest of my Providence visit in closed quarters." Then he gave a little laugh. Behind that stern exterior lived a genial man who could take a joke, even when it was on him.

But that lifelong dejection and abandonment overcame me. I turned and trudged up the stairs. When I closed my door behind me, all alone, with no one to hear me, I curled up on my bed.

"Oh, God above, I poisoned him!" I prayed hard for his recovery and berated myself, begging forgiveness, wailing over and over, "I knew not what I'd done!"

When would I ever speak to Papa again? I despaired. Oh, how I'd prepared for this moment with him, to finally tell him of our special bond.

I wondered where Aaron was, if he ever thought of me, if he read my letters. I missed him more than ever. I forced myself out of bed and over to my small table. I wrote him my most soul-bearing letter ever. But I didn't seal it. I slid it under my pillow and slept on it.

CHAPTER 17

THE DAYS GREW hotter and I grew larger. I was weepy for no reason but ignored the rude stares and clucks from the townswomen. Aaron stayed on my mind every moment. When I wrote to him, I kept theatrics to a minimum. He didn't write back. His silence kept my fantasies alive.

In the dry goods store, I fingered blue cambric for a post-birth dress. I gasped as a stab of pain pierced my gut. I doubled over, dropping the bolt. "It's time!" I stumbled into the street and flagged down a carriage.

"Please ..." I begged the coachman, hands over my swollen middle. "Take me to Ballou's on Charles Street. I'm about to birth my baby."

"Great Scott," he mumbled as the coach door opened and a dandy in silver-buttoned finery pulled me inside. "Miss ... Miss Bowen, is that you?"

Through my haze of pain, I recognized him as Congressman Benjamin Bourne, one of my customers. Another contraction shot through me like an arrow. I bellowed loud enough to hear on Narragansett Bay.

As the next contraction nearly blacked me out, the coach halted. The coachman and Congressman gathered me up and carried me on what seemed a journey. Aunt Free's voice commanded, "Bring her in here, Ben."

Delirious with pain, I lay back on Aunt Free's bed and she rubbed my belly. "Bring hot water! Bet is about to birth! I needs catnip and alder tea – and bring up an axe from the cellar!"

"An axe? What are you going to do, hack the child out of me?" I gasped one word at a time.

"No, love." She pushed back my damp hair. "The axe cuts the pain in half. It goes under the bed."

Someone propped me up on pillows and ran a cool cloth over my face.

"All right, love, push. I see the head!" She ordered water and soap. "Push again! The head's out," she announced as if giving me the time of day.

"A baby boy, Betsy." My first sight of my son was Aunt Free holding him, covered with a bloody blue-red sheen. As she wiped him, the pinkish hue of healthy flesh emerged. My baby's first sweet squall reached my ears.

Sobbing, I heaved a sigh of pride. "I have a son."

"Oh, he's just lovely, Betsy." Lavinia's voice sounded from afar. "So handsome. He's got a head of thick mahogany hair."

Hearing those words, I knew. "His name is George Washington Burr." I turned my head, and with a lazy smile, drifted off.

~

Aunt Free brought him to me, swaddled in pink. I looked at his face for the first time. Bright blue eyes offered the only resemblance to Papa. But I heard all babies had blue eyes. Soon they'd turn a sparkling brown – I was willing to wager my life on it. He sported fine, angular features, a straight nose, and strong chin. Well, why not? So did his father—the handsomest man in the world.

As I rocked and suckled my baby, Reuben came into the room. He held out a book, the pages yellowed with age, its cover worn and stained. Faded gold letters spelled out *The Holy Bible*. "This is for you and little George." He opened the cover. I read what he'd written inside, in bright blue ink. "*George Washington Burr, born of Eliza at my house in Providence. Reuben Ballou.*"

Tears filled my eyes. "Oh, Reuben, how beautiful, a heartfelt sentiment, and to write it in this precious artifact. You needn't have done that. But why write 'Eliza'?"

"To me, Eliza is more regal and majestic than Betsy. Reminiscent of a great queen. The only way to begin your new life."

"I reckoned I'd begun my new life in New York." I chuckled. "I need to start a third?"

"Lass, you have a son now. You're on your way to riches. This is your new life, not when you left here a ragamuffin with a few coppers to your name."

"I've a ways to go, Reuben." I chuckled. "I can't begin this minute."

"Oh, you know where to begin, my child. That is what keeps most of mankind behind." He bit off the end of a cheroot and spat it into the fireplace. "They don't know where they're going."

~

I had a tough decision to make. I needed that new life as Eliza. But George required the best of care. I couldn't do both.

Aunt Free offered—rather, begged me, "Go back to New York," when he was but a week old. "We'll raise him for you, feed, clothe, and educate him. No one in New York needs to know you have a child. Not till you're ready to tell."

My heart tore into pieces—between a loving home for George—and my goals.

Reuben was right; I wasn't the 7-year-old waif who stumbled through this door years ago. Like an outgrown dress, 'Betsy' simply no longer fit.

Could I bring George to New York? Who would care for him while I worked? How would I protect him from cruel barbs and bullies? How could I explain a baby with no father?

Oh, what to do? I paced the length of the porch and back.

I went to the desk and scribbled a hurried note to Aaron. "I'm returning. I offer you my heart and my fervent wishes to be with you soon." With a flourish, I signed my new name for the first time: Eliza Capet.

Why Capet? I followed all the news of the French Revolution. It fascinated me.

When the starving French rabble refused to 'eat cake' and ousted their monarchs, the new Republic gave headless Louis XVI the surname Capet, after Hugh Capet, who founded the Capetian dynasty. To me, the name sounded fit enough to tag onto the regal Eliza.

With my letter to Aaron posted and my trunk packed, I lifted George from his cradle, gathered him in my arms, and rocked him. Innocent blue eyes tugged at my heart. I ran a finger over his downy cheek and whispered, "Mamma loves you more than life itself." Tears blurred my vision.

The thought of separation produced a dull ache in my breast. I sighed, and my shoulders drooped. Going back to New York with an infant would not sit well with those I knew. It would make his childhood living hell.

I held him close to my heart, my love so fierce it hurt. Through my pain, I whispered, "You will have a much better life with the Ballous." Aunt Free fussed over him day and night. She snatched him from my arms when I walked the floors in the dead of night. She begged me to let her feed him the strained fruits and vegetables I hand-picked at the market. She told him the great George Washington was his Grandpapa, and he'd follow in those hallowed footsteps.

Snuggled on the window seat overlooking the river, I repeated Aunt Free's words of wisdom, "Yes, my son, you will bring our nation into the next century." I stroked the dark feathery hair, so like Aaron's. He gurgled. "Shh, baby, you will be fine. How can you not be destined for greatness, little George? You are a Burr. And you are a Washington." I touched my nose to his with a smile. "You're gifted with the blood of three fine bloodlines." I swear his lips curled in a smile. "You're blessed, my beautiful son. Truly blessed." Those bright eyes blinked. I marveled at how fragile he felt in my arms, yet knew the strong man he'd become.

On this warm sunny day, the saddest of my life, I never felt so alone as the boat pulled away. Reuben and Aunt Free holding my baby boy shrank from my sight. I waved and blew kisses until my arms ached. That vast gulf of sea now divided us. Briny wind blew through my hair. I'd learned about metaphors in *Julius Caesar*, so I turned and faced the bow. I vowed to look forward from this day on and recited one of my favorite Shakespeare metaphors: '*Lowliness is young ambition's ladder, Whereto the climber-upward turns his face.*' The ocean became a metaphor for my fate—vastness, empty space, and a clean slate awaiting me to fill it.

When the packet wound its way into New York Harbor, my past vanished.

I gathered my satchel. I wanted so badly to go straight to Aaron but was not ready—physically or emotionally. Slinging the satchel over my shoulder, I traipsed the dusty streets to William Dunlap's house. Too early for the matinee, I expected him home.

As he opened the door, the sight of him sent me back to the first time I called on him at home—tousled hair, rumpled shirt, sleeves rolled past his elbows. I dropped the satchel on his threshold, and we fell into each other's arms.

"Betsy, my Betsy, I'd given up hope of ever seeing you again." He slid my satchel inside and shut the door.

"I told you I'd be back." Arm in arm, we entered his cluttered sitting room. We sat on the settee, and I inhaled his familiar leathery scent. "I'm Eliza Capet now," I announced proudly.

"How posh. It suits you." He gave a reassuring nod. "Where is your child?"

"Back in Providence with the Ballous." I fought a pang of sadness. "I must be situated on firm ground before I call for him. Will, I must ask right out—what is your current situation with the theater?"

"I'm running *The Beggar's Opera*, but I fear there's no part for you at present. However, since I'm so happy to see you, when I end the play's run at month's end, I'll run..." He took a breath and gazed into my eyes. "Oh, you tell me. You name it, and I'll have the notices printed."

"Ah, I have so many favorites," I sang with joy at returning to theater, poor as I'd be. "I'll have to think this over back at Sally's, gather my wits, and think straight again."

As he walked me to the door, he commented, "I suppose you know your Burr is running for Philip Schuyler's Senate seat. I hope he wins." He gave me a sideways smile.

My heart leapt at the sound of Aaron's name. "Yes, I read about it. I know he will win."

"As Schuyler is Alexander Hamilton's father-in-law, fur is flying," he added. "A fair amount of mud-slinging, name-calling, and otherwise dirty looks between the two factions."

I smirked. "Schuyler deserves to lose. He is such a nob."

"You mean snob," he said as we stepped outside.

"That, too. Enough of counterfeit aristocrats," I spoke over a cart rumbling by. "Didn't France teach our citizens anything? We need to get nobs who think they're monarchs out of government and give it to the people. Who better to represent us than the future Senator Burr?"

"None I can think of." He shook his head. "But don't expect to see much of him if he wins that seat. The capital is moving soon, and your little fantasy may go back to dreamland."

"I know that. But I also know he belongs to my future. Lawyer, governor, senator, vice president, or president, his future and mine are one and the same." That familiar pang hit me. I longed for Aaron's touch. But I needed to prepare myself for him.

"You need no soothsayer, Bets—Eliza. You'll get there by sheer determination—and smarts." He tapped his noggin. "Not to mention beauty."

"Thank you, Will." I bade him farewell and headed to Sally's.

She greeted me with open arms. "Ah, lass, you're fit, fresh-eyed, and reborn as a new babe seeing our great big world for the first time."

I smiled. "I am reborn, Sally. I left Betsy Bowen in Providence, where she once trawled the streets. I am Eliza Capet, ready to take New York City by storm and rise to the peak of its rolling hills."

"You are Eliza Capet." She looked me over, made me stand and twirl this way and that. "Betsy Bowen was rough-and-tumble, but Eliza Capet is a desirable, worldly woman."

"Desirable enough that gents gladly part with their capital for my favors?" I hitched up my skirt to show some leg.

"Gladly? They'll shower you with it before they hang their breeches over the bedpost." She looked down. "But I've no longer room for you, Eliza. Your old room is occupied. I'm afraid you must find lodgings elsewhere."

I felt as though I'd fallen through the floor. "Oh, I so hoped you'd take me back in. I was so comfortable here."

She looked back at me and snapped her fingers. "Yes!" Her voice brightened. "I know of a French merchant looking for a housemaid. But that doesn't mean you'd *be* his housemaid." She gave me that 'saucy Sally' look, with raised brow and cheeky wink.

"Ah." My spirits lightened. "He seeks female companionship?"

She nodded. "A lady to entertain him, serve him... need I explain more... Miss Capet?"

With shivers of delight, goosebumps popped up on my arms. "Yes, you do. His age? His demeanor?"

"Not a day past thirty. The swarthy charm of a sea captain. Most magnificent mansion on Pearl Street. His own fleet of ships. A vast fortune, and a French name as *bon vivant* as your own."

My ears perked. My feet itched to run to his *château.* "And what is *Monsieur Bon Vivant's* name?"

"Stephen Jumel."

PART II
ELIZA JUMEL BURR

CHAPTER 18

I ALREADY KNEW the grand residence on Pearl Street. The yellow brick mansion graced the city's poshest neighborhood. Pearl Street got its name from the Dutch settlers who paved it with oyster shells. Gulping my anguish, I approached Number 24. Tall bow windows surrounded the black lacquered door and fan-shaped window above. I'd always slowed my pace and gawked when passing it, reckoning some rich swell who stuffed it with flash fawney dwelt there.

Now I knew who the swell was – and I was about to meet him face to face.

One snowy evening last winter, gleaming lights shone through the front windows of this palace, beckoning me like a beacon. I snuck up and peeked inside. "Holy macaroni!" I breathed my steamy breath on the window, ogling the opulent display of wealth beyond my reach—a chandelier ablaze with candles, a floor-to-ceiling mural that could've been painted by Leonardo himself, a gold clock atop an ornate marble hearth, and plush settees. A florid rug lay on a polished hardwood floor.

A gilded harpsichord, adorned with crystal candelabra, spanned nearly an entire wall. I fled before I got nabbed.

Chuckling at that memory, I lifted the gleaming knocker and rapped it against the door. A starchy servant opened it, broom in hand, and scanned me up and down. "And you are ..." she addressed me in a bored tone.

"Mademoiselle Eliza Capet." Why not French it up? I wore décolletage to match. "Monsieur Jumel expects me." He didn't, but I needn't explain. I'd save the explaining for Monsieur Jumel.

"A bit early, ain't you, Miz Caput?" She pronounced it *ka-PUT*. "The master don't see wenches of the night in the day." She glanced upward. "Sun's still up as I see. Till then, you ain't needed round here."

I could've shot back a snippy, *After I make Monsieur Jumel's acquaintance, we'll see who ain't needed round here,* but I never belittled even the most uppish servants. I simply stated, "Tell him I've arrived. Miss Marshall set the appointment."

"Miz Marshall?" She guffawed. "Now, that changes all, don't it just?"

Leaving me on the doorstep, she shuffled down the gleaming hallway. I brazenly stepped in, closing the door behind me. Finally, inside this castle! Fresh flowers and beeswax scented the air. My mouth hung open. Paintings ran the wall's length and along the curved staircase. But paintings, even by Leonardo himself, couldn't match the approaching vision. Tall and broad-chested, with a dusky complexion, the shadow of a beard over craggy cheeks, gray-sprinkled, sea-spray-tousled hair, and ocean-blue eyes, he regarded me as if he discovered the Northwest Passage at his door.

"Miss Marshall sent you? Why did she not send you sooner?" He folded his arms—arms that could steer a ship around the world. Even his words emerged salty and brackish, a man who knew what he wanted and seized it – or her. Soon that *her* would be me.

My anxiety bloomed into ardor as I drank in this powerful embodiment of man.

"Monsieur, I am here now." I made it clear I was his match and equal. The moment my eyes met those of Stephen Jumel, I knew nothing would stop our lives entwining – no sick spouses, no unplanned pregnancies.

He led me into his parlor and offered me a velvet chair. He served me brandy, which I didn't normally imbibe, but nothing was normal about this place or my host.

"Eliza Capet, I've seen you before, I know not where." He looked me up and down, but not in a liquorish way. "And I don't know the name. Where have I seen you? Certainly not Miss Marshall's."

"No, not there." I surely would've remembered him, dressed or not. "Perhaps on stage at the John Street Theater as Betsy Bowen?"

He shook his head. "I don't attend theater. I find it unrealistic and the seats uncomfortable."

Uncomfortable seats? From a man who spent half his life trawling the seas in a roiling sloop? I hid a laugh, more at ease now. I sat back and took a sip, holding back a grimace. "Then you may have seen me about town. The Queen's Head, perhaps?"

"That was it!" He leaned forward, splaying his hands. "How could I forget? Your escort was Colonel Burr."

I nodded. "Yes, he was." I tried to change the subject. "Did you attend the inauguration?"

"No, I was at sea." He swirled his brandy in the glass. "Do you still see Colonel Burr?"

Why did he want to talk about Aaron? I took another sip

and put the glass down, already tipsy. Any more and I'd forget I was Eliza Capet! "I haven't seen him since – since last year, when I left town, I went back home to Providence for family matters and ..." Just talking about Aaron made me long for him. Even this man's overwhelming presence didn't measure up to Aaron. But I raised a curious brow. "Why the interest in him?"

"I'm curious to know if you're his mistress."

I inched back, lifting my shoulder. "How brash, monsieur." I needn't feign offense, I was miffed for real.

"Let us not dilly-dally, Eliza. I ask because if you are his mistress, I will not ask you to move in with me. It would appear improper."

My jaw dropped, and I clamped it shut. "Uh ... you want me to ..." My hands fluttered and I clasped them over my widening grin. To live here, in opulence, servants at my beck and call, mistress to this gentleman merchant with a fortune to share, to help him invest, to grow, to see me to the top ...

Stop rushing, Bets ... Eliza! My eyes wandered the room – candles in gold sconces, a silver tea service, the portrait facing me – oh, God! The portrait was of Papa!

"Eliza?" He waved his hand in front of my eyes. "You look entranced."

"I'm sorry, I feel as if in a trance." Between that and the brandy ... I gave my head a rapid shake. My curls bounced. "What were you saying – oh, of course. No, I'm not Colonel Burr's mistress, but I do have feelings for him. To be blunt with you, I am in love with him." I'd said way too much already, and stopped there.

I didn't need to tell Stephen Jumel and Aaron was the father of my child and didn't even know.

"And you are not his mistress. That's enough for me." He held up his hand. "I need know no more. But I do not care to pursue a liaison between us when your heart belongs to another."

My shoulders relaxed. How gallant of him. But somehow I reckoned he had a mistress—or a few more—elsewhere. A dashing rich Frenchman? *Bien sûr!*

He stood and offered me his hand. "After our midday meal, I'll show you around. 'Tisn't much, only ten rooms and the outbuildings ..."

He showed me a lavishly furnished and appointed dining room, sitting room, south parlor, drawing room, and up the curving stairway to the bedrooms. I bit back an amused grin. *How will he show me these?* I wondered, but not for long.

"Do you care to move in this evening, Eliza?"

Care to? I needed to! "Why, of course, that's fine with me. Which boudoir is mine?" I left that hanging.

"Which do you prefer?" He showed me three. None were his. I chose the largest his because a bathing tub sat in the corner.

At dinner, he pulled out a chair for me at a table set for ten. "These are merely props, as I have no time to entertain."

I nibbled on my roast beef and potatoes and sipped Madeira.

"I supply this to the president," he boasted.

I saved my presidential boasting for another time. "So how did you come to settle here?" I knew his story would be as dramatic as any play I had acted in.

"I was born in Bordeaux, but with the sea in my blood, I made my way to Santo Domingo. I purchased a coffee plantation there. I did not simply rule the roost. I rose with the sun to sweat in the heat with my slaves. In the evenings, I indulged my vices – gambling, carousing, rum – which I believe gives immunity to malaria and yellow fever outbreaks. But the slavery there was horrific." His voice lowered, he closed his eyes and shook his head. "During the Revolution, I found my way here."

"Did you find it hard to settle here?" Would he be honest about how he made his fortune?

"Goodness, no." He laughed. His teeth gleamed, white and well-kept. "On the Fourth of July last, I stood in front of Federal Hall, and *La Marseillaise* drowned out *Yankee Doodle*." His gaze rested on his wine bottle. "Citizens here are much enamored of the French, I know not why."

"Then you decided importing wines was safer than slave-owning on a tropical island?"

"Safer and more profitable. A wine merchant, Jacques Desobru, was seeking a partner. We clicked like a well-oiled latch; he gave me a desk at his counting house. Now we charter our own ships to fetch the best wines of the world." He displayed a smug grin. "You have heard of Jumel and Desobru, have you not?"

"No, can't say I have." I shook my head. Why would I have heard of a hoity-toity company peddling fancy wines to swells?

We spoke of our new government. "I'm not political as a rule." He pushed his chair back and crossed ankle over knee, allowing me a gander at his manhood outlined under bulge-hugging breeches. "I go with the flow. The country is in good hands. I'm not a monarchist."

"Then you must mislike Hamilton," I presumed out loud.

"He is a customer of mine at times. I admire how he's shaping the Treasury. I do confess, at investing, I'm hardly savvy." He used the new word 'savvy' from the Spanish that I'd read in the *Gazette*. "But I know no one I can trust for advice, guidance – I considered consulting a soothsayer, but reckoned if ways to acquire wealth came to them by otherworldly means, they wouldn't read crystal balls for a living."

"I'm rather savvy," I informed him with all due confidence. "And no soothsayer."

"You?" came out in a surprised tone, but not condescending. He leaned forward, propped his elbows on the tablecloth, and fixed his sea-glass orbs on me. "Do tell."

"Land," I stated. "Fetch your compass, point yourself north, and it's at your feet."

"Land?" He scowled. "It's wilderness up there, forests, wildlife, Indians—"

I cut in, "For now. But millions of acres are there to be developed. And built on. Build and they will come. What to do with those buildings? Rent them and sell them as lots." I made a sweeping gesture with my hands. "Why is everyone so ... so provincial? And you, a seafaring man, not looking past Hester Street?"

"I'm a wine merchant, my pet." He guffawed. "Henry Hudson I'm not."

"I'm not talking about the North Pole. I'm talking about the rest of this island. To start with." I gestured towards his full-length windows looking out onto Pearl Street. "Why can no one under heaven take a few steps into the woods and not see what lies there? I have little capital yet, but mark my words – I plan to invest in whatever it can buy – even if it's a cemetery plot – and parlay and re-parlay and re-re-re-parlay. My credo, the same as Astor's, is 'buy acres, sell lots'."

I took another breath and proposed, "Do you care to join in my ventures?" I displayed a provocative half-smile and fluttered my lashes. I had coated them with that blasted sticky muck and they stuck together.

"I never heard a woman speak so." He laughed and looked me over. "*Mon Dieu*, I never even heard a man speak this way."

"You should get out more."

The irony sailed right over his head. "We can discuss this

further on the morrow. As of now, I have an appointment. But do make yourself at home." He waved his hand around. "And instruct the cooks on this evening's meal. Unless of course you'd rather sup out."

I glanced down at my half-eaten dinner. "Supper feels a million years hence. I'll surprise you."

He doffed his hat and bade me *au revoir* at the door. I closed it, leaned back, and looked around. Loss and despair overwhelmed me in this vast emptiness, but at the same time, I felt found. Yes, found – somehow I knew this was my home and Monsieur Jumel would give me the freedom to do as I pleased – from redecorating to planning menus to hiring more servants. This was the first rung on my climb to the top. I reached it sooner than I'd ever expected.

Standing alone in the parlor, I breathed in the aromas of polish and wax. The ticking clock echoed my heartbeat, and sounds of life outside cut me off from the world. I dashed to the door, threw it open, and filled my chest with city air – the earthy odors of sewage, smoke, and 30,000 living and even more dead people. I stood on the porch of the house I once peeked into with longing. Now I lived here. I peered up and down the street to catch anyone's eye passing by, to bid them *bonjour* from my lofty perch. But the street now stretched before me, empty.

CHAPTER 19

AT THIS POINT I was ready to call on Aaron. Rouging my cheeks to a modest blush, I left my lips bare, hoping to crush them to his. I grabbed my shawl and headed to Nassau Street.

Oh, to lose myself in those sparkling eyes, breathe in his essence, and melt in his embrace. I trembled with delight at the thought and tingled with anticipation all the way to his office. By the time I rapped on the door with my shaking hand, my breaths came in short, excited gasps.

But when a young clerk opened the door, my desire shriveled and died.

"Colonel Burr is in Albany and not expected back for several weeks ... madam," he added, as if not knowing how to address a finely dressed, coiffed, and made-up female barely older than him. "May I tell him who called?"

"No ...no need. Thank you." I turned, head down, heart heavy, leather soles dragging and catching cobbles as I slunk away.

But I had other things to do than wait. I picked up my step and hurried to the theater.

The cast was in dress rehearsal. I expected to see William in his office, adding sums and poring over scripts. I knocked on the open door and entered. A tall, rangy lad stood across from William at his desk.

"Eliza!" William greeted me with open arms, and I stepped into them as we kissed each other's cheeks. "Miss Eliza Capet, this is John Robinson, secretary to President Washington."

My heart tripped.

"He's come to tell me President Washington enjoys *The Tragedy of Lady Jane Grey*. According to custom, I shall run the play he wants to see."

"He enjoys that? Whew," I whistled in surprise.

William addressed the clerk, "You can tell His Presidency we'd be delighted to put on the performance for him and his guests."

The clerk gave a bow and backed out.

"Why does my father want to see that?" I shook my head in puzzlement. "Why sit through something so sad – a child queen beheaded after nine days?"

"He's an anglophile, obviously." William sounded proud to tell me facts I didn't know about my own father. "I read in the *Gazette* only last week, he loves Shakespeare. *Richard III* is his favorite."

"Then why not do *Richard*? I can recite every line backward in my sleep."

He shrugged. "I don't know. Perhaps he thinks it's too maudlin."

"And *Jane Grey* isn't?" I argued.

He gave me a wide-eyed questioning stare. "He thrives on melodrama. Perhaps that's where you get it from."

That sent a smug grin to my lips. "One of his many likes and talents I inherited. I shan't deny it."

"Aye. But he likes to watch from a theater box. You live it."

"Kiss my *derrière*, Will." I raised my chin and lowered my lashes.

"Later. Now, we begin casting *Jane Grey*. I can never find a good Richard." He combed his fingers through his hair. "They're all too dramaturgical."

"Where'd you get that word?" I wrinkled my nose, puzzled.

"Heard it just the other day. An actor just back from London. Come on! *Jane Grey* has dramaturgy written all over it!"

"Balderdash." I gave a dismissive wave. "'Tis merely capitalizing on a tragedy. You will cast me in this lead as Jane, will you not?"

"I had no idea you returned," he said. "You never wrote."

"I'm sorry. I had so much on my mind." I thought of my baby and a pang of motherly longing prodded me. "I miss my son more than I thought I would."

"I understand. But he's in the best of hands." We exchanged smiles.

"Perhaps I'll meet my father this time," I wished out loud, knowing these chances wouldn't keep falling into my lap. "We actually danced, at a ball my Aunt Free held at her home. As I started to tell him I'm his daughter, he broke away and ran to the privy. Bad oysters. Oysters I bought. Oh, I wanted to crawl under a rock."

William cringed. "I'll personally escort the president to your dressing room after the performance."

I gasped. "Oh, no! Make it before the show. I'll be a shaky wreck knowing he sits in his box. I need to rehearse my speech to him again." I cleared my throat. "Even I'm not that good an actress. I can act scripted parts, but in real life, I falter and stumble. Especially with the great man himself." I trembled at the thought of performing before Papa.

"Did you secure a room at Sally's?" he asked.

"Not exactly." I lowered my gaze.

"Where then?"

I met his stare. "I don't care to say, but since you'll hear it from one of the babblemouths, I'd rather you hear it from me – Stephen Jumel."

Sure enough, he nearly fell out of his chair. "How in God's good grace did you snag the richest wine merchant in New York?" His mouth gaped.

"Sally sent me. She had no room, which was my great fortune." I reclined and stretched my legs. "So I become his mistress – this evening, I presume."

"You haven't – yet?"

"Give me some credit, Will." I rolled my eyes. "I only just met him. Have you ever seen him around town?"

"Once or twice. He's not above frequenting the same watering holes as us peasants. Just to make sure they stock his wine. Produces at least half a dozen grades, from the lowliest plonk to the finest vintage."

Now feeling comfortable discussing Stephen, I should have known William would be more amused than jealous. After all, he went home to wifey many a night and left my bed cold. "He knows nothing of investing. I intend to employ my wily wheeling and dealing ways to grow his coffers. As his partner, of course. He's astonished to hear that Manhattan Island can grow and be developed. Imagine a man of the world – so savvy about the sea, yet so ignorant about land."

"Not all folk have your vision, Eliza." I sensed envy in his tone.

"Now that I have someone with deep pockets and faith in me, I shall take Manhattan by storm." I sighed and pressed my lips together. "Oh, if only I'd met him sooner. But what does it matter? He wouldn't have given a second glance to Betsy Bowen. But when Eliza Capet appeared at his door—"

He cut me off. "Come here, Eliza Capet. Show me what Betsy Bowen never learned."

I stood. "Betsy would've come to you. But Eliza wants you to come to her."

~

Rehearsals began the next day. William ordered notices that *Banquet* would end its run next week and *Jane Grey* would open the following Saturday.

I skipped to Pearl Street, my heart much lighter than when I dragged myself from Aaron's office. Monsieur wasn't in, so I had to knock and be admitted by another servant, who hadn't met me. I explained again who I was. She admitted me, ending with a curtsy.

I ordered her to rise, never to curtsy to me again. "We are no longer under Great Britain's rule. We are all equal in this nation. We have a president, not a king, and don't let anyone tell you otherwise."

She stammered "Yes, ma'am" and backed out, almost knocking over a table.

"Hell's bells, these people must learn they're no longer subjects of King George!" I stalked across the parlor and sat down at my ... what was Monsieur Jumel to me? My host? My landlord? Oh, I didn't care. He could call me what he wanted. I'd make us so successful, I'd chide senators for bowing to me.

Not a second later, the front door opened and shut, and Monsieur Jumel's frame filled the doorway, a figure Michelangelo could've chiseled out of marble.

Oh, what a physique! Ooh-la-la and *c'est magnifique*. I shut my mouth when I realized it was hanging open.

"*Bonsoir, mademoiselle.*"

I almost looked around, thinking he addressed someone

else. "Crikey, that's me!" My hand fluttered at my throat as a trickle of sweat ran down my back like a hot tear. "Good evening, monsieur."

He shook his head. "I'm Stephen to you." He approached and I stood, but he halted his steps. He didn't leer or hint that he wanted to touch me. Perhaps he was a true gentleman and respected my love for Aaron. Or—Jumpin' Jehoshaphat, could he be a molly?

"Did you order the evening meal?" He walked past me to a cabinet, unlocked it with a key from his pocket, and took out a bottle.

"No, I ... hadn't even thought of that. I went to the theater."

His eyes widened and his brows shot up as he opened the bottle. "Oh, the matinée?"

"No, I mean ... I went to see Will ... Mr. Dunlap, the manager, about a part in his next production." I thought of adding, "if it's all right with you," but didn't care to ask permission to resume my life.

"I prefer lighter amusements – cards, dice, chess. Never went in for make-believe." He poured amber liquid into a glass and offered it to me.

"No, thanks. Uh ... *Jane Grey* isn't make-believe. She was a pawn and beheaded at sixteen by a political faction who backed her own family. It's in production only because my ... our president ... wants to see it."

"Did you win a part?" He held up his glass to take a sip and it hovered near his lips.

It was easy to quash my smile of satisfaction because I still wondered why he hadn't taken my hand or kissed me or ... looked at me with liquorish eyes.

"Why, yes – Jane herself. I played her before, in the John Street Theater. Nicholas Rowe, the playwright, is my favorite."

"Does it not bother you to play a doomed young woman

murdered in the end?" He reclined on his settee and patted the place beside him, an arm's length away.

I sat closer than where he patted. After all, one of us had to get things started. "After the curtain goes down, I am Eliza again."

His eyes fastened upon me, pinning me as if he'd clamped his fingers around my wrists. A storm brewed in those eyes, but not the smoldering embers of lust. I sensed intense interest—in what was between my ears, nowhere else.

"I used my childhood name Betsy, but I was always me."

His lips curled and the smile touched his eyes. "Either Betsy or Eliza, I've wanted to meet you since I glimpsed you that evening, but you were too busy frisking with Burr to sweep a glance my way. He was my customer long before he became Attorney General, by the way."

How could I miss an imposing figure like Stephen Jumel? He already answered my question. I'd been drowning in Aaron's magical gaze.

"Then Ezra Weeks sang your praises." He added, "About your ambitions and knowledge of the arts, that is."

I basked in smugness. "Is that right? Ezra is a nice chap. I admire his work. He built City Hall, you know," I informed the foreigner, assuming him ignorant of city lore.

"Of course I know. He also built this house." His smile wavered.

"Then I'm doubly impressed. I plan to do my share of building myself."

"And I don't doubt that for a second. Now, what do you wish for the evening meal?" He stood and smoothed his breeches.

I believed I'd found a kindred soul with whom to conquer New York City. Meanwhile I would love Aaron from afar; I'd done it long enough.

CHAPTER 20

I STROLLED through the streets to the theater. When I closed that stage door, I shut out the world and entered my make-believe realm.

The cast passed around copies of *The Tragedy of Jane Grey*. Before we opened to the first page, William took center stage, waved his arms, and whistled to get everyone's attention. "Cast and crew, I have an announcement. It's not *Jane Grey* our president wants to see. His clerk misspoke. He requested us to perform *Jane Shore*."

Clearing throats, gasps, and titters scuttled around the stage and wings, with mumbles of, "*Jane Shore*? The president?"

I recoiled as if stung. Jane Shore happened to be the mistress of England's King Edward IV, and courtesan to other swells – one of history's most lascivious, licentious, libidinous harlots!

"Of course, Eliza will play the lead," William added. I knew *Jane Shore* better than *Richard III*. What my fellow players didn't know was that the real-life Mistress Shore and I were kindred souls with similar backgrounds, forced to face the disgrace of a strumpet. But the upstanding President Washington wanted to see this earthy play?

I scrapped the question, ashamed for even thinking it. So we had a day before new scripts were printed and scenery changed – as well as my approach. Quite a difference between Jane Grey and Jane Shore!

I cringed at the thought of performing this before Papa – yet at the same time, was glad he didn't know who I was—yet. He never would have requested this play knowing his daughter would be the lead.

~

I sat like a dumbstruck mule when Stephen spoke to me in French – and waited for me to answer that way. Bloomin' bollocks, I was still learning proper English! He told me in his gent's way that I should speak French, the language of the genteel. I didn't want to be part of nothing crusty, and told him so. He set me straight.

"You need to learn more than French if you want to be a society matron." He cocked a dark Bordeaux brow.

I shot back a dose of waterfront Providence: "Just 'cause I plan to better myself don't mean I'll behave like them blue-blooded nobs with noses in the air when they're not up someone's arse, or look down on the unwashed masses. I plan to stay the same humble salt of the earth I am now." I underscored that with a firm nod.

He chuckled. "How humble of you to proclaim yourself the salt of the earth. I applaud your humility, but once your coffers overflow, you'll see differently. If you want to be accepted into those circles, you must act accordingly. Your Burr speaks fluent French."

My eyes bugged at that delightful fact. Now that I knew

173

Aaron spoke French, I couldn't wait to learn. "All right. Teach me. Toot sweet! See, I know a little French!"

"*Bon*." He nodded. "Speaking French makes it evident you are refined and will separate you from the hoi polloi, as we say in Greek. It would help to know Latin and Greek. But one language at a time." He brandished a smug smile.

Hence, I studied French until *mes yeux sont tombés* – that is, my eyes fell out of my head.

After rehearsal, I changed into street garb, flipped a shawl around my shoulders, and headed to Little's Tavern. I entered through the snug and noticed Gertrude Meredith with pretty Elma Sands from the hat shop, and another lady sporting a smart lace-trimmed bonnet.

"Good day, Elma, Gertrude." I held my hand out to the third lady. "Eliza Capet. How do you do?"

"Pleasure to meet you, Eliza." She gave me a hearty handshake. "I am Catharine Ring, Elma's cousin. She's my star boarder at my boarding house on Greenwich Street."

"That's because I sell a lot of hats for her." Elma smiled. Her straw calash hat boasted a wider brim than mine.

"Oh, you're that Catharine!" I pulled up a chair. "Elma did tell me her cousin Catharine owned the hat shop. Well, ladies ..." I plunked down some coins and bought a round to celebrate my return to New York, my part in the play, and my new residence. "I now dwell with dashing Monsieur Jumel." I forced nonchalance into my voice as they fixed astonished eyes on me. "And I mean dwell, nothing more. He's ... er, I ... 'tis of convenience, a business arrangement."

"Have any of you seen Colonel Burr since he arrived

back?" Gertrude asked over a girly giggle, with no inkling about me and Aaron.

My mouth dried up. "He's back?" came out in a rushed breath.

She nodded. "I saw him, when was it ... yesterday. He must have just arrived. No one saw him before that. Did any of you?" She looked around the table.

The others shook their heads, but Elma piped up. "My new suitor is doing renovations on his house."

Should I be so bold as to call upon Aaron at this hour? A glance at the clock told me it was half-past eight, a bit late. *For God's sake, he's the father of your child!* I berated myself.

All the way to Nassau Street, too jumpy to walk at a normal pace, I tripped over cobbles in the gathering dusk.

The door opened to my knock, and there he stood. Those piercing eyes focused on me. With a simple "come here," he pulled me into his arms. Our lips met, and we kissed.

"Aaron, I missed you so ..." I was still the Betsy who fell in love with him so long ago.

"And I you." He released me, caressed my cheek.

I tingled. "Oh, it's been too long since you held me. I slept with your letters!" I blurted, but he already knew – I'd told him again and again, in every letter I wrote.

He guided me to a chair before his hearth, and we sat, clasping hands.

"How is Mrs. Burr?" I had to ask.

"Not at all well," he answered in a voice more resolute than I expected. "She's comfortable at the farm I bought her in Westchester. If she's not well enough to travel, she'll spend the rest of her days there."

"I'm so sorry."

His "thank you" hung in the air.

Now was not the time to tell him about our son.

Then he changed course. "How long have you been back?"

My heart calmed. "A few days. We're in rehearsals for *The Tragedy of Jane Shore* because Papa ... the president requested it. I got to meet him in Providence, as I wrote you, but I didn't tell you what else happened—and didn't happen."

He shook his head. "From the sound of your voice, I take it you didn't fare well."

I cringed and told him of the oyster disaster. "Just as I was about to tell him I'm his daughter."

His eyes regained that same resignation as when he opened the door. "Oh, that's too bad. But you will meet again. I wish he and I were on better terms. I'd arrange it." He shut his eyes for a few seconds.

"Enough about me." I crossed my ankles. "I heard you are running for Schuyler's Senate seat."

"Oh, yes, that I am." As if it was a common household chore.

"I'm so proud of you, Aaron."

"I haven't won yet." A small smile tugged at those full, just-kissed lips. "Have you seen the papers about my opposition?"

"No, just a glimpse this morn. I was busy studying French. *Je suis content de te revoir,*" I recited, albeit with a terrible accent.

His eyes brightened. "*Et je le suis aussi.* So why French?"

"Because Stephen Jumel told me you speak French. And... he is letting me live in his mansion," I told the truth. "Not as lovers," I added in the same breath. I paused as Aaron raised a brow. "I told him I am in love with you." I clasped his hands. "I was waiting for the right moment to tell you, but...I suppose this moment is good as any. He does not want me as his mistress, and we've no physical contact. He no doubt has a mistress elsewhere."

He offered a smile that didn't touch his eyes. "It's not that I don't love you back. But I can only do so much. I'm spread thin to breaking as it is."

So that was how Aaron told me he loved me. I'd been hoping for a more romantic setting, or a declaration of his love while in the throes of passion, but this needed to suffice for now.

He glanced at the clock in the corner. "I need to go meet a few colleagues to discuss some business." Ah, Aaron and work. That ended any more talk about love.

"I'll be out your way, then." But I wasn't capable of ending this visit. It was like cutting off my arm. "So you know where I live now." I needn't tell him where Stephen Jumel's mansion was; all of New York City knew that imposing palace.

I shall send you a note when more of my time is free and we can see a play or have dinner or..." His eyes pinned me. "Something else."

He already knew I was his for the asking, so all I needed to do was nod.

"Meanwhile, you've been keeping occupied, I trust?"

"Oh, yes." I nodded. "I'm back at the theater, and exploring the possibility of land development with Stephen. He has the means and I the vision."

"I'm bringing my own vision for the city to fruition. But not alone," he said in his unassuming way that set him apart from other great men, "That is what this meeting is about." He stood and reached for his coat.

"Tell me about your vision. I want to share everything – everything we can." I guided him back to sit down.

"The gist of it is, as you well know, many folk believe our putrid drinking water and dirty wells cause outbreaks of yellow fever, cholera and God knows what else. My brother-in-law Joseph worked to get clean water to the city. Those ponds they used were pestilential if not downright poisonous. But he got nowhere. I was an assemblyman, so he asked me to help. We assemblymen from around the city banded together and even secured support from Sandy Hamilton and his brother-in-law John Church. We managed to get a right to form a private water company using the Bronx River. We created a charter for the water company to be called the Manhattan Company. Back then, banks were under Federalist control – the national bank office and Sandy's Bank of New York. I had this idea, so I wrote the bill stating that the Manhattan Company's leftover funds will be used any way the stockholders see fit – in accordance with the Constitution and the state. I asked for investors to subscribe two million dollars to build waterworks. When the state passed this, we had the charter." The lilt of his tone told me he enjoyed bragging about this victory. "Now this is where I pulled my trick on the Federalists." He brandished a sly grin. "My friends and I used the excess funds to create a new bank, run by our people, in competition with the Bank of New York. Now common folk can get credit and loans." He emphasized "common folk" as a brickbat against Hamilton, that was obvious.

"I reckon the Feds aren't too chuffed about that." I matched his grin.

"Oh, the Feds were tipped over." His lips curled at the fond memory. "Enough to make us howl in glee. They couldn't do a thing. It was a bit through the back door, as it were, but completely legitimate. And that is how we secured the Manhattan Bank." He took a breath and lowered his voice. "Of course our opponents protested in ugly ways, especially Hamilton's cronies who accused us of setting up this bank in direct competition with his Bank of New York."

"What could be wrong with another bank?" I asked. "We surely need one. And ain't … is it not competition what keeps … that keeps competitors honest?"

His eyes fell upon me, wide with admiration. "Why, of course," he answered. "The monarchists don't want that. But this isn't England or France. It's America, a free nation, and I plan to grow it as such."

"That's brilliant! Why didn't I think of that?" We shared a laugh. "Would you consider me as an investor? Not in upcoming days, but down the pike? I want to be a part of my adopted city's growth, too. Water is as fundamental as it gets. I'd be proud to be your partner – or one of many partners, or shareholder, or whatever you're planning to organize."

He nodded. "I will keep you duly informed. Of that and other schemes – 'tis the term they use in the business, but I prefer 'plans' – for our city's growth. The city needs another source, and we're the ones to supply it. We'll lay wooden pipes from the Rye Ponds in Westchester through an open canal to the Haarlem River and down the island by a steam engine in Reade Street ..." He gestured along an imaginary pipe to illustrate, "... to pump water to an elevated pipe to a reservoir between the Broad Way and Center Street. We'll also lay six miles of pipe. Starting below the Broad Way on the west side and Pearl Street on the east. For now."

"Piped water all over the city, what bliss!" My eyes slid shut. Ah, to luxuriate in a tub of warm water from a pump in the yard.

"Don't think I'll stop at the tip of this island," he added. "I plan to grow with the entire nation. Just watch me." His smile brimmed with new confidence. During our time apart, he also evolved. I still believed our futures lay entwined. In every way.

But we couldn't share more 'schemes' at present, as he nudged me towards the door. "Aaron, I would like to attend this meeting with you. Or is it by invitation only?" Women were never welcomed with open arms at business meetings.

He gave a one-shouldered shrug. "Why not? Do join us.

We can refine some of our existing ideas, or even create some new ones."

I so respected Aaron for his equal treatment of women. Another reason I knew our shared future awaited us. He was my equal – and I his.

Scatty with joy at spending this time with him, I clasped his hand as he helped me into his coach.

I linked my arm through his on the way to the Tontine Coffee House. If only we were headed to a field of wildflowers to make love under the stars. But business came before pleasure with Aaron, I'd already learned.

"Tell me about these colleagues helping you set New York afire," I said as the carriage jounced over the cobbles.

"Robert served under me during the war in Malcolm's Regiment. He wanted to run for the Continental Congress, started making money in land spec, but prospered because he didn't get greedy. We're very close friends. My brother-in-law Joseph is a doctor. I met him when he was an army surgeon. He married my wife's sister and was my best man." He said no more about that and I didn't ask.

The carriage pulled over at the Tontine's entrance and rumbled to a stop. He helped me out, we entered through a side door and climbed a flight of stairs to a private room. Two gents sat chatting, glasses and a bottle of amber liquor on a table between them. As Aaron introduced me, they stood and looked me over, taking furtive glances at my décolletage.

Aaron cupped my elbow. "Miss Eliza Capet, this is Mr. Robert Swartwout and Doctor Joseph Browne. Doctor Browne is assisting me in planning the water works."

I held out my hand, not in the palm-down girly way expecting a touch of the lips, but sideways for the firm hand-shake I gave them both. "Good evening, gentlemen. I am pleased to make your acquaintance and equally pleased we'll be exchanging our plans to grow our city into a sprawling metropolis."

Their ogling turned into nods of grudging respect.

"Would you care to enlighten these men about your future plans for New York City, Eliza?" Aaron asked as we sat. He and Swartwout lit seegars and puffed away.

"Of course," I agreed as Swartwout poured me a glass. I took a sip and sputtered—this was stronger than anything Stephen served me. I couldn't quaff this, either, so I put it down. "It's not as if I'm afraid you'll steal my idea." I brandished a wily grin. "Tories once owned most of the land north of here, wilderness, as we all know, but vast land. It defaulted to New York's government after the Tories fled with the Red Coats. But Secretary Hamilton and our esteemed Colonel Burr here..." I gave him an adoring gaze, "...fought to restore ownership to Tories who returned to southern New York. They sued and regained most of their properties. What's left of the government-owned land can be affordable if bought in large quantities —and that land from eager sellers can be bought at reasonable prices."

They gaped at me with naked admiration. Aaron gave me an encouraging nod. I took a sip to wet my throat and went on, "The land is twelve cents an acre. Anyone with an adequate stash under the mattress would be unwise to let this chance pass them by. Once it's bought, it's ready to be built on. The growing populace'll need somewhere to live." The smoke bothered me. I cleared my throat. "I plan to start with coach houses and flats with storefronts at street level. And put renters in them, because not everyone will be able to buy—at first. They can buy from us later. Turnover, it's called. Or, in the cruder, quicker sense—flipping."

They leaned forward, rapt.

"But land shouldn't be bought and sold in haste. Land is a

long-term investment," I added. "For the most part. Some flipping may be done, in busy markets. But when the market slows, property may take years to appreciate. You take your equity and parlay it." I fought the urge to cough as clouds of seegar smoke billowed around me. So I took another sip of brandy and suppressed a shudder.

"What is equity?" Dr. Browne asked me.

Hiding my surprise, I explained: "The capital gain from holding on to your property. You buy for five hundred, a year later it's worth twelve hundred, and your equity is seven hundred. It's from the Old French, *equité*, meaning equal." They didn't need to know I'd learned the word twelve hours ago. I glanced at Aaron and he gave me a secret smile. I went hot all over.

"And what may be parlay?" Dr. Browne's eyes widened in fascination.

"Another fairly new word," I replied. "Means capitalize on it, pyramid it, take your earnings and add that to your next venture, then take those earnings and add them to your venture after that." My voice gained volume. "It piles up, compounds, as you'll see."

They sat speechless. Aaron leaned forward and flicked an ash into the ashtray. Swartwout asked me, "Miss Capet, when do you plan on making the first investment, and where?"

"I haven't decided yet," I replied. "I've yet to research each area and see which are best suited for growth. I'm leaning towards the west side of the island, on the bank of the Hudson River. Easier access to New Jersey—more land. Rather than the East River side, with only the ocean beyond. But these are only ideas, mind you—I'm no soothsayer."

"May I ask how you've accumulated your capital to date, Miss Capet?"

I smiled. "Shrewd, honest investing and parlaying, sir.

And putting a twenty percent stop loss on everything. That will save you from losing your shirt. Or in my case, my bodice."

They gave a concerted chuckle, then got back to business, discussing more about their water company and their bank. I itched to invest in both.

As the clock struck ten, Aaron and the men stood. Dr. Browne helped me rise. My fingers circled his.

"Miss Capet, charmed. And should I be so bold as to say I am greatly impressed with your intellect and forward vision."

"Is that because I'm a female?" I challenged, waiting for Aaron to chime in about his brilliant daughter.

"Not at all. I compliment anyone whose intellect surpasses mine."

"Now that is a compliment, sir!" I didn't hide my surprise. "Would that the world had more honest gentlemen as you and Colonel Burr."

Dr. Browne humbly admitted my intellect left his in the dust—who was I to argue?

Back in Aaron's coach, he looked at me as those other men had—as if I'd sprouted a set of gold talons. "You had Robert and Joseph tripping over their tongues. They've never encountered such a visionary and astute businesswoman."

"They should get out more," I remarked airily.

"Oh, Eliza..." he chortled. "They're sophisticated enough, but it's rare for any of us to meet a woman whose interest reaches beyond keeping house and rearing tots."

I leveled a sharp look at him. "Then it's up to us to try and change that, is it not? Because women can be business savvy *and* raise tots."

"I'm doing what I can, educating young Theodosia. And when I have the means, I try to help anyone else I can, male or female, but only if they want to learn."

"I make it a point to learn something every day, even if only one word," I said with a hint of pride.

"And where did you learn that word 'parlay'?" The coach lurched. He bumped against me and I took that chance to lean into him. "I must use it—it will be handy in the courtroom, too. It's always advantageous to baffle the opposing side."

"From the Italian. Stephen told me about it. He speaks several languages. And whilst on the subject, I'll ask him how much capital he cares to invest in your water company. Meanwhile—" We passed a lighted street lamp. The ride—and our evening—would soon be over. Disappointment crept through me. I dared ask, "Care for some company tonight?"

He stifled a yawn. "I was tired when you called on me. Now I am deathly tired. Forgive me for not inviting you in."

I wouldn't dare push myself on him. So I bade him good evening, with the comforting thought that we slept in the same city, if not in the same bed.

CHAPTER 21

STEPHEN GREETED me when I returned to his residence after the meeting. "Eliza, *bonsoir* to you." In the candle glow he looked every bit the weathered sailor. Arm muscles bulged beneath his laced shirt. His salty hair rippled like ocean waves. "Join me for a libation." Clasping my hand, he led me into the parlor. He poured two glasses from a crystal decanter and reclined in his plush chair. The furniture flickered in shadows – only two candles glowed on the mantel.

"And, if I may ask, where did you spend your evening?" He stretched his legs. "You needn't tell if you don't care to. I'm merely inquisitive."

That first sip of brandy gave me a second wind. I perked up with a surge of energy, ready to get on with business. I brimmed with happiness that Aaron was nearby once again. "I joined Aaron and two of his colleagues. We discussed the new Manhattan Bank financing a water company, and my ideas for building and renting. The two gents aren't the sharpest arrows in the quiver – they never even heard the word 'parlay', but they're monied. It would be to your benefit to attend next time they meet, as it's your capital we discussed investing. I mean 'we' as you and me. I didn't tell them about you yet."

"Then why do you want me to attend?" He swirled his brandy, sat back, and propped his feet on the table before him. Oh, he was a bachelor, all right.

"To keep you in the scheme of things." I took another sip. "I like that word 'scheme' and intend to use it when referring to business ventures."

He shook his head. "No, I'm of better use as a silent partner. Meetings bore me, frankly. I'd as soon play a hand of whist or trudge through the woods shooting game. You go ahead, take notes. I'll read them over and give you my blessing. As well as the necessary funds when the time comes."

A surprised "Huh?" escaped my lips. Not that meetings bored him, but that he trusted me so. It showed great faith in me – and of course in Aaron. Oh, how I wished I was back in Aaron's arms tonight!

Stephen gave me what passed for an adoring gaze as he held the brandy bottle up and poured a refill. I gazed right back, over my refilled glass – he was easy on the eyes, this churlish seadog.

To coin a cliché from the romances I read, he was ruggedly handsome. Dangle a sword from his hip and he could step right out of a Richardson novel.

"Do you believe business and brandy mix?" I knew the answer, after Aaron's meeting.

"Always," he said. "I once visited the tavern where our War for Independence was plotted, Boston's Green Dragon, and saw just how well they mix." He took a slow sip.

"Then I can tell you I'd like to start out slow," I said. "With the McAdams bookstore on Water Street. No construction involved. Simply exchanging money and rent."

"What do you know about running a bookstore?" He

twirled his glass by its stem, keeping that gaze, now scrutinizing, fixed on my eyes.

"I can read. It also has two floors of rooms above and one in the basement. All occupied so we need not scrounge for tenants."

"If it's so great a deal, why's McAdams selling?" he prodded.

"It's Mrs. McAdams," I said. "Her husband was killed in a duel. She's moving back to Baltimore with her daughter."

"How much is she asking?"

"Three hundred, but I can wheedle her down to two-fifty, perhaps two and a quarter. I read about the store and Mrs. McAdams's situation. It's clear she is motivated to sell. I'm an energetic negotiator." I kept the boasting tone from my voice.

"Are you?" He leaned forward. "Energetic, that is."

Taking that as a flirt – *it's about time!* – I flirted back. "The way things've been going between us, you might never know."

"I mean with your wheedling," he pressed. "This is a sweet old widow you're talking about wheedling."

I rolled my eyes at his complete miss of my tease. "I concede, she's a widow. I don't take advantage of the less fortunate. I will pay her asking price. But here on in, my motto will be 'business is business'. All personal feelings aside."

"Never do business with friends," he added. "And that goes double for in-laws."

"But we're friends," I stated.

"Are we?" His eyes widened as he baited me.

"What are we, Stephen?" I volleyed it back to him. "I'll take your lead – for Pete's sake, I'm inhabiting your house, not the other way around!"

"Why define anything? Who knows what tomorrow – and tomorrow night – will bring?" His voice rumbled.

A thrill made me shiver, picturing Stephen in my boudoir.

But I said, "Nothing changed between me and Aaron after this evening, if that's what you're hinting at."

He glanced out his window. "You were honest with me about your feelings for him, and I respect you for that. As such I'm not looking for you to be my mistress."

"This is none of my business, but do you already have one —or more?" I ventured. "I don't harbor any jealousy. I'm simply curious." If he lived chaster than a monk, I'd be all right with that, too—surprised as all heck, but all right with it. He called the shots.

"I'll be frank with you." His eyes narrowed. "I don't go to places like Sally Marshall's for entertainment of the base sort. I've loved one woman all my life. I asked her to marry me. She turned me down and married another man." His voice rasped. "I haven't yet found anyone to take her place. End of story." He quaffed his brandy, I reckoned without tasting it.

"Oh, I'm... I'm sorry." I fiddled with my cuff.

"Don't be." He drained his glass. "I don't want pity. I've survived well enough."

"I don't pity you, I'm... what do you want me to say?" I shrugged. "I'm glad the wench dumped you? I am sorry about it. I'm sorry for all sad stories. Perhaps that's why I strive to make my ending the opposite of my beginning. I don't want nobody to pity me, neither."

He studied his empty glass as if gazing into a crystal ball, beckoning the future from it.

"Listen to me." I raised my voice. "I know someone will replace her, whoever she was. You're handsome and sensual and... and dress foppishly—" I shut my mouth before I stuck my foot all the way in. It was halfway in already.

"As handsome and sensual as your Burr?" he prodded.

"Oh, no." I held up my palm. "I ain't comparin' you with

him or him with you. You're one part of my life, he's another. You made it mighty clear you want to keep it that way."

"As long as you have romantic feelings for him. I can live with that."

"You miss the point, Stephen." The titillating moment gone, I went on, "He has not hinted that he wants me to be his mistress. He's married and devoted to his ailing wife."

"And if she does not recover?" The question hung like a haunting spectre.

Now was my turn to empty the glass. I shuddered as it burnt down my throat.

"I'm realistic enough to know he won't ask. He knows who I...was."

"But you're no longer Betsy Bowen." His gaze assured me of that.

"There's a protocol among gentlemen of his ilk. They marry up, not down. I'll never be Mrs. Burr. Once I hoped, at the very beginning, before I knew his wife was ill, I hoped they'd divorce, but now as he moves up in government, that will never happen." My voice shook as I fought back tears. "But in my fantasies, I still—"

No, I couldn't share this with him. It wasn't right to tell Stephen I became Mrs. Burr in my private reveries.

"You'll move up yourself." He leaned towards me. "Someday you'll be above him. Then *he'll* be the one marrying up."

I laughed, amused at these predictions he made sitting over brandy. But I went dead serious all of a sudden. Someday I *could* be above him... "First things first. Let's buy that bookstore. Then, when the play ends its run, I'll quit theater and devote my time to building us a fortune—a second fortune."

"Why not build another theater?" Then he reminded me, "there's only one in the whole town."

"No." I shook my head. "I could never do that to William. He's far too good to me. Besides, you cannot get rich doing that. It's a labor of love. Theater isn't the real world in any way. Ask any player. We're no better than the whoring class. We act because of our love for make-believe. But now is the time to be real."

"Some brave playwright should pen a play about you someday. A musical." He gave an amused smile. I gave him one right back. The brandy warmed me, and his imposing presence intoxicated me even more.

"Impossible. No one could play me on stage. Besides, no one would ever believe any of it." My smile matched the pride in my voice.

CHAPTER 22

I PARTED the stage curtains an eye-width and peeked out. Fashionable patrons chatted and flipped through their programs. I trembled, not because it was nearly curtain time, but because the president's box was vacant.

"Where are you, Papa?" I released the curtain and on wobbly legs, exited stage left.

Jane Shore was to run tonight because Papa wanted to see it. Tonight was my last stage appearance—perhaps forever. William understood. He knew I wanted to move on and gave me every assurance I'd succeed. I promised I'd make a guest appearance if he wanted me. But would I have time between wheelings and dealings?

I gave all at my performance, not once looking out there, especially at the box. I knew Papa heard every line, saw every gesture, and applauded at the end.

I stepped to the edge of the stage, kissed my fingertips, and raised my arm high. I wiped away tears as I turned to the president's box. "I love you, Papa," I said softly, claps and cheers drowning out my declaration. He couldn't read my lips or hear my words. But for the first time in my life, I told my father I loved him—from the stage of a packed theater.

Back in my dressing room, I changed into my street raiment. As my dresser smoothed my overskirt, a knock sounded at the door. I stiffened, and my heart gave a joyous leap. *Here he is!*

I wrenched the door open. "Oh, it's you, Will. What happened this time?"

His sad eyes and grim lips said it all. "I'm sorry. President Washington left before I could address him. Senator Schuyler said he had to return to work. He left before curtain call."

My heart tripped and fell.

"Don't be disheartened." William's hopeful tone sounded forced. "You'll meet him someday, I feel it in my bones."

I bade William good eve and climbed into Stephen's coach. "Back to the residence, Miss Capet?" the coachman asked.

"No. Take me to Number Ten Gold Street instead."

Aaron opened the door and smiled, but the smile didn't touch his eyes.

"I know it's late. The play just ended, and I had to see you. He wasn't there. Again. I missed him. He left—" My voice broke.

"Who? Who left?"

I cleared my throat. "My father. William arranged for us to meet backstage and—oh, why bother? All I want is for you to hold me."

He gathered me into his arms, and I let it all out—my longing for him all these months, the father I might never meet...only one thing would comfort me: telling Aaron about the new life we created, the precious boy who waited to meet his own Papa.

He broke our embrace and stepped back. "Come in. The place is a shambles. I was about to retire—"

"I can take a hint, Aaron." I also took a small step back and half-turned away. "I need to tell you something I've been holding back, and need to tell you now."

He led me into his book-strewn study, and we sat in chairs before the fire. Not on the settee to invite embracing and fondling, but at a respectable distance. A table separated us, holding a book by Voltaire, a box of seegars, and a full ashtray.

I wrung my hands. This was harder than expected. Why? Because I knew the timing was bad—for him. I could have told him after he was settled in his Senate seat. "Aaron, whilst in Providence, I gave birth to a son. He's the spitting image of you. Your hair, your eyes, your chin—he's yours, I wouldn't lie. I needed to tell you tonight. I regret not telling you sooner. Please forgive me." My arms ached to hold our child right now.

His eyes brightened, but he didn't keel over in shock or lash out in anger. Of course, he'd heard this news before, from three different women—or more.

As he nodded with the hint of a gratified smile, I stopped sucking in my middle. My toes uncurled. My hands unclenched.

"What is our son's name?" he asked.

"I called him George Washington Bowen," I said with a proud lilt. "I hesitated to add Burr without your permission."

"Why, that's fine with me. You may add my name."

"I will ask him when he is older. I will leave it up to him," I replied.

"Bring him here," he said. "I want to meet him."

"Are you sure?" spilled from my lips.

"Of course. I have no reason to disbelieve you. You don't need my money – what I have. I trust you."

Now I knew, beyond question, I'd fallen deeply in love with him.

A wider smile tugged at his lips. "Do you already know I have more than one child besides Theodosia?"

I didn't let on that Sukie had already told me. "Who are they?" What a daft question. But my tongue lay in knots.

"A son of ten named Aaron Columbus. He's in Princeton with his mother. And two younger daughters, Frances and Elizabeth."

"Perhaps little George can meet his brother and sisters someday," I said.

"No reason he can't." His answer assured me.

Neither of us spoke again for a long while. We clasped hands over the table, the Voltaire, the seegars, and the overflowing ashtray.

The silence enveloped us like a blanket, cozy and comforting. We needn't keep a dialogue going.

I knew he was tired, and my own eyelids drooped. I stood, nestled into his lap, and with the steady thump of his heart next to mine, we dozed.

When we awoke at daybreak, he walked me to Stephen's coach. I assured him of one thing I knew for sure: "You will unseat Schuyler. No doubt."

"Nothing is set in stone yet," he muttered.

I pressed my lips to his. We enjoyed a leisurely kiss.

He pulled away and stifled a yawn. "I'm sorry, but I'm knackered."

"I fully understand. Good night, Senator Burr." I touched my fingertips to his kissable lips. "Until we meet again."

I nudged the coachman awake. Aaron helped me into the

coach and stood at the curb. I waved until we turned the corner.

What a night. Yawning, drained, I harbored both relief and sadness. I deeply loved the men – and the baby boy in my life, even if two of them didn't know who I was. Yet.

"They are moving to Philadelphia." Stephen folded the newspaper and placed it beside my breakfast plate.

"Who are they?" I held out my coffee cup to a new servant, and she filled it.

"The government, of course, the nation's capital. It's been in the planning for weeks. You knew about it, surely." He held out his cup for a refill.

"I did, but must have put it out of my mind." And I knew why: Papa would leave New York, possibly never to return. Every time the thought violated me, I shook it away and focused on French verbs. The table waiter brought in a tray heaped with scrambled eggs and biscuits. With no appetite, I excused myself, shuffled into the parlor, and gazed out the window onto the quiet street.

"Something bothering you?" Stephen placed his hands on my shoulders. I warmed to the contact, needing it so much.

I turned to face him, leaned forward, and nestled my head in the curve of his shoulder, breathing in the cedar scent of his shirt. "Oh, Stephen. I should have told you before but never had the right moment."

"Tell me what?"

I indulged in his closeness for another moment and drew away.

"You can trust me, Eliza. God knows I've grown to trust you."

Why not pour my heart out to this man who'd given me a magnificent home and the first step towards my future? "Stephen, I'm President Washington's daughter. He doesn't know it, and I've tried to tell him, but fate keeps us from sharing one cherished moment together. Now I fear he's not meant to know. I must accept I'll never see him again."

He rocked back on his heels and processed what I said. After a few beats, he brought me to him and stroked my hair with a touch lighter than I'd expected from those weathered hands.

"If he's meant to know, he will know. If you're meant to see him again, you will. Do what you can, and leave the rest in fate's capable hands." His warmth seeped through to me, and I longed for a more intimate touch.

He broke our embrace. Disappointment crushed me. "Breakfast waits without. You should eat."

I forced down the eggs and biscuits smothered in butter and fruit compote and perked up. I read the article about the capital moving to Philadelphia. Headlines screamed the president's upcoming departure, the parade that would escort him to his barge, and how happy he was to return to his beloved Mount Vernon before going to Philadelphia in November. I couldn't bear to be part of the crowd seeing him off, watching his barge float downriver, away from me forever.

Instead, with Stephen out conducting business, I strolled to the theater.

William's sudden news packed nearly the same punch. "I'm moving the theater company to Philadelphia," he informed me as he guided me to my favorite chair. "Of course, you're welcome to join us there. I will save every leading lady part for you."

I slumped over, head down. "I'm happy for you, but I cannot leave. I'm beginning a new life here with business ventures, and I'm gonna follow my dream to own a chunk of this city. I hope this theater finds a good manager, but no one can hold a candle to you."

"A speculator plans to knock this place down and build something else. But worry not – a new theater will be built somewhere. This is New York. I won't be surprised if a dozen theaters spring up before the decade is out." His voice carried hope I didn't feel.

I shook my head. "I fear not, but who knows – theaters may line the Broad Way one day. Look at me, dreaming again. I'm full of dreams, but unlike the average dreamer, I wake up and carry them out."

"I know, and when I come back to visit, you'll be the queen of this city." His voice rang with sincerity.

I managed a smile, the first in countless days. "I'm not keen on being queen lit'rally or figuratively. I am American and we no longer recognize royalty here. Chairwoman, perhaps."

We shared a glass of wine and an embrace before he returned to his duties. I sat in the last row watching the *School for Scandal* dress rehearsal. For once, I didn't wish I was parroting made-up lines, immersed in a make-believe setting. I didn't need that fantasy world anymore. My real world sprawled before me, love and success within my reach – just beyond that doorstep.

I got up, walked out, and left my youth behind.

Stephen swaggered into the parlor where I sat before a glowing candelabra reading Mercy Otis Warren's satire *The Group*. He tapped me lightly on the head with his rolled-up newspaper and unfolded it to reveal the front page. "Attorney General Burr is now Senator Burr, in case you haven't heard."

The book fell from my lap as I stood and grabbed the paper. I squealed in delight. "No, I've been here all day, reading – oh, that is wonderful news indeed."

"Old Schuyler is ousted and put to pasture." He smirked. "I wish our new senator all the best, and you can tell him I said that."

A knot of emotions stilled my heart. Aaron's star was rising alongside mine, but would our stars ever blaze the same path?

"Will you go congratulate him?" Stephen's voice came from a distance, even though he stood before me. I read the headline over and over ... Senator Burr ...

I put the paper down. "No, I'm sure he has enough to do. I'll drop him a note and see him when the hubbub dies down." I had another letter to write, even more urgent – to Aunt Free, asking her to bring baby George to meet his father.

Something else I should have told Stephen before now. But I wasn't ready to tell him about my son with Aaron – not yet. Perhaps not ever.

CHAPTER 23

AUNT FREE BACKED out and closed the door, leaving me alone with Aaron and our son. I never felt I belonged more than at that moment. We sat together on Aaron's settee, baby George on his lap. I wept with joy as we shared this family time.

"Hello, little lad. I am your *père* and will make sure you have every chance to be a wise and generous man." Father and son looked intently at each other. Pure love shone in Aaron's eyes.

Perched on his father's knee, he gurgled happily as he shut his eyes, the picture of contentment.

"He's big for his age. I wasn't quite as big." Aaron cupped George's head in his hand and rocked him into peaceful slumber. "But he does look like me," he added with a smile, his face aglow with relaxed ease I'd never seen before. Again, the sight of them together made me long for something I knew we wouldn't have – not quite like this – ever again.

"He's asleep." He stood and carried George to Theodosia's cradle. I didn't ask if his other children had used it.

Now was the time for the talk I dreaded. But I had to know. "When do you leave for Philadelphia, Aaron?"

"By Monday I will be packed and away, but I'll keep the house and office. I'll use them when Congress is in recess." He came back and sat next to me. I leaned into him, the sweet baby scent lingering on his shirt.

"Will you return here every recess?" I had to know. "I don't want to be a pest, but ... but I already miss you terribly."

He gave me a solemn nod. "There's nothing easy about this. My wife isn't fit to travel, so I need go and see her when I can." Careworn lines appeared around his eyes and a frown formed on his lips as he looked at me. "You don't have to answer me right away, but do you care to join me?"

I jumped. "What – to Philadelphia?" My mind raced in a thousand directions. William's offer was polite and dutiful, but we both knew he didn't need me. Aaron's question was not out of politeness or duty. The desire in his eyes said it all – he wanted me there. This request changed my plans, my business ventures ... my life.

"I want nothing more." Happiness flooded me. "If I could split myself in two, this would be the moment. How much I've grown to love New York, now owning part of it, but I love you so much more."

His eyes stayed fixed on mine. "You can buy real estate there, start a business, whatever you wish."

I shivered in delight, with a tinge of doubt. "This will be the second biggest move of my life. I'll join you the minute I finish packing." A thrill surged through me. I grasped his hands to make sure I wasn't dreaming. "Oh, Aaron, you don't know what this means to me, going to the capital with you."

I'd go to the edge of the earth with him, but Philadelphia was all I wanted for now. We embraced to the sounds of our slumbering son barely a step away, and the click-clack of Aunt Free's knitting needles in the next room.

~

With Aunt Free and baby George safely on their way home and Aaron journeying to the Senate, I wondered how to break the news to Stephen.

It turned out I didn't need to – he had news of his own. It knocked me on my bottom – for real.

When I entered the dining room at dinner hour, he sat at the table head as usual. A woman – rather, a *girl* – sat to his right. Her auburn hair fell in an attempt at ringlets around her full face, devoid of cosmetics. A smile hovered on her thin lips.

Stephen stood and led me to my chair. "Miss Eliza Capet, this is ... uh ... Mrs. Martha Ash," he mumbled his awkward introduction. We exchanged nods as he mumbled further: "Martha is ... she will be staying here with us for the time being. She's ... she's a widow. And, uh ... with child."

He needn't utter another syllable. I knew whose child she was ... uh ... *with*.

"Pleased to meet you, Mrs. Ash." I offered an outstretched hand across the posies in the centerpiece and grasped her limp fingers.

"So ... where did you live prior, Mrs. Ash?" I brought forth my theatrical tone, as if ad-libbing when another player flubbed lines.

"Number Ten Cherry Street." Her soft voice barely reached my ears. "I'm a seamstress with a shop there."

Between courses, it fell upon me to resurrect a new topic. "I'm seeking a good seamstress. May I give you some fabric I just bought for a new frock?"

Stephen minded out the way, intent on demolishing capon and asparagus tips.

When the meal ended I didn't know much more about Martha Ash than when I sat down. She excused herself and scuttled up the stairs. That left me and Stephen with a stretch of silence and an empty wine bottle.

"Now, then, will you fill me in on the backstory? Or do I guess?" I sat back, hoping he'd mimic me and relax, too, but he remained hunched over his empty plate, twisting his serviette into what I took to be a sailor's knot.

He sat up straight. "All right, Eliza. Her husband was my tailor and he died of smallpox a year ago, which narrows down the paternity of her expected arrival in a month or so. Anything else you care to know?"

"Well, yes." I folded my hands on the table. "Do you plan to marry her?"

He rang his little bell, and a servant scurried in. "More wine, please," he ordered. She nodded, backing out. "Martha doesn't want to marry. I offered to support her and her child, and that is suitable for her."

Before he had a chance to ask, I offered, "Do you want me to move out?"

He didn't blink. "Of course not."

Oh, he was French, all right. "Stephen, I need to tell you something. This might be better for all of us because I—"

A raw shriek cut off my words. We pushed back our chairs and ran to the stairs. Martha stood at the top, bent over the banister, clutching her middle, moaning, and gasping.

Stephen leapt the stairs two at a time and clasped her shoulders.

She wailed. "The baby is coming!"

I climbed the staircase. "Are you sure? Did your water break?"

Oh, yes, it had. All over Stephen's hickory floorboards.

"Get her in bed, call the servants, get hot water and towels. Now!" I demanded, and he looked relieved to dash out. I led her into the bedroom opposite mine and eased her onto the bed. "You'll be all right. Just lay there and relax," I soothed, or tried to, but her groans and gasps made me shudder.

Sweating more than she was, I rolled up my sleeves as the baby's head appeared. "Now push like you've never pushed before!" I gave one more tug and delivered my first – and I hoped my last – way smaller than George, but Martha was a month ahead of her time. "Fetch more water and towels!" Floorboards creaked as the servants bustled out. "You have a son, dear. Have you thought of a name?" As I tied the cord with a shoelace, I tried to get her mind off her pain.

"Stephen Jumel, after his father," she rasped, her voice hoarse from all the screaming.

"How apropos." I plopped onto the fainting couch by the bed. Maternal longing for George made my breast ache. Servants fussed over Martha and wrapped little Stephen in a blanket. Now his squalling replaced her shrieking.

I dragged myself down the hall and banged on the new father's door. "*Alors*, go say *bonjour* to your progeny!"

I stepped back as he opened the door and peered sleepily over my shoulder. "She had the baby already?"

"Already? Took three hours, no thanks to you, captain at the helm. You should'a stayed and saw the thing through." I shuffled back down the hall as he followed.

He hung back in the doorway, and I grabbed his arm. "Get in here. He's a baby, not a sea serpent. Go see your son." I laughed mockingly at the perplexed new father as I pushed past him and locked myself in my room. I washed up and fell into bed.

I'd served as midwife, but it hardly ended there. Next morning as I finished dressing, an urgent knock rattled my door. In two steps I threw it open.

"Martha has taken ill – the physician saw to her but she asks for you. Please sit with her, comfort her ..." Stephen pleaded, guiding me down the hallway to the sickbed.

"How is the baby?" I prayed this would not be another death from childbirth. The baby's early birth was enough to bear. My heart went out to Stephen. I'd never seen him uncomposed or distraught. His hair had escaped its queue, and his rumpled, sweat-stained clothes needed a change – and a laundering.

"Fine." His tone brightened. "She wants you. Something to do with stories about President Washington and singing."

"Oh, yes, desperate to cheer her last night, I told her the entire story of Papa and me."

That evening, Stephen wined and dined me with a meal from his favorite Belvedere chef. Over crème brûlée, the baby's faint cries floated down the stairs. He begged me, "Please, I need you to be Martha's companion and *Petit* Stevie's surrogate mother until she's up and about. I need someone to provide more than medical attention and feedings – and that someone is you, *chérie*. I know you will give Martha and our son what servants and physicians cannot – loving care."

"She won't be up and about any time soon," I told him what he already knew.

"I will buy you whatever you want, Eliza, I promise. I will buy you a mansion in any posh neighborhood you like." He clasped my hands.

"You need not bribe me. We can have the arrangement you ask for, but if you care to browse mansions, I won't protest ..." I squeezed his fingers with an attempt at levity, but he cracked not a slip of a smile.

He surprised me with this paternal side of him, and I told him so. "I thought your life and love was the sea, trading, collecting fees, and growing wealth."

"Is that good or bad?" he had to ask. He truly didn't know!

"Of course it's good. I know you have a heart under there. I never knew it was so big and caring. Martha must mean a lot to you. I gathered she was more than your seamstress. Do you two have a history or ..." I released his hands and poured myself a refill. "You need not tell me."

"I've known her and her husband John since I arrived on these shores," he explained in a controlled voice, eyes darting about. "I moved in with them, and we became a family of sorts. Before John died, he made me promise to take care of her. He gave me his blessing to have children with her, for it wasn't her who was barren, it was him – he'd had the pox and couldn't father any children."

"Which pox?" I asked. "The smallpox or *that* pox?"

"*Oui*, the 'night with Venus' sort. He was once a sailor and – well, you know the rest of that. So I kept my promise."

"Why not marry her after John passed?" I didn't believe that question too probing.

"She doesn't care to marry at all." He circled his temples with thumb and forefinger as if fighting off a headache. "We had ... what you'd call trysts. The result is the bundle of joy up there." He stood and added logs to the glowing embers. "Please, please stay," he begged, "and care for them. They—and I—need you."

"Of course I'll stay." With that, my Philadelphia plans went down the privy.

The fire blazed into warmth, and I splayed my cold fingers before it.

So when *Petit* Stevie wasn't wet-nursing or fussed over by the servants, I sang, read to him, and rocked his cradle. I suffered pangs of longing, knowing I should have done this for my own son. But he'd thank me someday for letting Aunt Free and Reuben raise him. Between me and his exalted father, George would be well provided for, well educated – and was already very well bred.

I wrote to Aaron on Stephen's cream stationery telling him my arrival in Philadelphia needed to be delayed, and why. He was likely too engaged in his new duties to give me a second thought.

CHAPTER 24

"Look, Stephen." I showed him a newspaper advert. "This is the one I want."

He kept his promise to buy me a mansion by taking me to Haarlem Heights. A two-hour coach ride north, Mount Morris stood at the end of a tree-lined driveway atop a hill on thirty-six acres of orchards and farmland. Standing on the porch under a portico held up by stately white columns, I shaded my eyes, taking in the spectacular view of the Haarlem River, the Bronx, and Long Island Sound to the east. I turned and gazed at the crowded church steeples and huddled roofs of Manhattan under a shroud of smoke to the south and the harbor beyond. I faced west to view the Hudson River, stretches of meadowlands, and New Jersey Palisades.

When I learned Mount Morris was Papa's headquarters during the War for Independence and he'd fêted founding fathers in the spacious dining room, a hunger akin to childhood homelessness gnawed at me.

"Oh, how I want this house!" I grasped the front doorknob

as if I already owned it. "I must sign that deed. This house is meant to be mine," I proclaimed to distant New York City.

But not yet.

"You cannot tell me you want that monstrosity and keep a straight face." Stephen scowled as we slid back into his carriage. He gave the mansion a crusty sneer as we lurched into motion. "That gaudy imitation of a sultan's palace? If you want to open a high-class brothel, I shall take you to Paris where it's much more acceptable – and profitable."

"You think it looks like a brothel?" I twisted around to get one last glimpse of the white Greek-style mansion, its imposing columns, lacy-railed balcony, front door graced with a lion's head knocker, fanlight window, and sidelights. "It has a rich history. It was once the home of a British colonel, Roger Morris, and our government confiscated it. Why would my father set up headquarters in a place that looks like a brothel?" I goaded, more determined to own this sumptuous dwelling – without Stephen's help.

"The location is strategic, and it's large enough to entertain cronies, not because he liked the looks of it," he countered. "Ponder the difference between this gaudy pile of blocks and graceful Mount Vernon. *That* is his style, not *this*. I wonder what the architect was drinking when he designed it." He waved a dismissive hand. I caught it in mine and gave it a squeeze.

"Next time this house goes up for sale, Stephen … just remember, if you don't buy it, I will," I assured him.

I added Mount Morris to my list of acquisitions. Someday that house would be mine. And perhaps I'd let Stephen stay there.

∾

After feeding the baby and singing his mother to sleep, I knocked on the door to Stephen's den and sauntered in. He sat before an open ledger, candles ablaze on either side of his desk, pen scratching paper, Ben Franklin wire specs perched at the tip of his nose.

"You should know I'm a sight better at accounts than I will ever be at speakin'," I said. "Uh ... speak-*ing*. Let me help you get your books in order."

He looked up over the rims of his specs, pinpoints of candlelight shining in his eyes. "You have a head for numbers? How can that be? You never had anything to count."

"I can still count!" I held up each finger. "One, two, three, four..."

He guffawed.

I dragged a chair around his desk and perched myself at the leather edge. "My first rule for success in business and take careful heed: paying interest is a chump's game."

"Tell that to Secretary Hamilton, who makes a religion out of establishing credit," he argued.

"Credit is wise," I agreed. "I mean sweating out payments when the interest rate is so high, you'll never get around to paying any principal. Double up your payments till the debts are paid."

He pulled off his specs and tossed them onto the open ledger. "Are you *fou?*"

"Pardon?"

"Daft. I cannot double up payments on everything I owe." He gestured at the ledger. "We'd starve."

"Not all at once. One at a time. And interest is negotiable, too, as you saw when we purchased the flat on Ann Street. He wanted three percent, but I haggled him down to two and a quarter."

"Perhaps he was bedazzled by your fast talking until it was too late," Stephen countered.

"He just knew he was being challenged and wanted to unload the property. But it saved us a few groats." I gave him a smug grin.

"Yes, Eliza," he conceded grudgingly as he doodled on his blotter. "But I'm a bit ahead of you there. I've been at this since I'm fifteen. I'm not sure what you can teach me. Besides ..." He leaned back and his chair groaned, "... your rule about paying interest."

"If I teach you a valuable lesson right now, will you gift me a sum adequate to purchase a new dress and hoopskirt?" I bargained.

"I offered to buy you a mansion and now all you want is a hoopskirt?"

I gave him a reassuring nod. "For now." I scanned his ledger and saw that he spent two hundred dollars boarding his horse in McSorley's stable.

"We can buy a stable for seven hundred. That will save two-fifty a year on renting. That's worth a dress, a hoopskirt, six pairs of satin gloves, a pair of shoes, and pearl earbobs. The mansion will come later. What say you to that?" I planted fists on hips.

He sat forward, slid his specs back up, and flipped through the pages of his book. When he added up how much he spent on renting the stable, his lips tightened into a thin line. He threw the quill down and eyeballed me as if I'd sprouted a halo. He opened his drawer with a key and grabbed a fistful of banknotes. "Spend it wisely."

I plucked the notes from his fingers, stacked them like a deck of cards, folded them, and nestled them in my cleavage. "As always. But I haven't given up on that mansion in Haarlem. And just to show how generous I am, I'm naming it after you."

I closed his ledger, blew out his candles, and bade him good eve. "Sleep tight. And dream of the Morris-Jumel Mansion."

～

Petit Stevie's very first word was 'Liza', but thank the stars no one else heard that gem. Ah, from the lips of children, as Jesus said.

The new *père* found a shaggy dog he named King Louie. Who trained *le chiot* to stop making deposits on the Turkish rugs? *Moi, bien sûr!*

When I walked in on them cuddled on the settee – mother, father, child, and dog – I felt shut out. An outsider. This was a family. I no longer belonged here.

I took the chance to talk with Stephen about moving out. Then Aaron changed my destiny. For a while, at least.

My passionate letters to him never stopped, but my heart stopped when I opened his latest letter. It began simply, "Dear Eliza, my wife Theodosia is not expected to live much longer."

I stood, stunned, unable to breathe. My eyes fixed on those words, reading them over and over. I sank to the bottom step and cradled my head in my hand as I read the rest: "I need you with me now. Please come to Phila—"

It slipped through my fingers to the floor.

Stephen Jumel no longer needs me. But Aaron Burr does.

～

With two new maids and a governess on duty, Stephen and I stood in the doorway to my bedroom. "This room will be yours when you return," he offered. "I mean, only if you want to."

"We are far from finished, Stephen. We've already started business ventures together. I'll return here when Congress is not in session. We have Manhattan Island to conquer." I took his hand and pressed it between my palms. "You've hardly seen the last of me."

"I would know that even if we never bought a door knocker together." He leaned forward and planted a kiss on my forehead. "My coach is yours if you want it for the journey."

I scowled. "That gaudy red-varnished brothel on wheels you bought from a ponce in Hoboken?"

"You'll fit right in if you hobnob with Federalists," he shot back.

"I don't, nor does Aaron. He's not of the party of monarchists and elitists. But I cannot arrive in a rickety old conveyance with anything less than that strong Arabian horse, and I insist on paying you for it."

I slipped out the door as light brightened the misty morning sky. Shivering and clutching my shawl about me, I let the coachman help me in. As the first jolt of motion threw me back against the plush seat, I did not look back.

I tried to force a happy mood, but couldn't. Exactly what had Aaron meant by "I need you with me now"? Hadn't he needed me before? I didn't ask those questions until this minute, with a hundred-mile journey before me.

Aaron boarded in a row house on Walnut and Fourth Street owned by a widow, Mrs. Todd. But I dared not go there, all disheveled and grimy. With a newspaper advert, I went to a boarding house around the corner and begged a room, any room, for I knew housing here was scarce. The landlady Mrs. Wright had no vacancy, but offered to share her own room for the night.

When I felt and looked respectable, with my new but wrinkled blouse and skirt, I walked to Walnut and Fourth, hoping Mrs. Todd had a private corner somewhere, for me and Aaron to be alone.

I couldn't have been more mistaken. I entered the house, as jammed as Fraunces Tavern on inauguration night. Men stood about in clusters, draining wine glasses and ale mugs, smoking pipes and seegars, in deep discussion or inflamed debate. Ladies perched on a settee, nattering away, fanning themselves. I elbowed my way across the stuffy parlor, sweat soaking my back. I reached the mantel, leaned against it, and scanned the room for that head of dark hair, those piercing eyes that melted me. But my Aaron was nowhere in sight.

One of the ladies flounced over, offering a slender hand. "I am Mrs. Todd, but everyone calls me Dolley. You must be Miss Capet? Senator Burr told me of your abundant red hair. Hence I knew it had to be you." Her eyes twinkled as she admired tendrils spilling from my bonnet.

Her sing-song voice, bright eyes, and wide smile bedazzled. Dressed in canary yellow, she smelled of lilacs.

"Yes, I'm here to see Senator Burr." I smiled back. "Is he about?"

"He's in his room, first on the right, top of the stairs, working." She added with a saucy smile, "But I'm sure he'll welcome your interrupting."

My heart quaked, with Aaron so close. I climbed the stairs and knocked on his door. It opened, and there he stood, exactly as I always remembered him. Only a trace of tiredness dimmed his eyes.

"Finally," he moaned. I fell into his arms. Holding him was heaven.

He had a bed, a desk, and two chairs. I avoided the bed. Yes, I wanted to be alone in complete privacy, but not in his room with the bed standing out like a giant meteor daring me to pretend it wasn't there. I stumbled over my skirts, heading for one of the chairs, and fell into it. He poured us both glasses of something and sat across from me.

"Whiskey." He gestured to the glasses. I took too big a gulp and choked. "You savor it, one sip at a time, you silly goose," he chided me.

I clutched the glass, knowing I needed something this strong, but wishing I could dip my feet in it for the same result.

"Well ... I'm here," was all I could think to say.

"How was the journey?"

"Slow – but the weather held up." I rolled my eyes and leaned forward. "Bloomin' Ada, enough with the idle chit-chat of strangers browsing the greengrocer's! Now I am here for you. Now and always. You are the only man I've ever loved, and I want to spend the rest of my life with you. There. I said it." I wished he'd said it first, but considering the tragedy that had brought me here, I couldn't expect any declarations of ever-afters from him now.

"Thank you." He nodded, and my heart danced as I grew warm all over. "Your being here means more to me than I can express. I'm not up to talking much, or ...anything at all, except work, and I hope you'll understand that. But having you near will make me feel alive again. Don't expect much right away. I need time alone, but will make it up to you, I promise," he said in a solemn tone, like a vow.

I put down the whiskey. "No promises. All I need now is a place to live. I found a room but just for tonight."

He stood and flipped through his calendar book. "I've an appointment at three. This house is full – Dolley will know where you can stay. I'll see you this evening, say seven? Just be forewarned, I'm not the liveliest company these days."

So here I was, in our new capital, with the man I loved. Why did my future make me quake in fear?

CHAPTER 25

Philadelphia was cleaner than New York, less crowded and more genteel. I went to William's theater just to say hello, for my acting days were over.

Dolley Todd sent me to a tidy boarding house on Walnut Street. No cobwebs hung in corners, no flies buzzed around the fruit bowl. I reacquainted myself with James Reynolds, who had just divorced his wife—or she had divorced him and married a dashing gent, Jacob Clingman. Aaron was her divorce lawyer.

I didn't know what led to the Reynolds breakup until one evening when Aaron and I left the City Tavern early. As we crept upstairs to my room, he pinched my behind. *Ah, yes, he's feeling his old self.* I reached back and grabbed him, shivering in delight at our night ahead.

After we made love, he told me of the scandal that still had everyone tittering—Alexander Hamilton and James Reynolds's wife, Maria, had an affair. None other than Senator Monroe and some congressmen got wind of it. They forced Hamilton to admit it publicly because he wouldn't sully his reputation as Treasury Secretary.

"How humiliating." I shuddered, picturing all that dirty laundry hanging in the halls of Congress. "What did Papa ... the president say?"

"Hamilton is his pet; he even calls him Sandy Boy." Aaron stretched his legs. "He could do no wrong. The president didn't offer a public statement, and of course, he and I never talk about it—I haven't had a private audience with him since I'm here—but I'm sure he has opinions. He hasn't relieved Hamilton of his position, so he obviously trusts him with the nation's money."

"Don't you?" I ran my fingertips over his chest.

"Yes," he answered without hesitation. "We don't see eye to eye on much of anything, but I cannot say I mistrust him when it comes to handling public funds. His private matters—that's a different story. I'm not one to judge, but he embroiled me in his messy *affaire de cœur*." He reached for a seegar and lit it from a candle.

"You? How? We're not talking *ménage à trois*, are we? You and Hamilton and Maria? Is that why you finalized her divorce?" I shot him a wry grin, but for a second, I envied Maria —if she did snag the two handsomest men in the entire nation.

But he set me straight: "Hardly. Monroe publicly admitted he'd kept copies of the letters between Hamilton and James Reynolds. Word leaked to the scandal sheet publisher James Callender, but Monroe denied having anything to do with it. Hamilton stomped up to Monroe one evening, branded him a liar, and that began an exchange of insulting, accusing letters between gentlemen that leads to you know what—Hamilton challenged Monroe to a duel. Monroe chose me to be his second."

I gasped. "Oh, my word. When was the duel?"

He shook his head. "I managed to call them together and appeased them so they ceased the fire that never got shot. I'm sure Monroe believed as I do, that Hamilton was innocent of illegal speculation with Reynolds, and I recommended saying so in a joint statement."

"You may have saved Hamilton's life. Or both of their lives," I marveled. "You are a hero."

He shook his head. "I'm no hero." He puffed on his seegar and exhaled a stream of smoke. "How I got pulled into that mess in the first place, I know not. I thought my part was done when I sent Maria her divorce papers—as she stood at the altar waiting to marry her paramour."

I whistled through my teeth. "She didn't waste time."

He stubbed out his seegar, leaned over, and caressed my cheek. "Enough talk of marriages, divorces, duels, and love affairs..."

"No, talking of a love affair isn't necessary when we've got one right here." Once again ready for him, I captured his lips.

Ecstatic as I was to be reunited with Aaron, he worked all day and I didn't. Purchasing Philadelphia land or real estate did not appeal to me. Hence, from the parlor, I took lessons in literature, French, and most importantly, English. Between lessons, I strolled to the Library Company on Fifth Street, Benjamin Franklin's legacy. Non-members like me could borrow books by leaving enough money to cover their cost. So, I raided my hidden stash of coin.

"What are you interested in?" the librarian asked.

"Everything," came my direct answer.

So he steered me to *Logic or the Art of Thinking* by a couple of French philosophers. It covered metaphysics, free will, the sacraments...and how to think right. A veritable one-volume lesson on life. That was worth plunking down a deposit.

I couldn't afford to borrow all the volumes I wanted, so I browsed the shelves and lugged armloads of books to a corner table. Hours flew by as I settled in for quiet study and learning.

One drizzly day, I studied until my brain drained, then I wandered over to the outdoor market.

At a cabbage stand, I bumped into that pretty 'servant' of Lady Washington's I'd met at Papa's inauguration. I never forgot her name, Ona. Her gingham frock, clean and pressed, fit her perfectly. My eyes bugged out at the pearl pendant suspended from a gold chain around her neck.

"Why, Ona, how nice to see you!" Not sure if she still obeyed the unwritten rule of never speaking to a white person until addressed, I extended the salutation. "I'm Eliza...well, I was Betsy when we met at my pa—at President Washington's first inauguration."

Her smile brightened the dreary day. "Yeah, I remember you." She held up a half-filled sack. "Just fetched some provisions, learning how to haggle prices."

By Jove, she didn't drop her 'g'! "Good for you! There's an art to haggling, and I'm dead sure a smart lady like you won't leave a shilling on the table." But never mind banter about haggling—I hankered to know about that trinket around her neck. "Mind if I ask who gave you that stunning pendant?"

She glanced down and brushed it lovingly with her fingertips. "Oh, Master General...er, the president let me pick it out when I went with Lady Washington to Mr. Bringhurst, her jeweler here. It's a reward for learning to tell time."

"Why, it's lovely. You have impeccable taste. The Washingtons are certainly generous." As I complimented Ona and the Washingtons on their stellar treatment of this prized 'servant,' a pang of longing tugged at my heart. For this was my own father she gushed about, the man I adored and longed to call Papa. How I wished for a gift from him—especially the Washington name. But I couldn't begrudge this charming lass her good fortune. Despite her kind owners, I knew her life wasn't easy— her life wasn't her own—her *self* wasn't her own.

We drifted into an easy chat as we browsed the stalls piled with produce. She picked up the occasional orange or melon for an expert inspection or squeeze. As we reached the exit, I didn't want to part company. "Ona, what say we duck into a café for a bit—I know you need to get back to work, but I've got nothing to do, and I'm sure Lady Washington won't mind your staying out just a little longer." I awaited a horrified gasp or immediate refusal in fear of defying her owner. But her eyes brightened, and she pointed to a café on the next corner. "Lady Washington brings us girls in there sometimes when we're out and about." She picked up her pace, and I followed. "Of course I wouldn't go in alone; they'd never serve me."

A torrent of anger tightened my chest and set my jaw. "Someday that won't be the case any longer," I voiced my prediction—in reality, a lofty hope.

Seated at a table, two lemonades before us, we chatted more about the new capital city and what it offered as amusements. She surprised me by revealing, "Lady Washington gives us ample time off to attend Shakespeare plays and lets me—but only me—study with a tutor."

Assuming she was literate, I mentioned some book titles.

"I can't read yet. Our cook, Hercules, has been teaching me my letters," she boasted, her grin wider than before. "I don't tell Lady Washington. She may not mind, but Master General might."

I decided to cut to the chase—I needed to know. This girl lived with my father and knew him better than I ever would. "How do you really feel about the Washingtons, Ona? Are they fair? Do you believe your...situation...is fair? I know they treat you well, but deep down, what do you hope for from them?"

She looked me straight in the eye and leaned forward. "What I hope for," she began, her tone low and intimate, just for my ears, "between us, they know what got them there and me here—an accident of birth. Those words never left me, once Lady Washington said 'em. An accident is something that shouldn't happen. So no accident will change nothing. It needs to be done on purpose."

"Ona, I feel you and I are nearly kin, and I'll tell you why in a minute. But first—are you telling me you want to be free?" I probed the depths of her soul, wanting to share some very special secrets with her.

She gave a determined nod. "All slaves want to be free. But it ain't possible unless she frees us. We're—me and my Mama and sister and brother—we're hers, not Master General's. When she dies, I'll belong to her grandkids. So it ain't never gonna happen." Tears welled up in her eyes.

I placed my hand upon hers and gave it a reassuring squeeze as my own tears blurred my vision. I swept at my eyes with my free hand. "Ona, every human being has a right to own his or her own body. This nation fought for and won independence despite overwhelming odds. But unfairly, and disgracefully, our leaders overlooked an enormous group of people. I can't say if the law will change in our lifetimes. But aside from the law, freedom is within your reach—if you really want it."

She shook her head. "Too dangerous. You know what happens to escapees?"

"How well do you really know General and Lady Washington, Ona?" I asked this for myself as well as her.

"As well as they let me. They're devoted, have their bickerings, but they always make up. Compared to what I hear about other masters and owners, they give us enough to eat, comfortable sleeping, nice clothes. Especially me. I'm her favorite. I get more than the rest of 'em." She held up her pendant to back up that claim.

"I'll let you in on a secret, Ona. I don't blab this to everybody." I took a deep breath, ready to spill. "First—I'd never own a slave, and if I inherited any, I'd set them free. But if that weren't possible, say as in your case, being my spouse's and not mine, if some of them escaped, I wouldn't punish them. I'd try to find them and bring them back, but I'd grant them their freedom then and there. You know why? Because I respect and admire anyone brave enough to take that risk."

She shrugged. "So, you're telling me what you'd do. That's you."

I gave her a warm smile, knowing what I was about to say. "But there's more. I'm not just the Betsy you met in New York. And what I do know of President Washington, we're very much alike. That's because he is my very own father."

"You...you his daughter?" Her voice rose, and she clapped her hand to her lips lest someone hear. But no heads turned. "How you know that?"

"My mother told me. Once in Providence..." I released a sigh. "Someday I'll meet him, and I know deep down he'll acknowledge me. But meanwhile...you never let go of that dream of freedom. And if you keep your eyes open, you'll find a way, and folks to help, but only if you're brave and determined enough to carry out your plan. And you won't get dragged back and punished. I'm telling you that as a Washington."

"But Lady Washington's my owner," Ona countered. "I don't dare disobey her."

I displayed a smug grin. "But General Washington is her

husband and her president. Lady Washington doesn't dare disobey *him*."

Ona sat in deep thought, eyes unfocused. When we got up to leave, she carried herself with a new confidence, head higher, shoulders squared.

Before we parted on the street, I clasped her hand. "Ona, we might not meet again, but I have a strong hunch I'll hear about you someday. And I can guarantee you'll hear about me. So this isn't quite goodbye."

"I know, Eliza. I know. And thank you." I could see it in her eyes—I'd gotten through to her. Did I change her life? I knew I'd find out someday.

I soon found out who Aaron's friends were—and more importantly, who his enemies were. The beginning of his Senate term marked the beginning of political parties. Once created, these opposing factions functioned like ant colonies.

It didn't take long for the town to brand me Senator Burr's mistress. When I attended dinner parties and levees on his arm, the bigwigs treated me as if I were the next Mrs. Burr.

At one dinner given by George Read, I caught Alexander Hamilton casting liquorish looks at me. Clearly he was in his cups, as was nearly everyone else. I avoided those violet eyes. Yes, he cut a dashing figure with his shock of copper hair – and he knew how to dress nattily enough. But he paled next to Aaron's midnight blue coat, brocaded waistcoat, breeches, and stockings that could've been painted on him by Gilbert Stuart. Silver buckles gleamed on his shoes. Being the one who polished them, I knew they gleamed.

One evening, Senator Robert Morris was fêted at the Hamilton home because when Papa chose Morris to be Treasury Secretary, Morris suggested Hamilton instead. Hamilton was in Morris's pocket from that day onward and spent most of his term licking Morris's boots. I didn't want to attend, but Aaron coaxed me: "It will be entertaining and amusing. Hamilton has the most colorful characters as guests, his in-laws, Jim and Eliza Van Rensselaer... Jim and I served under Monty, and Jim was at my side when Monty fell at Quebec. His sister Catherine is Hamilton's mother-in-law." He donned his jacket and buttoned it. "Then there's all his fawning flatterers. We always wind up engaging in friendly repartee and are careful to never let politics enter the room. The party ends when Mrs. Hamilton ushers everyone out at nine o'clock as is her custom. They have a brood of young ones, you see."

"Let's stay here tonight, Aaron. I want you all to myself. Besides, I don't like Hamilton. He's a cad. And when he's in his cups at these gatherings he gives me liquorish looks."

Aaron shrugged. "So what? He gives me liquorish looks, too."

"What?" I halted, rouge pot halfway to my cheek.

"Long as I don't look him in the eye I'm safe. Rumor has it he's..." Aaron flicked his wrist in an effeminate gesture. "Flexible. Of fur and feathers." With that, Aaron trotted down the stairs to fetch the carriage.

I sat there shaking my head. Could Hamilton be Double-Gaited? I gave it a brief thought. Come to think of it, he did appear a bit foppish at times.

I enjoyed myself at the party anyway, and Mrs. Hamilton was a charming hostess. When close up, I noticed her hair wasn't powdered but gray. I chalked that up to the humiliating public ordeal her straying husband put her through. The closest I came to drollery was with the bubbling Dolley Todd. She introduced me to her suitor James 'Jemmy' Madison, such a great man, and yet so diminutive. I felt uneasy looking down at him in my two-inch heels. Though he was a founder of the Democratic-Republican party, who opposed Hamilton and his cronies, Mr. Madison authored almost the entire Constitution and our Bill of Rights—and did we need that Bill of Rights!

"Did you know that Aaron introduced Jemmy and me?" the buxom Dolley gushed, clinging to Jemmy's arm and casting him an adoring gaze.

"No, I didn't. He never mentioned it." I suppose Aaron hadn't wanted to tell me, lest his matchmaking went awry and Dolley went on to greener pastures. But from the doe-eyes she cast upon Jemmy as he nuzzled her nose with his, it looked the perfect love match.

"It was quite by design," Jemmy explained, his eyes lighting up as he focused on his fond memory. "Aaron was already living in Dolley's mother's boarding house and helped her draw up a will leaving all her property to her son Payne—"

"Aaron is the executor," Dolley chimed in.

Jemmy continued, "I offered to back Aaron as the next ambassador to France and persuaded James Monroe to support him."

"Aaron did tell me that Monroe considered him too young." I nodded, secretly glad Aaron hadn't been appointed.

"Yes, ironically, Monroe is two years younger than Aaron," Jemmy said. "When I took the proposal to President Washington, he rejected the idea."

I knew why but didn't say a word. Aaron and Papa never got along. Some things were better left unsaid.

"Having tried to do this enormous favor, I asked Aaron if he'd formally introduce me to Dolley. We only lived three streets apart, and I'd bowed to her many times in the street. Now here we are!"

With Dolley the most eligible widow in town, Jemmy couldn't tarry much longer to pop the question.

They did make a sweet couple, although she was taller—and noticeably wider—than him.

~

Aaron came home to me after midnight on the day Congress began their August recess. I was packing for our return to New York until they reconvened. He splashed water on his face and dropped into his lounge chair.

"If you're this bedraggled from celebrating the Senate recess, I can imagine how the others fared. Did they drop in the streets on the way out the taverns?" I folded another chemise and placed it in my trunk.

"I wasn't celebrating, Eliza. I debated whether to tell you this and decided you'd rather hear it from me rather than from Sukie or some gossip hound." He pulled his shoes off and wiped his brow with his handkerchief.

"Tell me what?" I sat next to him. "Not another duel. And —oh, no." My heart tripped. "You were in it?"

"Nothing like that." He shook his head. "Mary Emmons, Theodosia's and my servant, has been living here in town since late last year. She gave birth to a baby boy today—mine," he added before I could take a breath or register a reaction. "She sent me a note this morning telling me she had just given birth and asked me very kindly to call on her and my new son."

Silence hung in the stuffy air as I took a few breaths. "She had another child of yours? You could have told me this sooner. I would have understood." I harbored no resentment, no jealousy. She was his servant, after all, and a woman of color. Colored servants did their masters' bidding, whether hunched over a washboard, on hands and knees scrubbing floors, or on their backs in bed.

"You did well to keep her under wraps. That's perfectly

understandable. But bloomin' blazes, you could have told *me*. I wouldn't have blabbed. Who is taking care of the child? And while we're on the subject, does he have a name? Besides Burr?"

One reason I greatly admired and respected Aaron—after all, slaves, servants, and their offspring had no status, in direct contradiction to Jefferson's famous line about all men being created equal. But Aaron gave his illegitimate children his name and treated them well.

"His name is Jean Pierre Burr. I hired a nurse to care for them. He looks like me—only a tad darker." He voiced a hint of pride.

"Congratulations, then. I would like to call on them. Where are they living?"

His brows shot up in surprise. I wasn't supposed to be the least interested in his progeny by a mere servant. "When she came to town—not long before you did—I settled her in a town-home on Pine Street. A safe area." His eyes continued to search mine as he shook his head in befuddlement. "I truly appreciate that, Eliza. My wife never cared to ask even one question about Mary or Louisa, and I have not even told her about Mary breeding again. She has too many concerns of her own."

I nodded. Of course. The woman was gravely ill. "I will call on the new mother and child tomorrow. But I would be much obliged if we can visit our own son after we return to New York. I'd like to tell him he has a new half-brother."

This brought the slightest hint of a smile to his lips. "It is done."

Hence I called on Mary and her new son. She remembered me and greeted me with all the respect befitting Marie Antoinette including a curtsy. "Do not dare curtsy to me! We are no longer subjects of the British king!" I commanded as the nurse, a portly German woman, handed me the newborn. Little Jean Pierre truly was the spitting image of Aaron, albeit darker. I held him in my arms, rocked him, and ached for my own child. "It is most honorable of Senator Burr to give your children that he fathered his surname, and I am happy they are Burrs," I voiced my true feelings, for offspring of slaves and serving wenches took either their mothers' surnames or the masters made one up. Hence the numerous Hemings children of Thomas Jefferson and Sally Hemings, upon whom he refused to bestow his surname.

The Senate reconvened, and we returned to Philadelphia. When not studying or attending galas on Aaron's arm, I corresponded with Stephen regarding our properties. He'd bought another few dozen acres near the East River and asked what I wanted built on it.

Aaron answered for me. "Farms, my dear. Be a planter, not a politician."

"I don't want to be a politician or a farmer," I countered. "I want to conquer New York City."

He laughed. "You're certainly off to a running start. And I have no doubt you will. But never stop studying people," he added. "That will teach you more about business than anything you could learn at King's College."

As I browsed the newspaper over coffee, an article caught my eye. Every Wednesday, they published the names of slaves who'd escaped their owners. Not being a slave owner, I always ignored this item, but I couldn't ignore the name in bold lettering, only because it was the most famous name in our nation – Washington.

It went on to announce that Lady Washington's slave Ona Judge had escaped.

Ona...the lass I'd befriended and urged to seek a path to her freedom. A surge of pride filled my heart. What a brave soul. "Ona, wherever you are, I pray you'll live out your life as a free woman, with God to guide you, and bless you for your courage. Go embrace your destiny," I spoke out loud to her. "And to the many still suffering in bondage, I pray you'll live to see your emancipation."

I never saw Papa at social events. Everyone knew the Philadelphia executive mansion on High Street – a three-story red brick with dormer windows that Benedict Arnold lived in during the war. I mustered the nerve to walk past it.

"Why doesn't my father attend soirees or social gatherings?" I asked Aaron.

"He does, but rarely. One sees his carriage about town, but he keeps the curtains shut and guards his privacy." He continued, in a casual tone, "I can arrange a meeting with you and your father, if you wish. He still mislikes me, but now that I'm a senator, he won't brush me off."

It hit me like a shot between the eyes. "No, don't—" I blurted out my gut reaction. "I've given up on it for now. I thought to wait until I'm wealthy and make him proud to call me his daughter."

"You're afraid he'll reject you if you're not rich yet?"

It hurt to talk about it, even with Aaron, but I couldn't open my heart to anyone else. "Since that ill-fated visit with the bad oysters, I gave it a lot of thought. Should I call on him, or should I write, or wait till he's retired..." My hands fluttered, my palms sweaty. "I've been at an impasse with myself about it." Letting it out was a relief, but I sat helpless, unable to make a decision.

"Don't be afraid of rejection if that's what you fear. He has a good heart. And never had a child to call his own. He'd never turn his only daughter away," he pushed on, as if convincing a jury. "You have Washington blood running through your veins – and your heart."

That convinced me. "I'll write him. Then it's up to fate." I squared my shoulders, strode to the desk and, with a trembling hand, penned the bravest, most sincere letter I'd ever written.

"My Dear President Washington,

We've met a few times in the past, and you saw me most recently at the John Street Theater, where I played the part of Jane Shore, the drama performed at your request. We met and danced at the Ballou home in Providence, when you fell ill from oysters. I truly hope your recovery was a speedy one. I request another meeting for a very special reason: I am your daughter. My mother was Phebe Bowen, from Providence. I was born in October 1775 and now live in Philadelphia. I would appreciate a private audience so that we can become acquainted.

Yours sincerely, your obedient serv't, Eliza Capet."

A fortnight later, a pale blue envelope dropped through the mail slot. I held my breath as I broke the wax seal. Dear God, could it be from *him*?

My heart fell to the depths of my soul as I scanned the terse message.

"Dear Miss Capet," it read: *'We are in receipt of your letter of 15 Sep.'* (Who is 'We'?) *"The President has divers matters on his mind. Therefor, I deemed it inapropriat to inform him of yr claim. Sinc'ly yours, Mrs. Martha Washington."*

How dare she read his mail! But he had a staff of secretaries who probably read it and passed it around over a laugh. Still, I resented her reply: my *'claim'*? I flung it to the floor, turned my back on it, and trudged up the stairs. Before I let resentment overtake my sensible side, I realized it was just a 'claim' until he acknowledged me.

"Someday she'll know the truth," I vowed. I did hope she would accept the truth, because if she didn't, it would be her problem, not mine.

When Congress adjourned again, Aaron told me to pack. "I cannot wait to return to New York." He tossed his valise on the bed and began stuffing it with his clothes.

Until we returned, his daughter Theodosia was mistress of the house.

I dreaded meeting this educated, exalted princess. I cringed with inferiority.

"I will feel wholly inadequate in her presence," I lamented as the carriage lumbered over Philadelphia's dusty streets and onto the road cleared through the New Jersey wilderness.

"You will get on like a house on fire," he assured me.

The evening of our meeting, every thread I wore was new, clean, and pressed. Lilac netting draped my purple silk gown, trimmed in gold tinsel and embroidered in white silk.

One of the servants opened the front door and admitted us with a curtsy. Theodosia swept down the staircase in regal grace, her dark hair upswept with cascading curls, her eyes more ravishing than Aaron's. Her tailored masterpiece of pale yellow brocade fit her budding figure to perfection. She greeted me with a cordial kiss on both cheeks and a dazzling smile. As we sat in Aaron's parlor, she engaged me and her father in a lively discussion about Miss Wollstonecraft, the theater, and she complimented my performance in *Jane Shore*. Aaron allowed her to see that?

My fears were unfounded—she put me completely at ease and treated me as her equal. I thoroughly enjoyed her company.

That night, Aaron bade me good eve at the top of the staircase. The servant, Ellen, showed me to a boudoir right out of Versailles. My jaw dropped. "Posh, ain't it?" I muttered. A gold-trimmed bureau stood across from the bed draped in a canopy of silk and lace. A gilded-framed mirror above the mantel reflected candles glowing from sconces. Who decorated this place? Queen Charlotte? Then I knew. If Theodosia's advanced education was any hint, her lessons included the art of home décor. She clearly took to this art as she did the others.

Aaron didn't need to tell me why we bedded separately.

Theodosia was at her studies the next morning when we departed. I could hear the clear, clean notes of Bach on the harpsichord. Somehow I knew it wasn't her instructor.

I sent for little George and we had an emotional reunion. Aaron and I introduced him to his half-siblings and we enjoyed picnics in the country, pony rides, and lawn bowling. Watching the children play together, I longed for us to be a real family. I asked George to stay with me in New York, but he shook his head, regarding me with his father's dazzling eyes. "No, Mamma, Providence is my home with Aunt Free and Uncle Rube. But I do love visiting here and my Papa and brothers and sisters – and I love you most of all!" He wrapped his young arms around me and I hugged him with a longing that pained me. But I had to respect his wishes. He thrived under Aunt Free's wing, as I indulged him in the best schools. I had no doubt he'd "make a noise in this world," as Mozart said about the young Beethoven.

Before we parted, I addressed them both with something that came to the forefront of my mind all of a sudden: "Aaron, remember when you agreed to bestow your surname upon our son?"

"Why, of course," came Aaron's immediate reply. "You wanted to ask George when he was older."

I turned to our son. "George, would you care to be George Washington Bowen Burr?"

He regarded Aaron with all the respect due his father but shook his little head. "Uh-uh, Mama, I am happy having three names for now. When I am a grownup, I may add Papa's name, for I am proud to be a Burr as well as a Washington. It is enough to explain to people why my name is George Washington—a lot of explaining for a little boy."

We both chuckled at his honest assessment, and I wrapped my arms around him. "Well, you have a heritage to be mighty proud of! You go right ahead and explain away. And believe me when I say Papa and I are truly pleased you are so proud of it." As I was proud to be Washington. No one could take that away from me.

I stayed on in New York to tend to some business, visit Stephen and his little family, and buy some new raiment as Aaron returned to Philadelphia. As I labored over my ledgers and paid bills, I heard the post drop through the mail slot. Expecting nothing important, I let it lie there a few more hours. When I tore into a letter from him, my heart stopped. It began simply, *"Dear Eliza, my wife Theodosia is no more."*

I stood, stunned, unable to breathe. My eyes fixed on those words, reading them over and over. I sank to the bottom step and cradled my head in my hand as I read the rest: *"Please come back to me..."*

It slipped through my fingers to the floor and I ran to pack.

CHAPTER 26

I HARDLY LEFT Aaron's side through the remainder of his Senate term. He never spoke of his late wife. When his term ended, he sold his coach and horses at a loss to cover debts. I didn't know this until one evening when we stepped out for dinner. "Where's the coach?" I looked up and down the street.

"Oh, it's gone. I needed to pay creditors. I'll go rent one..." He started to walk away and I pulled him back.

"Never mind, we can walk the nine blocks." I tucked my hand in the crook of his elbow, shaking my head in dismay. He never discussed financial matters with me, as I did with him. Was his salary as a senator not sufficient to support his life-style? Unlike Papa, he didn't own a plantation, a mansion, or hundreds of slaves. I itched to ask how he spent money he didn't have. But I bit my tongue.

Aaron easily won election to the New York State Assembly. On the evening of departure, I paid for the Belvedere's chef to cook us a meal of mushroom soup, broiled bass, and roast beef. Over a bottle of vintage cognac, I asked him to marry me.

He looked me straight in the eye and grasped my hands. "Eliza, I need to be sensible right now. Another marriage—I'm not quite ready for that. Not yet. In the future, perhaps. When I am sound financially."

"Or when *I* am," I corrected.

"Surely you don't believe I'd marry you for your fortune." He freed my hands and sat back, regarding me now more frostily from the added distance.

"What good is a fortune if I cannot share it with my husband?" By now I owned ten—or was it twelve?—apartment buildings in New York City, a tract of land in Brooklyn, two stables, and I'd 'flipped' a dry goods store. I bought a shop that sold intimate apparel and whalebone stays.

I'd acquired all this property with rental income and took out small mortgages but never spent money I didn't have. I also bought Aaron a new coach and two matched grays. He, on the other hand, owed his soul to creditors all over the city. But it didn't bother him. All high-ranking politicians and lawyers lived beyond their means.

Even Papa was in debt, so I heard—living in grand style, but on borrowed money. I wondered how anyone could enjoy a mansion or a coach or splendid raiment if they didn't own any of it.

"I am not a leech," Aaron retorted and drank his cognac.

I snatched the glass from him and plunked it down. "I never said you were a leech. You never will be. And there'll be no more liquor tonight. I want our last night together to be passionate, hard-driving, and engorged with fortitude—if you catch my *entendre*." I made my voice breathy and seductive.

"I intend to wear you out." He stood and took my hand. His eyes glowed like a pair of citrines in the candlelight.

A delightful warmth spread through me as he led me up the stairs, shucking off his raiment along the way. "At least once tonight, and once at daybreak. I'm not greedy," I murmured as I ran my lips down his lean torso, planting kisses all the way. "But when you're president, it had better be three times a day."

"How about if I only make vice president?" He unwound my chignon, tossing pins aside. My hair tumbled down in lustrous waves.

"Then I'll be easy on you till you become president," I gave him the answer he wanted, for though he wouldn't admit it, he wanted the highest office in our land.

"You want two short ones or one long one?" He unbuttoned my blouse.

"Any way you want to give it to me, Mr. Future President." I sighed. "As long as you give it to me when you're Mr. President."

"Fate is fickle, my darling," he replied. "And voters are even more fickle."

As Mr. Future President's coach pulled away from the curb next morn, a familiar emptiness gripped me. A haunting specter, it revisited me at times like this. Would I ever learn to ward it off? A lady and a gent walked by, glanced at me, and exchanged a knowing look. They knew Aaron lived there.

I did an abrupt about-face, packed my valise, and got out.

I went to the livery stable on Broad Street to hire a coach. "Take me to Maiden Lane," I told the coachman. Bedazzling jewelry always brightened my spirits. I deserved a bracelet or two—with a brooch to match. As my eyes swept over the rainbow of gemstones in a fine jewelry store, I assured myself, "You're almost at the top, Mademoiselle Capet!" But

I could not wrap my arms around empty lots or brick buildings.

Whilst strolling past another jeweler, my newest purchases —er, investments—gracing my wrists, I spotted the pretty Elma Sands with a tall wiry gent, at least mid-thirties. *Is that the generous suitor she blushed and gushed over?* I wondered. Leaving them to their tryst, I kept walking.

The evening after next, I again espied them outside the Three Bells Tavern in a heated argument. He pushed her, and she stumbled. As I charged over to the scene, my pointer finger at the ready for a chest-poking what-for, she gave him a shove, knocking him off his feet. "Keep 'im down for the count, honey," I voiced the term from the new sport I liked—boxing— and sauntered away.

Wishing to add to my collection of jewels—for investments, of course, not to flash around—I browsed in one of the Broad Way's posh jewelry stores. As my eye caught a pink pearl necklace, a familiar voice piped up behind me. "Oh, this is lovely, Levi. And it fits me like a glove."

I turned to face the beaming Gertrude Meredith holding her arm out to admire a dazzling sapphire on her ring finger. A lanky chap stood beside her, nodding his agreement. "It matches your eyes, my pet."

She spotted me and grinned. "Eliza! How nice to see you!" She clutched her beau's arm and trotted him over. "This is Levi Weeks. Levi, Miss Eliza Capet."

"Levi?" I held out my hand, and he grasped my fingers. "I know your brother Ezra quite well." I needn't say how well. But I did recall Sally's claim that these brothers sometimes shared their ladies of the evening—on the same evening.

"Ah, yes, Miss Capet, everyone in town knows Ezra," he said over a chuckle as Gertrude clung to him, turning her be-ringed finger this way and that. The stone caught the light and sparkled.

"That is a stunning ring, Gertrude." I gave it an admiring nod. "Is this a precursor to wedding bells?"

"It very well may be." She flaunted a smile.

Levi went to the counter and came back with a heart-shaped ruby brooch. "And this is just because." He pinned it to her collar.

Gertrude squealed with delight and threw her arms around her betrothed—if that's what he was. I recently saw someone wearing a lovely cameo brooch and complimented her on it—oh, who was it?

Then I remembered—pretty Elma Sands, who gushed about her new suitor, a boarder where she lived. Bloomin' blazes, some generous suitors lived in this town—but none to equal my Aaron.

"Well, here's to much happiness," I extended my wishes as the lovebirds waltzed over to the clerk. Levi dug into his pocket—he'd need to dig deep for those baubles.

Not a week later did I see the bridegroom-to-be canoodling with a willowy blonde at a performance of *As You Like It*. I knew that girl from somewhere...but where?

Did she know Levi was also courting Gertrude? I didn't venture to guess. I kept my distance and pretended I never saw them.

Papa left public life and retired to Mount Vernon. But I hadn't given up on a private audience. A meeting would be easier now. Getting to Mount Vernon would be the hard part.

I had one of those 'a-ha' moments the next day. That willowy blonde with Levi—now I remembered who she was: Anna Gardie, the dancer. I'd seen her in the ballet a few times as the company's principal dancer. She also played one of the singing and dancing witches in *Macbeth* when William ran it at John Street. She was from the Dominican Republic and had a French husband.

But did Levi know Anna was married? I reckoned Anna did not care.

I sent Papa one letter a month. But I never received a reply. I guessed his secretary—and interceptor—was now his wife. Hence no response.

I now dwelt in a brick townhouse on Orchard Street. I purchased it with the proceeds from four lots I sold. I later learned the buyer was John Jacob Astor. He was an investor, not a developer. Why he wanted these, I knew not. But when Aaron returned from Albany, we went to see *Othello* at the Park Theater, which Astor co-owned. The box I rented was next to Astor's, and Aaron introduced us. With the show about to start, I couldn't engross him in chit-chat or probe his reasons for buying my four measly parcels. I said hello and admired his slick silvery hair and Roman nose, knowing I'd reach his level of success someday. But for now, trading up was good enough—with that Haarlem mansion on the hill my ultimate prize.

As I passed the hall table next morn, I noticed a cream envelope. I didn't recognize the penmanship but saw the return address, 'Mount Vernon, Virginia,' across the top left. My heart stopped. My shaking hands tore it open. I skimmed the body of the letter until my eyes reached the signature. *"George Washington,"* it read, with the flourish I'd seen so many years ago and never forgot.

"Aaron!" I backed into the wall and slid to the floor, inhaling fresh wax.

He clattered down the stairs and knelt by my side. "What's wrong?"

My voice gone, I held the letter out.

"God's sakes, I thought you were having an attack..." He read the letter. "Why, this is wonderful news."

Our arms wound around each other, the letter pressed between us. Tears of joy spilled down my cheeks.

He sat beside me as I read it again, out loud: *"My dear Eliza, forgive me for not having written sooner, for my chores here are many and time is growing ever shorter. I am in receipt of your letters of March and April. If you can see your way clear to travel here to Mount Vernon, I will be pleased to honor you as my guest so that we can discuss the subject of your correspondence. I fondly recall my visit to Providence in 1774 and the charming Phebe Bowen and do remember our visits and your stellar performances in the theater. I await your arrival. I remain, Yours, George Washington."*

"He received only my March and April letters. I can guess with certainty how the others met their fate." A tinge of bitterness invaded my joy.

"What does it matter?" Aaron drew me close to him. "He wants to see you. And I could not be happier for you, my darling."

"I know!" I squealed with childlike glee.

I tore my eyes away from Papa's exquisite writing and looked at my beloved Aaron. Tears shone in his eyes, too.

CHAPTER 27

"PLEASE GO WITH ME," I begged, but Aaron shook his head.

"Too many legislative duties, and I must return to Albany," was his excuse, but Papa had not invited Aaron. He had no reason to believe I even knew Aaron. "Besides, you should be alone with him, not with me tagging along."

"He would welcome you. I hear visitors swarm in on Mount Vernon in droves, even complete strangers," I argued as he refused for the tenth time in as many minutes.

"If he and I were complete strangers, Perhaps I would go," he reasoned. "But I could not make an appearance at Mount Vernon. I am more than cocksure I am not welcome there."

I packed my best raiment and hired a coach and four for the journey. Being December, daylight faded by 4:30. I wanted so badly for Aaron to join me, for the two men I loved so dearly to greet each other with fellowship and amity. But he wished me well and saw me off. As I blew him a farewell kiss, I leaned out the carriage and waved my handkerchief. "Keep our bed warm till I return!"

As the journey dragged on over rutted roads, I saw our

nation by land for the first time. Breathing the cleanest air ever, I gazed out the jouncing carriage past rolling fields and farmhouses.

Late afternoon of the fourth day, the carriage wheels crunched on a long gravel drive. Before me stood magnificent Mount Vernon. Curved colonnades on either side of the red-roofed mansion led to smaller outbuildings, red brick walkways, and rows of bare trees, branches shivering in the wind. Finally – journey's end. My heart slammed.

The carriage halted, and the coachman helped me down. Four brick steps led up to a large framed door. I knocked, and a light-skinned servant in a white apron and turban greeted me. "I am here to see General— President Washington. I am Eliza Capet."

"He receives visitors in the little parlor, this way, Miss Capet." She led me into a room with a harpsichord and left me alone. "I cannot believe I'm actually here," I repeated in breathless whispers. The room's six walls glowed in soothing yellow trimmed in spring green. I walked over wide polished floorboards and studied pictures on the walls: oval portraits of Papa, Benjamin Franklin, and Lafayette. Two chairs covered with fringed cushions stood in the corner.

As I peeked into the next room displaying a huge looking glass, I heard footsteps.

"Eliza?" came a deep booming voice.

I turned and faced my father.

Love and longing washed over me as I beheld his magnificent bearing. Tall and muscular, he filled the doorway with his imposing presence, dressed in the richest burgundy – brocaded jacket, waistcoat, breeches, and riding boots. His face bore deeper lines than I remembered from before. His eyes shone brilliant blue as ever. I stood rooted to the spot, knowing not what to do or say – so I dipped in a curtsy. He strode up to me in two steps and held out his hand. As I rose, we touched. Finally – George Washington and Eliza Washington, meeting as father and daughter. I choked back a torrent of tears and found my voice. "I am so happy to see you, your highness. I am honored to be in your presence."

"No need for that, I am not a king, lass. Never wanted to be." He struggled to move his lips, his teeth larger and worse-fitting than last time.

"I know, but you're a king to me, sir."

"Balderdash. We are now Americans." Which is what I always said. He guided me over to the chairs and sat across from me. I sank into the cushion. "Shall I order refreshment?"

"No, sir – nothing, thank you." My mouth dry, I trembled. However rude, I couldn't stop staring. I silently begged, *please don't let Lady Washington appear. I need to be alone with him.* "This cushion is plushy, sir," I commented dumbly, my tongue in knots.

"Lady Washington made them."

"She's truly gifted. And that harpsichord is lovely." I pointed at it. "Do you play it, sir?"

"No, and you needn't 'sir' me," he returned, tightening his lips. "I can neither sing one of the songs, nor raise a single note on any instrument. Lady Washington's granddaughter Nelly plays it. She was married on my last birthday and promised to come back to remove it to her home."

"An excuse to visit, perhaps?" I blurted, my eyes wide and unblinking.

He nodded. "We're never without company here. And how was your journey?"

"Long, but the scenery is so lovely. It makes me proud of my country." I studied his features, for last time we met was so brief, amazed at the similarities between us – the light fringe of lashes over the blue eyes, the strong chin, the low forehead.

"I ordered your coachman inside. It's cold, and the sun hasn't been out." His eyes wandered over me, taking in my hair, my eyes – did he see similarities, too? Oh, how badly I wanted to ask him what he felt at this moment.

Here I sat, finally alone with the greatest man in our nation, my own father, and we prattled about the weather! But who would bring the crucial subject up first? To my intense relief, he did.

"I received your letters. I remember that … that time I spent with Phebe Bowen in Providence, and I shan't deny it. You and I share many features. I have no other children of my own, as you know. I'm proud to call you my only daughter." His voice carried pleasure. With a slight bow of his head, he smiled.

I tried to smile back, but my lips quivered. "Then … may I … may I call you Papa?" stumbled out of my mouth, I know not how, beyond thinking clearly.

"You may in private, but it's unwise to let anyone else know just yet."

Dumbly, I nodded. I wanted to ask why but didn't dare. His accepting me as his daughter was the greatest gift of my lifetime. I ached to hold his hands and feel his arms embrace me, but he didn't seem demonstrative or affectionate. We chatted some more about my journey, my purchases of real estate, our favorite books. Aaron's name never came up.

But I did tell him about my son—his grandson. "You have a namesake, Papa." Oh, what a thrill to call this great man Papa! "My son, George Washington Bowen."

"So I have a true grandson!" His eyes twinkled with joy that brought tears to mine.

Someday his grandson would tell anyone who asked why he was named after our great president, but neither of us mentioned this now—it remained unsaid, but I knew he was thinking the same thing.

After a lengthy pause as we stood looking at each other, lost in our own thoughts, he reached for my hand. "Come, let me introduce you to Lady Washington."

I didn't want to meet her—I needed more time alone with him—but didn't dare refuse. He brought me to a closed door and knocked. Another light-skinned servant – a slave? – opened it, and Martha Washington approached, plain and plump, wearing neutral homespun and a lacy cap.

Papa presented me as Eliza Capet, but whether he discussed me and my mother in the privacy of their boudoir, I'd never know. She already knew who I was from the letter she intercepted, and likely others. She was neither cordial nor hostile. She let me lodge in the downstairs bedroom, so I never got to climb the grand central staircase. But that night, snug in my comfy canopy bed, I sat up and gazed around the room by the glow of a candle, moonlight streaming through the Venetian blinds. If only he'd married Mamma, all of this would have been mine someday. But my destiny was to succeed on my own. All I wanted was for him to call me his daughter. I snuggled into the warm feather mattress, content and loved.

Daring not to overstay my welcome, I prepared to leave the following day, after breakfast in an elegant dining room with a fire blazing in the hearth and liveried servants – slaves? – lined up. Again, Papa engaged me in a chat about books, theater, and the history of Mount Vernon. Clearly, he had no desire to talk politics.

When he walked me to the door, his wife excused herself and vanished into the depths of the mansion. I was grateful she let us bid farewell alone. As we stood in the chilly wind on his doorstep, Papa and I faced each other, my head barely reaching his chin. He held out his arms in a wide circle and let me in. We embraced, and I rested my cheek on his chest. I wanted him to hold me forever. He pulled away, and I looked into his eyes one last time – eyes so much like mine.

"Oh, yes, the resemblance is plain as day, Eliza. I have the deepest regret our circumstances couldn't have been otherwise. In time, I will make it public that you are my daughter." His voice wavered, pent-up emotion behind his words.

"I want nothing more, Papa." Just saying it bonded me to him. Sharing his smile, I sensed his joy. He finally had the child he longed for.

"I will write and let you know the best time to return. Thereafter, if you wish, you may call yourself Eliza Washington."

"Thank you so much." I couldn't hold back any longer. A stream of tears spilled down my cheeks. He took out a handkerchief and dabbed at my tears, then handed it to me. I knew I'd cherish it for the rest of my life.

He helped me into the coach. As it lurched into motion, I held his handkerchief and waved. I didn't look back, but knew he stood there until my carriage vanished from his sight.

After a rollicking pre-holiday tavern crawl with my old friend Sukie, we slipped into the Tontine Coffee House. Once again, I glimpsed Elma Sands with that chap. "Poor lass, such a sweet girl, and saddled with that wastrel," I murmured. "I would stop and wish her season's greetings, but she's rather occupied."

Sukie said, "I've never seen him, but I do know her. Elma Sands, she works in her cousin Catharine's milliner's and lives in her boarding house. Last time I saw her, Levi Weeks was escorting her."

"Yes, I know Elma. But ... Levi Weeks and her?" I puzzled. "I saw him with Gertrude, showering her with pricey baubles in a jewelry store. Then I saw him with Anna Gardie, the ballet dancer."

Sukie snickered. "Levi gets around. He lives in Catharine's boarding house, too. Rumor has it his bedpost is worn to a twig with notches. He needn't even leave the room."

I made a note to advise Elma to drop the wandering Levi. But not to give back the jewelry.

I trudged down the Broad Way to purchase some gloves. My shoes crunched over dirty snow. Christmas was nearly upon us, but the city was quieter than usual. Streets lay eerily deserted. People and even stray animals seemed to be in hiding. Was there a killer on the loose?

As I crossed the street, Alexander Hamilton stood on the corner, alone, head down. Dear God, he was weeping.

I approached him and stood at a respectable distance. He looked up, and his teary eyes met mine.

"Colonel Hamilton, are you all right?" I asked in a soft voice.

He wiped his eyes. "I just heard terrible news. Terrible, terrible news." He drew a ragged breath. Senator Mason informed me ... President Washington died."

Stunned numb with shock, unable to breathe, I fell into his arms. "No! I just saw him. I went to see him at Mount Vernon. I am his daughter – I am his only blood daughter, and he finally acknowledged me, he let me call him Papa ..." I babbled on and on, uncaring if I abused protocol, but I needed to share my raw excruciating grief. "He told me he would make it public ..." I sobbed. "It took years. Someone threw my letters to him away, then he finally received one letter and invited me ..." My legs gave way beneath me. He clutched my arms to hold me up.

"I never knew. I am so sorry, my dear." He guided me to his townhouse down the street, unlocked the door, and led me in. Children's voices and footsteps echoed in the distance.

He ushered me into a parlor and sat me down, repeating how sorry he was. "No friend of his has more cause to lament on personal account than myself ... he was an aegis very essential to me ... oh, he was nothing less than a father to me!" He broke down and cried as he spoke.

We must have sat for an hour talking, sharing, grieving. As his clock struck the noon hour, he walked me home. "Call upon me if you need anything, lass. Anything at all."

"Thank you, Alexander," I whispered, thinking *he's not such a prat after all.*

CHAPTER 28

DAY AFTER DAY, I wandered the snowy streets, tripping over cobbles, animal bones, and refuse, my mind a blur. My breath emerged in puffs of steam. My face stung, numb with cold, yet sweat soaked my woolen cloak and skirt. Black shrouds hung from windows, casting a mournful pall over the city. People wandered in silence, staring straight ahead, black bands around their arms. Plangent church bells tolled.

On the fourth day—or the fifth, I'd lost track of time—I stumbled home, fell through the door, and hurled myself onto the settee. Grieving for Papa, I wanted Aaron with me so badly. I pushed myself upright, staggered to the desk, and with a trembling hand, scratched out a letter, begging him to come to me, for I couldn't bear this alone.

I remember not how or when I posted it. All I did was sit at the window staring blankly into the street until darkness fell. When the sun rose, still I sat.

Christmas passed me by. With the new century a few weeks old, I tore open the letter that fell through the mail slot, recognizing Aaron's penmanship.

My eyes halted on *"I am so very sorry"* and *"do come to Albany."* I kissed his name at the bottom, imagining his lips kissing mine. I dashed upstairs to pack.

Under leaden skies and two soakers, my three-day journey ended at his elegant house on Albany's Washington Street. My pulse quickened as he embraced me. "You make me feel alive again," I whispered, kissing his neck.

"You have everything to live for, Eliza." His voice caressed me. "You had each other in the end. You loved him, and he loved you, and that's all that matters. He's watching over you and is very proud of his only daughter. You hold the truth, and no one can ever take that away from you."

With those words, my mind reawakened. A surge of energy tingled my fingertips. "Thank you," I spoke with a renewed will to live.

He guided me in, and we sat on his settee as darkness fell. One flickering flame glowed in the distance. "Aaron, please relight the fire. That candle is not giving off any heat."

He released me and turned around. "There is no candle, Eliza."

At that moment I knew—*Papa really is watching over me.*

I returned home and threw myself into work. The daily papers piled up on the table. I spilled some coffee and grabbed the top paper to sop it up. When I saw the front page, I gasped as if struck. "Oh, no..."

MURDER AT THE MANHATTAN WELL... the headline screamed. I sickened at the sight of the victim's name—

Elma Sands. As I reeled in that tragedy, my eyes halted on the name I knew so well, the Manhattan Well's owner—Aaron Burr.

His Manhattan Company had built it at the edge of Greenwich Village. Rendered unsuitable, they covered it with wooden planks. It stood abandoned in Lispenard's Meadow, swampland to the city's north. How could she drown in a covered well in the wilderness?

No more moping around feeling sorry for myself. I donned my cloak and trudged through the snow to Elma's Greenwich Street boarding house. Her cousin Catharine answered the door, pale and shaken.

"I just read the newspaper, Catharine. I'm so sorry." I stepped inside and slipped my cloak off. She wept as I gave her a heartfelt hug. "Have they a suspect?"

"Oh, indeed they have." Her voice shook with rage. "Levi Weeks."

I blinked in shock. "Levi? No, he wouldn't. He couldn't..."

"He could, and he did." Her shrill tone curdled my blood. "They were to be secretly married that eve. He made sure it didn't happen."

I followed her into the parlor. We sat in facing chairs. "A boy found a muff near the well, a muff Elma borrowed from a neighbor. My husband Elias and the boy's father looked down into the well and didn't see anything. But when they dipped a pole in, they found her..." She paused over a ragged breath. "Several men joined Elias and improvised a set of hooks, fetched some ropes, and lifted... lifted Elma out." Her voice broke. I reached across and clasped her hand. "Her hair hung in a tangled mess, her bonnet askew, her shoulders and feet bare, and..." Her voice quivered, "... her dress torn near to shreds."

The image formed in my mind. I couldn't bear it. A sob caught in my throat. "Oh, dear God."

But Catharine wasn't finished. "Her neck and shoulders were bruised, with a ring of marks around her throat. She died a violent, excruciating death." She broke down and sobbed. I went over and held her until she caught her breath.

"When did Levi become a suspect?" I asked when her breathing calmed.

"It was he Elma was with last. When a constable arrived, the men with Elias reported Levi's name. The constable brought them to Levi in his workshop. They pegged him, all right. They brought him to view Elma's body, and he admitted it—I mean, he admitted he knew Elma. He'll never admit he killed her." Her voice dripped with venom.

"Where is Levi now?" I asked.

"In Bridewell where he belongs," came her short reply.

I didn't dare blab that I'd seen Levi buying Gertrude Meredith baubles or squiring Anna Gardie around town. He could be a rogue. But hell's bells, that didn't mean he murdered Elma.

"He had no reason to kill her, Catharine," I offered my platitudes to the stricken woman.

She glared daggers. "Then who did murder her? Or do you suppose she threw herself down that well and strangled herself?"

"N-no," I stammered. "She wouldn't. She was happy..." But was she? She was obviously smitten with Levi. But what about that wastrel I saw her arguing with outside the tavern? She didn't look smitten with him.

Catharine confirmed what Sukie and Sally Marshall told me. "He was a cad. He chased after my sister and Margaret Clark, who also live here. He just wanted Elma out of the way to pursue his... other interests."

"Did he have an alibi?" I wanted to know the facts, not how many more notches he nicked into his bedpost.

"Ezra said Levi was with him. The night Elma vanished, she asked me to help her dress, and Levi asked me to tie his hair. He went out while Elma went to borrow the muff. At eight, Levi came back in and said he was going out a third time."

She went on as if testifying, "Elias and I went to bed, and Levi went out. I heard someone follow him down the hall and whisper. The door closed and..." She splayed her fingers, "... nothing. He returned at ten, asked me about Elma, and I told him she'd gone out. He...ha!"

She gave off a bitter laugh. "He expressed surprise she'd go out alone so late. But I had no reason to think she went alone, and told him so. Next morn, she was still gone. I looked into her room some fifty times, and Levi claimed he looked more than fifty times. As if."

She sniffed. "That night, she still hadn't returned. Then another. Levi's sleigh was gone the evening she vanished, and it didn't have bells. People saw two men and a lady in a sleigh without bells. Others heard a woman scream 'Murder!' and 'Lord help me!' from the well area..." She heaved a shaky breath, "... it all adds up. He will not get away with this."

I shook my head in disbelief. "Even if Levi is a cad, he can't be a murderer. Someone else did away with Elma. But who? And good Lord, why?"

Catharine picked up her Bible and held it in clenched hands. "There is no one else, Eliza. She was a good girl."

I didn't dare dispute that. I gave Catharine a warm hug. She stiffened up but relaxed as I soothed her. "I'll be here for you if you need me, dear. Elma's at peace now."

Levi's brother Ezra Weeks hired the best team of lawyers in town: Henry Livingston, Alexander Hamilton—and Aaron. Aaron returned from Albany to prepare for the case. He wouldn't discuss the upcoming trial or his strategy for finding Levi innocent. Meanwhile, it tore me to pieces—in my heart, I knew he didn't kill that sweet girl. But Catharine was hell-bent on getting Levi hanged. One visit became frightening.

"Elma would want you to have this, she bought it with her own money." Catharine handed me a gold ring with three round sapphires, as delicate as Elma herself.

"How thoughtful of you, I'm touched." I slipped the ring on and touched it to my lips. Then I opened my big mouth and started yammering about Aaron and Hamilton getting along so well working the case. "I'm glad to see them on the same side for a change. Perhaps they'll put their differences aside and become friends."

"And don't you itch to see your fast-talking lawyer lover strut from that courtroom in victory, a freed murderer at his heels," she spat. "If Hamilton and Burr have that evil soul acquitted and they die a natural death, then there is no justice in heaven."

I blanched. "Oh, Catharine, surely you don't mean that. Of course, they want justice served." But I knew two more reasons Aaron and Hamilton put their mutual contempt aside for this case: business and politics.

Ezra was building Hamilton's estate on Convent Avenue, and Aaron's water company pipes, among other dealings. Aaron and Hamilton also knew the value of publicity: with the presidential election coming up, this sensational murder case thrust them into the center of attention, keeping their names before the public.

I knew this election would result in one or both of them

achieving greatness. 'President Burr' rolled off my tongue like honey.

"No one else had reason to kill her," Catharine insisted, pacing the floor in a figure eight like a caged tigress. "It was not suicide, though I wager that's what your silver-tongued lawyers will dredge up, and I'm no soothsayer."

I should've said something about that wastrel I'd seen Elma arguing with, but kept my mouth shut.

Instead, I told Aaron.

He scoffed, "There's no way to find this person, and that doesn't prove he killed her, just because they had a tussle. We can't go and question every tall thin wastrel in New York. Our job isn't to convict someone else. It's to secure an acquittal for our client."

Convicting 'someone else' was my notion of justice. But I wasn't a prominent lawyer. Still, Catharine's rant about Aaron and Hamilton not deserving a natural death rang in my ears. I didn't mention that to Aaron. He'd scoff at it.

"I fear she will harm me now. Or even kill me." I struggled to keep my voice steady. "She was on the verge of madness when I visited her last."

This got an understanding nod. "People get emotional when a loved one is murdered. We'll be careful with her on the stand."

"Even though I cannot serve on the jury, I believe Levi innocent until proven guilty," I declared.

Then I saw something that knocked me off my feet.

CHAPTER 29

WE PASSED on the street in bright daylight. I couldn't mistake him—that wastrel I'd seen arguing with Elma Sands. A willowy blonde clutched his arm—and there was no mistaking her: Anna Gardie, the dancer I'd seen with Levi. But what struck me dumb was the blue and white cameo brooch at her throat.

Elma's brooch.

I'd seen it at Elma's throat, admired it, studied it up close, complimented her on it. A jeweler had custom made it, she'd said... and a suitor had given it to her.

How in blazes did Anna Gardie get it?

I wouldn't relax a muscle until I found out. The strangest hunch hovered over me—if I found out how Anna got Elma's brooch, I'd have a clue as to who killed her. Somehow I sensed the pieces would fall into place. I could solve the most prominent murder case in New York history, save an innocent man, and bring a murderer to justice.

As the couple brushed past me, I turned on my heel and followed them for one block, then two... to 54 Pearl Street, a boarding house I'd considered buying until I found it housed more bugs than boarders.

I tarried on the street a moment, then marched up to the door and pushed my way in. Boarders sat in the parlor reading the papers, playing cards, idling.

"Excuse me, sir." I strode up to a gent glancing at his pocket watch.

He stood to address me. "No need to stand for me, sir. All I need to know is about a couple who board here—he's tall and wiry, she's blonde and willowy. I know she's Anna Gardie. But do you know his name by chance?"

He nodded. "Why, yes, he's her husband Maurison. He's a musician in the Park Theater's orchestra."

So that was her French husband. "Maurison, of course." I nodded as if I knew all along. "Many thanks for reminding me, sir." I twirled and dashed out, straight for Aaron's office.

Striding at a brisk pace, I released puffs of steam and pondered the mystery. Maurison must've taken the brooch from Elma and given it to Anna.

A wave of disgust sickened me. But I couldn't let personal feelings hinder my mission. I strode on and reached Aaron's office, panting with exertion.

His clerk answered. "Attorney Burr is in court, madam."

Unwilling to trust the clerk's memory with such crucial information, I dipped one of Aaron's pens into an inkpot and wrote on a sheet of clean parchment: "*Go question Anna Gardie's husband Maurison at 54 Pearl Street immediately. A clue he killed Elma: Anna is wearing Elma's brooch, and I will swear under oath he is the man I saw arguing with Elma. No time to waste. Your Eliza.*"

I placed it dead center on his desk, and took the next step to clear Levi. I had to work fast—the trial would start at ten the next morn.

Aaron sat me down that evening and lit a seegar. "I read your note and went to question Maurison and his wife Anna."

"Well? What did they say?" I held my breath.

"Nothing. They're both dead. Murder-suicide. Stab wounds." He puffed on his seegar and paced back and forth.

I sprang up, unable to sit. "Dear God, how awful! What happened? Do you think it had anything to do with Levi's case?"

He halted and our eyes met. "I talked to the boarding house owner, Mrs. Orcet. She and Anna were cordial. Anna said at the threat of deportation she decided to return to the Dominican Republic and Maurison back to France. He wanted her to go with him, but she refused. He plunged into severe depression over money problems and the removal of the ballet establishment from the theater. When she prepared to depart, he stabbed her to death and slit his wrists."

Unable to sit, I trod circles around him. "I'm convinced Maurison killed Elma. And I have a way to find out. I only hope it'll be before the trial."

He shrugged into his coat. "Are you attending?"

"No... no. But I know you'll get Levi acquitted. I have the utmost faith in you." I approached him and clasped his hands.

"The evidence is thin." He buttoned his coat. "We have a few things up our sleeves that will create much doubt. The judge knows me and my family. I have every confidence he'll instruct the jury to acquit Weeks. It's politics, you know. Not justice, sadly."

I walked him to the door. "Politics or not, justice will prevail. He's innocent."

We bade each other good evening and I prepared my own defense of Levi Weeks.

I didn't join the shoving mob outside City Hall the next morning. Instead, I went to 54 Pearl Street to call on the owner, Mrs. Orcet.

She offered tea and cakes but I had no time for trifles. "Mrs. Orcet, I have a mission of utmost importance." I recited my rehearsed speech. "I am Anna Gardie's first cousin, her only relative in this country. I gave her a cameo brooch that I can describe in explicit detail if you so desire. I would like to have it back. May I look around Anna and Maurison's room to retrieve it?"

How could she refuse? My tears were real even if my story wasn't. I needed part of Elma to hold in my hands, and whatever I could find to prove Levi's innocence—and Maurison's guilt.

"Why, of course." She led me up the stairs to the first room on the left, opened the door with a key on her brass ring, and stepped aside. "I'll be in the kitchen." She left me alone in the silent room that smelled of death, the air charged with tension and tragedy.

I found the cameo brooch in a small box atop the dressing table. Knowing definitive evidence was waiting for me to find it, I kept poking around. I opened drawers, tossed undergarments, flipped through private papers... and there I found the truth.

Letters... dozens of them, in neat expressive hand on quality parchment. I skimmed each one... "*My dear Mauri, I've never loved anyone the way I love you... don't ever leave me... I cannot live without you... you're the love of my life now and forever... why won't you leave Anna? She's no good for you... if you don't leave her I'll tell Anna everything...*"

Each letter bore the same signature... "*Elma.*"

Now I knew Levi Weeks was innocent.

~

So did the jury. After the forty-three-hour trial, they acquitted Levi.

Was it politics rather than justice? Some believed so. But as Aaron told me, the prosecution couldn't produce any physical evidence. They could prove neither cause nor place of death. No eyewitnesses were present. Levi had a solid alibi and no motive.

Poor dear Elma. I shook my head as I knelt at her grave. With a garden shovel, I dug up a small mound of earth and buried her brooch next to her gravestone. "Rest in peace, sweet one. Now we know the truth." I stood, brushed dirt from my hands, and blew her a kiss.

Levi fled town. I didn't blame him. Even though he was acquitted, the city stood divided. If he stayed, they'd have crucified him.

My mission wasn't ended yet. I wrote him a letter telling him I found Elma's killer.

"*Thank you,*" he wrote from Mississippi. "*You gave me my life back. I couldn't go on without your quest for the truth.*"

I invited him back to New York City to go into business with me. But I never heard from him.

I asked Aaron to destroy the Manhattan Well. "I'll get around to it," came his reply as he dashed off to another committment.

I hoped that well would fall apart, and not survive as a curiosity in a Greenwich Village basement in the distant future.

~

At the threshold of this 19th century, I witnessed my second most exciting event—the presidential election of 1800. Aaron became vice president, but should have won the presidency.

It couldn't have stung worse than if I'd lost the election myself. But Aaron's reaction floored me. He walked in and stated, "Jefferson won," his tone so vacant I thought him joshing.

"Yea, right! C'mere, let me take my new president to bed." I sidled up to him and fondled him through his tight breeches. Ah, bedding the president of the United States, the man I loved. I tingled at the thought.

He stood unresponsive and removed my hand. "It is no joke, Eliza. Jefferson was elected. He is the president."

My arousal dissolved. I stepped away. "God's truth, you are dead serious. What on earth happened?"

"To put it simply, we each got seventy-three electoral votes, so the House of Representatives needed to break the tie," he explained, his voice devoid of emotion. "With Hamilton's maneuverings, or more aptly put, shenanigans, the majority of the House voted for Jefferson, on the thirty-sixth ballot."

My blood simmered as my fists clenched. "You could have won that election!" My voice loudened with every word. "Why did you never leave New York to convince Federalists to vote for you? You did want the presidency, did you not?"

"Not yet," he replied without hesitation. I hoped he wasn't rationalizing, but Aaron never made up excuses.

"I need to grow my New York base first. New York is a state of factions." He smoothed the front of his breeches. "I'm competing with upstate Democratic-Republicans and Federalists. My interests right now are in New York."

"You're not just letting Hamilton off the hook?" Incredulous, I placed a fist on my hip.

"I'll never let Hamilton off the hook for anything," he stated with conviction.

That slowed my pulse, but my resentment still bristled.

He lit a seegar and puffed. "Certain Federalists in the House could have swung the election my way." He exhaled smoke. "I know because we talked about it at length." He spat tobacco into the ashtray. "They would have voted for me if I'd gone to Washington City to face them. Some did approach me with seductive advances to give me the presidency, but I want nothing to do with a defeated party."

He walked over and flicked ashes into the fire. "The House is overwhelmingly Democratic-Republican and with Jefferson as their leader, they're inclined to stay with him. I discussed it with these Federalists, and not just over a glass of flip. Hamilton despises Jefferson politically, but he despises me more, and gave the election to his lesser enemy. Isn't democracy grand?"

"And you sit back and let Hamilton get away with this?" My voice rose with my growing ire. "But he was so kind to me when he heard Papa died. We shed tears together."

"He'll not get away with anything." His voice remained steady. "I can outfox him. He's not as clever as he thinks he is. Besides, I'm not going anywhere with Theodosia's wedding coming up."

That was all he had to say. Yes, he put party loyalty above personal ambition. That's what made him the gentleman he was, in that den of mercenaries. But in the end, he'd given up the presidency for his daughter.

I admired his devotion as a father but... why put this wedding before the presidency? I didn't dare question him. Theodosia came first, before me, before the presidency, before his career, before his own life. "You'll have another chance." I believed it. "It's not up to Hamilton. It's up to you."

"Of course," he declared with lawyerly self-assurance. "But for now, I'll serve as Jefferson's vice president and let him have his day. It will pay off in spades, believe me. I know what I'm doing."

"You don't want to go down there and join in the debates?"

He looked me in the eye. "No, and let's hear no more about it, shall we?"

I wouldn't call it an argument, but he curtly called it a night. What I didn't plan for was his departure for the capital without a goodbye.

I stayed out of his way. After all, he had the second most important position in our nation – a heartbeat from the presidency. He did not need me badgering him. My pride prevented me from doing so anyway.

But I had a surprise visitor at my doorstep. While dressing, I heard a knock at the front door.

The knocking persisted but my servant still didn't open the door. As I headed downstairs, the insistent raps grew louder. "Alright, alright, hold your bloomin' horses!" I unlatched the door, pulled it open, and stood face to face with Stephen Jumel.

CHAPTER 30

"Jumpin' Jehoshaphat, Jumel, it's been a long time!" I stood back for him to enter, and he gave me a shaky smile. "All right, out with it, Stephen. Then you may have a brandy."

"Oh, Eliza, *mon Dieu*, I wanted to call on you for so long, but one thing after another got in the way."

Too early for me to imbibe, I poured him a brandy.

Streaming sunlight caught his abundant mass of hair, casting a glow about his shoulders. His black jacket matched his breeches and boots. He still cut an elegant figure, yet the raiment darkened his eyes, turned his complexion sallow, and cast a somber mood over his being. I almost asked him if he was in mourning, but he spoke first.

"Martha left me and took our son. I miss you terribly and would ask that you move back into the house with me."

I halted, my hand halfway to handing him his glass. He reached out and took it.

"What happened?" But I bloody well knew. "You wouldn't marry her, and didn't knock yourself out to convince her, I assume."

He drained half his brandy before I finished speaking. "She did not want to marry me. And just as well. I've more on my mind than getting embroiled in that. She wanted to own me, my businesses, the house, the silver, the furnishings, the rugs, the clavichord or whatever the hell it's called... and she wanted it all neatly spelled out in a document, final and legal. But not in a marriage certificate. Why hand over to her all I've worked so hard for? Truth be told, I don't even like her!"

I sat on the settee and gestured next to me.

He sank down, leaned back, and crossed left ankle over right leg. "She wanted to control my assets. I showed her the door and bolted it after her and told her not to let it hit her in the bum on her way out."

I tried not to smile. The situation wasn't amusing, only the way he said it. "Where did she go?"

"Back to the peat bogs of Ireland. I gave a tidy sum to provide for the baby, and she promised to bring him back when he's old enough to hold a conversation."

I took the glass from his hand, put it on the table, and brought his head down to rest on my shoulder. "We can spend time together and invest in more real estate, but I'd rather not cohabitate."

"Eliza, I know damn well you miss your vice president like hell and spend every night apart from him in a cold bed – not that I'm hinting to be your bed-warmer – that is not what I ask. I just reckon why have two cold empty houses when we can have one warm one?"

"Now that Aaron is widowed, I hope to marry him – soon."

"So he proposed," Stephen stated, rather than asked.

"Well, no, not...not yet." I wasn't about to blab that I'd proposed to him and he'd turned me down. "I love you in a special way, Stephen. There will always be a place in my heart for you. But it wouldn't be right to live together at this point."

He straightened and cupped my chin in his hand. "I didn't realize you were planning on marrying him—soon. But I respect your wishes."

"I don't suppose you changed your mind about Mount Morris," I said. "It's not on the market, but the owner will sell if I make a good enough offer. Everybody's got his price."

"Not that ramshackle pleasure palace in Haarlem again," he scoffed. "You still harping on that old hovel, and willing to pay top dollar? Where's your business sense, Eliza? Would Astor overpay for a piece of property?"

"'Tis anything but a hovel. I am connected to that house. It was my father's headquarters. A sitting gold mine. I'm going to own that house. With or without your help." My vow hung in the air.

He threw his hands up. "*Sacré bleu!* Very well, make an offer. If it means that much to you."

I sat up and clapped. "Splendid! Let's celebrate. Dinner at Sweeney's Porter House is on me!"

But the owners wouldn't sell, at any price. Bugger them. I'd wait. I bought a few acres nearby instead. I planned to build livery stables on them, breed horses, and rent them out. Perhaps a carriage or two. Nothing fancy, for I was designing my own carriage – the grandest in New York City. I already had it sketched on paper and pinned to my wall – next to my sketch of Mount Morris – both in perfect proportion. "I will live and die in that house," I promised myself, "as Mrs. Burr."

When I arrived home from collecting rents the next day, I found a polished trunk in my foyer. Crafted of dark hardwood, it featured gold hinges and a gold latch. I knelt before it. It was unlocked. I wiggled the latch open and lifted the lid.

It contained a pile of books with a sealed letter atop them. *"Mount Vernon"* in a lacy scrawl looked vaguely familiar. Of course. Lady Washington. My heart took a dive. I broke the seal and read the letter. According to Papa's will, he bequeathed me these books and his favorite signet ring with the Washington coat of arms. Signet ring? I dug past the books and found a small box. I flipped it open. My eyes popped. Inside nestled a gold ring displaying three stars and two stripes. I held it to the light to look for an inscription. The engraving said *"Eliza Washington."* Sometime over the years, he received at least one of my letters and had this ring engraved for me to have upon his death. He'd known I was his daughter but couldn't proclaim it. My vision blurred with tears.

I lifted out the books – books we talked about during my visit: *Gulliver's Travels* and *A Modest Proposal* by Swift; the romantic novel *Julie ou la nouvelle Héloïse* by Rousseau because he knew I liked romantic novels; all six volumes of *The History of the Decline and Fall of the Roman Empire*; some books on European history, art, and geography. I would cherish these for the rest of my life.

I planned to display them in the front parlor of Mount Morris when it became mine. Meanwhile, I spent day and night poring through them, lost in my own world, his ring gleaming on my thumb.

Next morning, a cart halted at my door. It contained several crates, *"Mount Vernon"* stamped on the sides. I pried one open with a knife and gazed upon the silver tea service I'd admired on my visit, matching cups and plates, and service for twelve. I opened a long thin crate to reveal an exquisite oil painting of Papa in military regalia. The portrait stood nearly as tall as me. I knelt before it, eye to eye with his image. "I love you, Papa." I kissed his face and grieved some more.

In the 1804 election, Jefferson stabbed Aaron in the back with a mutton dagger, and that's putting it mildly. He dropped Aaron as his vice president, with a fraudulent claim that Aaron 'stole' the 1800 election from him.

I fumed. "That vindictive lying old scoundrel! Oh, how I want him drummed out of the Executive Mansion! If only women could vote..."

Spiteful, malicious Thomas Jefferson all but froze Aaron out of his administration. Jefferson hated sharing victory with anyone. But it didn't faze Aaron a whit. He had the skin of a reptile.

Not missing a beat, he collected covert backing from Federalist 'Burrites'. But again, Hamilton stood in his way and unleashed a slew of attacks in the papers. He called Aaron 'a dangerous man, one who ought not be trusted with the reins of government', and compared him to the Roman dictator Catiline.

"Now he's gone too far," I declared.

Aaron brushed off those hateful remarks like a pesky housefly. Almost nightly, he read me Hamilton's scathing assaults, snickered with a devilish gleam in his eye, and tossed the newspaper aside.

"Does this not infuriate you one half of how much it boils my blood?" I nearly shrieked, shaking the newspaper at him.

"Not one bit." He shook his head, a wry smile playing upon his lips. "Let him slander me, let him spew forth his venom.

The more, the better. His rantings about me will be his undoing. Trust me on that," he assured me in his calm, even tone.

"I'll put this in the privy." I folded the *Gazette*. "We're low on paper."

"Don't bother," he answered. "It's not even fit for that."

I didn't see much of him these days. He stayed busy journeying to South Carolina to see Theodosia and his baby grandson Aaron. He adored the little boy and nicknamed him Gampy. Oh, he never stopped boasting about Gampy! "You'd think he was the only man in the world to have a grandson," Dolley Madison remarked. I shared Aaron's happiness over his little family, yet I envied him. Even when he invited me to gatherings with his children, I blended in but didn't feel I belonged. If only ... if we married, I'd be their stepmama, and that would change everything. Until then, I was a mere visitor, my own family still in faraway Providence. Aunt Free wrote weekly, and I wrote to her and George, telling him how much I loved and missed him.

When Aaron left town, I studied with tutors, collected rents, and bid on properties with Stephen, but at night in my cold empty bed, I longed for life as Mrs. Burr.

Aaron finally came home to me one evening as I sat writing to him. The door knocker banged. Not expecting anyone, I ignored it, but it could be a renter or a sick neighbor. I opened the door and screamed as if I saw a ghost. "Oh, my love!" I fell into his arms.

"I'm here, knackered, but here," he said as I dragged him inside, and he was knackered, all right. We spent the night reclining – but naught else – on my settee, arms entwined.

Next morn, he returned to his own dwelling to entertain his

coterie of statesmen and New York cronies, Hamilton among them. He invited no wives or females of other persuasion. I waited at my own empty house, spirits soaring as I sprinkled *Jacinthe Fleurs* over clean sheets. I lingered at my toilette and made myself ravishing.

But he never came back. At midnight, my coach brought me to his house. I knew his party must be over, but I couldn't bear to spend the night alone.

His servant admitted me into his study. He sat at his desk, scratching out a letter, deep in concentration, specs perched on his nose, brow furrowed. I didn't dare interrupt.

He put the pen down, flexed his fingers, and looked up. "Oh, Eliza, I didn't hear you come in. What time is it?" He pulled off his specs.

"After midnight. Who are you writing to?"

"Hamilton." He spat out the name as if it tasted sour and blotted the page.

I approached him. "What about? He was just here, was he not?"

"Yes, he was. I am giving him one warning—just one. And he should consider that generous." He pushed back the chair, stood, approached, and enclosed me in a welcoming embrace. But as I held him, I sensed tension.

I didn't ask what he meant by that vague remark. They likely argued over how Republicans are taking the nation to the dogs, or what the Federalists want to add to the Constitution. "I'm all politicked out for the time being." I grasped his hand and pulled him from his chair. "Finish your letter tomorrow. I'll take your mind off Hamilton." I lured him up to his bedroom, but he fell asleep before I slid off my shoes.

∾

Aaron went back to the capital without telling me his latest conflict with Hamilton. Oh, if only he'd shared what vexed him about his political nemesis. I could have calmed him. He would have ripped up his letter. I would have changed the course of history. And I would have saved two lives.

CHAPTER 31

THIS ENTIRE TOWN, from market to coffee house, devoured gossip – who stepped out on his wife, who missed church, who cheated customers—everyone knew everyone else's business. I clamped my lips shut and didn't contribute any more trivial chatter.

But I could not ignore this. Within a week, it made the *Albany Register.*

On page two was a reprint of a letter from an Albany physician Charles Cooper to Hamilton's father-in-law Philip Schuyler. He claimed that whilst at a dinner party, he heard 'a still more despicable opinion which General Hamilton has expressed of Mr. Burr.'

What was so despicable? I wondered.

Bypassing tavern chatter and fishwives' finger-pointing, I went straight to my own intimate source. I took my carriage through the empty streets that evening, knowing I'd find Aaron home. He answered the door himself, barefoot and in rolled-up shirtsleeves, chomping on a chicken leg.

"A bit late for nibbling, is it not?" I opened my satchel and pulled out a brandy bottle.

"A bit late for a visit, is it not?" He turned and held out his hand for me to enter. "But I'll take the brandy. And if you offer anything else, I'm limp and will stay that way. I rose with the sun."

"We'll see about that. But first, Aaron, once and for all, I need to know what's going on with you and Hamilton. It scares me. I read some unnerving articles in the papers and this time I fear it's no idle gossip. It's coming to a head. You'd be wise not to be so blasé about it any more." We sat in his front parlor. As I poured our brandies, he set his chicken leg on a plate and wiped his hands on a napkin.

"I had every reason to be blasé. I made sure to give himself enough rope to hang himself with—from the highest bough." He sipped his brandy. "He received my warning and did not heed it. He just did not know when to stop. He will know shortly."

I released an impatient breath. "Stop being so coy and aloof. It vexes me so, I want to shake you." I tried to keep my voice down. "That letter in the Albany paper – what more despicable opinion Hamilton expressed of you at a dinner party did Schuyler refer to? It sounds ill-omened. And from everything else I heard, I'm afraid this will eventually lead to your challenging him on the field of honor."

His eyes darted around and he blinked a few times.

I went on, "I can't think of anything else. I'm ... I'm frightened, Aaron. Please talk to me. Don't shut me out." I couldn't keep the pleading from my voice.

He rested his head against the back of the settee and closed his eyes. "Well, you asked for it. It's not eventually. It's Wednesday. I challenged Hamilton and we're meeting on the field in Weehawken at dawn."

I blanched in shock. "Why so soon? God almighty, why?"

"The 'despicable opinion'—accusation—is more disgusting than despicable. He'd insulted me time and time again. I waited patiently, for he was causing his own impending doom. But this time he implied that I engage in incestuous relations with my daughter," he stated, his voice flat and weary, eyes still shut. "That was the last—" Then he swore and I'd never heard him say that word before, "—straw. The time for the inevitable duel has come. I've had it up to here." He drew his finger across his throat.

I sprang to my feet. "How dare he! He's the despicable one, the cur! But, Aaron, must you duel?"

"You cannot seriously blame me for calling him out at this point. I tolerated his vitriolic venom, he ruined the election for me, he accused me of horrific behavior with my daughter, and now he's pushed me to the breaking point. He'll have to meet my challenge."

My heart twisted into knots. I nearly choked. "No, please don't do this. One of you will get killed, I know it. Please—" I rushed to him and embraced him. "You want to be president some day – think what this will do to your reputation and your future." A terrifying image flashed before me – Aaron lying dead on that field, blood gushing from a gunshot wound ... I shuddered. Hairs stood on the back of my neck. "Aaron, please, I beg you, don't go through with this!"

"It is all but over, Eliza." His voice rattled my ears as he gave me a piercing stare. "I've sent him the formal challenge. He accepted. William Van Ness is my second."

Terror rent my heart into shards, for I knew I couldn't stop him. "I'm going to lose you, I know it." I sobbed.

He rolled his eyes. "Have some confidence in my aim of a

pistol, for God's sake." I couldn't utter another word. I brought his lips to mine, we stumbled into bed, made impassioned love, and my sighs of pleasure became sobs of fear. He wiped away my tears.

We parted the next morning, but I couldn't bear to let him go. "This cannot be goodbye." I clung to him, my arms clasped around his waist.

"I must do what I must," he near-whispered. "I will be the one walking away from this."

"I'll never understand gentlemen pointing guns at each other," I insisted.

"He dueled before and had his jacket button shot off. All gentlemen duel," I kept muttering to myself on the bumpy ride. Reaching home, I staggered up the steps and collapsed on my bed, frantic at the possibility of Wednesday's newspaper reporting tragic news.

Oh, if only they could have a simple urinating contest. But honorable gentlemen met on a field and shot at each other.

Wednesday, July 11, 1804, a day I'll never forget, I rose early from fitful sleep. Two of my cooks huddled in the kitchen, murmuring instead of cooking. They held the newspaper wide open.

When I walked in, they froze as if turned to stone, and held the paper out to me.

"What is it?" Seeing the paper, I trembled. My mouth dried up. "Oh, no ..." I hid my eyes with my hands, I couldn't bear to look.

"M-Miss Eliza ..." Mary stammered. "Vice President Burr shot General Hamilton in a duel."

Too weak to stand, I grabbed a chair and sank into it. "He ...

shot Hamilton?" My head spun, dizzy with relief. But I still didn't know about Aaron. "Is he all right? The vice president?"

"It doesn't say, ma'am. It just says General Hamilton was mortally wounded."

Without another word, I ran down the hall, threw open the front door, not closing it behind me, and raced to Gold Street in the gathering morning heat. Humidity soaked my clothes. I mopped sweat from my face.

I banged on his door. No answer. "Aaron, please open the door, we need to talk!" I banged again. Echoes answered me. I stepped back and squinted into the sunlight, shading my eyes to see the upper windows. Nothing stirred. The house was shut tight. He'd fled. But where? When would I see my beloved again?

Hamilton died the next day, and the city fell to its knees in mourning. It was even more pronounced than when Papa passed – because Hamilton was one of New York's own.

Public grief over Hamilton paled beside the anger at Aaron. As I approached Trinity Church for the funeral, Gouverneur Morris greeted me. "I'm to deliver the eulogy. But indignation mounts to a frenzy already," he cautioned me, eyeing the mob.

The tolling church bells and muffled drumbeats echoed through the sweltering city air. I thought of every place Aaron could be. I knew he hadn't meant for this to happen. It was a tragic twist of fate. I also knew Aaron's political career was over. He'd never be president.

"Oh, Aaron," I wailed, "Where are you, my love?"

But his prediction had come true. He was the one who walked away.

I heard nothing from him as each empty day slipped away. Desperate, I wrote to his daughter Theodosia but received no reply. I contacted his friends, but no one knew his whereabouts.

I saw Mrs. Hamilton on the Broad Way, head to toe in widow's weeds. I wanted to approach her and offer my condolences, but she knew I was intimate with the vice president, so I kept my distance. Their country home, The Grange, was not far from the Mount Morris mansion I planned to buy. We'd be neighbors someday.

Hamilton was laid to rest in Trinity churchyard. I didn't attend the burial, but at dusk, I went alone and stood at his grave. Head bowed, I whispered, "I know you are in a better place, General. May your soul be at peace. I'm so sorry I could not stop the duel. But, oh, how I tried. Please forgive me." I blessed myself with the sign of the cross and turned from the fresh mound of dirt.

Craving human contact, I walked to Stephen's house. He staggered in surprise. "I couldn't wish for anything better."

But he quieted when I tearfully relived my last few days. "It's heartbreaking, Stephen. I grieve for both of them – our martyred treasury secretary and our disgraced vice president."

"Yes, what a tragedy to befall the young nation." He led me into the parlor and poured me a cordial. We settled into our usual seats, as if I'd come home from a day's work and this evening were like any other.

"I wish I could have prevented it." I barely tasted the spicy cinnamon sweetening my tongue. I cast my eyes to the floorboards and clasped my fingers around the glass.

"How? Was it about you? If it was, I care not to hear about

it." He crossed his ankle over his other knee and lit a seegar, blowing the smoke away from me.

"No, not me. But I went to Aaron two nights before. He told me they would duel Wednesday morning. I begged him to call it off, but he wouldn't budge." Tears blurred my vision, rendering Stephen a runny watercolor portrait. "The only consolation I have is that he won the duel."

"He won?" Stephen's tone dripped with cynicism. "He fled the city and the vice presidency and is God knows where. His career is ruined."

I wiped my tears and glared at him. "He hasn't fled, Stephen. He's no coward. He will come back. He's probably with his daughter." I defended him now and would defend him to the death.

"Only time will tell," came his dismissive answer. I detected an undertone of 'let us change this tedious subject.'

He wasted no time changing it. "Our house in Varick Street still hasn't attracted a buyer. Should we lower the price?"

"I cannot think about wheeling and dealing right now." I finished the drink with one more gulp and eyed the decanter, glad it was near full. I needed more.

"Look, Eliza, I know you won't calm down till you hear from him. But take your mind off it. As you said, he will come back," he assured me. "He needs to cool his heels and rein in his spur if you ask me."

I looked away. "I'll get no comfort from you this evening." I placed the glass down with a clink in the center of his chessboard, gathered my skirts, and stood.

"Sit down." He sprang up and sat on the settee, pulling me down to him with his powerful grasp. "You'll not spend tonight alone, nor any other. Fetch your things and move in here with me. I will not take no for an answer." His tone was gentle yet strong.

"Then my answer is yes. I hope I can repay you for all you do for me."

"Coming here to stay is more than enough. I've missed you more than you'll ever know," he spoke the most sentimental words he'd ever said to me. I'd finally chipped away that gruff exterior and found the soft heart inside.

Together we went to my house. I packed my ledgers, books, raiment, and cosmetics. But not my *Jacinthe Fleurs* perfume. I wore that only for Aaron and had no desire to seduce Stephen. Intending to stay cleansed, I packed my lavender bath salts.

Another month and no word from him. I flung the mail on the desk with a huff of frustration and unfolded the newspaper on the dining table. I scoured each page searching for his name. Not a word about him in the papers either. He seemed to have disappeared off the face of the earth. "Do we no longer have a vice president? Aaron, my love, please tell me where you are!" I raised my eyes to the heavens and begged. My throat rumbled in an exasperated growl.

Each morning I started my routine by going to my townhouse and tearing through my post. Then I scoured each newspaper looking for his name. I couldn't eat a bite or drink a sip before this ritual.

I finally saw his name in print and nearly fainted. The news terrified me. Grand juries in New York and New Jersey indicted Aaron for murder.

"Murder?" My voice broke. I trembled in shock as the papers slid from my hands and scattered on the floor. "Since when is killing someone in a duel on a field of honor murder? If he'd snuck into Hamilton's house in the dead of night and strangled him in his bed, that would be murder. But not this!"

Too shaken to sit, I circled the room, standing by the window to catch a breeze, but it only carried heat and the rotten stench of trash and sewage. I unbuttoned my blouse and wiped my handkerchief over my chest. I sweated profusely – and not from the heat: I feared for Aaron's life.

Stephen picked up the newspaper and folded it. "He knows he must continue to serve as vice president. He can't let his murdering Hamilton keep him from that." His voice carried a tone of sarcasm that spiked my ire.

I yelled, "He did *not* murder him, *durement tête*! Perhaps, someday you'll be a gentleman and understand what the field of honor is about!" I couldn't un-say those words but spoke out of exasperation. "I'm sorry, I didn't mean it. I'm not thinking clearly ..."

"I know," he replied, calm now. "Neither is Burr, by the look of things."

CHAPTER 32

WEEKS STRETCHED INTO MONTHS, and I hibernated at Stephen's mansion, my mind on studies and business. Every time I rifled through my post and found nothing from Aaron, my heart fell.

I forced myself to read the obituaries every day, drunk with relief when I didn't see his name.

When I read that the New Jersey Supreme Court quashed the indictment against him, I breathed easy for the first time in months. It gave me some hope that he'd come home. But he didn't. Not until November did I read in the papers that he resumed his duties as vice president and was presiding over the impeachment trial of Justice Samuel Chase.

Disappointment pelted me like a hailstorm. Back for days if not weeks and he never contacted me. But I thanked God he was alive and safe as warm tingly comfort overcame my despair.

Justice Chase was acquitted on March 1. Aaron's term as vice president ended three days later. I finally received a letter from him. Holding my breath, I tore it open. As I guessed, he went to his daughter in South Carolina after the duel. He then wandered the South before heading back to finish his term. He told me of his last speech to the Senate as vice president. In his unassuming manner, he stated simply, *"The speech was unprepared. I neither shed tears nor assumed tenderness, but tears did flow in abundance."*

I rushed to the desk, pen scratching paper fast as my hand could write: *"I miss you so much ... when will I hold you in my arms again?"* On and on.

In the evening paper, I read his last speech as vice president:

"I favored no party, no cause, no friend, but had striven to be absolutely impartial. I'd done my best as vice president but knew my mistakes, and for these I pray your forgiveness. As I bid you goodbye, perhaps forever, I am leaving with high personal respect for each member, and the thought that we will continue to work for the cause of freedom and a better social order."

I read it out loud, hearing his voice in every word. It was so eloquent, so honest, so Aaron. I kissed his name. The article ended with a statement by our New York Senator Samuel Mitchill: *"When Mr. Burr had concluded, he descended from the chair, and in a dignified manner walked to the door, which resounded with some force when he shut it after him. On this the resolution of many senators gave way, and they burst into tears. There was a solemn and silent weeping for perhaps five minutes."*

I then read that one senator had wept profusely and laid his head on his desk unable to recover from his emotion for more than a quarter of an hour.

Aaron had known with this soul-bearing speech that he would never again hold public office. And he'd made grown men cry.

Oh, how my arms ached to hold him.

My sister Polly died, and I adopted her daughter Mary, a budding beauty at fourteen. She needed education and refinement. I hired Mr. Martel, who tutored Theodosia Burr. I sat in on their history, Latin, and mathematics classes and re-learned what I'd forgotten. I then sent Mary to the school once attended by Washington Irving. As Aaron did, I believed women had souls and the right to a quality education.

Aaron's next letter came from Ohio. He used an assumed name, R. King.

Financed by his son-in-law Joseph, he bought the rights to the Bastrop Grant – a half-million acres of uncharted Texas frontier. He planned to create a new state, settle it with pioneer men, attract a slew of settlers, and make himself governor.

"Since war with Spain is imminent," he wrote, *"I will lead an army into Texas and on to Mexico, and liberate Mexico from Spain."*

Great balls of fire! I nearly fell off my chair. Was this the same altruistic self-sacrificer who gave up his only chance at the presidency?

I wrote back: *"I hope you succeed. Afterwards, please come home to me. Please,"* I pleaded, with no pride or shame, *"I am so in love with you and want you back with me where you belong."*

My jaw dropped when, not a week later, another letter arrived, now from Natchez, Mississippi. *"I've assembled 100 adventurers, including women and children, and personally led them down the riverways south."*

Why not ask me to join him? Or at least why not ask me for financial backing? Once again, that stark feeling of abandonment came over me, but it didn't kick me to the ground. Perhaps I'd grown old enough to handle it.

Aaron knew I was conquering my own world in New York. But I would rush to his side if he asked me to join him on this bold expedition.

I had little time to dwell on it, for he sent me a hurried missive saying he abandoned the entire plan. Why? He didn't say. But the newspaper told me days later. President Jefferson filed a formal charge of treason against Aaron. He was summoned to Richmond for trial.

Once again, he cast me aside. Crushing emotions of my girlhood revisited me ...how I mourned all the men I loved after they rejected me, deserted me, died on me ...

I longed to be with him, no matter where his zealous schemes took him.

Every morning I tore through the post for a letter and foraged through the papers for word of him. I wrote him a pile of letters, but not knowing where to send them, stashed them away.

On this raw and chilly spring Thursday, I sat in the dining room of the City Hotel with a banker, negotiating the price of a townhouse on East Tenth Street. Without warning, some inner voice bid me look up – and there at the entrance stood Aaron. I gasped. My breath caught. My heart slammed.

His sharp eyes searched the room. I sprang to my feet and knocked the chair over. "I must leave, sir."

The banker grasped my elbow. "But, Miss Capet, we're in the middle of—"

"Here. Take this as a deposit. We'll close the deal later." I stuffed some money into his hand and tore across the room into Aaron's arms.

I pulled back and searched his eyes. How I hungered to lavish kisses all over him. It pained me to restrain myself. "When did you get back?"

"Late last night," he said. "Your housekeeper told me you were staying at Jumel's, and when I went there, another housekeeper told me you were here."

I led him outside and turned to face him. "We'll go back to my house – where is your carriage?"

"I have no carriage, Eliza. In fact, I've not much of anything."

But his dress was hardly shabby. His chocolate brown trousers and jacket must have been part of the new wardrobe he'd written me about from Richmond.

"We'll use mine." My third coach, which I bought out of boredom, sported white wheels and a black varnished body with my initials in gold on the sides.

"What sturdy horses." Aaron admired the matched bays, running his hand over their manes. "And silver harnesses?" He looked at me and nodded, clearly impressed.

"I named the bays Cain and Abel. They're brothers." I directed the coachman to bring us to my house, my adoring gaze on the man who still sent shivers through me. His hair had thinned on top and grayed at the temples. His eyes shone as brilliantly as before, now with lines at the corners. Creases lined his forehead.

"It appears you're prosperous and living your dream." He helped me in and I settled into the blue Moroccan leather seat.

"I'm getting there. Not at the top yet, but getting closer all the time." I snuggled up to him. "I adopted my niece, I keep busy – but I've missed you so. Stephen invited me to move in again after your duel knowing how lonely we both were. And he was right. I have a drawer full of letters to you," I rambled. "I knew in my heart you'd come home to me. That's what got me out of bed every morning."

"I'm not exactly coming home to you – I sail for England tomorrow." He patted down his pockets and drew out a seegar. "Unfortunately, I still use an assumed name. No one else knows I'm here, except Theodosia."

"What?" Spirit crushed, I clutched his arm. "I have you back for moments and I'm losing you again?" I heaved a sob. "Please stay. You're much better off here, I'll take care of you ..."

The pleading and beseeching went on as we entered my house and settled on the settee. I wasted not a moment more. "Aaron, marry me, please, we've spent enough time apart. We will be so happy. I've enough money for us to live comfortably ..."

He shook his head as I spoke. "I've no inclination to marry. Go back to Jumel if he assuages your loneliness and you his." He looked for something to light the seegar with.

"I'm not in love with him. I'm in love with you, always have been and always will be." Not wanting to provide a light so he could smoke, I leaned forward and embraced him.

"I'm too dispirited after the trials, I need time to recover from that – from everything. I sought you out to ask a small loan of just five hundred dollars, till I get on my feet."

I released him and heaved an exasperated sigh. "I'll give you the money, never mind a loan. Just stay with me. Don't leave again, please. What in England is so important anyway?"

"I hope to find European sponsors for my plan to march into Vera Cruz and free Mexico." He slid the seegar back into his pocket.

"You're still hell-bent on that reckless death-defying misadventure?" I shook my head in disbelief. "Did you not learn your lesson yet?" Anger tightened my chest. "Oh, I could tie you down and shake you to your senses!"

"It is a just cause." He stood, drew himself up to his full height, and stared me down.

"Then resume your law practice," I suggested. "That's a just cause."

He shook his head – again. "'Tis too soon. Why do you not understand that?"

"Perhaps I'm too stupid for you." I sprang up and strode past him, pulled the drapes open and stared out the window.

He said nothing. Another word on the subject would be a waste of time. He was leaving me – again. Another abandonment. I prolonged the agony by enticing him to stay the night.

I attempted to seduce him again next morning, but did not succeed. "How long do you plan to stay there?" I asked as he dressed.

"I cannot see beyond the ship's bow. But I shall be back. This is my home." The slanting sun shone in his dark eyes.

"I know you will. You wouldn't dare *not* come back to me," I demanded.

"And suffer your wrath? No matter how many times I circle the earth, my travels will end back here with you." A parenthesis formed around his mouth as he smiled.

"Damned good thing the earth is round then."

Once more, he left me. I did not look back.

Next evening as sleet lashed against the windows, Stephen and I sat by his fire sharing a cordial. On impulse, I gave up my customary seat and boldly slid onto his lap. Before he could say a word, I looked into his eyes and blurted, "Stephen, will you marry me?"

He looked at me as if my brain had leaked out my ears. "You claim you're so in love with Burr. How would marriage benefit either of us?"

"Marriage is not in the cards for me and Aaron. Your life will be so much easier as my husband." I twirled his queue around my finger.

"No, perhaps your life. I'm not the one whose lover killed Alexander Hamilton. Not much that I can see is in it for me." He waved his hand as if shooing a fly and looked away, his signal that the matter was closed.

"Do you want to be a bachelor all your life?" I prodded, determined not to suffer another rejection. "You know what Mozart said, 'a bachelor is only half alive'."

"Yea, what wisdom from a married chap dead at thirty-five," he scoffed.

"I shall not leave this room till you agree to be my husband," I badgered him. "Why can't you see that benefits us both? I daresay you haven't bedded anyone since I moved in here again. You need me in bed even more than you love me, admit it."

"Oh, now you're offering yourself to me – but only if we're married. You drive a hard bargain, Eliza. No wonder you're making a fortune in real estate. When it comes to convincing a buyer, Astor has nothing on you."

"No need to wait till we're legally wed. One night in my bed will have you tripping to the altar before your breeches are buttoned back up." I stood and pulled him to his feet. Keeping a firm grip on his hand, I led him upstairs. Truth told, I'd had more resistance uncorking wine bottles.

∼

But he still wouldn't marry me. Not until I showed him some world-class acting.

CHAPTER 33

P<small>APA WAS GONE</small> and Aaron only needed me for money. But life was meaningless if I could not share it.

Hence, two days before Stephen left for Philadelphia on business, I performed my most major acting role. I needed not rehearse.

Scene One began during supper on Thursday. "I cannot eat a bite." I rubbed my head, groaning.

"What is wrong?" Stephen bit into his leg of lamb.

"I am ill, Stephen. I have a splitting headache and am weak. I must take to my bed. "*Excusez-moi.*" I placed my serviette down. Palms to my head, I trudged up the stairs. I indeed took to my bed, but only after devouring the bread, cheese, and apples I'd stowed away.

Next morning, he brought breakfast on a tray. I lay on my back, hand shielding my eyes. "How considerate of you to bring this, *mon chéri,* but I fare worse than before." I made my voice weak and whispery.

"I'll leave it here." He placed it on the nightstand. "I hope your appetite returns." He leaned over and brushed my hair from my forehead. "Do you have a fever?"

"No, just headache and weakness." I turned away. "Go on your way, do not worry about me."

"I should stay—"

"No!" I cut him off. "No," I repeated more calmly. "You go along." I tried to hide my anxiety, for now I trembled in panic. "I promise I will recover before you return."

But he sent for our physician Dr. Gray first. He probed my head and my middle and gave me a bottle of laudanum. "Take this thrice a day. But if you worsen, call on me again." He tipped his hat and bustled out.

Stephen knelt beside me and kissed my hands, my cheeks, my lips. "You may worsen. I can stay—"

"Please go, Stephen, I will recover, I've had these spells before," I assured him, and it must have convinced him, for he left me with the promise of a hasty return.

"I shan't be long, no more than a week." He showered me with kisses and exited my room.

After a long-enough wait, I sprang from bed and pulled the servant bell cord. I gave her a flat bottle. "Fill it with hot water," I instructed her. "And call Dr. Gray. Then get a stable-hand to find Monsieur Jumel on the road to Philadelphia and tell him I am breathing my last."

She stumbled backward. "Miss Capet, what—" The color drained from her face as her eyes widened in terror.

"Nothing is wrong with me. This is what I must tell Monsieur Jumel. Trust me. And now I must trust you." I pulled ten bank notes from under my pillow and pressed them into her hand. "Will this ensure your silence?"

She stared at the notes in her open palm as if I'd dropped the crown jewels into it.

"Y-yes, Miss Capet." She bobbed a curtsy and fled.

When I heard the clip-clop of the doctor's horse outside, I

plunged the thermometer into the bottle of hot water and slipped it under my tongue.

Dr. Gray slid the thermometer from my mouth and flinched at my flaming temperature. "Miss Capet, you are gravely ill. I suggest you send for your husband immediately. He needs to be at your side, for I cannot predict—"

"I understand, Doctor," I cut him off, my voice as weak as the dying. "I shall send for him."

But our stable-hand was already on his way to intercept Stephen.

When Dr. Gray departed, I leapt out of bed and patted Stephen's white hair powder over my face until I rivaled the picture of death. I climbed back into bed and, hungry as a wolf, devoured the crumpets he left me. I washed it down with ale I'd stashed.

Sunlight danced through my curtains as Stephen tiptoed up to my bed. He knelt by my side, hands clasped, head down, as if in prayer.

"Please don't cry," I whispered.

"I'll summon Father Michael." His voice quivered.

"That would be fitting. I believe my final hour is near," I rasped.

While we waited for Father Michael, Stephen held me, rocked me, and pressed his lips to my forehead. "Your fever rages."

It wouldn't rage much longer, for the water grew cold, and I couldn't summon more hot water. I hoped the priest would make haste in arriving.

I wasted not a moment. "Stephen," my voice strained, and he moved close to my lips, "before I leave this world, it would mean so much to me to become Madame Jumel. Please make me your bride."

"Of course," he agreed without hesitation. "As soon as

Father Michael enters the room, I'll have him marry us before he administers extreme unction."

"Oh, *merci*, you don't know how happy you've made me." I tried not to smile too broadly, peeking out and struggling to grasp his hand.

"Save your strength for the wedding vows." He placed my hand back on the bed.

When Father Michael arrived, Stephen propped me up on a pile of pillows, we exchanged vows, and became man and wife. My groom knelt and kissed my fevered lips for what he believed was the last time. Then the priest administered last rites.

My new husband sat by me and read me Voltaire, brought me dinner, and wiped my brow. When darkness fell, Dr. Gray paid another call. But this time when he took my temperature, his eyes crossed. "God above, 'tis a miracle. Your temperature – why, it's normal as the day is long."

My eyes met Stephen's, and we breathed a collective sigh. "I shall live! Stephen, you are the reason for my recovery. I would have perished had you not come back to me."

He pulled back, shaking his head. "No, not my doing. It was otherworldly intervention." He embraced the doctor in a grateful bear hug. "Doctor, how can I ever repay you?"

"By paying me, I suppose," came his answer.

Should I feel guilty for my devious act? No, I told myself – he needed me as much as I needed him. Two lonely souls united – and I hadn't tricked him at all. It was fate I tricked this time. Kiss my *derrière*, fate!

"I am taking you to France tomorrow for your birthday," Stephen told me as if planning a stroll through the park.

Amidst my jumps and squeals, he gave me details. "We embark on my brig, the *Eliza*, at noon and will be at sea for—"

"*Ah, très bon!*" I cut him off, twirling around the room, arms straight out like a windmill. "It is my dream to see France!" I dragged him upstairs to show my gratitude.

Later, as we lounged before the fire, he told me he'd planned this trip anyway. "Your birthday is a lucky coincidence."

His reason? "I had a rather tart falling-out with my business partner that nearly came to physical blows."

"What happened?" I sat up.

"He's a cheat," Stephen spat, his tone flat and defeated. "And I don't suffer cheats. I've been cheated too many times before."

"I'm sorry to hear that, Stephen. The business world, unfortunately, is dreadfully corrupt. It can be tempting to swindle at times, quite frankly. But I could never cheat at business. I treat others the way I care to be treated."

He turned my face to his and looked me in the eye. "And I so respect that about you." His expression gentled and his tone grew solemn. "Enough about business. You are going to hear this whether you want to or not. I am hopelessly love with you, Eliza. I fell head over heels when you first appeared on my doorstep." He grimaced as if it pained him to confess it.

Joy fluttered through me. "You're hopelessly in love with me? Hell's bells, why did you never tell me?"

"I feared you'd flee to the other side of the world, or run off with Burr, anywhere to be away from me. An ambitious, independent woman as you hardly needs a man telling her he's hopelessly in love with her. Especially if it is not mutual."

I shook my head. "Oh, the irony. How little you know my needs. Since I was born, the love of a man was snatched away from me, starting with my very own father. I am this ambitious, independent woman because the love I crave always eludes me. But now that I have it with you, I have all I ever strived for."

He nodded in agreement. "Yes, you're devoted, loyal, content ... but not romantically, passionately, hopelessly in love." He added in the same breath, "Not with me, that is."

I knew what he meant. He knew I was in love with Aaron, I'd told him enough times. I moved closer and lay his hand on my heart, to show him it was his. "But I do love you, Stephen. That needs to suffice. And we will make this work."

"I know we will." When our eyes met and held, we connected as never before. Whatever he called it, we had it.

As if we both knew what would happen next, our arms wound around each other and his lips devoured mine. Tingles danced through me as I pictured us gliding down the Champs Elysées in a plush coach and six.

Under a warm drizzle, the *Eliza* glided into southwest France's Gironde Estuary. I leaned over the rail, breathed misty air, and through hazy fog, took my first glimpse of the most romantic nation on Earth. During the month-long voyage, I wondered whom we'd meet in France – counts and countesses? Dukes and duchesses? A dauphin at least?

Mon Dieu, was I in for a surprise. As I returned to our cabin, Stephen approached with a short, compact man. His jacket with a double row of gold buttons, fitted trousers, and leather boots told me he was *bourgeois*. A fellow merchant, perhaps? An old *ami* of his come aboard for a spot of sherry? As I continued to size him up, Stephen introduced us. "Eliza, this is His Imperial Majesty Napoleon Bonaparte."

I nearly keeled over. My eyes bugged out and my mouth fell open. "*The* Napoleon Bonaparte?" As if there was another.

I stood, dumbstruck, not knowing what in bloomin' creation I said.

Bonaparte stepped forward and plucked my hand from my side, holding it between short fingers. Tingles zinged up my arm.

"Your Imperial Majesty, my wife, Madame Jumel," Stephen presented me.

He released my hand. Still stunned out of my senses, my tongue stuck in my mouth. I wanted to drag Stephen below decks and hammer him with questions: "How in God's holy heaven did the invincible emperor Napoleon Bonaparte stumble onto our two-masted brig?"

He explained as if he read my mind. "I offered the *Eliza* as a means of escape for His Imperial Majesty."

Escape? I knew he'd just fled Elba, but was he in more trouble? And how did Stephen get embroiled? Would we abet a crime by one of history's most notorious emperors? Oh, I hoped so! The intrigue thrilled me to my tingling fingertips where Bonaparte touched them.

"Madame," Bonaparte spoke, "I have no intention of taking power again. I will command the Army ... defeat the enemy ... crush him." He clenched his fists and smacked them together. "Then I will depart. Since France disclaims me, I wish to begin a new life in the new world. My banker prepared a frigate, *LaSalle*, for my voyage. I traveled as far as Rochefort in my calèche."

He let out a bitter laugh. "But wily France and her bedfellow England ambushed me with a blockade." His eyes pleaded as he spoke. "*LaSalle's* captain vowed he'd rather sink than cease fire before I give the order. But I did not want to meet my end retreating from the British." His eyes narrowed to slits. "I could not imagine a more undignified death – hence I trust an American vessel will ensure my safe escape." He slid his hand inside the front of his jacket and stood at attention.

"Your Imperial Majesty, you're more than welcome to the *Eliza*," I repeated Stephen's invitation.

Then Stephen delivered an offer with all seriousness, "I have a wine keg you can stow away in, Your Imperial Majesty."

If I didn't know Stephen, I'd have thought he was teasing the little emperor.

Bonaparte certainly thought so, for he laughed. "Very well, Monsieur Jumel, roll it out and I shall climb in."

"Oh, I cannot roll it out." Stephen turned towards the stairs. "Come down with me and I'll help you in. It sits below decks."

The emperor stomped his foot and glared daggers at Stephen. "Monsieur, you jest. I will not suffer the indignity of stowing away!"

"I do not jest. You did ask." Stephen gave a half-hearted shrug.

In order to ease the gathering tautness between the two Frenchmen, and knowing what Napoleon Bonaparte was capable of, I interjected: "Your Imperial Majesty, you are more than welcome to stay with us in New York City."

"*Merci.*" Without another word to Stephen, he granted me a polite bow, made an about-face, and strode away, heels clicking on the deck.

"*Bienvenue à la France,*" Stephen muttered as he rolled his eyes and gazed up at his mainmast.

Two days later, we reached our rented *château* on the Rue de Rivoli. As I stood on our boudoir balcony, a canary yellow calèche emblazoned with a gilded eagle rolled up to the front door.

"Holy smokes, it's him!" Not knowing Napoleon's where-abouts, I naturally assumed he'd made peace with France. Had he come back to engage in witty banter, or at least a game of *mille bornes?* But the man who alighted wasn't the little emperor. He presented himself as General Henri Bertrand. The calèche belonged to Napoleon– well, not anymore, I learned. "It is now yours, Madame Jumel." He waved at it with a flourish. *"Alors."*

"Merci beaucoup, mon général!" I climbed inside, squealing in delight. I trailed my fingertips over the velvet seats, slid out the opposite door, and gazed upon the gilded eagle. What a sensation I'd make trundling the streets of Paris in such a conveyance of elegance!

"I must thank His Imperial Majesty!" I gushed.

But the next morning, in a hair salon having my locks curled about my feathered *chapeau,* I read in *Le Journal des Débats* that Napoleon never made it to the new world. After surrendering to the British on HMS *Northumberland,* they exiled him to a volcanic rock in the South Atlantic called Saint Helena. But his captors did allow him some indulgences, to the tune of 40 kilos of meat, seventeen bottles of wine, and nine chickens per day.

Will I ever see Napoleon again? I wondered. I wrote a letter, thanking him for the calèche and repeating my invita-tion: *"... and offer Your Imperial Majesty much more than wine and chickens."*

Stephen's business connections afforded us introduction to the upper echelons of Paris society. I promenaded with the

Duchess de Berry, the Duchess de Charost, and Countess Marcelle de la Pagerie, a relative of Empress Josephine. With my niece Mary away at school and Stephen on his business ventures, I wandered the empty *château*, longing for company. Desperate, I invited Marcelle to move in. Being connected to Napoleon, she held several artifacts of his, which I bought from her: a silver tea service; chairs upholstered in rose silk that matched my dining room; Napoleon's bed; a gold clock that I had engraved with his and my names; and most magnificent of all, Josephine's tiara, necklaces, bracelets, and ear bobs, all encrusted with diamonds set in gold and filigree. I also took possession of several bottles of the perfume Napoleon had especially made for Josephine and named after her.

Later that day, on my knees in Notre Dame Cathedral, I spoke to my father. "Oh, Papa, if only you lived to see this ... I'd invite you to visit me here." My words echoed through the cathedral's depths and faded. I enfolded that powerful spirit within my own, that unflinching Washington spirit I carried like a banner.

I returned to the *château* and wrote to King Louis, requesting formal acceptance at court. I hired a scribe for the occasion and dictated it as a manicurist buffed my nails.

"Sire, each time I have the honor of seeing Your Majesty, the graciousness with which you have deigned to notice my carriage and the great kindness with which you bow to me, make me feel like writing to you. But once out of Your presence, courage fails me."

(So I was prone to trite exaggeration.)

I gave him Stephen's abbreviated background, to ingratiate him into French royalty: *"... he is so patriotic, he's unwilling to have commercial relations anywhere except with France ... he was the first to introduce* la Soirée *at wholesale in the United States..."*

I hoped King Louis wouldn't drown in my bathos ...

"*... we came to Paris and he was moved by his kindness of heart to set up several manufacturers who today prosper. His lofty nature does not allow him to ask for a place at Court himself. Knowing Your Majesty's extreme kindness, I hope you will not ignore a subject so worthy as Stephen Jumel. Your Majesty will find in Stephen a faithful subject and in his wife, eternal gratitude.*"

I posted it before Stephen came back. But I told him about the letter – my version of it, anyway. He was not amused, especially at the king's finding about my tarnished – in name only – yellow calèche.

"You are *abruti dans la tête!*" He made a circle with his fingers around an invisible throat – mine. "If he gets wind of that carriage's provenance, you'll not be invited to scour the court privy!"

I tossed my head. "I should have known better than to beg your acceptance to the royal court. You are every bit a *paysan* at heart, monsieur. Go eat cake." I twirled around in a whorl of silk skirts and stormed out to my calèche. "Take me through the streets until the horses drop," I ordered the driver. But I did not get far. An angry mob on the Voie Georges Pompidou, espying the grand eagle, blocked the carriage and would not let me pass. Two gendarmes held back the rabble, but two more arrested me.

I spent two nights in a dark musty cell ignoring the glares and obscene French remarks of my cellmates – three frowzy prostitutes. To their rude questions, I replied, "No parlee Fransaze," in my worst Yankee accent.

On the third morning, Stephen bailed me out. But he would not speak to me.

I spoke to him. "I am going home." He relented long

enough to take me to Bordeaux. I boarded the *Eliza*, without him, without Mary. Only my Bonaparte treasures kept me company.

CHAPTER 34

Majestic Mount Morris finally came up for sale, and I tore up the road to Haarlem to make the first offer.

After rapid negotiating with its owner, Leonard Parkinson, I made my final offer. I left not a shilling on the table. For ten thousand dollars, Mount Morris was mine. Stephen deeded it to me, 'in consideration of the love and affection he bore her, for and during her natural life.'

As my signature dried on the deed, I declared, "It is now the Morris-Jumel Mansion, as promised." I went out and gazed at its elegant façade. "Oh, Papa, I hope you're proud." I vowed to make this the most beautiful home in all of New York City.

I bought the adjacent thirty-nine acres for farming and building a wharf. I hired Ezra Weeks to make renovations. The house became my toy. I sent to Paris for exact reproductions of the original flowered wallpaper. Ezra replaced siding, shutters, painted the exterior white, and I furnished its thirteen rooms in the elegant French Empire style. I added finishing touches: Napoleon Bonaparte's bed went into my room, and his gold clock sat atop the parlor mantel. His chairs graced my dining room table. Stephen enjoyed his new role as country squire while I held lavish soirées.

I had everything – almost. I was in love, but not with my husband.

Aaron's letters made his absence bearable. No two came from the same place. He wrote from Tennessee, Ohio, Louisiana – his adventures boggled my mind. Nearly every day, I wrote him an entreaty to "*come back home where you belong ... to people who love and adore you.*" I listed every reason, from his children to financial stability to a longer life.

None budged him. Not even the death of his beloved grandson at the pitiful age of ten. But he came home anyway – for a short while.

His latest letter arrived on a cold spring morning. I instructed the servants to place his letters atop the others when the post arrived. I tore it open. When I saw the return address "*23 Nassau Street,*" my heart tripped.

"You're home, Aaron, you're home." I embraced his words, feeling as close to him as if his arms encircled me.

"*I settled in Tuesday last and hung out a shingle. I'm resuming my law practice and eagerly await your response – do I travel there, or you to here? Yours, I am, AB*"

I ran to the carriage house as fast as my legs could take me. Two hours and ten minutes later, his arms encircled me for real. A flood of emotion swept us up in a whirling torrent. We clung to each other in longing, sadness, hopelessness, and grief from which I never fully recovered.

With his own dealings, tending his farm and running his ships across the ocean, Stephen didn't notice my comings and goings. I had my Aaron back, and my life was complete. But something changed. That spark no longer glittered in his eyes.

One evening as we lay before the crackling fire at his Richmond Hill estate, I coaxed it out of him. "Tell me what's gone missing, Aaron."

"I feel as if my life ended the same day as Hamilton's," he admitted. "I committed suicide that day, Eliza. His bullet may as well have pierced my gut instead."

"I pleaded with you not to go through with it, but your cockiness got the best of you," I chided. "But what good is 'I told you so'? Hamilton is dead, and your life is in ruins. Neither I nor God could have stopped that." I sat up with a burst of energy and optimism. "But you can start over. Hamilton can't."

His eyes slid shut, and he lay his head in my lap. I stroked his hair and looked down upon him. "Listen to me good now. You resumed your practice and within weeks you'll bring in a huge income. You're home where you belong. You have me, you have our son, and your other children. And most of all – *most* of all ..." I raised my voice for emphasis, "...you're Aaron Burr, damn it, and don't ever forget it!"

His eyes stayed shut, but those kissable lips spread in that fearless smile that always melted me.

Yes, he was Aaron Burr, all right. As I predicted, within weeks he was commanding huge fees. He spent freely and gave money to whomever walked through his door for a handout. When he hired my nephew-in-law Nelson as his law clerk, Nelson sang his praises: "Mr. Burr can teach me more in a year than I can learn anywhere else in ten!"

At the end of 1812, I finally learned the limits of Aaron's endurance. One excruciatingly tragic event nearly stripped him of his will to live.

Hamilton's widow Elizabeth, of all people, was the one to tell me what happened. We were now neighbors, and as I passed by her estate in my carriage, she stood chatting with some folk. She waved me down and I halted the carriage.

"Mrs. Hamilton, good day." Close up, I saw her furrowed brow and deep frown. "What is it? Something wrong?"

Eyes downcast, she delivered the news: "Theodosia Burr's ship never arrived from South Carolina, and is believed shipwrecked."

I stared straight ahead, stunned with disbelief. It sounded right out of James Callender's filthy rag sheets. "Where did you hear that?"

"My son told me. I was going to call on you later. I thought you should know," she added in a softer voice. After all, she knew who I was – and who I was to Aaron. "I'm so sorry." Only a person with a forgiving heart of solid gold could say that.

I closed my eyes and lowered my head as the blood drained from my face. "Dear God. He must be devastated."

The rest of the day went by in a blur until I got to him. He saw me but stared blankly, eyes dull, dark. He looked dazed. I held out my arms, and after a moment's hesitation, he stepped into them as if afraid to let anyone else near him.

"You will survive, my love," I assured him.

We sat on his settee together, his arm draped around my shoulders. "Any chance you can come to Europe with me?" It seemed out of the blue, but I knew he'd planned it.

"Why are you going this time?" I asked.

"I have to go somewhere far away," was his answer, and I understood. I knew the feeling – the need to escape reality. I'd done it at a much younger age.

"I want nothing more than to be with you every minute, but Stephen's health is worsening, I've properties to run – I cannot possibly leave." I did not ask him to stay here with me this time. It was far too selfish.

So off to Europe he went. He wrote from France, Germany, Sweden, Denmark. Royalty wined and dined him, authors and statesmen fêted him. He charmed the pantaloons off them all.

But he soon ran out of money. In heartbreaking letters, he described the unheated hovels, existing on a diet of potatoes, no money to claim his shoes from the cobblers – dire poverty. He had to sell his collection of books and gifts he'd bought for Theodosia. I sent five hundred dollars to his latest address in Sweden.

He returned eventually, but did not contact me for at least a month. I only found out he was home when I read his ad in the newspaper – he re-started his law firm at 30 Partition Street.

Knowing he was in the same city was good enough for me. I didn't need to rush into his arms this time. I finally made my way to him when I arranged my schedule to fit in a visit.

He looked reborn – his eyes shone with that old spark. His hair, now salt and pepper, still crowned his head. He dressed as a king. He made me feel twenty years younger – and here he was, twenty years older than me!

With Stephen away on business, I read in the papers that the great Shakespearean actor, Junius Brutus Booth, was going to perform *Richard III* at the Park Theater on October 6. Seeing Booth, the most famous actor of our time, was the next best thing to Richard III himself coming back from the dead to drag his club foot across the stage.

Aaron and I slogged through a torrential rainstorm to witness the brilliant Booth as Richard III. My ears rang for hours after the ten-minute applauding, thundering, clamoring ovation. Booth's sons Junius Jr., Edwin, and John Wilkes were gifted actors, and it was inevitable that at least one of them would become as famous as their father.

Spring finally arrived, but Stephen dressed as if the dead of winter still gripped us. He rocked before a blazing fire, wrapped in a shawl, clasping his gnarled hands, staring into the flames as if he could see eternity.

"Stephen, get out and about. It's a lovely day." I twirled my parasol as I rang for the coachman.

"I feel so old of late ..." His voice barely reached me, gravelly and defeated.

"You feel old because you act old. Visit your farmlands, plant some seeds."

That great head nodded. He stood, bones popping and cracking as he stretched his still-lean muscular frame. "Perhaps you're right. Is winter truly over with? I feel rheumy."

"It is over and done with. Just step outside." My coach now waited, and I turned to leave. "I'm off to the shops. The Astors are dining with us should you be back in time."

Confident I'd convinced him to get up and enjoy his spread of earth, I headed out, taking in a lungful of sweet spring air.

That evening, about to enter the parlor with my decorator to measure the windows for new draperies, I heard insistent pounding on the front door. My butler was not close by, so I answered it.

Two farmhands plowed past me carrying a lifeless figure. "Where can we put him, Mrs. Jumel?"

Before my lips formed "Put who?" I saw Stephen, eyes shut, head and arm wrapped in bloody bandages.

"My God, what happened?" I staggered into the wall behind me.

"He fell from his hay cart on the King's Bridge Road. Hit his head and broke his arm. Been sliding in and out of wakefulness the better part of the journey back."

"Bring him upstairs ... no, here!" I led them into the parlor and pulled the throw off the settee. "Lay him down here."

I summoned Dr. Gray, and he had Stephen moved to an upper floor room. It was warmer there. He slurred his speech and didn't recognize me at times. My name finally escaped his lips when I read him the Jane Shore play.

Dr. Gray made a splint and set Stephen's broken arm. He forced cognac between Stephen's lips, inserted a lancet in his good arm, bled him, and gave him a draught of laudanum, nitre, and other savory elixirs.

"Oh, Stephen," I beseeched him, not knowing if he could hear me. "Please recover." I stroked his brow, bent over and kissed his lips. "You have so much more to live for. I do appreciate all you've done for me. You gave me a life worth living ..." My voice wavered as I broke down in tears.

To make the tragedy more unbearable, I knew he lay here at death's door because I'd nagged him to go out. The sight of his suffering drowned me in guilt. He heaved a sigh. "I'm here for you, as you stood by my bed and married me, making me so happy." I turned away.

I sat vigil over him for two days, or was it three? I lost track of time, seeing one sunset, then two, and perhaps a sunrise. As I clasped his hand, I thanked God he had the strength to clasp back. "The doctor says you will rally," I assured him, my voice light and chirpy.

"I'd better," he rasped. "Desobru must be robbing me blind."

Yes, he is about to rally, I assured myself over and over.

But it was not meant to be. In the dead of night as I dozed on the floor by his side, a loud wail jarred me awake. I sat up as Stephen slammed his fist against the wall.

I scrambled to my feet, bent over and tried to hold him down. His savage strength overpowered me. He threw my hands off him and began to rip the bandages off his arm.

"No, stop!" We struggled until my energy drained. I collapsed on my knees.

He tore the blood-encrusted bandages from his arm and flung them aside. I clamped my fingers around his arm and tried to still him. His other arm began to bleed where Dr. Gray had inserted the lancet. I tore my skirt in strips and wound them tight around his arm, but blood soaked them within seconds. His body spasmed.

My breath heaved with the effort to hold him still. "I am here with you." I grasped his hand. He squeezed mine, then his hand fell limp.

"Eliza ..." With my name on his last breath, he slipped away. I felt for a pulse. Nothing.

He lost his fight. I couldn't save him. I let out a ragged breath, sweat-soaked hair falling from my cap into my eyes. Rage at myself for letting this happen dissolved into grief.

I closed his eyelids and whispered a prayer for his soul. "Now you're in heaven with Papa." I sat with my husband's body until the sun came up, then stumbled down the stairs. I roused the servants, babbled about Stephen, and pointed upwards. Then I collapsed from exhaustion.

When I returned home from his burial at Saint Patrick's on Mott Street, a carriage blocked the drive. Before I could step from my coach, a constable strode up and served me with a summons.

Because no witnesses were present at his death, a Grand Jury indicted me for Stephen's murder.

"Sweet Jesus." The summons fluttered to the ground. I staggered to my porch steps and collapsed. How could they be so cruel? Why on earth would I murder my husband?

I needed Aaron. He would convince a jury that I couldn't commit murder, the way he secured the innocent Levi Weeks's acquittal. But first, I stumbled up my steps and through the front door. I couldn't even make it to my bedroom. I fell onto the settee into a dead sleep.

Through God's great mercy, the case was dismissed before I could even engage Aaron for my defense.

But that did not end my torment. Loud footsteps clomped past my bedroom door in the dead of night. The house creaked and groaned. I snatched my candle and prowled over squeaking floorboards, attempting to glimpse a shadowy figure lurking in the hallway. Clutching my nightdress, I crept down the stairs, unlatched the front door, and peered into the darkness. But only the breeze rustled the leaves. Shivering, I turned and went back inside. As I latched the door, the candle's flame vanished, plunging me into darkness. I groped my way back upstairs, shaken.

A presence surrounded me, a restless spirit unable to cross to the beyond, tormented and trapped between two worlds. Believing it my departed husband, I stood in the room where he died.

"Stephen, if your spirit is here, I implore you, please go to the light and rest in peace. We will meet in the next world, I promise." Not another sound echoed through the house – until the next night, footsteps thumped outside my door. The next morning, I hired builders to tighten the joists and reinforce the beams. The haunting ceased. But looming over me, tormenting me more than any mad ghost, was the belief that I'd killed him.

Without another thought, I ran to Aaron.

CHAPTER 35

Aaron opened his arms to me. "I'm so sorry, my darling. You should have contacted me when he had the accident, I'd have been at your side."

Hugging him tight, I asked, "Oh, why couldn't we stay together all those years ago?"

"Our lives kept us apart," he answered. "Simple as that."

He walked me to his settee. We sat side by side, comfortably, like an old married couple. That familiar fire still warmed me with delicious delight. I pushed it away. I shouldn't feel like this! I was newly widowed, and demonic guilt still haunted me ... "Aaron, I need to get something off my chest."

He moved closer. "And I am here for you, Eliza."

A mess of emotions flooded me. "It was sudden and the burial swift. Stephen wasn't religious. He didn't care to be buried in consecrated ground, but I insisted." I rambled, releasing my torment, my guilt, my self-loathing. "He'd be alive today if I hadn't pestered him to go visit his farmlands. I almost physically forced him out of his chair and out the door ..." I sobbed as gradual hints of relief calmed me.

Aaron handed me his handkerchief and drew me to him as I wiped my eyes. "He wouldn't go anywhere he didn't want to, Eliza. You did not push him out at gunpoint. He had a mind of his own and he used it. You have no reason to harbor any guilt."

"He blames me, I know it." My voice quivered. "His angry spirit will not cross over, he stomps around the house, shakes the rafters, rattles the windowpanes, books fall off shelves ..."

Aaron cupped my face between his palms. "Stop that supernatural humbug. He's gone, and no spirit is haunting you, the house, or anything else. I'm surprised at you, Eliza. A sensible intelligent woman like you ..."

His harsh words strangely soothed me. "Oh, Aaron, you have such a way of uttering a phrase, you could cast a spell over the harshest critic. If only you pushed harder, you'd have been our third president ..."

"Let's not dredge that up." He waved a dismissive hand.

"I find it hard to move on from this," I went on. "All my life, I juggled dozens of balls at once. But this – how do I move on?"

"I can tell you how," he replied without missing a beat. "You no longer need to be a widow."

I looked up at him through misty eyes. His gaze bored through me. "Are you asking me ..." My heart leapt with a burst of joy. I wanted to hear it from him before I said another word.

"That is what I am asking you. Eliza, will you be my wife?" The moment couldn't have been more romantic if he'd dropped to one knee.

"Now you ask? Now? After all these years of my hinting, cajoling, outwardly proposing, making a bloody fool of myself ..."

"You never made a fool of yourself. Did you ever see me crack a smile?" he demanded.

"You didn't have to," I quipped back. "You're too well-trained. Trial lawyers don't laugh in public. Ever."

He laughed now. "Oh, you'd be surprised. Gallows humor abounds in court. It has to. But never did I think you a buffoon."

"When did I say buffoon?"

"Oh, what was the word – fool, was it?" He sat back and rested his arm along the top of the settee, his fingertips playing with my hair. "I never thought that. I simply was not ready for another marriage."

"And now you are? At this age? Now? Why now? Why not twenty years ago?" I badgered.

He rolled his eyes. "Eliza, twenty years stretch between our ages. I was always old enough to be your father."

"So what? Now you're old enough to be my grandfather."

His expression hardened, and he instantly appeared older. "I give you my hand, madam. My heart has long been yours."

Now was my turn to be coy. "I shall think about it. This is not a decision I can make in haste."

"Haste?" He glared at me. "When I am rejected, I do not return for a second entreaty."

"I know. That's why you never became president," I stated the truth.

He nodded. "Touché." He went on, "But I wasn't in the right place at the right time for that. I'm here now, however. And so are you. Now what are we waiting for? Both single and alone when we can live together in wedded bliss." He held out his hands, and I clasped them.

"I should spend the customary year in widow's weeds." I looked down at my skirts and blouse of yellow, my favorite color, as was Anne Boleyn's. She didn't make any hasty decisions to marry.

"You in widow's weeds for a year?" He clucked. "I can only hope you give me the honor of twenty-four hours. Black does not become you. Nor does widowhood. Nor does custom.

Accordingly, to that end … our wedding naturally follows this course of events."

"Give me some time to think about it," I tormented him.

"How much time do you think we have?" he prodded.

"More than you think. You don't look a day over my age," I insisted in the flattering tone of a seasoned flirter.

"Take as long as you want. As long as your answer is yes."

He knew bloody well the answer would be yes. I just wanted to take him for the same ride he took me for – and saying yes would be all the sweeter.

I didn't want to be his wife right away. I wanted him to court me. To pursue me. To revel in the chase. And enjoy the ritual of courtship we did. He called at the mansion nightly to play bid whist and chess, and I held sumptuous dinners in his honor. I hired a string quartet, and we danced to celebrate my birthday. We attended plays, luncheons, and dinners in the city. He knew I was close to accepting his proposal when I shared something most private with him: my account books.

"How romantic," he commented as we sat at my desk and pored through ledgers over claret and candlelight. "Frankly, I am astounded at how much property I've accumulated." I'd long since reached my goal to be the richest woman in New York City.

Before my open books, he slipped a gold band around my finger. "Now will you become Mrs. Colonel Attorney General Senator Vice President Burr?"

I could no longer hold off. I quivered with a surge of bliss as when I was a love-struck maiden! "Call on me Friday evening at seven, and we'll make plans. I want a simple ceremony with family present. I want to order proper raiment. I can't wed you in something I've worn before."

"I care not what you wear." He put down his reading specs and closed the books.

"Well, I do. And I want music. And flowers."

"Why do you want to play the blushing bride?" he asked.

"Because I feel like one. Just give me this chance to star in our show, as I always dreamed."

He grinned with a nod, but that twinkle in his eye told me he had something up his sleeve.

The following evening as I entertained our son George, my niece Mary, her husband Nelson, and their children William and Eliza, the knocker clanged against the front door.

"Colonel Burr to see you, madam," the butler announced a moment later. There stood Aaron with an elderly gent, both dressed in sumptuous evening attire. Aaron's burgundy coat and trousers hugged his lean form.

He gave me a valiant bow as he introduced his companion. "Eliza, this is Reverend Bogart."

"Good evening, Aaron, Reverend." Awww, he wanted to rehearse the wedding ... how sweet.

But I found out he wanted to do more than rehearse: "The good reverend has accompanied me here so that I may marry you. Now." Before I could make sense of those words, he took my hand, lifted it to his lips in a soft kiss, and pressed it to his cheek.

Still holding my hand, he dropped to one knee and nearly toppled over before regaining his balance. "Eliza, love of my life, woman of my desires, will you make me the happiest man on earth and marry me? Tonight, in this very room?"

I looked around the parlor. My family beamed at the romantic tableau before them. They nodded, goading me on. I looked back at him. His hair shone, his sharp eyes gleamed with that spark of youth.

"Get up." I drew my hand away and helped him to his feet. "Yes, I accept and would be honored to be Mrs. Burr tonight ..."

... *finally*, I added under my breath.

His smile displayed perfect white false teeth. "Let us proceed, then." He clutched the minister's arm. "Before she changes her mind."

"Your mind is more changeable than mine, dear fiancé," I quipped. "But I must don proper raiment." I turned to my niece. "Mary, please come and assist me to dress." I leapt upstairs as fast as my aging legs would take me. I donned my most splendid dress of gold brocaded satin and my gold lace fichu with tulle trimmings. I dabbed extra rouge on my cheeks, applied lip stain – and did not forget to splash *Jacinthe Fleurs* on a few special spots. Mary brushed my hair and arranged my diamond tiara on my head.

As I descended the grand staircase, my groom stood waiting at the bottom, handsome and dashing as the first day we met. Those same shivers ran down my body, and I stared just as yearningly, unable to wrench my gaze away. He smiled, pinning me with those lustrous eyes.

His nearness tripped my heart. After all these years, he still aroused me like that blushing Betsy Bowen outside Federal Hall, when we met for the first time. I knew he was my destiny then, and I knew it now.

He took my hand and led me into the parlor.

My groom and I stood side by side before the hearth. Our family gathered around as servants crowded the doorway. We faced Reverend Bogart, exchanged our vows, and I became Mrs. Aaron Burr.

Finally.

Everything I ever achieved, all I ever accomplished in life, nothing compared to this holy union with my only love, the man I waited for all these years. We kissed for the first time as husband and wife. Now I truly belonged.

CHAPTER 36

WE SPENT our wedding night fully clothed, sprawled on the settee, exhausted. We talked about everything – our son, his children, my niece and nephew, their children, our past, our future. He rested his head on my shoulder, our fingers inter-twined. I relaxed, more content than I'd been in ages. Yet regret tugged at my heart. "I wasted years longing for you instead of holding you." So I added another wedding vow: "I shall cherish every moment we have left."

As sunlight peeked through the drawn drapes, I asked him which bedroom he wanted.

He leveled a glare at me. "I cannot share a bedroom with my wife?"

"How *bourgeois*," I quipped. "But seriously, my Napoleon bed is barely a single. I'd kick you to the floor, not intentionally, of course."

"Is the bed in that red bedroom big enough for both of us?" he persisted.

I nodded. "I suppose."

"Then I'll take it and you can join me when the occasion

arises." He ran his finger along my jawline and his thumb brushed my lips.

I pushed myself up on my elbows to study him, so youthful in the weak rays of dawn. "Does your – occasion still arise?" I tried not to sound skeptical, it just came out that way.

"As long as I have a heart pumping blood, it still pumps to all the vital places, dear bride. Care for a demonstration?" He grasped my hand and placed it between his legs – oh, yes, blood still pumped.

I gave him a wicked smile. "Not till I've had my morning coffee."

For our wedding trip, our liveried coachman brought us to Connecticut to visit relatives, including his nephew John Trumbull, the famous artist. We first stopped at Hartford on the way, where I owned stock in the toll bridge.

"I saw that on your books," Aaron commented as we crossed the bridge. "I know ways you can put those dividends to much better use."

I took a breath to speak, but he proceeded in his lawyerly manner: "The Boston and Providence Railroad was incorporated three years ago almost to the day." His wizened eyes glittered. "The first section, Boston to Canton, opened but three weeks ago. The rail will reach New York. You'd enjoy being part of the expansion of your hometown," he concluded with the practiced mastery of his art.

Hearing all this, especially how it connected to New York, I relished my high hopes and coddled my new husband, tucking my hands around his arm.

That afternoon, on his advice, I sold the toll bridge stock for six thousand dollars. As the banker handed me the cash, I waved it away. "Pay it to my husband." I enjoyed being able to say that. It empowered me somehow.

But letting him pocket that six thousand became the first of many regrets.

Like clockwork, he pitched scheme after scheme, each more chancy than the last. One evening after supper, he finished his glass of vintage Heidsieck champagne and told me, "A land agent by the name of McManus and his daughter are settling German immigrants in Texas." My steward refilled his glass. "If all goes to plan, we realize a sizable return on our investment."

With those last two words, I knew – "You already plowed money into this venture, didn't you, Aaron?"

"It's a sure thing," he insisted, cracking his knuckles.

Arguing was a waste of time. I couldn't get my money back. I mentally chalked up another loss, waving it aside – *oh, it's not much, we're wealthy, not every investment is a pot of gold* ... I rationalized as I went about my shopping and foot massages... *Aaron is still the love of my life and he's in charge now.*

But deep down I knew I was acting the part of the helpless bride. Offstage, I'd started to lose control.

"Money always slipped through his fingers. It was the tragedy of his life, except that he made it a comedy." –Gamaliel Bradford, on Aaron Burr

Aaron spent money as if my coffers were bottomless. He wined and dined cronies at the Astor House with hundred-year-old cognac, stuffed his wardrobes with custom-made attire, supported his wards in style with posh boarding schools and French lessons.

Then he didn't come home for a few nights. I waited in his

bed ready to surprise him, ears perked because I knew he'd come home. *He's at an all-night card game,* I convinced myself. Restless, I arose and waited on the balcony in the evening chill, peering down the drive. No sign of him.

Next day, my nephew Nelson told me the cold hard truth about Attorney Burr, his employer. He and others had seen my husband cavorting with Jane McManus, publicist for his ill-fated Texas colony.

I was too sickened to confront Aaron. Of course, I blamed myself. What did I do – or not do – to make him want another woman? I listed my shortcomings – I'd gained some weight, I feigned a headache last time he wanted a romp ...

Then I looked at it from his point of view. What was provoking him? It hit me like a sack of feed: Jane McManus was twenty years younger than me. I smacked the side of my head, it was so bloomin' obvious. He was aging, and the chit made him feel young. We needed to sit down and work this out. I knew we could. After all, he asked *me* to marry *him* this time.

I ordered a sumptuous dinner and plumped the cushions for us to lie on afterward. He wasn't home yet, but a tailor shop delivered another crate of velvet jackets and trousers. *Oh, well,* I laughed it off. *I like my husband to be well dressed.* As my butler rang the dinner bell, he still wasn't home. *Give him another ten minutes.*

An hour later, dinner long gone cold, he waltzed into the parlor and announced, "Eliza, I need a thousand dollars." He walked over to the desk and fetched the ledger. I'd given him access to my ledgers, my biggest blunder since saying "I do."

"Whatever for now?" I demanded, my cheeks growing hot. "What happened to the thousands you sank into the Texas land deal? The 'ground floor opportunity'?"

He waved as if swatting a fly. "Oh, that fell through." As if he'd lost some pocket change at bid whist.

"You're an hour late for dinner. I don't even want to know why." I brushed past him, snapped up the ledger, and opened it. I blinked, not believing what I saw. In his tidy penmanship, the dwindling sums ran down the column until it ended on the next page with a minus sign. I added up all the debits and broke into a drenching sweat. During our short marriage, he'd plowed through thirteen thousand dollars.

"Christ Almighty, what did you spend all this on?" I swept the sweat from my brow. "Aaron, we have to ..." I turned around. But I was talking to the wall.

I found him out back mounting Silver Surrey, the Arabian stud he bought last week. I grabbed the reins. "Whoa, buckaroo, before you trot off into the sunset, rein in your spur. We need to talk."

He slid down and leaned against the sturdy horse. "Shoot."

"Despite what it might seem, my money does not grow on these trees. Look around, Aaron." I gestured at the apple trees. "Those are leaves, not bank notes. You need to stop this reckless spending."

He drew himself up to his full height. "As your husband, I am legally entitled to all your rents, goods, and chattels. You now have a master, and I manage all your funds."

"This is what you call managing? I am cutting you off this minute." I nudged him aside. As an amused smile played on his lips, I hoisted myself into the saddle and took Silver for a canter around the fields – and a good long think.

"Dear God," I admitted out loud, "I made a terrible mistake. I regret this marriage." After decades of waiting and hoping, the bare facts struck me. We weren't meant to be husband and wife. We were much better off as widowed lovers.

I came back in to find my husband lounging on the settee reading law briefs, smoking a seegar, and sipping cognac. I fetched a sheet of paper listing my faults and brought it over to him. "Aaron, we need to talk."

He looked up at me over his specs. "What about?"

"What do you think?" I thrust the list at him. "You plow through all that money, but stay out all night ..." I couldn't bring myself to put into words what my nephew had told me. "What did I do to cause this ... your lack of interest in me?" Before he could answer, I flung the list into his lap. "Here. These are the reasons I believe I'm at fault. Things I couldn't say out loud, so I wrote them. I took a long time on this, looking myself over real careful. And that's what I've come up with. Perhaps you should do the same."

He glanced at the list and tossed it to the floor. My heart plummeted, as if he'd tossed *me* to the floor. "Don't go all Descartes on me," he said. "You don't have to examine our minds."

"All I'm trying to do is save our marriage." My voice broke with emotion as a sob caught in my throat. "Lord knows you took decades to ask me, now you act as if you're still breezing through bachelorhood. We did exchange vows, you know. Remember 'forsaking all others'?"

His sharp eyes left me. He tossed his head. "Oh, that." He waved the hand holding the cognac glass. "She doesn't mean anything to me. It's just a bit of fun, nothing more."

God help me, I didn't want to know but I asked anyway. "Aaron, look me in the eye and tell me you haven't slept with her."

He looked me in the eye. "I haven't slept with her."

"Then why did you come home reeking of cheap perfume?"

"A man can reek of perfume without a night-long romp. It proves nothing," was his defense attorney answer. "Now, do you want to be my cross-examiner or my wife? If the former, don't waste your time. If it's the latter, come here and be a wife." He put down the glass and opened his arms. The lovesick fool I was, I reclined with him on the settee. The stallion he was, he wore me out.

Oh, why couldn't I resist him, even after all that?

Next evening he went to visit his adopted son. I tore up my list of faults and stuffed his tailor-made raiment into trunks.

"I tried, God, I tried," I voiced, unable to stop myself from glancing out the window. *I'll give him another chance if he's home in a half hour* – but he didn't come home that night.

When he showed up next morning, I asked him to move out. When he refused, I *told* him to move out. He took Silver Surrey, and I assume he went back to his mistress. As much as it hurt, I didn't chase him or bribe him or beg him to stay.

No, Eliza, this isn't your failure, I assured myself as I fought conflicting emotions: fury at him for treating our marriage as an amusement, and all-consuming desire that tempted me to go and drag him home. I admitted the truth: *I'm still madly in love with the cad.*

But what would chasing him accomplish? He didn't want to be with me – he preferred *her* company. I walked to the river and took a cool cleansing soak. As the water washed over me, I marked the end of a lifelong behavior pattern. Never again would I chase a man who'd left me. Never again would I beg for love or crawl back after being flung aside. Today marked the last time I'd ever be jilted. Little Betsy Bowen still lived inside me, but on the bank of the Hudson River, the grown Eliza told young Betsy, "No man will ever break your heart again."

There were no men left to love.

CHAPTER 37

IN TRUTH, I didn't 'have it all'. I longed for the friendship of another escapee from starvation – a kindred soul to share memories of privation, hardship, the gouge in my heart from an absentee father. Oh, for another gal to share all that and more, to fill my lonely hours ...

But I couldn't *will* her to knock on the door. Or could I? On this clear morn, trying to put Aaron out of my mind, I did chores and paperwork. My butler busy in the pantry, I answered the front door myself. A young lady faced me and her jaw dropped. A peddler, I assumed. "Sorry, don't need any sundries. Thanks just the same, but—"

"Well, butter me and call me a biscuit! Madame Eliza Jumel Burr, answering her own door!" She gaped at me and bobbed a curtsy.

"No bowing and scraping, I ain't Queen Louise. And I never deny access to my doorstep. So what wares do you peddle, may I ask?" I smiled, mildly amused, glad for this diversion.

Her smile matched mine. "The world's oldest."

"A-ha, you're in the business. You're too well dressed for the merchant class, and girls on the town now shun that archaic custom of having escorts." I dropped my gaze from her dainty azure hat to the matching tailored dress. The lace parasol and satin satchel couldn't claim a previous owner. But by the mettle in her nut-brown eyes, I already knew this gal clawed a long hard path to her perch.

She bobbed me another undeserved curtsy. "Rosina Townsend, and I would have called sooner, but unlike yourself, I needed to gather the resolve and – I trust you'll appreciate this – the raw grit."

I couldn't let her stand on my threshold another second. "Enter and sit, my dear. Yes, you may sit in my presence. And no more curtsying. Hells bells, I'll brew and serve you the bloomin' tea myself, unless you hanker for a dose of spirits."

"I don't imbibe in the day, tea suits me fine ..." She stepped in and gazed upwards, across and back again, as if drinking in treasures much dearer than my Napoleonic bric-a-brac. "What an exquisite home, but I expected this splendor, having passed by it so many times, so tempted to peek in ..."

"You need to acquire more raw grit, honey. I would've peeked in." I led her into the parlor and motioned to the settee. "Why didn't you call on me before, you silly goose? The house is cavernous, but it's not a cloister." One of my servers entered the hall, and I called out, "A pot of tea and a plate of crumpets, please, Edwina."

Rosina, yet on her feet, whistled at the courtesy I granted Edwina. "You say please to servers?"

"The most worthwhile acquisition one can make is manners." I gave a gentle nudge, her knees bent and she sat on the settee. "If you heard anything about the travails of my journey here, you'll know I never look down on anyone or turn away a caller serious enough to appeal to me." I snickered.

"Bloomin' blazes, hasn't my reputation spread around town yet?" I sat next to her. Her wide-eyed gaze landed on each flower vase, each painting, each doily.

I relaxed into the cushion, but she stayed ramrod straight. "I presume your business has its ups and downs," I teased with a friendly poke of her arm. "Now what do you propose?"

Her tension melted with a deep breath and a relieved sigh. "I manage a posh Thomas Street house, but I'm looking to expand. I've my eye on a desirable property in Jersey City, eight rooms with a tavern on the ground floor and a carriage house. Under a decade of age. The owner is looking for a ready cash buyer, but I've not enough to meet his price."

I reached over and clasped her hands. "A woman who haggles over real estate is a woman after my own heart. If this place is what you claim and is free of vermin, you got yourself a partner. Contingent upon inspection and the right price, of course."

Her smile lit up the room. I added, "I've never been in the tavern business but will gladly venture into it. Men's vices will never be satiated." I jumped to my feet. "Let's hop the ferry and take a gander."

As Rosina Townsend and I linked arms, we skipped out the door in delight over another common trait – we put business before tea and crumpets. So began our lifelong kinship. As my calèche conveyed us to the pier, she sat in awestruck silence. She gawked at the velvet interior and swept her fingers across the fringe on the curtains as if strings on a harp.

"What is it, Rosie?" I crossed my legs and settled in. "It can't be the carriage. You must have one of your own. Running a prosperous brothel allows for a few perks."

She turned to me. "Oh, it's just being in your company, madam ...though the coach is splendid. I'm not able to afford a new one. I send the bulk of my earnings back to the folks."

I gave an admiring nod. "That's very honorable of you. And drop the 'madam' already. I'm Eliza to you, and that's how I insist everyone from Haarlem Heights to the Bowery address me."

Her mumbled, "Much obliged," told me now was the time for that great equalizer: "I'm where I am today because of where I'm from. I came up the hard way, from the streets of Providence ..."

She nodded in soul-fusing empathy as I related my childhood labors at the workhouse and my efforts to escape poverty. As I got to "I pushed open the John Street Theater's door," the carriage approached the pier. The coachman helped us out, and we boarded the ferry.

"My given name's Rosanna Brown, native to Castleton, up Albany way." She heaved a wistful sigh. "But itchy feet drew me here after I saved enough from chambermaiding. A chance encounter with Henry Beekman of Greenwich Street was my ticket out of my hovel. He offered me a taste of fineries beyond my reach. Of course, a taste wasn't hardly enough." A wry grin curled her lips.

"That name leaves a sour taste in my mouth." I scowled. "When did you work there?"

"Oh ..." She tapped her gloved finger to her chin. "Seven, eight years ago, I believe. Didn't stay long. Mr. Beekman, shall I say, angled for liberties I cared not to yield. When he dismissed me, I had no choice but to take refuge in a house of assignation."

I shook my head and let out a whoosh of disgust. "I trust you swung him a swift kick like I did."

She recoiled. "Heavens, no. I couldn't take no chances miffing his kind. Hence the assignation house stood between me and the curb. Soon I wangled my way up to Thomas Street. I manage the business, but John Livingston owns the building."

"That's a flush neighborhood. Can't go much farther up from there," I commented as the return ferry approached and passed us. Our boat swayed on the waves.

She nodded, hanging onto the seat. "It was two houses, but now it's one. A yard with gardens, benches, a piazza and a parlor where the wall was knocked out. But Livingston built these to be brothels. He never made improper overtures and chose me to manage the business after I moved in." Her voice lilted with pride.

"Forward-thinking move on his part. An asset well acquired."

"I'm bookkeeper, overseer, supervise the maids." She raised her head and lowered her lashes. "I entertain when I'm in the mood – and not just at the piano."

I patted her shoulder. "You're well on your way to getting a rise out of these parts."

By then we'd reached riverbank on the Jersey side, a wilderness of brush and dirt roads leading to Hoboken and Jersey City.

She sealed her deal – with me, anyways – after I inspected the Wayne Street Tavern, its tidy bug-free flats, and empty scrubbed chamber pots. "Let's drink to our health here, and I'll leave a calling card for the owner." I dug through my satchel.

We settled on three-legged stools before the blazing hearth in the smoky taproom. A scattering of patrons swilled ale or nursed whiskey, some played cards, two sat in deep discussion.

"Not a bad turnout for daytime," I observed as we warmed up by the fire. "We'll pack it to the rafters when we're in charge," I promised her. "After we buy this place, I'll drum up some lively discourse."

"Oh, won't you ever." She gave me a knowing smile.

We approached the long polished bar with its spit-shined rail. "I am Mrs. Vice President Aaron Burr and this is my partner Miss Townsend," I told the barkeep. "Please summon the proprietor so we may negotiate the purchase of this establishment."

His jaw dropped. "Why, I am the propri—er, the owner, John Fulton."

I held out my hand. "Miss Townsend and I spoke to your partner, Mr. Lempio, and arrived at a tentative price."

"Right ... I work here in the daytime, keeps me off the streets." He smiled, displaying a full set of tobacco-stained choppers, and shook my hand.

"Then I'll let you keep working here." I displayed my sauciest smile, my tried-and-true negotiating supplement – knocked the price down every time.

When the ink dried, Rosie and I owned The Wayne Street Tavern, which, of course, wouldn't keep that moniker another day.

On the sidewalk, I turned to Rosie. "Put 'er there, partner." I pumped her hand. "Old Mr. Fulton just sold his watering hole to a couple of dames. And this is just the beginning."

A smile lit up her eyes. "Eliza, you're a woman among women."

"Yeah. And in good company."

The Wayne Street Tavern became Rosie's Tavern, and I got my wish – a kindred soul cut from the same threadbare cloth.

"You knocked on my door when I needed a close lady friend the most," I admitted a few evenings later as we drew up the tavern's business plan. My grandfather clock chimed two of the morn, and I rubbed my eyes. "I've had too many men friends and too few ladies."

"Me, too," she revealed, and I marveled at another common trait. Could she be a long-lost sister?

"You're not from a Providence slum, are you?" I joked.

"Older men appeal to me because they remind me of my real father." Her eyes grew round and sad.

That revelation knocked me backward. I sat silent, mind whirring. Her admission churned up a mélange of buried emotions, turning up like long-lost orphans.

I tensed, prepared to share my most cherished secret. "Couldn't have said it better myself. This sticks to me like a scab I can't pull off. It's painful, yet I'm proud of it at the same time."

"What? Do tell." She busied her hands straightening her stack of papers, her eyes still on me.

"It's my father. He was President George Washington."

She dropped her papers. "Great Caesar's ghost!"

"He fathered me before that, of course."

She didn't ask me to reveal more, but I had to. I told her about Papa acknowledging me and our visit a week before his death. But this time, it didn't drain me empty. "I feel like I just finished reading a sweeping saga, and the ending satisfied me."

"That's hardly the ending, Eliza. You're the one who said this is just the beginning." Her eyes met mine. "My father abandoned us on my tenth birthday, and Mother died two weeks later." She looked away, focused on a distant memory. "I tried to find him but couldn't. I forced myself to look forward and – well, here I am."

I nodded, Papa's vision before my eyes. "You're right. What the hell was I talking about, endings?"

After two weeks, I hadn't heard a word from my husband. Whilst riding in my carriage, I spotted a familiar form strolling down the road.

I ordered the driver to stop and hopped out. "Yes, it is you! As I live and breathe!"

"Eliza! My, are you a sight!" William Dunlap held out his arms to me. We clasped hands and kissed — on the cheek. "How do you do all these years?"

"Still thriving, I expect. And you?"

Ah, he went on and on ... bankruptcy, failure, family deaths, illness ... he had me in tears. "Will, why did you never call on me? I'd have been there for you. All we meant to each other ... "

"No," he broke in gently. "You were busy living your extraordinary life. You didn't need me irking you. I managed to survive. Speaking of survivors, how does Colonel Burr do?"

I cast my eyes away and gazed over the river. "I don't see him anymore. He got thirteen thousand dollars of my property and spent it all or gave it away. I had a new carriage and pair of horses cost me a thousand dollars. He took them and sold them for five hundred. Does that tell you enough?" I looked back into his eyes, my youth rushing back to me — my surprise as William told me he was the theater's manager, the first role he gave me, scraping by to my last shilling. Here we stood, as if that gaping stretch of time had never passed.

I had to smile at the absurdity of it all, and he met it with a grin of his own, shaking his head in wonder.

"Where does Colonel Burr reside now?" He had the wherewithal to conclude I still kept tabs on my beloved, wayward husband.

"With a silversmith in the Bowery by the name of Burr — Aaron Burr. His adopted son."

"Oh." He then murmured, "I'm sorry."

"So am I. But I married him on my own terms. And keep in mind, Aaron is my walking, breathing, living proof that you must be careful what you ask for. You might get it."

He clasped my hand. I took a step closer, so happy to be here with him. "Eliza, I never had any doubt you would someday rule our fair city on your terms. But to the Colonel's credit, his marrying you makes anything told of him credible."

I laughed. "And should you care to write a play about him, I'll do all in my power to make sure it's the most rollicking comedy ever performed on a stage."

"Ah, yes. If anyone can adapt Aaron Burr's life into a stage comedy, you can."

"He already did himself. But he wouldn't appreciate calling it comedy. Let us say melodrama." I gave him a wink and a grin.

We shared those decades-old grins and as we talked, he never let go of my hand.

"Whether or not you write a play about Aaron, I expect to see you again. We have a lot of catching up to do." We exchanged farewells and I smiled all the way home — not at the delight of seeing Will, but at my husband, who'd raised melodrama to its highest art form.

CHAPTER 38

GENTS PACKED Rosie's Tavern after we painted, replaced rickety furniture, installed a new stove, hired a cook, and opened. We turned the carriage house into a parlor with Brussels carpet, crystal chandelier, velvet settees, divans, and ottomans, all upholstered in crimson, the color of kings. I placed the latest issues of the scholarly *Knickerbocker* on the tables. But what brought them in droves? The unusual name on the sign hanging outside. A tavern named for a lady. Not an Irish surname preceded by a 'Mc' or a nondescript chestnut like 'The Ten Bells'. They ventured through the door trusting the feminine moniker would guarantee fine ales in clean glasses, home cooking – and if there really was a Rosie, a glimpse of her countenance, if not her décolletage.

What brought them back was a treat this land of ours never gave them – not only a tavern owned by 'dames' but those 'dames' greeted them at the door, served them their potations, and pulled up a chair to chat.

I spent most evenings at the tavern, warming up to our

patrons. One such gent was New York's comptroller. I knew him through Aaron's cronies. As he entered, I did a double take at his false whiskers. Seeing through the disguise, I greeted him, "Good evening, Mr. Comptroller," as I handed him a glass of single malt Scotch. "You needn't hide from us, we're discreet as the confessional. But why a disguise to sit in a tavern? You're not known as a teetotaler – or did you turn a new leaf for the temperance movement?"

"No, madam, uh ..." he sputtered, struggling to pull the whiskers off.

"I'm Eliza to you."

"Forgive me, Eliza, but the buzz around town is you opened a brothel upstairs." His cheeks reddened. "That's what steers the not inconsequential traffic here and drudging back across river harboring the crushing blow that it's simply a tavern."

"Now how did that rumor spring up?" I puzzled, drumming on the table. Then like lightning, a renegade idea flashed before my eyes. I saved it for after hours with Rosie.

I pulled Comptroller Marcy into a discussion about Manhattan real estate, praising him for his generous donations for internal improvements. In return, he uttered, "to the victor the spoils," and I couldn't agree more.

Before he departed, I pumped his hand. "I won't disappoint you or our 'not inconsequential traffic'. The next visit is on the house," I extended the invite. "Don't bring the whiskers, just your appetite. And I don't mean for chicken livers." I wiggled a brow.

He took the hint, for he displayed a toothbrushed smile, a jaunty spring to his step on his way out.

That evening, I proposed my venture to Rosie. "Bloomin' bollocks, they thought we ran a bordello," I marveled as we sat in the quiet provided by the 'Closed' sign. "Mr. Marcy brought the rumor right back here that we serve more than spirits and light fare." I held my hands up and splayed my fingers. "We have clean rooms upstairs. Let's tart them up and run a gent's bordello. It's a crying shame, but there are pitiful few high-class brothels around here. This whole area's our oyster."

Rosie's grin brightened the candlelit room. "Why not indeed? But why did we not think of this before?" She picked up one of her kid gloves and slapped her cheek with it.

"Didn't see the forest for the trees, I suppose." I shrugged. "So, what are we waiting for? The night is young." My grandfather clock's chimes gonged twice from the far corner. "Let's list what we'll need and what it'll cost. We'll start with featherbeds. We'll need eight ...and extras for the occasional ménage." I fetched pen and paper from behind the bar.

"Don't we need fillies first?" Rosie wiped a smudge on the table.

"Fillies with no beds?" I tossed her a grin. "We run a high-class bordello, *chérie*, not a stable."

We built it, and they came. The door never closed. We had to turn many away, as we operated by appointment only.

Another gray-haired gent entered *sans* disguise, for he clearly didn't give a whit who saw him. I greeted and seated him at my private table. "As I live and breathe – Senator Martin Van Buren himself. And what brings such a distinguished statesman to our humble establishment?"

"Same as what brings the others. And I daresay there's naught humble about it." He gave me an admiring gaze rather than a Hamiltonesque leer. "Your pulchritude is as alluring as rumor hints. But why, dear lady, why do you toil here rather than luxuriate in your mansion with servants at your beck and call?"

"I'll give you the first two reasons off the top, Senator. One: I've ample eggs in this basket and want to keep an eye on it. Two: what's not to enjoy, being here among guests such as yourself? I can hardly compare bid whist and growing lilies to this. Now what is your pleasure, if I may qualify that question, of the liquid variety?"

"Whatever you're imbibing, dear madam."

"That's single malt Scotch, and I'm Eliza to you." I waved to our new barmaid and ordered.

"And where is the elusive Rosie whose name graces your shingle?" Van Buren's eyes roamed the room.

"She's running her other business in the city." Need I expand? "I hope you'll stay till she arrives. She'll be thrilled to meet you."

He looked at my grandfather clock. "Why, what a stunning clock. I collect them, you know."

"I bought it from Mr. Tyler of the Washington Garden," I said. "It has special sentimental value." I didn't tell Van Buren that clock had ticked away the precious minutes of my first private meeting with Aaron. "When Mr. Tyler retired, I made a generous offer on the clock, to remind me how precious time really is."

"I don't suppose you care to sell it." He went to admire it up close and I followed.

"Never." I shook my head. "Care for anything from the kitchen?" I offered. "We have a Viennese cook. His frankfurters and wiener schnitzel are out of this world." My mouth watered.

"Much obliged, dear, but ..." He patted his paunch, "...I've cut back to keep the trousers buttoned."

"Yes, our president needs to be fit." I led him back to our table.

He blinked in surprise, as if a fortune teller turned over his destiny card. "And what provokes that prediction, my wily Eliza?"

"Don't be coy, my crafty Martin." I reached over and smoothed down his collar. "And if I may address you that way ..."

He agreed before the words were out my mouth.

"Just a variety of variables." I brushed lint off his coat. "Not the least of which is your probable opponent, Mr. Harrison. He hasn't the vision, the aplomb, you have."

"But I haven't even considered tossing my hat in the ring." He shook his head, jowls jiggling.

"Not till now, you mean?" When our shots arrived, I toasted him, "To our eighth president. May peace reign over our nation as you rule with a sharp vision for the future."

As he tipped his glass to his lips, Rosie flounced in, saw the guest at our table, and dropped her jaw.

"There she is!" I waved her over. "Rosie, meet our newest patron."

She paced as if approaching an altar. Van Buren stood, hand extended. "Rosie, if I may address you as such?"

I stood and completed the introduction. "This is Senator Martin Van Buren, our next president."

She neither bobbed a curtsy nor lost her footing. "A finer president we couldn't have." With a glance at me, she added, "...aside from our first, of course."

I heard not a word from Aaron. *Maybe he'll change, maybe he'll tire of her and run back to me*, I kept hoping, then berated myself – how naïve, how Betsy Bowen of me. It no longer mattered whose fault it was. I stared reality in the face. With a heavy heart, I called on my neighbor, a lawyer who specialized in divorces.

Alexander Hamilton Jr. Yes, the son of *that* Alexander Hamilton.

Strikingly similar in stature to his late father, he greeted me at his door and offered me sherry, but my stomach could handle not a drop nor a bite. "I wish it hadn't come to this," I told him as he seated me across from his desk. "But I must file divorce papers."

He nodded, not showing a shred of sympathy. In fact, I could see him struggling to keep a straight face. "Thank you for engaging my services, Mrs. Burr. I shall make it my first priority."

No joshing, I thought. He likely started proceedings before I stepped out the door.

Meanwhile, Rosie and I had a ball running the tavern. Until Mr. Livingston complained of Rosie's neglect of the Thomas Street business. I approached the dandy with an offer to buy him out. Well aware of his mattress-covered gold mine, he refused my first bid. He caved in at my second offer and sold me controlling ownership.

We ran our Thomas Street brothel and hopped over to our tavern/brothel in Jersey City. Some eves, as Rosie and I took respite at our corner table, we shared past lives and future hopes.

Rosie's 'just-us' tea parties in our Thomas Street parlor became our escape from the hustle and bustle. Fridays at four, we perched on the settee and sipped Earl Grey like the proper ladies we'd seemingly become. Our tête-à-têtes became farcical as we affected British accents, held our cups with pinkies extended, ankles crossed.

On this Friday, as we sipped tea and nibbled scones, a stunning young lady sauntered in, her azure dress tailored to her form. Accenting emeralds dazzled at her throat – these were no fakes. Rosie stood – was she a French marchioness? Should I stand? But I remained on my *derrière*, fixated on her beauty as she strode up to me and offered a hand.

"Good afternoon, I am Helen Jewett. I believe you are Mrs. Burr." No marchioness this, her accent from these parts or farther north.

"In formal circles, but I'm Eliza around here. Pleased to meet you." I clasped her fingers, matching her firm handshake. *Now here's a pistol who knows what she wants and gets it*, that grip told me. If she wasn't already striding in my footsteps, she soon would be.

Rosie said, "Helen just moved back after living at other places for a while. We're so pleased to have her back."

Helen draped her arm around Rosie's shoulders. "Pleasure to meet you, Mrs. —Eliza. I've a full evening ahead, so I'll go to my room and rest." She held up a book, finger stuck in the pages. "I just bought *The Vindication of the Rights of Women* and started reading it walking down the street. I cannot put it down."

"A kindred soul!" I turned to my tea party co-star. "Rosie, may I be so bold as to invite Miss Jewett to tea with us?"

Rosie pulled the bell cord. "Splendid idea. Helen, you'll join our little party, will you not?"

I patted the settee cushion next to me. "Sit here, dear, and let's talk books. I reckon you've read a stack of 'em."

Her enthusiastic nod told me she did. "I have a small library upstairs."

"What else have you read that's memorable?"

She sat and crossed her ankles. "There are so many …whatever my gentlemen recommend, or what I see reviewed in the press. The last book I read was *The Disowned* by Bulwer-Lytton. I read anything by Lord Byron or Sir Walter Scott. I like that new author from Massachusetts – Nathaniel Hawthorne. He wrote a novel, *Fanshawe*. I especially enjoyed it because the heroine's name is Ellen – that's a pet name of mine – her two suitors are rivals. Then my favorite play by far is *Jane Shore*."

"Ah, *Jane Shore*." I closed my eyes in wistful reverie as the years melted away. "I have fond memories of her." I focused on Helen, wide-eyed with intent. "You're too young to have seen me when I trod the boards, but I was a thespian in my youth, and Jane was my favorite role." I winked. "For obvious reasons."

Rosie's maid placed a fresh teapot on the table. Rosie pulled up a chair. "Eliza's led a fascinating life, sweet pea. I hope she'll tell you about it sometime."

"Save my tales for later." I flipped my hand. "Tell me about you, Helen. You reeled me in with your appetite for books. You can hear about me any old time."

"I was born Dorcas Dorrance," came her answer, "and abandoned."

I nodded in empathy. Another kindred soul.

"I came here via Portland and Boston, worked at houses of ill fame till I came here four years ago and lived – well, worked my way up to prosperous places: brothels on Chapel, on Duane, Mrs. Cunningham's on Franklin …" She counted on her fingers. "But the most respectable brothel, second only to Rosina's, was Mrs. Welden's at 55 Leonard. The previous renter, Mr. Dunlap, left her some sumptuous furnishings and tasteful décor."

"You mean my dear old William?" I shrieked in glee.

"Why, yes. You know him?"

"Oh, do I ever!" I shut my eyes and basked in memories. "He managed the theater where I went to beg work, and he saved me from extinction."

"He's a gem." She nodded. "Then I came back here to Rosina's. I feel right at home. We're more of a family here than anywhere I ever stayed."

I studied those bright eyes as she sipped her tea. "It's like looking into a mirror. A three-way mirror," I added, fixing my gaze on Rosie.

"Eliza and I own a tavern with an upstairs brothel together in Jersey City," Rosie bragged. "Eliza is a business genius."

As Helen gaped in wonder, I prepared to brush off Rosie's superlative when she added, "And the richest woman in New York City. Made her fortune in real estate."

My counterclaim of, "Well, I did take some weighty risks …" drowned in Helen's ocean of exclamations.

"Oh, how I admire a woman who made her own way in this world."

"You're not doing too badly yourself, dearie." I served this compliment with a gesture at her finery – and looking closer at those emeralds, I saw they had a few companions in the form of diamonds nestled above her *décolletage*.

"I get by." She tittered with a modest wave of her teacup. "I plan to have my own business someday," she stated with conviction. "After all, a lady can't make a living on her back when parts start to sag and lose their bounce." She hefted her breasts. "My current suitor is a success in the making."

I let my other shoe flop off, wiggling my toes. "Who is he? Someone prominent?"

"His name is Richard Robinson, but he goes by Frank Rivers at times. For business reasons." Plucking at the lace on her sleeve, she stated this as if businessmen took aliases every day.

I plowed on, "What business is he in?"

"He's a clerk at Mr. Hoxie's store and comes from a respectable family with a pure pedigree. He's an upstanding Republican and voted for Henry Clay," she boasted.

Sensing she'd tried too hard to sing his praises, I dug deeper. "Honey, how well do you really know this fellow?"

CHAPTER 39

HELEN RAISED HER CHIN, fists curling into loose clenches. "Intimately." Gazing into space, a dreamy smile on her lips, she went on, "He's personable, bright, generous, well-read, easy of manner, an avid theater- and opera-goer ..." She took a breath, "... uncontaminated by the vicious, and a gifted athlete. He *golfs!*" She punctuated his string of virtues with a smug twitch of her mouth.

Before she began praising his prowess between the sheets, which I knew would come next, I interjected: "How does he *show* he's in love with you?"

She blinked as she scrambled to answer a question she clearly never pondered. "Why, he treats me like a queen. Look at this necklace." She plucked it between her fingers and leaned towards me, as if lending a third ear.

"It's a stunner," I admitted. "Clearly genuine and costly. But how does he treat you other than lavishing jewels upon your person?" I dug to get to the heart of her relationship with this paramour.

"He, uh ..." This being the first pause, I withheld further

volleys. "Well, uh ... he's never broken a date with me. He's never kept me waiting. He's a considerate lover."

Ah, I knew that would make the shortlist. "How do you know he's faithful?" I penetrated those layers while all she did was skim the surface.

"He, uh ..." She fingered her necklace, as if to mine it for reassurance, and cast a pleading glance at Rosie. But a frown pulled at Rosie's lips.

"Tell her, Helen." Rosie gestured 'and now for the main attraction,' as her words hung in the air.

"He doesn't see me exclusively. But I live with it and look the other way." The droop of her shoulders spoke volumes.

"You don't have to live with it or look the other way, Helen," I corrected her, my tone stern as a schoolmarm's. "Simply put, he's a philanderer. I'm angry at this cad and I don't even know him! A beautiful, intelligent woman as you should not tolerate philandering."

"An occasional romp is hardly philandering," she jumped to his defense. "You only heard a few details of my past, Eliza. You don't know what I've endured – my mother's death, my father's abandonment, shunted from one house to the next, treated like a servant, fought off lechers that would turn a weaker woman against the entire male sex for life. Richard stepping out with some doxy pales in comparison."

Rosie poured a splash of gin into my cup and handed it to me. I accepted it, not for refreshment, but for fortification. Not that my tongue needed more loosening, but ...

"Dearie, heed my most obtrusive trait: I say what's on my mind, and I don't give two plums who I offend. I offer unsolicited advice to the young when I see promise. And I don't just mean how to invest your shillings. I mean affairs of the heart, which take the majority of our energies. You'll hear what may sound like a quest to run your bloody life. Are we in agreement?"

Her eyes lit up to rival the necklace between her breasts. "How can I disagree with the shrewdest woman in New York City? I'm sure every affair of your heart brought you more happiness than any of us dream of."

I had to laugh. "Ha! Keep thinking that." I shared a smile with Rosie. "Abide by this pearl of wisdom – learn from other people's mistakes. And, being presumptuous as holy hell, I'll give you another dose of advice, which you can take to heart or toss out with tonight's rubbish." My voice gathered volume. "Ditch this scoundrel. You're too good for him. If he's cheating now, he'll cheat after the wedding."

"But ... but ..." she sputtered. "I already said I can forgive his dalliances. After all, I'm the one he comes back to. Besides – don't all men step out on their women?"

"If their women let them," I informed her. "If they know they can get away with it. Just what is it you deprive him of that he needs to get elsewhere?"

Stumped again. "Well, I, uh ..." Her hands fluttered at her throat. "It's not what I don't give him, it's what I do." She frowned, not looking all too pleased with herself.

Holding up my ginned-up Earl Grey, I told Rosie, "You'd best pour her one of these." Rosie got busy.

Helen cleared her throat. "As long as we're being upfront here, I'll list my faults, as we all have them. I'm feisty, willful, stubborn, possessive, and can be a shrew when I don't get my way."

"Those are faults?" I laughed as Rosie passed a cup of spiked tea to Helen.

She took it and gulped. "At times I push him over the edge, we engage in loud rows, and he storms out – into the arms of a doxy who won't dare talk back."

"What causes these rows?" I asked.

"He drinks too much. He hit me – but just once. I hit him back." Her voice grew more bitter with every item on her list.

"And you tolerate this? Why, Helen?" I shook my head. "I feel like I'm talking to my younger self. I so wish to save you from my past mistakes. You can do so much better."

"That's what I've been asking her," Rosie spoke up. "She never has an answer."

"We're in love." Helen pumped her balled fists. "I was meant for him. Don't ask me how, I just know."

"It's not otherworldly, Helen." I attempted to pull her back to earth. "You need to go out and find someone worthy of your love. It's not him. I know his kind. There's one born every minute."

"I can change him," she declared.

"Oh, how many times have I heard that old chestnut – and said it my very self – until I learned the hard way? You have work to do." This would take more than one tea party – with or without a splash of gin.

Rosie's girls – Helen, Elizabeth Salters, Caroline Stewart, Maria Stevens, and Amelia Elliot, 'adopted' me as their auntie. They joined our tea parties, and we shared our stories as 'girls on the town'. I treated them to the theater and carriage rides. Meanwhile, Helen fretted over her philandering beau, but when I met Mr. Robinson in all his charming ardor, I couldn't believe it was the same person.

"*Bonsoir*, Madam Burr," he addressed me with a click of his heels and a kiss of my hand. He didn't *faire taire* until I told him, "All right already, you sold me. Now if you really want to impress me, speak English."

He was everything she described, and more striking in person. Blond, blue-eyed, well-built, and would've charmed the pantaloons off Betsy Bowen back in the day. Too bad he was the good-for-nothing he was – or so Helen claimed. I believe in giving the benefit of the doubt, until doubt outweighs the benefit.

One Thursday evening, it did. Servants dismissed, I answered a banging on the door of my Orchard Street town-house, where I stayed some weeknights. A teary Helen stormed in and slammed the door. Her frock rustled as she kicked the bottom step and pounded the banister with her fists.

I grasped her hands before she pummeled them to pulps. "Hell's bells, what happened?"

"That filthy swine is parading Emma Chancellor around town making a fool of me, that's what happened!" Her shrieks echoed down the hall. She collapsed on the bottom step in a torrent of sobs. I sat beside her and gave her my hankie.

"I don't want to say I told you so, sweet pea."

"Then don't tell me so," she cut into my words and swiped a hand across her teary eyes.

"So why come here? Not for a hand of bid whist by the looks of things."

Her breathing calmed as she glared daggers at me. I didn't take it personally. Her fury was directed at her filthy swine, not her adopted auntie. "Revenge is what I want. To get back at both of them."

"Oh, how I see the young Betsy Bowen in you!" I sat beside her. "Revenge, or even pondering it, is a waste of effort. Success is the best revenge. Follow in my footsteps. It'll kill him."

"That will take eons. He is cavorting with her now." She folded my hankie and blew her nose.

"When I told you to jilt him, you seemed able to grin and bear it. What turned that grin into raging desire for payback?" I helped her up, sat her in the parlor, and fixed us both a mix of gin and vermouth.

"She's not just another doxy. He buys her gifts. Not cheap gewgaws, but fine jewelry, raiment, dinners at Delmonico's, operas ... he's never taken me to any opera. All I get out of him is a stroll around Sybil's Cave in Hoboken."

"You told me you hate opera." I sipped my drink.

She downed hers. "That's not the point! He never takes me anywhere."

"But why the vendetta against what's-'er-name?" I dropped my slippers from my feet and dug my toes into the plush rug. "To her, he's likely just a meal ticket."

"That and much more." Her eyes narrowed. She rolled the glass between her hands. "She knows me, all right. She insults me – goes around blabbing that he plans to jilt me for her. Calls me a second-rate whore."

"And what is she?"

"A third-rate whore." She smirked. "Not fit to lick his boots. Nor mine."

"She must lick something, for him to keep going back to her," I ventured.

Her smirk lingered. "I know not what he sees in that sow." She poured another drink, this time in a larger glass.

"A bit of strange, I expect. He'll tire of the romps. They're called romps for a reason. Meanwhile, you're wasting your beauty sitting with me. Go find another charmer to squire you around town. That's your revenge. For starters," I advised her.

Her glass already half empty, she sidled over to the chessboard and fiddled with the white king. "Have you ever been betrayed, Eliza?"

"Yes. Most recently by my soon-to-be former husband." Why not tell her the illustrious Aaron Burr was a cheat? "But I was never bent on revenge against any man. I simply took my favors and bestowed them on someone deserving. We're talking about the game of love here. Men are so inept at it. They are ruled by their privy parts, you almost can't blame them."

She calmed enough to put the drink down, lips in a straight line, all the smirking and hissing over with. "Where would I be without you, Eliza?"

"Wasting even more time on him than you are now, I suppose."

That got half a smile out of her. "I know a few gents I can use my feminine wiles on to squire me about. If you think that'll awaken a bit of jealousy in him."

"Men are fragile, my dear," I educated her. "Seeing you on the arm of another gent, even hearing about it, will get a rise out of him."

She downed the other half of her drink. "I shall keep you informed." She headed for the door and turned to face me. "Every man I ever knew hurt me or left me. That must be why I'm incapable of letting him go."

I slid back into my carpet slippers and stood to see her out. "I've been down the exact same road many times, dearie. You know my history. Concentrate your efforts on yourself, not on him. That's where I channeled all the hurt and abandonment. It made me who I am. You can do the same."

"I think not." She opened the door. "I don't have your spunk. It's not something one can learn. One is born with it. Your father gave you yours when he sired you." With a kiss to my cheek, she flounced into the street.

"I like to think that ..." I mused, returning to my settee and my book. "Papa gave me some spunk. I earned the rest of it in Providence."

CHAPTER 40

After looking at a tavern for sale on Fourteenth Street, I went to tell Rosie. She'd like the place – the owner had been jailed, and his wife couldn't afford the upkeep.

Rosie wasn't in, but I found Helen standing in the parlor reading *Macbeth* out loud. She poured us some sherry, and we sat on the settee to chat.

"So, how goes the love triangle?" I sipped my drink. "I hope you've acquired a few beaux of your own."

She nodded without enthusiasm. "A few. But Richard's still squiring Emma around town. I let him call on me last evening, and after a blow-up that woke the neighborhood, we made up – all night. He doesn't deny he's interested in the doxy. But he denies he loves her, and proclaims his eternal love for me. When our Elizabeth saw them head into the theater, Emma flashed yet another bauble he gave her. And hear this – Mary Berry told me he squires Hannah Blisset around town, too."

"I'm tired of hearing my own voice, but I'll say it again. Give him his walking papers," I badgered this babe in the woods.

"No, he's mine and I'm going to fight for my man!" she proclaimed. Oh, how she'd missed her calling. She made Charlotte Cushman look like a summer stock player.

"If you can love him, you can love someone who deserves you," I lectured, knowing my words fell on deaf ears, for she crossed the room to Rosie's desk and retrieved a letter.

"I wrote him this." She handed it to me. "We send each other letters all the time. They're nearly as passionate as our trysts. But I'm especially distraught." She sighed. "I haven't heard from him since Wednesday. Reading it over, I think I may sound too forceful. I value your opinion."

I recited it out loud as if reading a script: "*My dear, you have passed your promise by two nights, and yet you have not thought proper to send me a single line, even in the shape of an excuse. Do you think I will endure this? Come to see me tonight or tomorrow night, and tell me how we may renew the sweetness of our earlier acquaintance, and forget all our past unhappiness. Slight me no more. Trample on me no further. Oh, do not provoke the experiment of seeing how I can hate. But in hate or in love, your Helen.*"

I shook my head and met her questioning eyes.

"Well?" She took a step closer, hands on hips.

"You'll be sorry you asked."

Her lips curved down in a scowl.

"I hope you come to your senses on the way to post it," I gave it to her straight. "You sound like a bloomin' shrew. I'll eat my hat if he doesn't hop the next boat to China after reading this." I glanced down at the turgid prose. "A subpoena is romantic by comparison."

I put the letter down as something occurred to me. "Helen, where does he get the money for all these costly gifts, dinners, and carriages? He's a clerk in a hardware store."

She sat next to me and wet her lips. "I need to tell you this, only if you promise not to go to the police." Her gaze pinned me.

Uh-oh. I frowned. "Of course you have my word. What is it?"

"Richard is ... that is, he's been ... he embezzles from Mr. Hoxie. He's been going at it over a year now, and Mr. Hoxie is none the wiser. But as long as no one gets hurt, I keep quiet. Hoxie can afford it."

"You're embroiled in a dangerous plot here," I warned. "He will get caught. And he'll take you down right with him. You could be an accessory to his crime if you don't inform the authorities."

She winced and covered her ears. "I've never met a man so intelligent. He can discuss any topic, you know that, having met him. What did you discuss? The French Revolution? Physics? He knows it all."

I let out an impatient whoosh. "What has book learning got to do with his criminal activities? You're so taken with this scoundrel you can't see straight. I'm not moralizing, dearie. But you're headed for trouble. You can do so much better. And remember, the sooner you jilt him, he won't have the chance to jilt you. Hence you will not be abandoned."

We sat in silence for several minutes. The clock gonged. How many times, I didn't count.

She looked partly convinced but wouldn't admit it.

"Oh, how I hope you'll come to your senses." I gave her a motherly hug and she left.

The 'doxy' Emma Chancellor called on me soon after. I was now officially embroiled in this love triangle.

A week later, I saw Helen at the apothecary buying arsenic. A few of Rosie's girls, Elizabeth and Caroline, stood behind me. They saw it, too. They whispered to each other. I turned and left. Perhaps they knew more than I did. But I knew Helen by then. *Oh, well, it's for her complexion,* I rationalized. Then I forgot about it, until ...

... I was planting some posies in my front window boxes when I heard, "Excuse me, Mrs. Burr ..." in a timid voice.

I turned and there stood another stunner ... not endowed with Helen's classic beauty, but her blue-black hair reflected the sun with glints of sapphire. Her milky skin glowed in stark contrast. Shorter and plumper than Helen, she fidgeted with a ruby pendant that accented the pink of her dress. More rubies dripped from her wrist. I instantly knew who she was.

I brushed soil from my hands and approached her. "Let me guess. Emma Chancellor."

She nodded as we shook hands, her eyes the silver-gray of tarnished pewter, her lashes black-coated. "How do you know who I am, madam?"

My eye-roll came in concert with my smile. "First, dispense with the madam. I'm Eliza to all the girls on the town, you included. But you're awful young to be in the business. You barely appear at the edge of seventeen."

"Seventeen and a half," she declared, "and not in the business. I keep house for Mayor Lawrence and his family. But I live on Reade Street. And that is not a brothel. Who told you I was in ... that business? Helen, no doubt." Her eyes narrowed to stormy slits.

I shrugged, but jumped to Helen's defense. "Perhaps she's misinformed. It's neither here nor there to me. But if you don't want that rumor spread, I suggest you correct her." I guided her inside. "You're here for advice, I take it." I couldn't help chuckling. "My word, since I met Rosie, I'm the quintessential mother hen. Though the girls call me 'auntie'. Are you seeking an opinion on your entanglement? Otherwise, I'm happy to oblige you in French lessons."

We headed for the settee, and I rang for tea.

"That's what it is, Eliza." She gave her head a rapid shake. "I cannot address you thusly. Do let me call you Aunt Eliza. Please? I've no aunts of my own, and always wanted one."

As I studied her features, once again I looked into a mirror, backward. But even farther back than with the other girls ... she was the youngest. "Then Aunt it is. Now, I know what's on your mind, I've heard the other side of this story. But as every story has at least two sides, settle in and recite yours. I'll interject when it suits me, beware of that."

She spread her skirt and folded her hands. I didn't notice if she crossed her ankles, but she was the most poised and mannered of all the girls. "Our mutual friends tell me that Helen rants about how much she hates me, because Richard courts me. She's threatened both of us many times. She also physically assaulted me." She pushed back a sleeve to reveal a bruise in ten shades of purple. Lowering her head, pointing to her crown, she added, "She knocked me to the ground Friday last, but the bump has gone down."

My tongue in knots, I sat, stunned. "This doesn't sound like Helen. She has a jealous streak that could wipe up the streets, but violence?"

She went on, "I tell everyone, including Rosina, that if I turn up dead, chances are Helen murdered me."

She stopped and took a breath. Now it was my turn. "I know crimes of passion happen, but I truly doubt Helen is capable of murder." That scene flashed before my eyes: Helen buying arsenic. I kept that to myself.

"It's more complicated than passion. When I stood up to Richard and said, 'if you go back to Helen, I'll expose your embezzlement,' he said, 'you wouldn't dare,' and went back to Helen. He told her my threat. She confronted me. 'Don't you dare threaten Richard,' she snarled at me. She pushed me, smacked me, then her parting words were to the effect of 'Richard is mine. Stay away or else ...' and she made a slicing gesture with her hand." Emma shuddered, holding her neck. It reminded me of Anne Boleyn the night before her beheading: 'I have such a little neck ...'

"The game of love is dangerous," I cautioned, for her silence invited my advice. "But if you want to stay safe, heed her warning. Stay away from Richard. Don't accept any more of his advances – or his gifts."

Her eyes shone with tears. "But I love him so, Aunt Eliza. I never loved anyone the way I love him."

"Hmm ... what is it about this chap?" Of course, I fell madly in love with Aaron – but Richard Robinson was no Aaron. "It's not worth the risk, dearie. Find a suitor who's not embroiled with another gal. And who's not a thief. That's more dangerous than invading another gal's boy territory. Cheating is despicable, but you can't go to jail for it."

"I hoped you'd tell me how to win Richard back and make him jilt Helen." The tea came, but neither of us picked up a cup. "But since you didn't, I ask you—please tell Helen to give up Richard. It's me he loves, not her."

I raised my brows. "Now that's bold. I already told Helen to give up on Richard. For the same reasons I gave you. She ignores my warnings. Hence, I'll tell you right out: I wouldn't wish Richard Robinson on my deadliest enemy," I set out the bare facts. "He cheats, he embezzles ... that leads to more serious crimes. Before long, and mark my word, he'll be a hardened criminal. You deserve better. And, I daresay, so does Helen. Let your mind lead your heart."

Did she heed the advice she came to me for? I'll never know.

Three days later, Emma Chancellor was dead.

We sat in Rosie's parlor with a few of the girls, Helen among them. She shook like a leaf. Caroline and Elizabeth sat stone-still. Neither Rosie nor I could calm Helen with tea, sweets, or soothing affirmations.

As I hugged Helen and stroked her hair, she told us, "Richard said he'd blow out the brains of any woman who exposed him."

"Emma must have exposed him, then," Rosie said. "I hope none of you other girls have – have you, Helen?" she quizzed her protégée with a shaky voice.

Helen gave a rapid shake of her head. "No ... I was going to, but ... I didn't like Emma, she was my rival, but I didn't want her to die!" She buried her face in my shoulder.

"Now will you listen to us and tell him to stay out of your life, Helen?" Elizabeth demanded. "You may be next."

"Be easy on her, Elizabeth, she's shaken up enough as it is," Rosie chided.

"His last letter to me chilled me to the bone." Helen left the room and returned with a folded sheet. She handed it to me.

I skimmed the first half then read out loud: "*Nelly, I cannot sit with you in the presence of one who has, and may again, purchase you as his; do you really think I can? I repeat I cannot. I am never more unhappy than when with you at the theater. I cannot come till Saturday night. I have read your note with pain, I ought to say displeasure; nay, anger. Women are never so foolish as when they threaten. You are never so foolish as when you threaten me. Keep quiet until I come on Saturday night, and then we will see if we cannot be better friends hereafter. I must shorten my letter, for I have not much time to write you as we are about shutting up. Goodbye.*"

"I suggest you never threaten him again, Helen," Rosie warned her.

"Have the police made any arrests?" I asked.

"No." Rosie shook her head. "Everybody they questioned has an alibi. They came here and questioned all of us. I believe they questioned everyone Emma knew, and that was a lot of people – the mayor and his family, the house where she lived, her friends, past suitors. All the evidence is circumstantial."

Those words hung in the air. No one said another word. I wondered why. Later, as Rosie and I sat in the tavern after closing, I found out.

"I didn't want to say anything in front of the girls, but they already know." Rosie's hands and voice shook.

"They know what?" My grandfather clock tick-tocked. When it gonged, it shattered the silence like a clap of thunder.

"Richard didn't kill Emma." Rosie took a breath and paused. "Helen did."

The words smacked me with the force of a horsewhip. I gasped and clutched my chest. "What? How do you know?"

"Helen told me. This morning, before anyone came to breakfast. She went to Emma's house on the pretense to mend fences between them, brought a flask of arsenic-laced whiskey. When Emma left the room, she emptied it into Emma's teacup. She watched Emma drink it, sat there while Emma collapsed in a heap on the floor, and snuck out the back door, leaving her there."

I slumped over, unbelieving.

Rosie went on, "She didn't mean to kill Emma, she just wanted to debilitate her and make her suffer. She miscalculated the dose. Arsenic does kill slowly, but in large amounts, kills instantly."

I steadied my hands on the scarred tabletop. "What happens now? Will you turn her in?"

She shook her head. "None of us will ever go to the police. They want nothing to do with prostitutes."

"But all suspicion points to Richard," I countered. "I wonder if he's living in fear of being accused of the murder. He certainly could have committed it – easily – and with motive."

"He gave the police his airtight alibi. He was working at his store. Plenty of witnesses back him up. No, this is a dead-end. An unsolved murder – to the rest of the world." Rosie gave a warning glare that dared me to 'solve' this case by blabbing to the police.

CHAPTER 41

"I won't say a word to the police," I assured Rosie. "But I'm shocked. And so disappointed in Helen. How can she live with this?"

"Perhaps she's so wracked with guilt, she'll confess, who knows? Now I'm not convinced she only tried to debilitate Emma." Rosie trailed her fingers along scratches on the tabletop. "She may have had murder on her agenda the whole time. I don't know what or who to believe anymore." She looked up. "Now for some good news. We have a new patron at Thomas Street – the governor of New York himself, Enos Throop. And he doesn't wear false whiskers."

No one saw Helen the next day, or the next.

Rosie didn't show at our Jersey City tavern that night. *Something's amiss,* I feared. My skin crawled with dread. I tried to push it from my mind by starting a game of bid whist with some gents. I lost every hand.

Hoping nothing horrific happened to Rosie, I went back to our brothel in the city the next morning. A pushing, shoving mob milled around the door and spilled into the street. Voices buzzed like a swarm of flies. I elbowed my way up the porch steps. Two policemen blocked the entrance.

"What happened?" I demanded.

Busy pushing the crowd back, they ignored me. I caught a glimpse of Rosie in the entry hall. "Let me by, I own this building."

They parted to let me enter. I reached her and gasped at the sight before me – eyes red from crying, unable to focus, hands shaking. "Rosie, what happened?"

"Helen." Her voice reached my ears, barely audible. "Helen was murdered."

I recoiled as if slammed against the wall. I didn't find out what happened until the next day – in the papers.

Helen Jewett was murdered in her bed in the middle of the night. Her head struck thrice with an axe, and the bed set afire. Her charred body lay on its back and side, with no sign of struggle. The axe lay next to the bed, a cloak lay in the yard. The axe was from Hoxie's Store – where Richard Robinson worked. It wasn't yet known whose cloak it was – but Richard owned one just like it.

Wanting Helen to have a respectable funeral, I paid for it. She was interred at Saint John's Burying Ground.

After the funeral I sat down with Rosie in our parlor. Much calmer now, she told me, "Watchmen fetched Richard and brought him here at eight this morning. He was unexcited looking at Helen's body, even when they arrested him for her murder. Now he's in jail. The house was so crowded..."

She heaved a deep breath and glanced around. "All my girls, the watchmen, the coroner, the police magistrate... Mrs. Gallagher, a neighbor, asked him right out: 'What induced you to commit so cruel and barbarous an act?' He shot back, 'Do you think I would blast my brilliant prospects by so ridiculous an act? I am a young man of only nineteen yesterday. Besides, there's another man's handkerchief under the pillow with his name in full upon it,'" she mimicked his reedy voice.

"Was there another handkerchief?" I asked.

"Yes, George Marston's. But he was questioned and released fast enough. Mrs. Gallagher then took pity on Richard, putting her arm around him and saying, 'God grant that you may prove innocent for the sake of your poor mother.' As if Richard Robinson cares. When they showed him Helen's charred body, he stood in apathy as if viewing a dead bug." Rosie shuddered. So did I, and I hadn't even been there.

She went on, "They brought that unemotional wretch to Bridewell, and he wasted no time shouting, 'I am innocent, and I shall prove it tomorrow!' out the jailhouse window."

"Poor Helen," I moaned, waves of guilt torturing me. "I could have kept her from him, I could have taken her up to my mansion in Haarlem, she would have been safe there..." *Will I ever quit blaming myself?* I wondered.

As soon as I heard his employer retained the wily Ogden Hoffman as defense counsel, I knew Richard Robinson would walk free. Richard heeded his crafty counsel's advice from the start, ceasing his open-window rants.

Just because the prime suspect was behind bars, Rosie wasn't off the hook. James Gordon Bennett from the *Herald* swooped in even before Helen was cold in her grave. With that, the public divided into two camps – pro-Richard and anti-Richard.

"Some folk think I did it," Rosie's voice trembled. "Just because I was the last one to see her alive."

"You obviously weren't," I reasoned. "The killer was."

"That's not good enough for them. They don't want to be confused with facts. And the facts are that at eleven that night, Helen called for champagne, which I brought her, and saw Richard reading in her bed. I didn't see his face, but I recognized his bald spot. My caller, Charlie Humphrey, left at 11:30. Then at midnight, Richard had the gall to knock on my door to be let out. I told him to get Helen to let him out. At three, I smelled smoke, saw the back door open, and sounded the alarm. When they found his cloak in the yard, I knew he left through the back door. He had no other way out."

"If they haven't arrested you by now, they won't," I assured her. "Ogden is a fast-talking lawyer. He'll secure Richard's acquittal, I'll wager my fortune on that. But you?" I shook my head. "You have witnesses to back your alibi, and no motive."

"That vulture Bennett implied I killed Helen because I was in debt to her," she went on. "I never borrowed a shilling from her. Then he suggests I was after Helen's jewels, which might've gone missing. May have, might have!" She pounded the table with her fist. "How dare he!"

This boiled my blood, too. "Why can't the press simply report news instead of implying, supposing, butting in?"

"Oh, poor Helen," she wept. "How many times did we warn her? I hope they lock him up and throw away the key!"

Then I heard who the presiding judge would be – the misogynistic Ogden Edwards. Aaron's cousin – and his complete opposite. That sealed it for me. Richard Robinson would go free.

There was too much murder going on around here. I longed for the good old days when our biggest killer was the pox – *that* pox. The 'night with Venus' sort.

~

The trial started on June 9, a drizzly sticky Thursday. The jurors were young men of Richard's age. Rosie and the girls would be called to testify. "Just tell the truth," I urged them.

But poor Maria Stevens didn't get to testify. Not in court anyway. She fell ill that Monday and called me to her bed. Unable to sit up, she reached out and grasped my hand. Her weak grip alarmed me. Her face was paler than mine when I'd slapped on powder to fake the pallor of death, to hasten Stephen's marriage proposal. A kerchief covered her head. "Is Rosie taking care of you? Did she call a doctor?"

"Yes, he gave me huge doses of laudanum and poppy oil but told me I burst a blood vessel. My head is splitting." She grimaced, rubbing the side of her head with the heel of her hand.

"Here, I'll do that." I leaned over and began to rub both sides of her head. Her eyes slid shut. She sighed. "He said to call in a priest, but I've no faith."

"Oh, Maria..." Despair flooded me. This poor girl, so young. Another death, and this one by life's most heinous killer, illness. "Can I do anything? Please, just tell me." My fingers cramped, yet I still rubbed, trying to ease her suffering to make her final hours a bit easier.

"There's something you need to know. They'll never tell you so I will." Her weak voice barely reached my ears.

"What is it?" I leaned closer.

"Help me sit." She struggled to prop herself up. I grabbed a cushion from the foot of the bed and wedged it behind her back. I got her to a sitting position. Her eyes, dulled with pain, focused on me. "Richard Robinson didn't kill Helen. We did."

Her words struck me numb. "We?"

"Me, Caroline, Amelia, and Elizabeth. To get back at her for killing Emma. She deserved it. Emma was innocent as driven snow and didn't deserve Helen's treatment of her. So we murdered Helen and set it up to look like Richard did it. A clerk from Hoxie's store, Gilbert, came here to visit Caroline. She took his key to the store, went in and got a hatchet, and left the key in the store. The cloak is Richard's – Helen was mending it.

"At midnight, me, Caroline, and Amelia, with Elizabeth on lookout, went into Helen's room after Richard left. Me and Amelia took turns with the axe and hacked her. Then Caroline set the bed on fire. We left the axe with a string attached that matches his cloak – to make it look like he tied the axe under his cloak. I dropped his cloak over the fence. We went back to our rooms before Rosina sounded the alarm." She seemed to run out of breath, for she turned away.

"But why, Maria? Why did you do such a thing?" The words scraped my throat.

She turned and looked at me. "Revenge, why else? We hated what she did to Emma. She was never kind to us either. She stole our beaux. She looked down on us. We couldn't stand having her around. When she killed Emma, we had to see justice."

"Oh, Lord above." As shock wore off, pity flooded my heart. Pity for all poor girls who never have a chance, including this waif, who had nothing in this world, except perhaps a clean conscience.

She reached for my hand. "I know you won't turn the girls in. I told you because I'll not leave this bed alive, and I trust you. I had to tell you... because you share so much with me. I feel you deserve the truth."

"Have you told Rosie?" I voiced my concern in a whisper.

"No one else knows. Just me, the girls, and you."

"I'll never turn them in, you know that," I assured her.

"Besides, the police will look the other way. They don't bother with prostitutes." I knew that well enough.

Maria died that night, taking her secret to the grave.

CHAPTER 42

THE TRIAL BEGAN. What a farce.

I didn't attend, but Judge Edwards steered the jury to a verdict of not guilty. Not for lack of proof, but because the testimony of prostitutes, without other testimony 'from better sources,' was not to be received.

Truth be told, there was no proof Richard killed Helen. The girls, in their plot to frame him, didn't consider that no juror would think Richard foolish enough to leave an axe and his cloak behind.

Rosie went through hell during this spectacle. She got death threats in the post: 'You'll suffer the same fate as Helen if you testify against Richard!' She handed her mail over to me, terrified to open it. At least the police sent a guard to protect her. But the crowd's hisses and jibes made her an emotional wreck as she entered the courtroom.

The defense crucified Rosie on the witness stand. After testifying, she came to my door and fell into my arms, so shaken I had trouble getting her to the settee. "It's over, honey, they won't question you anymore," I soothed, rubbing the knotted muscles in her back.

"His lawyer tried to blame me..." she choked out between sips of whiskey. I held it to her lips, her hands too shaky to hold the glass. "Will Price, with a slicker tongue than the slipperiest snake oil salesman..." Her voice faltered, "...rammed home that my debased status rendered my word worthless. I was little more than a criminal myself, murdering beautiful girls' souls. When he told them to presume I was 'the one,' the entire courtroom burst into applause, like a packed theater. He said I had plenty of motive, I burnt Helen's bed to collect insurance!"

"That despicable sod," I hissed through clenched teeth. "That's not evidence to arrest you. That's just him shooting his mouth off."

The whiskey and my comfort seemed to calm her. She sat back, knocked back the whiskey, and held out the glass for more.

My morals warred with me in a mental fistfight until I made that crucial decision. "Rosie, I must tell you this. Richard is not guilty of this crime."

She opened her eyes and stared at me.

"Maria confessed to me in her final hour that she, Elizabeth, Caroline, and Amelia killed Helen and set the bed on fire. In revenge for Helen killing Emma." I gave a resolute nod. "I could not keep this from you. You have a right to know."

I breathed deep. Now I knew how Maria felt when she confessed: cleansed, purified. Able to die with a clean conscience.

"May the Lord have mercy upon their souls," Rosie whispered, and went limp.

Hence, a jury of Richard's peers found him not guilty. I was glad he went free because he was innocent. The entire city knew those men wouldn't let Richard Robinson rot in prison on the testimony of prostitutes. I had mixed emotions about the girls who got away with murder...

...until Rosie burst through the door. She sobbed, collapsing on my settee.

"What happened now?" I sat beside her, helpless to coax a word out of her.

"The girls..." Her voice shook. She trembled. "They committed suicide. Elizabeth, Caroline, and Amelia. With that damned arsenic."

I sat there, stunned. "Why? Because of Helen?"

She pulled a crumpled note from her pocket and handed it to me with a shaky hand. I unfolded it and read: "*Please forgive us.*" It was signed: "*Elizabeth, Caroline, and Amelia.*"

We wound our arms around each other in grief. I prayed to the Lord for mercy upon more souls.

Rosie held a police-escorted auction of the furniture from her house. I bought most of it and gave it to charity. When a fiendish snake started to chop up Helen's scorched footboard, I had him arrested.

Rosie moved in with me when she began seeing ghosts in her parlor.

"She's a young woman with blood upon her face and hair streaming as if on wings. She haunts me so, I spend every waking moment looking over my shoulder." Trembling and pale, she voiced her fears.

She should've kept her sightings to herself. Her blabbing to neighbors attracted crowds to the house. They jammed the street and halted traffic. Ghouls peered in the window and claimed to see a man brandishing an axe, chasing that hapless ghost. Poor Mr. Livingston would have one heck of a time selling that house.

I had one more task before putting this matter to bed. I called on the acquitted Richard. Too surprised to invite me in, he stood in his doorway stammering. I let myself in and faced him with my usual volley of advice.

"You'd best leave town, son. The sensation this caused isn't going away anytime soon. They're selling lithographs of you leaving Helen's bed with a hatchet in your hand and pictures of dead Helen half-naked. Robinsonian juntos are harassing prostitutes, dressing like you..."

"I cannot control dandies or bandits," came his curt answer.

"No, you can't. But half this city still wants to see you stretch hemp. You can't be so bold as to keep strutting the pavement thinking some thug won't reverse the jury's decision on his own. But, Richard... I know you're innocent."

He gaped at me, as if I possessed otherworldly powers.

"Have a good life." I turned to leave.

"Wait!" He stopped me at the bottom of the outside steps. He glanced up and down the street, found it empty of onlookers, and blurted, "You know the killer? If so, I need you to tell me. I want justice for Helen."

What tenacity. I had to applaud it. "There was more than one killer. And they're all dead. Helen got her justice." I turned toward the door but not without my final word. "Don't ask who they were. Some things you aren't meant to know. Richard, I'll tell you something I never tell anyone. I'm intent on finding real killers because when I was much younger, two men rescued me and faced being hanged for a murder they didn't commit. I went to the judge and told him who the real murderer was. I knew because the murderer was me."

He leveled a stare at me. "You murdered someone?"

"Yes, it was self-defense. But I couldn't let someone else suffer for my deed. That's why I'm hell-bent on justice. I know how the system collars innocent people." I paused as he drank that in. "And heed this pearl of wisdom—cease your embezzling. You won't be acquitted next time. Mark my word on that." I made my tone menacing enough so he caught my drift. I turned and headed for my calèche.

Holding a steaming mug of coffee in my hand, I glanced down at the opened *New York Times* on the table. An article caught my attention. That name—Richard Robinson—it stood out, catching my breath in my throat. A flood of memories returned...Helen's declarations of love, her jealous rants, the shock of her murder, Maria's deathbed confession, the girls' suicide pact.

Now it came full circle. Richard died in a Louisville hotel. New York City may have forgotten the sensational murder and farcical trial, but he hadn't. The elderly woman who attended him in his last hours relayed to the press that he died of a fever, calling out a name over and over: "Helen Jewett."

Grasping the paper, I went down the corridor to tell Rosie.

Mixed emotions crossed her features. "Do you think he knew who killed Helen?" she asked, the first time we'd talked about this in ages.

"I wouldn't tell him. But chances are he knows now," I answered, and tossed the paper into the glowing hearth.

Alexander Hamilton Jr. was quite the detective as well as an astute lawyer. He discovered that Aaron and his paramour Jane McManus were cohabitating. This gave me everything I needed. In New York, adultery was necessary to file for divorce. I had him dead to rights.

My husband's quick reply showed he would always be New York's top attorney. He stated I was 'disobedient and insulting,' and I had a 'violent and ferocious temper.'

But he let it go uncontested. What else could he do? My maid Maria testified that she'd literally caught him with his breeches down.

After the court ordered the divorce, he asked for a re-hearing. His grounds? "I am too old to commit adultery."

I hrrumphed. "He wasn't too old last July Fourth on the terrace as fireworks exploded all around."

The vice-chancellor denied him. He must have known Aaron.

The following day, my butler knocked on my parlor door as I sat at my desk paying bills.

"Colonel Burr received the divorce papers, Mrs. Burr." His voice trembled, and his hands shook.

"It's all right, he can handle it." I gave a dismissive wave and went back to my ledger.

"N-n-no he can't, Mrs. Burr. He died."

"Christ Almighty," came out of me in a hoarse whisper. I stood, and my pen slid to the floor. I clasped my hands. "Oh, Aaron," I sobbed. "Why did it have to come to this? You know I would have taken you back."

He died of a stroke, I later heard. The funeral was to be at the Chapel of the College of New Jersey in Princeton, and he would be interred next to his father.

I did not want to attend, to face phony gestures of sympathy. All I wanted was to be alone with him and leave with a heart full of memories. Draped in widow's weeds, I entered the chapel, inhaling candle wax and sweet incense. As my eyes adjusted to the dim light, the sight of the black coffin startled me. Some unknown force pushed me forth, and I approached it. I peered inside at the silver hair, the closed eyes, the thin trace of a smile, his last pleasurable thought frozen on his lips forever. Bits of clay, remnants of a death mask, stuck to his face.

Seeing him in eternal rest didn't strike me as I feared. He was finally at peace, for I knew since his first stroke, he'd suffered, unable to use his limbs, unable to speak. His release was a blessing. "It was the divorce papers, wasn't it?" I whispered. Oh, the irony. I knew he'd gotten a chuckle out of it. "Divorce papers from Alexander Hamilton," I pictured him saying. "That's the final *touché.*"

I knelt beside him and laid my hand upon his. "You haven't seen the last of me, my precious rascal," I promised, as I took out my tiny sewing scissors. I snipped off a lock of his hair and wrapped it in my handkerchief. I didn't have much else to remember him by that I could hold or look at. We'd been apart more than we'd been together, but our fleeting moments were worth the wait.

He did leave me one thing I'll treasure until the day I die— his name. For the remainder of my days, I am Mrs. Vice President Aaron Burr, and proud of it.

Finally, I stood, my legs wobbly from kneeling. I turned and walked down the aisle in silence. I blew him one last kiss before I opened the door to the outside world.

A soft breeze fluttered through my hair as I climbed back into my calèche.

"Where to now, Mrs. Burr?" the coachman asked.

Where to now, indeed. My tavern? The crowded streets of New York City? The gaudy salons of Paris? Some exotic far-reaching land I only dreamed of? Egypt? Greece? Morocco? To buy more mansions, brothels, land, jewelry, and coaches with matched bays? To solve another murder? To find another man who'd promise never to leave me? No. All the men I loved—and hated—were gone. But they all made me strong and independent.

My family waited at home. Now was the time to gather them around me, count my blessings, and say thank you.

I settled back in my seat and looked straight ahead. "Just take me home to my family. Someone needs *me* for a change."

The End

AUTHOR'S NOTE

Eliza lived another thirty years after Aaron. She died on July 16, 1865, at age 90. She is buried at Trinity Church Cemetery and Mausoleum in Manhattan. Her son, George Washington Bowen, lived to be 90. His photo shows a strong resemblance to our first president. There is no historical evidence that Aaron was his father; I added that to the story.

Some of the dialogue was actually spoken, such as Senator Maclay's tavern discussions and Aaron's farewell speech to the Senate, which did make grown men cry. Eliza's last conversation with Aaron before their divorce actually took place, as spoken, as did her chat with William Dunlap when they ran into each other on the street. Eliza truly faked her own impending death to trick Stephen Jumel into marrying her.

She did meet Napoleon Bonaparte in France. Many of the gifts he gave her are on display at the Morris-Jumel Mansion in Harlem, which is now a museum and open to the public. (morrisjumel.org)

Stephen Jumel actually offered Napoleon Bonaparte a

wine barrel to hide in aboard his brig, the *Eliza*. The emperor's indignant refusal took place, as written.

The fragrance that Napoleon had a perfumer create for Josephine and named after her is still on the market.

Eliza appreciated irony and hired Alexander Hamilton Jr. to serve Aaron with divorce papers, charging him with adultery, the only grounds for divorce in New York at the time. He did say he was too old for adultery and died of a stroke later that day, in Staten Island, New York, at age 80.

The 1799 murder of Elma Sands and the Levi Weeks trial were very high-profile and made major headlines. Ezra Weeks indeed did hire the 'dream team' of Hamilton and Burr to defend his brother Levi. After his acquittal, he left town. The dancer Anna Gardie and her husband Maurison did live at 54 Pearl Street and were found dead together from stab wounds. Police ruled it a murder-suicide. Their story is true, as written.

Determined to find out the name of Anna Gardie's husband, I scoured the internet, and after an extensive search, finally discovered his name was Maurison. It was like striking gold. I was so glad I did not need to make up a name.

The murders of Helen Jewett and Emma Chancellor did take place; the trial proceeded as written in the story, with Aaron's cousin Ogden Edwards as presiding judge. Richard Robinson's and Helen Jewett's letters to each other, as written in the story, still survive. Richard Robinson was acquitted and moved out west. He died soon after. On the coffee table in his Texas parlor, he kept a book telling the story of the murder of Helen Jewett.

The two-volume set George Washington sent Eliza in the trunk, *The Law of Nations*, was the property of the New York Society Library, America's first lending library. President Washington checked the books out on October 5, 1789, and never returned them. Librarians discovered this while digitizing the library's ledger in 2009. One of Washington's secretaries had signed 'president' next to the titles, which were due back a month later.

Aaron Burr's death mask is at the New-York Historical Society on Central Park West in Manhattan.

As all historical novelists, I need to take license with facts and events, and make up what is not on the historical record. While I pointed out many of the historical facts above, I didn't list every one, nor everything in the story that is fiction. We blend fact and fiction, and though I strive to stay as close to the historical record as possible, I must adhere to the Mark Twain quote, "Never let the truth get in the way of a good story." That's what makes it fiction. There are many nonfiction books which I list in the bibliography for further reading on Eliza, Aaron, and their times.

ACKNOWLEDGMENTS

I am happy to be a member of the Aaron Burr Association, which I discovered when researching my biographical novel of Hamilton. Many members are descendants of Aaron Burr. They strive to promote Aaron Burr's life and legacy. I thoroughly enjoy our gatherings and value the many friendships I've formed. I appreciate the support they've given me as I researched and wrote this book.

For more information, please go to Aaronburrassociation.org.

Many thanks to Stuart Johnson, Frank Burr, my beta readers Piper Huguley and Bonnie Schutzman, my team and editors at Next Chapter Publishing, and of course, my husband, Chris.

SELECTED BIBLIOGRAPHY

Brierly, Earnest, *The Streets of Old New York*, Hastings House, 1953

Canary, Robert, *William Dunlap*, Twayne Publishers, Inc., New York, 1970

Carson, Cary; Hoffman, Ronald; Albert, Peter, eds., *Of Consuming Interests: The Style of Life in the Eighteenth Century*, University Press of Virginia, Charlottesville, 1994

Cohen, Patricia Cline, *The Murder of Helen Jewett*, Random House, New York, 1998

Custis, George Washington Parke, *Private Memoirs of Washington by His Adopted Son George Washington Parke Custis with a Memoir of the Author by His Daughter; and Illustrative and Explanatory Notes*, Union Publishing House, New York, 1859

Davis, Mathew, *Memoirs of Aaron Burr*, Harper & Bros., 1837

Duncan, Lois, *Sukie*, Little, Brown and Company, Boston, 1970

Duncan, William, *Amazing Madame Jumel*, Frederick A. Stokes Company, New York, 1935

Dunlap, William, *Diary of William Dunlap, the memoirs of a dramatist, theatrical manager, painter, critic, novelist, and historian*, Benjamin Blom, Inc., New York/London, 1930

Durant, Will and Ariel, *The Age of Napoleon, A History of European Civilization from 1789 to 1815*, Simon and Schuster, New York, 1975

Falkner, Leonard, *Painted Lady, Eliza Jumel, Her Life and Times*, E.P. Dutton & Co., Inc., New York, 1962

Fisher, William, *The Music That Washington Knew, A Program of Authentic Music, vocal and instrumental, with historical data, for the use of Musical Societies, Music Clubs, and Historical Celebrations*, Oliver Ditson Company, Inc., New York, 1931

Ford, Paul Leicester, *George Washington*, J.B. Lippincott Co., Phila., 1896

Gilfoyle, Timothy J., *City of Eros, New York City, Prostitution, and the Commercialization of Sex, 1790-1920*, W.W. Norton & Company, New York, 1992

Hampden, John, ed., *Eighteenth Century Plays*, J.M. Dent & Sons Ltd., London, 1928

Hogeland, William, *Declaration, The Nine Tumultuous Weeks When America Became Independent*, Simon & Schuster, New York, 2010

Homberger, Eric, *The Historical Atlas of New York City*, Henry Holt and Company, New York, 1994

Maclay, William, *The Journal of William Maclay*, Frederick Ungar Publishing Co., New York, 1890

Maginnes, F. Arant, *Thomas Abthorpe Cooper, Father of the American Stage*, McFarland & Co., Inc., London, 2004

Meese, Edwin III, *The Heritage Guide to the Constitution*, The Heritage Foundation, Washington D.C., 2005

Monaghan, Frank, and Lowenthal, Marvin, *This Was New York*, Doubleday, New York, 1943

Nolan, Charles, *Aaron Burr and the American Literary Imagination*, Greenwood Press, Westport, CT, 1980

Parmet, Herbert, and Hecht, Marie, *Aaron Burr, Portrait of an Ambitious Man*, The Macmillan Company, New York, 1967

Paul, Raymond, *The Thomas Street Horror, An Historical Novel of Murder*, The Viking Press, New York, 1982

Perrottet, Tony, *Napoleon's Privates*, HarperCollins Publishers, New York, 2008

Pidgin, Charles, *Theodosia, the First Gentlewoman of Her Time*, C.M. Clark Publishing Co., Boston, 1907

Porta, John Baptista, *Natural Magick*, Naples, 1558

Ribblett, David, *Nelly Custis*, Mount Vernon Ladies' Association, Mount Vernon, VA, 1993

Seton, Anya, *My Theodosia*, Houghton Mifflin Company, Boston, 1941

Shelton, William Henry, *The Jumel Mansion*, Houghton Mifflin Company, Boston, 1916

Singleton, Esther, *Social New York Under the Georges*, D. Appleton and Company, New York, 1902

Tebbel, John, *George Washington's America*, E.P. Dutton and Company, Inc., New York, 1954

Van Doren, Mark, *Correspondence of Aaron Burr and His Daughter Theodosia*, Covici-Friede Inc., New York, 1929

Weisberger, Bernard, *America Afire*, HarperCollins Publishers, New York, 2000

Wollstonecraft, Mary, *A Vindication of the Rights of Woman*, Joseph Johnson Publisher, London, 1792

ABOUT THE AUTHOR

 Diana Rubino writes about folks through history who shook things up. Her passion for history, travel, and the paranormal has taken her to every locale of her books: Medieval and Renaissance England, Egypt, the Mediterranean, colonial Virginia, New England, and New York. Her urban fantasy romance FAKIN' IT won a Top Pick award from Romantic Times. She is a member of the Richard III Society and the Aaron Burr Association. With her husband Chris, she owns CostPro, Inc., a construction cost consulting business. In her spare time, Diana bicycles, golfs, practices yoga, lifts weights, plays her piano, devours books, and lives the dream on Cape Cod.

To learn more about Diana Rubino and discover more Next Chapter authors, visit our website at www.nextchapter.pub.

Printed in Great Britain
by Amazon

57169401R00219